A STEVE CANNON NOVEL

THE KNIGHTS OF NAUVOO

B. R. LAUE

ISBN: 978-0-9973419-7-3

Brandy Hill Publishing

P.O. Box 1202

Morgan Hill, CA 95038

brandyhillpublish@gmail.com

Join the mailing list (no spam) for advance notice of new books in this series, and to periodically receive free Steve Cannon short stories.

Cover by Sandy Laue

For Sandy, my
beautiful muse

OTHER STEVE CANNON TITLES

Vegas Wash
A Song for Desmond
Lost and Found
The Mayor of Burro Springs
Palaces of Sand
Seven Come Eleven

FOREWORD

IN AN IRONIC twist, the history, as well as the pre-history of Las Vegas is inextricably bound up with the Mormon church. The failed Mormon settlements in the middle of the 19th century were the first attempts at white occupation of the valley and were the precursors of the railroad town that formed the basis of the present day city. A significant portion of the residents were members of the church up until the last twenty years when the population boom pushed the percentage of Mormons below two percent. In the heyday of wide open gambling in the city, the Church of the Latter Day Saints was as much of a power broker as many of the mob organizations. In fact, one could argue that with many state offices and gaming posts held by Mormons, they had more say in the way that gambling was conducted in the state of Nevada than other single entity.

JUNE 30, 1965

STEVE CANNON PULLED his wallet from his back pocket and handed over a dollar bill to the man behind the counter. He unfolded the Las Vegas Sun newspaper and holding it up to the streetlight, scanned the headlines while he waited for his change.

'Las Vegas Man Murdered'. A smaller headline underneath called attention to the fact that this was the second murder of a prominent Mormon in as many weeks. He grunted to himself as he folded the paper under his arm and looked up the street. Though it was two o'clock in the morning, the air was still warm as Steve walked toward the empty bench that was under the brightly lit Greyhound Bus sign. A few minutes later, Steve glanced at his watch just before he caught sight of the silver bus as it turned the corner a block away and moved slowly in his direction, the air brakes hissing as it slowed to a stop. Steve could feel the heat from the engine as it radiated over the sidewalk. He moved a few feet back toward the news stand as the door swung open making the same noise the brakes had made.

The driver waited with his hand on the big silver lever and watched as the sole rider moved past him and descended the metal steps. The driver pulled back on the lever and glancing in his side mirror pulled the bus away from the curb, leaving a cloud of blue exhaust hovering over the street. Steve smiled and held out his hand as the smaller man lowered his suitcase to the ground and moved forward. Steve shook the newly extended hand and pulled the man toward him with the arm holding the paper, hugging him closely. Steve took a step backward.

"You look good, Skipper, you look real good." Skipper smiled and bent slightly to pick up the case.

"So do you Stevie, how long has it been? A year?" Steve shook his head. "Almost, Skip, a year ago next month." Skipper nodded thoughtfully, his short brown hair framing his tanned face. Steve held out his hand toward the suitcase and gestured to the corner, where Skipper could see the back end of the red Jeep Wagoneer parked by the curb.

"You hungry?" Skipper nodded as he released the handle of the case. "I was asleep when the bus stopped in Bakersfield." Steve smiled as he led the way across the short distance and slid the case in the passenger rear door of the Jeep. When Skipper was seated comfortably in the front seat, Steve turned on the engine and waited a few seconds before he turned to his boyhood friend.

"Well, as they say, Skip, the world is your oyster. Where do you want to go?" Skipper smiled.

"How about the Golden Nugget?" Steve nodded as he pulled away from the curb and started up Fremont Street. "Sounds good to me."

"Do you think Nick will be there, Stevie?" Steve shrugged as he slowed for the left hand turn into the Nugget parking lot.

"Maybe. It's a Thursday night right before a holiday weekend, Nick usually likes to keep a close tab on things when it gets busy."

Skipper smiled as they moved through the casino toward the restaurant in the far corner of the building. Steve had to stop and wait for his friend several times as Skipper paused by some of the crowded gaming tables to watch the action. When they were seated in one of the booths that looked out over the casino, Skipper grinned and gestured out the window.

"Forgot how noisy these places are. I spent the last two months by the beach. Hard to imagine a place farther away from there than here." Steve leaned back in the booth.

"Was it hard to make the decision to come back, Skip?" He watched while Skipper gazed at the table, turning the salt shaker in small circles on the tablecloth. He didn't look up as he spoke.

"Maybe, a little. The last few months I have been a counselor for some of the new guys entering the program and the more I talked with them, the more I realized that until I came back here and faced what I had become, I could never be sure I was truly well." Steve nodded thoughtfully and picked up the menu when he saw a waitress heading for their table. Though Steve did not remember her name, he recognized her face and read her name tag as she pulled the short tablet from the front pocket of her apron and retrieved a pencil from behind her ear.

"Hi Grace, do you know if Nick Montero is around tonight?" She smiled as she wrote something on the top of the tablet.

"Yes, he was just in here. Want me to page him for you?" Steve looked across at Skipper who responded with a slight nod.

"That would be great, Grace, if it is not too much trouble."

"No trouble at all. What can I get for you two?" Steve looked across at Skipper before he held out the menu to Grace.

"A New York steak, rare, and a glass of sweet tea." They both looked at Skipper as he grunted to get Steve's attention. He had a calm composed look on his face that Steve struggled to recall having seen before.

"In all the years I have known you Stevie, I have never seen you eat a steak without a beer, and I have never once seen you drink ice tea." Steve sat up in the booth to say something when Skipper continued. "The last thing I want, or need is for you to start changing your behavior around me. Will you promise me?" Skipper gazed intently across the table. Steve looked into the dark brown eyes and the face he had known since he was seven. He smiled, nodded and stretched his hand across the table. When Skipper had grasped it, Steve spoke.

"It's good to have you back, Skip, I missed you." Steve's voice caught as he looked back at Grace.

"I will have a Coors with that steak, Grace." She nodded as she wrote it down and then looked at Skipper. Skipper laughed as he handed her the menu.

"I'll have the same, except without the Coors. Sweet tea will suit me fine, Grace."

They were halfway through their meal when Steve saw Nick Montero moving through the crowded casino. He was stopped just outside of the entrance to the restaurant by an employee who thrust a piece of paper toward him to sign. As he put his pen back in his pocket, he looked up and saw Steve through the window. He smiled, pointed and made his way through the small crowd of gamblers just inside the entrance waiting to be seated. When he rounded the corner and walked to their booth, the smile got even wider when he spied Skipper. Nick grasped Skipper's hand and gestured for him to slide further into the booth to make room for Nick to sit down. Nick smiled and waved Grace off as she moved toward the table. He winked at Steve before he crossed his arms on the table and looked over at Skipper.

"Well, Mr. John, it is good to see you hale and hearty." He patted Skipper's shoulder, and sat back slightly when he saw the serious look that crossed Skipper's face. Nick looked quickly across the table at Steve just as Skipper cleared his throat. Skipper sat upright with his hands in his lap and looked steadily at Nick.

"When Steve asked me where I wanted to go, I chose the Nugget so I could talk to you, Nick. I want to apologize for the way I have acted in your casino over the last five years." Nick started to make a sound in protest, but stopped when Skipper grasped his wrist. "No, Nick, hear me out. I lost respect for myself and in doing that I disrespected you and Steve and everyone else that tried to help me. It was selfish of me and I know that I can't change the past, but maybe in time, my behavior will show that your efforts were not entirely wasted." Skipper sat back and smiled at Nick. Nick nodded his head thoughtfully and extended his hand once more toward Skipper.

"You know, Skipper, I believe you. Good to have you back."

JULY 1

NOISES FROM THE kitchen woke Steve the next morning. He lay blinking at the ceiling for a few seconds before he remembered that he had a houseguest. He looked at his watch and smiled. 8:30. He sat up on the side of his bed and pushed his feet into a pair of slippers. He was cinching up his bathrobe as he moved through the short hallway that led to the kitchen. Skipper was seated at the table and pouring coffee from the percolator. He smiled when he saw Steve.

"I couldn't sleep. Hope I didn't wake you." Steve waved dismissively as he waited while Skipper poured coffee in his cup.

"No, it's fine, Skip. We're due at the Casablanca by ten, so I'm glad you woke me." He took a big sip and looked across at his friend.

"You know, Skip, I had forgotten what you look like in a suit." Skipper smiled as he looked down at the gray suit and burgundy tie. His look was more serious when he glanced back up across the table.

"Publicity Director. Sounds like a lot is riding on this, Stevie." Steve nodded from behind his coffee cup as he lowered it to the table.

"You've handled plenty of big publicity jobs for the hotels over the years. This is the same thing, only this is a long term position for Bernie's hotel. Most of the other directors on the Strip are still the same ones you have worked with in the past, and the only new wrinkle is getting to know the folks over at the convention center." Skipper nodded absentmindedly as he stared at his coffee cup.

"You're right, Stevie. I have sent many guys back out there to resume their careers, I just have to remember what I told them and follow my own advice." Steve smiled and patted Skipper's arm as he stood up.

"You'll do fine. I need to get dressed so we don't make you late on your first day."

An hour later, Steve and Skipper stood in the lobby of the Casablanca. All around them, workers and bellhops were scurrying across the Italian marble floor, all intent on their tasks in the final two weeks of preparation that led to the grand opening. Steve pointed to the staircase just to their left.

"Before we go and find Bernie, I want you to meet Miss Perone." Skipper fell in behind Steve as they ascended the wide staircase to the second floor. Steve stopped at the thick glass door and waved at his receptionist and pulled the door handle when she buzzed them in. Just inside the doorway, Steve turned and put his arm around Skipper's shoulders as he grinned down at Steffi Perone.

"Miss Perone, this is Mr. Skipper John. Skipper, this is Miss Steffi Perone." Miss Perone stood up behind her desk smoothing her bright red dress before extending her hand toward Skipper.

"So nice to meet you, Mr. John. Mr. Cannon and I have been looking forward to this day for a long time." Skipper shook the petite hand gently as he blushed.

"It is my pleasure, Miss Perone, I have heard many good things about you." It was Steffi's turn to blush as she quickly sat down and waved her hand toward Steve.

"Don't believe him, Mr. John, he will say anything to get on my good side." Steve laughed and gestured toward his office.

"Let's go in there, Skip." He looked back at Miss Perone as Skipper stepped into the hallway.

"Miss Perone, could you see if you can locate Mr. Gold and tell him Mr. John is my office?" Steffi smiled as she picked up the phone.

Steve found Skipper at the window gazing up at the five story room tower that loomed over the property.

"Quite a sight, huh, Skip?" Skipper turned and smiled. He waited while Steve pulled another of the gold brocade wing chairs into place next to the one that always sat in front of his desk. He sat down before he replied.

"Man, you go away for a year and the whole place changes. This was just the old boarded up Three Coins Motel and the lot across the street was just dirt and look at it now." Steve shook his head as he sat down.

"Caesars Palace should be done in the next eight months. Remind me to take you over there and introduce you to Jay Sarno soon. You should hear some of the ideas he has for that place." Steve pulled out a new pack of Pall Malls and gestured with the pack toward Skipper. Skipper waved his hand and smiled.

"Another thing I gave up, Stevie, but you go ahead." Steve shrugged and lit up his first cigarette of the day. The intercom buzzed and crackled on.

"Mr. Cannon, Mr. Gold is here." Steve leaned forward and pressed down the small lever as he smiled across the desk at Skipper. At the same time, he crushed out the cigarette.

"Send him in, Miss Perone." Steve and Skipper both stood and turned toward the door as the wide smile of Bernie Gold entered the room. Bernie headed straight for Skipper and gave him a big bear hug, then stepped back and looked up at the slightly taller man.

"Skipper, you look great. Man, am I glad to see you. I was worried when you didn't come back right away, but Leo and Steve kept me up to date on your progress. How you doin'?" Bernie stepped forward and hugged him again. Skipper laughed and winked at Steve over Bernie's shoulder.

"I'm doing good, Bernie, looking forward to getting started." Bernie turned and pushed one of the chairs back and sat down, still smiling.

"That's good, because I have cleared all morning to work with you. We got a meeting in…" Bernie looked at his watch before he continued. "ten minutes with all the casino people, then the entertainment director, and then I am going to take you downtown to meet the ad execs at both papers and lunch with the new head of the Chamber of Commerce." Bernie stopped for air and laughed when he saw Steve shaking his head at Skipper.

"I told you this was going to be a wild ride for all of us." Skipper nodded his agreement.

"I hope so. You can't make up for lost time, but it will feel good to be productive again." Bernie interrupted.

"You'll do fine, just wait and see, but listen, I took the liberty of leasing one of the units two doors down from me out in the valley. If you want to stay here, there is an empty four room suite on the other side of Jack Cathay's you can have if you want." Skipper grinned and held up his hand.

"Out there with you will be fine, Bernie, I think at this point I prefer the quiet, especially after all day in this hustle and bustle." Bernie stood up.

"All settled, then. Let's get started." He snapped his fingers and looked at Steve.

"I saw Remy an hour ago and she told me to tell you to drop in and see her after the meeting. I will call you when we are through." Steve nodded as he followed the two men to the door. He waved as Miss Perone buzzed them out onto the mezzanine. He had just finished his second smoke and second cup of coffee when Miss Perone's voice came over the intercom.

"Mr. Cannon, there is a Mr. Benjamin Stanwick here to see you." Steve frowned at the unfamiliar name.

"Send him in, Miss Perone." Steve stood up, walked to the door and watched as his visitor approached. He was a medium height man in his mid-fifties, with light sandy hair, and a slightly ruddy complexion. His conservative dark blue suit was expensive and well-tailored.

Steve stepped back from the door and waited until the man stopped in the center of the room before he closed it behind them. He walked behind his desk and motioned to the chair that Bernie had just left.

"Sit down, Mr. Stanwick, can we get you some coffee?" The man shook his head and looked down at the half full ashtray perched on the edge of the desk.

"No, thank you, Mr. Cannon." He sat back in the chair and crossed his legs. Steve sat down and leaned forward on his arms gazing intently at the gray eyes across the desk.

"How can I help you, Mr. Stanwick?" The gray eyes flitted around the room quickly before they settled back on Steve.

"I want to hire you, Mr. Cannon. Or more accurately, the organization I represent would like for me to hire you." Steve sat back and adopted the same casual position as his guest.

"And what organization is that, Mr. Stanwick?"

"The Church of Jesus Christ of Latter Day Saints." Steve stopped his face from frowning, but instead adopted a blank gaze as he replied.

"The Mormons?" The man shook his head.

"We prefer our proper title, Mr. Cannon." Steve snorted softly.

"Doesn't matter much to me what you call yourselves as long as we both know who we are talking about. Just so we are clear, what is your position in the church?"

"I am a bishop and the council of bishops has delegated me to approach you." Steve nodded.

"So, you are the bishop of Las Vegas, right?" Steve's question was met with a shrug.

"If you wish, Mr. Cannon, but it matters less who I am, than whether you will help us or not."

"Help you, how?" Stanwick scowled and sat forward in his chair.

"We need you to prove that the church is not involved in any way with the recent murders." It was Steve's turn to scowl.

"Prove a negative? How do I go about doing that, and if I could, why do you care so much? I haven't heard anyone suggest that the church is involved…unless… of course!" Steve snapped his fingers. "The Danite angle." He smiled slightly at the instant discomfiture that was displayed from across the desk. Benjamin Stanwick shook his head forcefully, his voice harsh and urgent.

"There is no such thing as 'Danites', Mr. Cannon." Steve interrupted him.

"Then why hire me to prove that something which doesn't exist, didn't commit a couple of murders?" Steve drummed his fingers loudly on the green desk blotter. The gray eyes slowly lost their glint of anger as Mr. Stanwick held his hands open in front of him and spoke in a smooth, cool voice.

"Perhaps I have presented my request badly, Mr. Cannon. The church would like you to conduct a private investigation separate from the police, to find out who the murder or murderers are and in so doing prove that the church is not involved. We will pay you handsomely." Steve scowled again.

"If I take the case, you will pay me what I decide to charge, period. Which will be what I normally charge. But just so we are clear, I haven't accepted the case, and I don't know as I sit here, if I will." The gray eyes squinted slightly and the voice that followed was a little less smooth.

"How and when are you going to decide, Mr. Cannon?" Steve's frown was punctuated by a hard stare out of the brown eyes.

"Don't push me, Stanwick. You want some 'yes' man, there are plenty of other gumshoes in this dusty town, use one of them." Steve sat back and swiveled his chair so that his profile was presented as he waited. Mr. Stanwick sighed and sat back in his chair.

"Are you a religious man, Mr. Cannon?" Steve regarded him out of the corner of his eye.

"No. But I believe in God, if that counts."

"And 'Mormons', as you call us, do you have anything against us?" Steve shrugged.

"Not particularly, don't have a strong opinion one way or the other. Mormons make good neighbors, at least those that don't pester you to join. I'm more of a live and let live type, Mr. Stanwick." Steve swiveled his chair around and faced his visitor.

"This is as far as I go right now. I will check with the police and with Rita Malone down at the Sun. If I hear anything from them that warrants me getting involved, then we will talk again, but I wouldn't get my hopes up were I you." Steve stood up and waited until Stanwick did the same, then walking behind him, Steve opened the door. Stanwick looked into his eyes for a brief moment before he strode rapidly through the reception area and out the front door. Steve waited until the door closed completely before he approached Miss Perone's desk.

"Miss Perone, would you get Rita Malone on the phone for me, please?" Steffi nodded and started dialing the number as Steve walked back into his office. He had just lit a cigarette when his line buzzed.

"Rita?"

"Hi, Steve how are you?" Steve swiveled slightly in his chair as he pulled a yellow writing tablet from his top drawer.

"I am doing well. Do you have a few minutes to fill me in on the Mormon murders?"

"Sure, what would you like to know?"

"Well for starters, you know a bishop named Benjamin Stanwick?" There was a low chuckle on the other end of the line.

"I can't say I know him. Most of the few short conversations I have had with him end with 'no comment'. Why do you ask?"

"He was just in here trying to hire me to look into the murders. Why is he being uncooperative with you?"

"I received some information from an anonymous source that I checked out with a history professor out at NSU. I used it as background in the story I wrote after the second murder. Mr. Stanwick didn't like it and now nobody connected with the church will talk to me." Steve snorted softly.

"Yeah, I mentioned the 'D' word myself and he almost came

un-flanged. How much cooperation are you getting from the police?" It was Rita's turn to respond with derision.

"The usual brush-off. You know how Samuels is. There is evidence from both crime scenes they are not releasing to me or anybody for that matter, but what I have been able to glean suggests that the two murders are the work of the same person or persons and that there is plenty of evidence to suggest that members of the church are involved." Steve wrote quickly across the yellow pad.

"Thanks, Rita, that is a good start. I am going to see what I can find out from the police. If I decide to take the case, I might be in a position to help you fill in some blanks down the road. If I get anything out of the cops I can share, I will. I think you should be careful. Danites or not, everybody seems to think a lot is at stake here." Rita chuckled softly.

"Well if the past is any guide, having you involved will certainly take the heat off me." Steve smiled into the phone.

"I will try to keep my head down as well. Let's agree to call each other and share any information we can, OK?"

"I certainly will, Steve, goodbye." Steve hung up the phone and was writing notes in the small book he carried when the intercom buzzed.

"Mr. Gold, is on the phone."

"Thank you, Miss Perone."

"Hi Bernie, how'd the meeting go?" He waited as Bernie spun out the highlights of the meeting.

"Yeah. I told him he could handle it, and that it would all come back to him."

"Thanks. Tell her to wait there, I am coming down to see her." Steve hung up the phone and after walking across the hall, waited at Steffi Perone's desk while she finished a call. When she had hung up the phone she held out two sheets of paper to Steve.

"That was Jack Cathay. Here is the schedule of security meetings for the next three days." Steve frowned at the list of dates and times.

"I have to be at all these?" Steffi Perone nodded.

"And at the twelve hour casino run-through next week." Steve shook his head as he slipped the schedule into the notebook he kept in his pocket.

"Much easier being a private detective. I will be down with Miss DeMarche for the next half hour. Can you call Tam Polhaus and tell him I want to take him to lunch." He glanced at the clock on the wall behind Miss Perone's desk. "Tell him I will be there by 12:30 at the latest."

Steve made his way down the wide stairway and made a quick right through a narrow service hallway that emptied into the outdoor courtyard that held several fountains, two al fresco restaurants and the spacious pool area. He reentered the hotel and the west wing of the casino on his way to the small showroom. Since it had been built using the casino floor of the previous structure, all the finish work had been completed for several months. He walked under the crystal chandeliers that hung over every round table on his way to the stage. When he didn't see anyone around, he walked quickly down a small flight of stairs behind the stage and knocked on the first green door he came to. A small dark haired woman in her mid-twenties opened the door and smiled at Steve.

"Hello, Anita, is Remy here?" Anita nodded and opened the door wider so Steve could enter.

"She is on a call, but go on in." Steve walked through the dressing room portion of the space and through an archway that led to a spacious office with two desks and a conference table in the center of the room. Remy sat at one of the desks. She smiled and indicated a chair right beside her when she looked up and saw Steve. A few minutes later when she had hung up the phone, Steve leaned over and gently kissed her lips.

"How you been, Gem, I haven't seen you for three days." She ran her fingers through his dark brown hair and smiled.

"These last two weeks are going to be rough. You think you got it all planned out and then every day there are four or five new things to consider and work into the schedule." Steve smiled as she held up a large desk calendar with every space filled with tiny scribbles.

"How is the entertainment coming along?" Remy chuckled as she slipped on a light blue sweater that had been draped on the back of her chair.

"Believe it or not, the easy part has been lining up the talent for the opening week. Bernie's idea of booking people that are between their month or two month long shows at the other hotels has caught on. I have entertainment directors from other hotels calling me to see if they can get their stars in. Look at this." Remy held a mock-up of the billboard that would appear on the large neon sign that would be lowered into place by a crane the next day. Steve took it from her hands and held it up. In addition to the two showgirl revues, there were two other showrooms in the Casablanca. The main show-room would rotate three shows a night between Tony Bennet, Danny Thomas, and Milton Berle for the first week, before the next rotation which included Phil Harris, Jimmy Durante and Mitzi Gaynor. Steve shook his head as he placed the large card on the desk.

"That is an amazing line up. Are you still working on Frank?" Remy smiled, nodded and held up a small stack of messages.

"These are just for the last two days. We just have to clear up a few legal details with the management at the Sands and Warner Brothers and he will probably do two weeks in August." Steve leaned back in the chair, shook his head in mock disbelief and jiggled several casino chips in his pants pocket.

"I thought if you weren't knocking off too late, we could catch dinner somewhere." Remy smiled and leaned forward kissing him on the lips.

"I will be done by seven. But don't you have Skipper staying with you?" Steve stood up and caressed the back of Remy's head.

"No. Bernie has him already settled into a condo out at his place.

How did Skipper do today?" Remy was searching through her purse for her hairbrush as she looked up at Steve.

"He did great in the meeting I was in. He had several good ideas for promotion that no one had thought of and he has Bernie upstairs right now going over the changes he is suggesting in the printed materials." Steve smiled as Remy ran the brush in several quick strokes through her shoulder length dark blond hair. As she slowed the strokes she looked up at Steve.

"Pick me up?" Steve leaned down and gently took the brush from her hands as he kissed her passionately for several long seconds. He straightened and handed her back the brush.

"Seven o'clock, right here." He gently squeezed her shoulder as he turned for the door. He was almost to the archway when she called after him.

"Steve. I forgot to tell you. Tomorrow night is the first rehearsal for the café shows. Rita Malone will be going on about eight. I heard her last week at the auditions, and she is great." Steve smiled.

"Wouldn't miss it. Let's make it a date." He waved as he smiled and nodded to Anita on the way out of the door.

*

Steve stood in the doorway of Tam Polhaus' office and surveyed the empty room. He had just turned to leave when a uniform cop walked by.

"You looking for Tam?"

"Yeah, you seen him?" The cop pointed down the hallway in the direction he had just come.

"They are all in the war room." Steve squinted down the hall.

"The war room, what the hell is that?" The cop laughed and spoke over his shoulder as he continued in the opposite direction.

"The Mormon murders, got everybody in a big tizzy." Steve snorted in reply and walked toward the end of the hall and a large storage room. He pulled open one of the double metal doors and peered in. The space had been converted into a makeshift command center with two rows of long tables down the center holding several telephones. The walls were covered with photos and documents and a large green chalkboard stood against the far wall. Though there were only three people in the room, Steve could see from the overflowing trash cans beside him that things had been busy. He sauntered into the middle of the room and waited until Tam finished his conversation with another detective. Tam jerked his head back slightly in recognition when he saw Steve.

"This better be good. I turned down two other lunch invitations waiting on you, one from the Chief." Steve didn't change his expression.

"Sorry you missed your chance to kiss up to Samuels. How much time you got?" Tam's face was dark.

"I wasn't talking about Samuels. As long as I want, why?" Steve jiggled the tokens as he turned around.

"Let's go to the Embers. Quiet. Nobody to bother us there." Tam fell in behind Steve as he headed for the door.

"I don't know who would care what we say, but suit yourself." Steve waited for Tam to catch up when they had exited the glass doors and the air conditioning and stood in the hot sun. He squared up and looked the Irish-German detective in the face and waited until he had his full attention.

"The subject is going to be the Mormon murders, so if you don't want to spill, tell me now, and I will go waste my time somewhere else." Tam took a step back and shook his head.

"Always something with you, isn't it? And always something that gets everybody's knickers in a twist." Tam shook his head again and looked at the ground. "OK, I'll bite, but only because you're buying and my natural curiosity, which always gets the best of me where you are concerned." Steve laughed and slapped the detective on the shoulder.

"That's big of you, Tammy boy. Come on, this won't hurt that much at all." Steve was still laughing when he reached across the bench seat of the Jeep and pulled up the small knob to open the passenger door.

The Embers restaurant on West Charleston Boulevard was dark and cool when Steve and Tam opened the big wooden door and stood blinking on the red tiles of the foyer as their eyes grew accustomed to the lack of light. When their beers had been delivered to the corner booth that Steve had selected, Steve pulled out his notebook and frowned across the table at his lunch companion.

"Well, Tam, who is chopping up the church elders?" Tam snorted and took a long drink of the pale beer.

"How do I know? I just work here." Steve took a small sip of his beer and motioned to the waitress to bring another round.

"You have no suspects?" Steve leaned across the table and peered intently at Tam. The detective shook his head sullenly and looked at his half empty glass.

"Nope. Just two hacked up bodies, a whole lot of blood and a bunch of clues that make no sense." He shook his head disgustedly and hurriedly finished his beer when he spied the waitress heading toward them. Steve waited until the woman had placed the two beers on the table and left with Tam's empty glass.

"Let's start with the clues." Steve pushed his notebook into the center of the table with his pencil poised over it as Tam leaned forward.

"Anything I tell you about the clues goes no further, especially not to Rita Malone. I got your word on that?" Steve nodded his head slowly.

"Of course, Tam, if that is the way you want it. Why all the hush-hush?" Tam leaned back against the cool vinyl of the booth.

"Because, the higher-ups think we are dealing with a serial killer here, and they don't want any clues that only us and the killer know about to get out." Steve held his hands out and widened his eyes.

"So?"

"So, this. First victim, Magnus Pearce, 52, owner of Pearce

construction, the words: '3M' written in blood on the wall of his study where his body was found, or the pieces, I should say. Coroner says he was killed with some kind of hatchet. Second guy, Hiram Dame, 53, state legislator, some talk a few years back of his being Sawyers' pick to fill the vacant senate seat, killed in the same fashion, the words 'wild bill' on his wall. And here is the strange part: At both scenes there was the words, 'Knights of Nauvoo' written in blood on the back of a door." Tam picked up his beer and took two quick sips.

"Well, there you are, what do you make of that?" Steve sat up as the waitress set down the white oval platters that held the rare steaks and asked him if they needed anything else. Steve looked over at Tam as she moved away from the table.

"Don't make much of it, one way or the other. Any connection between the two victims?" Tam shook his head as he chewed.

"None that have shown up, but that isn't an avenue that Samuels is pursuing aggressively, if you know what I mean."

Steve wrote in his notebook between bites. He waited until they were nearly finished before he spoke again.

"So, this Nauvoo Knights thing, is that where the Danite angle comes in?" Tam shrugged.

"I don't know. That came from Rita, what she based it on is anybody's guess. Samuels has no time for speculation about the church. He even gets upset if any of us call it the 'Mormon murders'. Just a murder case to him." Steve snorted.

"Well as usual, time will prove him wrong on that, just like everything else." Tam looked up from the last bite of his steak quizzically.

"So, your turn. Who you working for?" Steve laughed and sat back in the booth as he pushed his plate into the middle of the table and picked up his beer, stopping it halfway to his mouth.

"The Church of Jesus Christ of Latter Day Saints, that is if I decide to take the job." Tam looked blankly across the table

"You're kidding." Steve shook his head.

"Nope. The bishop of Las Vegas himself appeared in my office and wanted to write a big check to get this monkey off their back."

"Well, I'll be. It's a strange world alright." Tam's eyes narrowed.

"But why you? They got all kinds of guys from Salt Lake in town, asking everybody questions and bugging us every two minutes. Why hire a gum shoe that probably doesn't know the angel Moroni from a halibut?" Steve shrugged.

"Probably figures that unless it is an objective source, nobody will pay any attention. Or maybe they know how strong my connections are to the Las Vegas Police department." Both men laughed heartily and clinked their glasses. Tam grew serious.

"Samuels is not going to like this one little bit when he finds out." Steve interrupted.

"So, we don't tell him, that's all." Tam scoffed.

"How's that worked out in the past? No, your best bet is to forget about this case and tell the bishop to get himself another boy." Steve stared out across the restaurant for several seconds.

"Oh, I don't know, Tam, might be fun. Most of the cases I have now are pretty cut and dried, might be worth the try, don't you think?" Tam screwed his face into a frown and shook his head as he hoisted the beer glass to his mouth. Steve waited until Tam had put the glass back on the table.

"I'll make you a deal. I promise to keep out of Samuel's sights, if you keep feeding me any new developments. In return, I will share anything I come across that adds to the evidence and if I figure out who the murderer is, I will come to you and you can make the collar. How's that sound?" Tam 's eyes roamed around the restaurant, before he looked back at Steve.

"Yeah, that's fine with me. Most of our resources are working on this case, so leaks could come from anywhere." He pointed a finger across the table before he continued. "Just make sure that none of them can be traced back to you, and we will be OK." Steve sat back in the booth and raised his hands in mock surrender.

"Don't worry about me, Tam, worry about Samuels. He's the loose cannon." They both laughed at the joke as they left the table and walked toward the front door. When they were on the hot sidewalk, Tam turned and stopped Steve with a hand on his shoulder.

"This has gotten very hot politically, Steve. The governor calls the chief every day for updates and his office hears about it every day from Salt Lake City. With Samuels heading this up, we both know anything could happen, and I don't want either of us in the line of fire if it does." Steve smiled and turned Tam by the shoulder as he started walking toward the Jeep.

"Don't worry, Tam, nothing bad is going to happen. I still need to talk with Rita before I decide to take the case. I will let you know one way or the other."

*

Steve parked in front of the Las Vegas Sun building. He was putting two nickels in the meter in front of the Jeep when he heard his name being called from behind. He turned to see the owner and publisher, Hank Greenspun, walking toward him with a sheaf of papers under his arm. Hank held out his free hand.

"Steve, how are you doing? What brings you down here?" Steve shook the extended hand and smiled at the shorter man. He had known the editor and owner of the Las Vegas Sun for over ten years and while they enjoyed a very good working relationship, Steve had always tried to keep a professional distance.

"Doing good, Hank, how's things in the fourth estate?" Hank laughed and shifted the papers he carried to his other hand.

"Always a laugh a minute. You here to see me?" Steve shook his head and indicated the building with a short wave.

"No, here to see Rita Malone." Hank's eyes narrowed slightly, even as he smiled.

"Something tells me we're talking about the 'Mormon murders', am I right?" Steve chuckled and nodded.

"Yeah, you're right, but I had the bishop of Las Vegas in my office this morning and he is none too happy with that sobriquet." Hank snorted softly.

"I bet not. Are you going to get involved in this mess?" Steve leaned over and locked the Jeep as he spoke.

"Don't know yet. Thought I would talk to Rita and see what's what before I decide. But let me ask you something that may be rather personal, Hank." Steve straightened up and waited for a reaction. Hank squinted at Steve for a second.

"Sure, what is it?" Steve motioned that they should start walking toward the building a few yards away. He kept his voice low.

"Let's just say that you and the LDS church are on the same page a lot of times when it comes to some of the seamier aspects of this town. Why are you and Rita pushing back on this one?" Hank stopped just outside the door and waited as one of his younger staffers pushed through the revolving glass. He acknowledged the young man and waited for him to travel out of earshot before he replied.

"I just hate power applied for power's sake. The church has no business telling us how we should frame a story, that stuff just gets my goat, always has." Steve nodded thoughtfully as he held the door open for the editor.

"I thought as much, Hank, thanks for giving me a straightforward answer. Is Rita's desk this way?" Steve pointed down a long row of metal desks lined up by the window that ran the length of the wall. Hank shook his head and pointed at the ceiling.

"Has her own office. Second floor, third one on the left when you hit the top of the stairs." Hank reached out and touched Steve's arm as he turned toward the steps.

"Let's have a drink in the next week or so. By then we might have some notes to compare, and I want to ask you some questions I have about Bernie and the Casablanca." Steve smiled as he put his foot on the first step.

"That sounds good, Hank. When you see an opening in your

schedule, call Miss Perone and set it up." Steve waved, turned, and took the stairs two at a time.

Rita Malone was at her typewriter with her back to him when Steve rapped on the open door frame. Rita held a heavily braceleted hand up in the air.

"Put it on the desk, please," drawing out the syllables of the last word. Steve chuckled. Rita swiveled in her chair when she heard him and smiled.

"Steve Cannon. I don't think I have ever seen you down here." Steve slipped into one of the chairs in front of the gray metal desk.

"I was just downtown talking to the cops and I thought I might pop in and see if you had a few minutes." Rita moved her wheeled chair toward the desk. She put a finger to her lips and motioned toward the door. Steve stood up and closed it, sitting back down in the suddenly quiet office. Rita smiled again and pushed an ashtray toward Steve's side of the desk, her gold bracelets shining brightly against her dark skin. She sat back in her chair and watched as Steve pulled a zippo lighter from his back pocket and lit a Pall Mall. Her eyes held an inquisitive gaze.

"Talking to the cops? What do they have to say for themselves?" Steve took a small drag on the cigarette.

"The usual. Though it is obvious they are making the big push on this one. Between the governor and the church, they are feeling the heat. Problem is Samuels. He has no imagination and is more interested in how he looks than solving crimes." Steve leaned forward and flicked the ash off the end of the cigarette and into the tray.

"That all?" Rita's face wore a half smile. Steve smiled back, but more broadly.

"You know I found out some things I can't divulge just yet." Rita nodded quickly and picked up a small piece of paper from her desk.

"My guess is that you want the name of my source out at NSU, right?" Steve put the cigarette to his lips and nodded.

"If it doesn't put you in a bind, yeah, that would be helpful." Rita leaned across the desk and placed the paper in front of Steve. Steve picked it up with the hand holding the cigarette.

"Maggie Hannigan?" Steve folded the paper and slipped it into his shirt pocket. Rita clasped her hands in front of her on the desk.

"You know I will interview her again after you talk to her." Steve agreed with a smile.

"Yes, I do. I will caution her to keep our talk to herself, but ultimately, it is up to her. But on to brighter things. Are you ready for tomorrow night?" A quick look of panic crossed Rita's face.

"You heard about that? You aren't going to be there are you?" Steve chuckled as he stood up and crushed his smoke out in the tray.

"Of course, wouldn't miss it, and Bernie would drag me down there anyway even if I tried to stay away. Remy is excited about it, which is enough for me, I look forward to it." Rita shook her head as she rose and moved toward the open doorway where Steve was leaning.

"I should have my head examined for ever agreeing to this, but I must admit that it has been great fun so far, Oscar Aleman and Stephane Grapelli have been so nice and supportive, and it does sound good if I do say so myself. Plus, the money. I was surprised at Bernie's generosity." Steve stepped out into the narrow hallway.

"Top drawer all the way for that man." Steve held out his hand. "Keep in touch. I will call Maggie Hannigan, today or tomorrow." Rita shook Steve's hand.

"Be careful, Steve, she is no pushover." Steve smiled as he turned toward the stairs.

*

Steffi Perone sat in the gold brocade chair in front of Steve as he read the calendar she had placed on his desk. After a minute, he looked up.

"Is this everything, Miss Perone?"

"Yes, Mr. Cannon. I am sorry it is so full, but between Mr. Cathay and Mr. Gold, I am afraid they are relying heavily on you and require a lot of your time leading up to the opening." Steve nodded thoughtfully.

"You said there was something else, Miss Perone?"

"Oh yes, I almost forgot, Mr. Cannon. Mr. Stanwick called again this afternoon when you were out. He seemed anxious to get hold of you."

"Did he leave a number?" Steffi nodded. Steve sighed.

"Alright, Miss Perone. If he calls again, tell him that I will be in touch by early next week at the latest." Steffi stood to go. Steve held up his hand and smiled.

"Miss Perone. Rita Malone is putting on a dress rehearsal tomorrow night in the 'Rick's Café Theater'. Would you like to go take in the show with Remy and me? In fact, maybe Ida would like to join us as well." Steffi shook her head sadly.

"Mother doesn't go out, Mr. Cannon, not for many years." Her expression brightened. "But I would love to go." Steve stood up.

"Great. It starts at eight, so we will pick you up at seven. Is that OK?"

"Of course, Mr. Cannon." Steffi's face lost the smile as she started toward the door.

"I have to go home and decide what I am going to wear." Steve chuckled as the door to his office closed behind her. He picked up the phone and dialed the number on the small piece of paper that Rita had given him. After three rings he heard someone pick up the phone, but whoever it was didn't speak.

"Hello?" There was a two second pause before Maggie Hannigan spoke.

"Who is this?" The voice was high and reedy and definitely belonged to an older woman. Steve also thought he detected a slight southern accent.

"Hello, Miss Hannigan. My name is Steve Cannon and I had some questions about the recent murders and I thought perhaps you could help me." This time the pause was two beats longer.

"Questions? Why would you think I could help you with that?" Steve decided to wait a few beats himself before he answered.

"Rita Malone down at the Sun says that you are an expert on all things Mormon." He counted the seconds. Five, until he heard a scoff.

"Hardly, Mr. Cannon. I teach Nevada history to young numb-skulls and as most everyone that lives here knows, the Mormons are as much a part of the landscape in this state as sand and saltbush. I have an outsiders' knowledge at best. Why are you so interested in the murders?" Steve smiled to himself.

"Sometimes I work with the police, Miss Hannigan, and they have some clues that are rather cryptic. I think you can help decipher them for me."

"What kind of clues, Mr. Cannon?"

"The kind that are written in blood, Miss Hannigan." Another interval of five seconds ensued.

"I see, Mr. Cannon." Steve broke the pattern and replied quickly.

"I don't feel comfortable talking about this on the phone, Miss Hannigan. Are you available tomorrow sometime? I can come to you."

"Yes, Mr. Cannon, I will be back home from the university by noon. Shall we say one o'clock? I am out in the valley just past the Rocking Horse Bar."

"That would be fine, Miss Hannigan." Steve wrote down the address and then hung up.

JULY 2

STEVE TURNED AROUND carefully in the confined space. He pivoted again and took two steps to his right. He peered down at a craps table twenty feet below. He noted his location on a piece of paper he kept on a clipboard. Several minutes later he emerged into an 4x8 low ceilinged room that was formed by the intersection of three catwalks. He handed the clipboard to Jack Cathay who looked down skeptically at the sheet in his hand before he fastened his watery blue eyes on Steve and spoke in his guttural growl.

"Bad news?" Steve shrugged.

"You're gonna need two more guys per shift minimum, and on busy nights even more."

"Why?" Steve looked evenly at the older man, turned, and indicated the portion of the catwalk he had just come from.

"When you have the casino run-through, put twenty-five or thirty of the shills two people deep, around those two tables. You'll see that half the action is obscured unless you have a guy at every position in there. Sorry, that's just how I see it." Jack sighed and looked at the sheet in his hands.

"Already got more guys than the Desert Inn ever had." His voice trailed off into a grumble. Steve pointed down the long catwalk behind Jack.

"Then I guess you don't want to hear about the poker room." Jack scowled and made an exasperated motion with his shoulders.

"What about the poker room?"

"There's no catwalk over the area where Bernie and Milton put the private poker room. Now, granted, poker isn't the biggest cheating problem, never has been, but once word gets around, you and I both know that the card cheats will convene." Jack nodded.

"Any ideas?" Steve nodded and reached for the clipboard. He started writing on the bottom of the top sheet as he spoke.

"Have Bernie hire two more baccarat dealers per shift. Position the extras in the poker room, here, here and here." Steve held up the sheet for Jack to see.

"You and I will hold a special meeting next week in the poker room with all the baccarat dealers. We will run through procedures and I will show them the likely scams. Just having them in there moving around behind the players might be enough of a deterrent." Jack took the clipboard out of Steve's hands and studied it for a few seconds. He looked up Steve.

"Yeah, I'll make sure Bernie gets this." Steve looked at his watch.

"I have been here an hour longer than we had scheduled. I have a meeting out in the valley. When can you and I get together and go over the cage procedures?" Jack swiveled around quickly and Steve could see he was bristling, the color above his neck redder than usual.

"Nobody told me about that. I handle the cages," he hissed. Steve looked evenly at his friend.

"That's not how it works, Jack and you know it. Everybody is checked out on all aspects of security and money handling. Now, if you're unclear on that, let's go to Bernie right now and get it settled. Otherwise, meet me here tomorrow at ten." Steve stared directly at the blue eyes. He could see Jack weighing the options in his mind. After several seconds, Jack shrugged.

"What the hell, I got nothing to hide. Tomorrow at ten, at the central cage." Steve nodded and smiled. Jack did not smile back.

"See you then Jack." Steve patted him on the arm as he brushed by him and headed down the catwalk that would lead him to the narrow stairs and out onto the casino floor.

A strong wind was blowing up the valley and made the ninety-nine degree heat seem cooler as Steve drove deep into Paradise Valley. He slowed as he came to the turn-off that lead to the Rocking Horse Bar, and as the Jeep plowed through the corner he could see that the dirt parking lot was full as usual for a Saturday afternoon. He took a left turn and drove until he reached a cattle guard and a long pipe gate across the road. He climbed out of the Jeep and stepped carefully across the guard. The gate was chained, but not locked. Steve unwound the chain and swung the gate inward. He drove through and swung the gate back into position, wrapping the chain as he had found it. He drove slowly through a thick grove of willows until the road widened into an area of hard-packed dirt and crushed granite in front of a large rambling Spanish style one story house. Steve figured it was probably built in the 1880's and was likely one of the many old haciendas that dotted the valley, the last remnants of the large Spanish land grants.

Steve had just stepped out of the Jeep and was looking at an old well that sat ten yards from the car when he heard a screen door slam shut behind him. He turned and watched as a tall thin woman in khaki shorts and a red flannel shirt stopped at the edge of the wooden steps that lead into the house. Her head was full of short reddish curls and her face sat on top of a long thin neck. Her eyes were squinted from the sun and her skin was wrinkled and tanned as she peered at her visitor.

"You, Cannon?" Steve stepped around in front of the Jeep and stopped.

"Yes, I am." He waited and gazed evenly at the woman fifteen feet away, guessing that the same conversational cadence as the phone call was in store. After a few seconds, she stepped to the side, her hiking boots scraping on the rough surface.

"Well come on in, then, you don't have a hat and you will stroke out in the sun." Steve snorted to himself and followed her into the coolness of the front room. There was a fan spinning lazily in the ceiling, the room was lined with glass cabinets and there were three leather club chairs in the middle on top of a Navajo rug. Steve bent down and peered at the first cabinet he came to. It was filled with Navajo and Hopi pottery and baskets. Steve was very familiar with most of the material culture of the native inhabitants of the Great Basin, but there were several examples presented that he had never seen. He was examining some stone projectiles in the next case when Maggie Hannigan came back into the room with two tall glasses of lemonade. She held one of the moist glasses out to Steve and indicated the chairs in the middle of the room.

"Lemonade is all I have, don't drink, don't smoke." She eyed Steve suspiciously as she settled down in the farthest chair. Steve chose the one directly across from her and sat down. He took a big sip of the lemonade and smiled across the space that separated them.

"That is kind of ironic, given the likely topic of our conversation, don't you think Miss Hannigan?" She snorted into her glass.

"Like a Mormon, you're thinking, right? Nothing like it at all. Just had two brothers and a father that died from drink and I never could see the point of cigarettes, so there you are." She indicated the wider room before her dark eyes settled back on Steve.

"I don't see much use in you and me spinning the small talk, so why don't you tell me about these clues you are so interested in." Steve shrugged and pulled out his notebook.

"First of all Miss Hannigan.."

"Maggie."

"OK, Maggie. What does the 'Knights of Nauvoo' mean?" She took a small sip from her glass and shrugged.

"Nothing, in and of itself. The significance probably lies in what someone wants it to mean." Steve held out his hands in a questioning gesture.

"I would guess it is a reference to the original Danites, that were formed in the city of Nauvoo, Illinois. Their main purpose was to defend the Mormons from the persecutions, but they branched out, began to intimidate and kill apostates and anyone trying to leave the church. Someone made it up is my opinion, I have never heard the Danites referred to by that name." Steve wrote in his notebook.

"Does the name 'Wild Bill' ring a bell." Maggie smiled.

"Of course it does, 'Wild Bill Hickman', he was the original leader of the Danites in Illinois." Steve scribbled a few more lines. He drew a figure in the notebook and looked across at the tall woman, then waited several seconds before he asked his next question.

"The symbol '3M' was scrawled in blood at the scene of one of the murders." He stood up and held the notebook in front of Maggie. She peered at it for a few seconds before she rose and walked into the next room. Ten seconds later she returned and held a book out toward Steve. Steve took the slim tome and sat back in the chair. He turned the spine toward the light.

'The Mountain Meadows Massacre' by Jaunita Brooks.

Steve thumbed the pages and looked up at Maggie.

"You know about the massacre, Mr. Cannon?"

"Vaguely." Maggie pointed to the book.

"120 wagon train settlers were traveling through southern Utah in 1857. A company of Mormons dressed as Paiutes ambushed them just southwest of Cedar City, at a place called Mountain Meadows. The settlers held out for four days. The Mormons shed their war paint and gained access to the encampment by pretending to be their saviors. When the settlers laid down their arms, they were all killed except for seventeen children under the age of seven. Several of the women and older girls were interfered with before they were hacked to death with tomahawks." Maggie stopped and stared quietly at Steve.

"The code word inside the church for that event is the one

you've got written there." Steve nodded and turned the book over in his hands for a few seconds.

"May I keep this for a few days?" Maggie considered Steve's face for several seconds before she nodded. Steve stood from his chair and walked to a case directly behind Maggie. He waited for her to turn her head before he pointed to one of the pictures.

"That is Marcus Boomer when he was young." Maggie stood up and bent over slightly, peering at the faded photograph from five feet away.

"You are right, but how did you know that?" Steve returned to his chair.

"I have known Marcus since I was twelve." Maggie shook her head.

"I find that hard to believe, Mr. Cannon. Marcus Boomer is a recluse and doesn't like white people." Steve smiled thinly.

"Would you like me to describe the rusted table and chairs, the old wrecked '46 Chevy, the line-up of oil paintings inside his trailer?" Maggie shook her head.

"Well you must be someone special, Mr. Cannon, I have only been there once and it was with a delegation from the legislature, a tribal centennial, if I remember." Steve shrugged.

"Hard to say why someone has an affinity for someone else in this world, Maggie, just as big a mystery as to why 120 people had to die for no other reason than they were in the wrong place at the wrong time, or why upstanding pillars of the community end their lives lying in pieces in their own blood." He held up the book. "Any theories as to who might be committing these murders?" Steve passed the time counting in his head. Eleven.

"None spring to mind, Mr. Cannon."

"Do you believe in Danites, Maggie?" Maggie scoffed. Five beats later, she replied.

"Yes, I do, Mr. Cannon, but these days I believe they wear three piece suits and went to law schools back east." Steve stood up.

"Well, Maggie Hannigan, keep reading the newspaper articles, and if anything occurs to you, let me know." Steve slipped his wallet from his back pocket and extracted one of his business cards. He held it out toward the woman. She leaned forward in the chair and took it from his hand. He waited until she had read it and slipped it into one of the front pockets of her shorts.

"The police would rather the public not know about the clues we discussed. I am sure that Rita Malone will call you soon with her inquiries. I can't tell you what to do or say, Miss Hannigan, but I think it would be better if we kept this between ourselves." Maggie stood up and looked straight at Steve, their eyes at the same height.

"Not promising anything, Mr. Cannon, but I would be lying if I tried to tell you I am not intrigued." Steve smiled as he turned toward the front door.

"Thank you for the lemonade, Maggie." She followed him out onto the porch, stopping at the top of the two wooden steps as he walked toward the Jeep.

"Mr. Cannon." Steve turned just as he reached the driver's door and waited for her to continue.

"The church is a very different organization than any you have likely come across. Things are seldom what they seem." Steve nodded and waved before he climbed into the hot interior of the red Jeep.

*

Steve took a window seat in the rundown diner across the street from the parking lot that was connected to the Police Station. He had just ordered coffee when he saw Tam on the other side of the road waiting for the traffic to clear. Steve caught the eye of the waitress and motioned that she should bring another cup of coffee. Tam stood in the doorway and moved to the booth when he saw Steve wave his hand. He stood while the waitress put two full coffee cups and two menus in the middle of the table. Tam slid carefully into the cramped space and reached for the small metal creamer and two sugar packs before he grunted a greeting. Steve smiled serenely and snorted to himself as he took his first sip.

"Lovely day, don't you think?" Tam let out a slightly longer grunt as he reached across the table to pick up Steve's spoon. He stirred the light brown liquid as he looked across at Steve.

"Glad you called. I needed a break from that grind."

"You guys any further along than when I last saw you?" Tam shook his head and stared down into his cup.

"Nope, most of everybody's time is split between interviewing possible suspects and witnesses and trying to keep the governor and the press happy. Not to mention the church guys from Salt Lake that are camped out at the motel down the street." Tam used his thumb to indicate the direction.

"You narrowed down the suspect list yet?" Tam looked blankly at the private detective.

"If they have, they haven't told me, but I don't think so. Everyone I have talked to has an alibi or no motive, or both. What did you find out from Miss Malone?"

"Not much that isn't in her stories, except she mentioned that she has received some of her information from an anonymous caller. She also gave me the name of a history lecturer out at NSU. I interviewed her an hour ago." Steve pulled out his notebook, and flipped to the last page. Tam pulled a larger one from inside his suit coat pocket.

"The Knights of Nauvoo is probably a reference to the Danites, but apparently not one that anybody has ever used before, 'Wild Bill', last name, 'Hickman', was the leader of the original group of Danites in Illinois, and '3M' is how the church refers to the Mountain Meadows Massacre. You know what that is?" Tam scoffed as he scribbled hurriedly, using large block letters and three pages in the process.

"Yes, of course, I do, but that was a hundred years ago. What's the connection to the here and now?" Steve shrugged as he flipped through several pages of his book before he put it down.

"Who knows? Maybe something. Maybe nothing." Tam made a disgusted look and crammed the notebook back into his pocket.

"I could have stayed across the street and learned that much." Steve smiled.

"Well, according to you, nobody over there was able to put the clues into any sort of context, so I would say, that crossing the street, was worth your while." Tam leaned back against the cracked black vinyl of the booth and stretched his hands over his head. Yawning, he looked across the table and folded his arms.

"Maybe. Give me the name of this history gal. Samuels will want to know where this stuff came from." Steve tore a page from the back of the notebook, but paused, his pencil poised above the small lined sheet.

"How about a list of the people that have been interviewed so far, and what they said." Tam stared into the dark brown eyes for several seconds before he sighed and sat back in the booth his arms dangling loose at his sides.

"I'll see what I can do. Samuels and the other guys won't be around tomorrow. Let's meet and I can let you see what we have so far." Steve quickly copied Maggie Hannigan's name and number and pushed it across the table toward Tam. Steve slid out of the booth and reached into his pants pocket, extracting a silver dollar and spinning it on top of the formica table. It was still spinning as Tam followed him to the door. Steve pointed to the Jeep ten paces away.

"That's me. How about one o'clock tomorrow?"

"Sure, see you then." Tam looked quickly in both directions before he stepped off the curb and jogged to the other side of the street. Steve watched him disappear behind several black and white police cars before he pulled a new pack of cigarettes out of his coat pocket. He lit the smoke and began walking toward Fremont Street. A half block later, he came to a motor lodge that promised free hot coffee and air conditioning on the tall marquee that loomed over the small office. 'No Vacancy' flashed on and off in the window.

Steve walked slowly toward the building. From the street he could see a man inside leaning on the counter and watching as Steve approached. Steve bent over and stubbed out his smoke in the sand of an ashtray just outside the door. He was smiling as he straightened up and pushed through the door. He stopped just inside the door and still smiling, hitched up his pants. The man glanced at him briefly, before resuming his long stare down the street. He was thin and nearly bald and did not look any too well.

"Full up?" The man didn't move his gaze as he replied.

"That's what 'No Vacancy' generally means." Steve chuckled, grinned and moved to a chair that was next to a table stacked with several magazines. He sat down and gazed at the man's profile for a few seconds.

"Most of the places around here are almost empty. How'd you get so lucky?" The man glanced over at Steve again.

"I got customers, they don't." Steve smiled thinly.

"Yeah, and they all dress and look alike. Kind of your own private convention." The man sighed and stood upright. He turned and faced Steve.

"You cops are all alike. Say what you got to say, or get out of here." Steve shook his head and stood up. He was at least four inches taller than the man in front of him.

"I'm no cop. But I do have something that might interest you." Steve pulled out his wallet and laid a new twenty dollar bill on the counter just out of the man's reach. Steve's hand rested on the cool granite a few inches away from the currency. The man glanced down but didn't look up at Steve.

"What's that for?" Steve smiled and leaned casually on the counter his hands clasped in front of him.

"It's for the answer to one small question." The man now looked blankly at Steve.

"What question?" Steve held his gaze steadily on the small wizened face.

"How long is this convention booked for?" The man looked quickly at the bill before he met Steve's gaze.

"Til the end of next week."

"What is the name of their leader?" The man scoffed and reached for the money.

"That's two questions, mister." Steve pulled the bill back and held it up.

"Yeah, twenty clams doesn't go as far as it used to. Ten apiece, and if I ask a third, I'll give you another ten."

"Show me." Steve pulled his wallet out and extracted two fives and held them up in the opposite hand from the one that held the twenty.

"Amis Kinsley." Steve folded the bill lengthways with two fingers as he handed it across the counter. He folded the other two bills into his front pocket as he turned to go.

"Room 22, if you want to talk with him." Steve turned back and he put his hand on the chrome bar of the door and pushed it open.

"Thanks. I may do that."

*

The blue spotlight cut through the smoke that filled the air in light gray layers and illuminated a microphone standing alone on center stage. A rhythm guitarist began to play at a brisk pace, his outline silhouetted by a deep blue backlight. A paler spotlight came on just as the thin mustachioed Oscar Aleman began the fast hot jazz runs that punctuated one of his signature Irving Berlin tunes. After five bars, Stephane Grappellli came in, and used his violin to weave the rhythm and the melody together. The trio played on for twenty bars and then brought the volume down slightly for three more bars. Out of the blue smoke of the backstage, Rita Malone moved forward in a slow stroll that emulated the quick gypsy beat. She wore a bright red, full length dress, her hair was swept up with a matching red rose behind her left ear. She stepped into the spotlight and one bar later, she placed her hand gently on the microphone and beneath lightly glittered eyelids, looked out over the heads of the audience as she began to sing.

"Every night you hear her croon, a Russian lullaby."

Her voice was low and smoky and a counterpoint to the accompaniment behind her. Her body swayed to the pulse as her voice grew in volume to match the instruments.

"Rock a bye my baby, somewhere there may be, a land that's free for you and me and a Russian lullaby."

She turned and swayed gently in place as Oscar and Stephane took instrumental breaks, speeding up the tempo as Rita's voice slid back in underneath them and scatted the melody for eight bars, before the final chorus.

"Just a plaintive little tune when baby starts to cry. Rock a bye my baby, somewhere there may be, a land that's free for you and me and a Russian lullaby."

The lights came up bathing the stage in a soft yellow glow as the trio led out with ten more bars of the torrid beat. When they finished, everyone in the showroom rose to their feet clapping, and drowning out the slow, mournful sound of Grappellis' violin. When they had quieted and began to take their seats again, they recognized the Hoagy Carmichael song as Rita stepped once more to the mic.

"Sometimes I wonder why I spend the lonely nights... dreaming of a song."

Her voice was low and smooth and her phrasing and inflections matched the gypsy jazz the three musicians were pouring forth. As she reached the final chorus, her voice and the staccato single notes of Oscar Aleman's guitar created a seamless sound.

"Though I dream in vain, in my heart, there always will remain....... my stardust melody... the memory of love's refrain."

Rita smiled as the last notes of Stephane's violin faded. She stepped back from the microphone and took a small bow. Most of the crowd was still cheering when she left the stage and moved toward the table where Bernie, Remy, Steve and Steffi were seated. She sat down, her breathing heavy as she accepted a cloth napkin from Remy and quickly dabbed her forehead. Remy hugged her and kissed her on both cheeks and whispered something to her while looking into her light brown eyes. Bernie poured a glass of champagne for everyone before he leaned over the table toward Rita. He held up his glass.

"To one of the prettiest voices I have heard in a long, long, time." All except Rita raised their glasses. After the toast, Rita shook her head and looked around the table.

"I can't believe how exciting that was. I had doubts this week that I could do it, but Remy convinced me I could, and now I know she was right." Remy smiled from her place beside Steve.

"Bernie and I knew that you were perfect to front the trio. It made me homesick for Paris. But we still get three more numbers from you, right?" Rita smiled.

"If I have the energy, yes. I forgot how draining live performing can be." The last few syllables were drowned out by the trio reaching the climax of 'Minor Swing.' As the last flourishes of the finish died away, Rita took another sip from her champagne glass and stood up.

"Thank you all for coming. It made all the difference." She turned and to another round of applause, climbed the two steps back onto the stage.

JULY 3

STEVE WALKED TWENTY yards and up a floor up from his office and knocked on the white door. He waited for a few seconds and then knocked again. When he heard a muffled reply from inside, he thumbed the large gold handle and opened the door partway.

"Jack?" He heard noises coming from the kitchen two rooms away. Jack Cathay came around the corner holding a chrome coffee carafe in one hand and two white porcelain cups in the other.

"You need saucers?" The normally growly voice held an extra edge from the early hour. Steve chuckled, stepped into the foyer and closed the door behind him.

"No, Jack, just the cups." Jack rolled his eyes as he gestured to two wing chairs and a coffee table in the middle of the room. There were several stacks of paper neatly arranged on the round glass. Steve sat down and accepted one of the cups and held it steady as a thick stream of hot black liquid sloshed into the cup. Steve sat back in the chair and pulled one of the pages from the stack nearest him and deposited his cup on top of it. Jack set the carafe down in the middle of the table and still bent over, looked at Steve.

"What? You need a napkin or something? I'm fresh out of doilies so you're gonna have to rough it." Steve laughed and picked up his cup, blowing softly across the surface before he tested it with a small sip.

"Sit down, Jack and relax. I'm not the enemy, I just need to understand how your system works." Jack gazed back at Steve with his watery blue eyes.

"Hmmph."

Steve shook his head, smiled and took several more sips of the coffee. He put down his cup and pulled out his cigarettes. He took his time lighting up and watched as Jack reached behind him and picked up an ashtray from the small bar. He slid it across to Steve. Steve put the crumpled cellophane from the fresh pack in the round tray.

"So, Jack, give me a quick and dirty rundown on how the counting is going to work." Jack sat back and shrugged.

"Pretty straightforward. Every eight hours, all of the three cages get counted on a staggered schedule. Once every twenty four hours, all the bagged currency and coins get transferred upstairs to the main safe, ready for the armored car when it comes at one. I figure the transfers should happen at six in the morning, less people around to get wise, right?" Steve nodded.

"So, three trips up, one from each cage?" Jack nodded.

"Lighter and quicker that way. Takes more guys, but the safety factor is higher."

"What about the counters? Different crew for each cage?" Jack shook his head.

"No, same crew for all of them. Either, Bernie, me or Andy will be at each counting, along with my two other guys, Mitch and Rocco, on days, and Melvin and Bobby doing nights. After the opening and we see how people shake out, we will add more guys."

"How much does the Gaming Control Board say needs to be on hand for the opening?" Jack's thick stubby fingers sorted quickly through the stack in front of him. He pulled out a piece of light blue paper and handed it to Steve.

"$750,000, minimum." Steve frowned at the paper.

"That's pretty steep, why so much?" Jack pointed at the paper.

"I had it down to $450,000, but then Bernie let the cat out of the bag about the no limit on twenty-one, baccarat and roulette."

"I thought that the 'no limit' was only for baccarat." Jack held out his hands and rolled his eyes.

"Me, too." Steve handed the paper back to the ex-mobster and waited until Jack had carefully placed it back into the stack and was looking at him.

"How much did you usually carry at the Desert Inn, the juice part aside?" Jack looked up blankly at the ceiling before he answered.

"Two fifty, three tops, maybe a bit more if there was a lot of high rollers in the hotel. But Tommy always insists that there is another 500 G's ten minutes away in the bank vault just in case."

"How is Bernie set up on that score?" Jack screwed his mouth into a downward frown.

"Don't know. I asked him three days ago after the Gaming Control guys left, but he got distracted and never gave me an answer." Steve pulled a new notebook from his shirt pocket. He talked as he wrote.

"I'll check with him on that, Jack and let you know. How many of the slots have been certified by the Control Board?"

"Last I heard, most of them. Bernie is still waiting on those machines from Perone Mechanicals, so that has probably slowed things down a bit." Steve scribbled quickly across a blank page.

"Well, we have less than two weeks to get them going. How many certified slots would we have up and ready to go if we opened tonight?" Jack shuffled through the papers and read one four pages down the stack.

"Two hundred sixty-eight as of Thursday, but that doesn't include any dollar machines only the nickels, dimes and quarters." Steve frowned.

"Bernie may be wearing too many hats here. He still insisting on being the casino manager?" Jack nodded.

"Just like Tommy Carmino. Who you gonna find just standing around that can pull rank on Bernie?" Steve laughed and sat back in the chair, taking a drag on the cigarette before he took another sip from his coffee cup.

"Yeah, that can be a problem. Let's put our heads together over the next few days and see if between the two of us we can come up with some names that Bernie could go for and that might get past the gaming commission."

"Might be worth a shot. Tommy always rotates the floor managers and box men pretty routinely, but then again, Tommy has other problems we don't have." Both men nodded knowingly. Steve stood up.

"I'm going to get out of your hair. We have plenty of meetings scheduled this week, to get most of this covered and put to bed. You going to Bernie's BBQ?" Jack stood up and walked to the front door.

"Yeah. How about you?" Steve opened the door and walked out onto the promenade.

"Wouldn't miss it."

*

Steve drove up the Strip, past the Sahara Hotel and into the business district. Instead of the usual shortcut, he continued on until he made a right turn in front of the train station and slowed for the traffic that jammed Fremont Street most afternoons. The colorful mix of locals, tourists and cruising high school kids, added even more bustle to the narrow canyon formed by the tall brightly lit facades of the downtown casinos. Twenty minutes and four blocks later, Steve turned off Fremont and traveled the three short blocks to the Police Station in less than thirty seconds. When he reached the war room, he stopped and held his ear close to the door. Hearing no voices, he swung the silver handle down and pushed the heavy metal slab open a few inches. Tam was all alone at one of the center tables, smoking a cigarette and looking at the large boards arrayed around the room. Steve stepped inside letting the door clang shut. Tam didn't move from his position, but turned his head to the side.

"That you, Cannon?" Steve didn't reply, but walked into the detective's peripheral vision and stood looking at the pictures and documents spread across the front of the room. He took two steps forward and bent over to look at three black and white photos of the second crime scene. The least gory one was a close-up of the phrase: 'Knights of Nauvoo' written in blood. In the photo the scrawl looked like it was made with a thick black tarry substance. He straightened and looked down at the sandy hair that was beginning to thin on top.

"Been here long?" Tam sighed and looked down at his watch, before he turned in his chair and stubbed out his cigarette.

"Half an hour." He stood up wearily and gestured to the front of the room.

"Well, there it all is. Have at it." Steve grinned across the four feet that separated them.

"Not so fast, my friend, you are going to give me the guided tour." Steve pulled out a notebook and held it up. "I got a fresh notebook just for this case, and I expect to fill it up." Tam stared at the private detective for several seconds before he turned and walked over to the board that was nearest the door.

"It flows left to right. Here is the first murder, all the inquiries, the people that were questioned, the follow-ups and any new leads. Second murder is right in front of you, with the same information, third board over there, the one with precious little on it, is possible connections between the two men. I'm going to hit the head, and get a coke, you want one?" Steve shook his head and took Tam's place in front of the first board as the older detective disappeared into the hallway.

Steve moved from board to board, copying down several names and numbers from each. When Tam came back, Steve showed him the list.

"I am going to talk to some of these people myself. After I do, I will need to compare their statements with the ones taken earlier.

That going to be possible?" Tam took the notebook from Steve's hand and flipped through the four pages he had filled up.

"Yeah, maybe, are you going to need all of them?" Steve shook his head as he retrieved the book and held it up.

"I don't know yet. Tell you what. It would take me at least three or four days to work through this list even if I use the telephone for some of it. I'll cull through them, then I'll call you at home and give you a list of names I want to check. That way, you can steal the statements a few at a time." Tam snorted.

"Great. Give me even more chances to get caught." Steve grinned and sat down on the nearest table.

"Well you don't seem to be making much progress doing it Samuels' way." Tam didn't say anything but looked at the boards. Steve lit a cigarette and took two long puffs before he spoke again.

"Funny way to work a case. Samuels seems to be treating each one as separate event. Has he put any time into thinking about who might be next?" Tam pulled out a chair from the table Steve was sitting on and turned it so he could see Steve and still look at the boards. He leaned over the back and looked at Steve through a pall of smoke.

"Next? How could we possibly figure that out?" Steve shrugged and flicked some ash to the floor that was littered with empty paper coffee cups and sandwich wrappers.

"Both prominent Mormon business men, both the same age. Likely there is a connection somewhere, if not in their past, there is something they have in common. Where did they go to high school, where did they go to college? Where did they go on their missions? What kind of business or investment deals could they both be involved in? You see? Someone should be working those angles. Somehow they have made someone mad enough to kill them." Tam shifted in his chair and considered the boards for a few moments.

"You know what gets me? Why leave clues like that?" He looked at Steve and Steve could see the questioning behind his eyes. Steve took a drag and looked down at his smoke.

"Could be several reasons. Wants to throw Samuels off the scent, which isn't a big feat, or they want to implicate someone else, or it's their way of giving us the motive. Could be any one of those or any combination. Could be one person, could be two, or a group. But most likely it is one person. The physical evidence is too consistent. If a group were involved, there would be some difference in the writing or where they placed the clues, or something that would be amiss because there was more than one person at the scene. Too clean, too tidy for that. They were both killed in roughly the same time period, both on a weekend. This is methodical and well thought out, which means his next move and the one after that are going to be thought out as well." Tam's brow furrowed.

"You seem pretty sure there are going to be more." Steve nodded and sucked carefully on the short length of cigarette left between his fingers. He turned and tossed it into a half empty coffee cup, making a small hissing sound.

"Yeah, Tam, I'm pretty sure. Samuel's right about one thing. This is the work of a serial killer, but not a random one. These victims are hand-picked and he knows who the next ones are. My guess is that like most of these guys, a least the smart ones, he is biding his time, gauging the reaction, seeing if he has to make adjustments in his methods before he resumes." Tam shook his head and looked at the floor.

"Christ. That's all we need. As if the pressure around here isn't enough." Steve slid off the table and pushed the notebook deep into his coat pocket. Tam looked up.

"Tam. You want to get a beer?" Tam looked at his watch.

"Sure. I got an hour to kill before I pick up Lisa at my sisters' place." Steve pointed to the door and the two of them emerged into the hallway. At the entrance, Tam swung the big glass door open and held it as Steve moved through, stopping on the concrete just outside the entrance.

"Where we going?" Steve pointed north.

"You like Japanese beer?" Tam shrugged as he fell in behind Steve.

"Dunno. Had some on the troop ship coming back from the war. Can't remember what it tasted like, we were just all trying to get as much in our bellies as fast as we could." Steve snorted and nodded.

"I know a place."

*

Tam wiped the foam from his lips and watched as Steve tossed several small rice crackers into his mouth from a bowl that sat between them. Tam plucked one from the bowl and chewed it slowly.

"Wow. These are strong. What are the little green spots?" Steve smiled.

"Seaweed. An acquired taste, Tam, just like most things in life." Tam grunted and looked around the small sushi restaurant.

"How'd you find this place?"

"Remember the Martin Ogawa case last spring? Well, his father brought me here. I kind of like the atmosphere." Tam swiveled his head and looked toward the door where two elderly Japanese men were arguing over a board game. Tam turned back toward Steve.

"Yeah, swell. But the beer is pretty good. Sooo…" Tam drew out the syllables and waited until Steve had put his beer glass down. "I guess you are taking this case, right?" Steve shrugged and fished several more crackers out of the bowl.

"I am going to work it, that I know. I'm still not sure that I want to work for the church, but having someone foot the expenses is tempting."

"You'd do it without getting paid? All that time…" Steve smiled.

"Are you saying you guys don't need the help?" Tam scowled.

"Very funny, but I'm serious. Why let yourself in for the headaches? What do you care?" Steve turned in his chair.

"Suko?" A quick answer came back from behind the split blue curtains.

"Hai!!" Sukos' pale, delicate face appeared at almost the same time. She hurried to the table and bowed. Steve bowed his head slightly.

"Two more beers?" Suko bowed quickly and turned toward the back.

"Domo arigato." Steve smiled and turned back to Tam who was shaking his head.

"Now you speak Jap?" Steve continued to smile.

"Just enough to show proper respect, Tam." Tam ignored the reply and instead held the two empty beer bottles up when he saw Suko coming back to the table. When she had left, he took a large gulp and looked at his companion.

"You didn't answer me. Why take this on, especially if no one is paying you?" Steve stared toward the door without seeing.

"I don't know, it is just interesting that's all." His eyes snapped into focus and he peered intently at Tam.

"Tam, did you know that all the murder victims in the Mountain Meadows Massacre, came from the same small county in Arkansas?" Tam shook his head as he washed down several of the rice crackers with a swig of beer.

"No, I didn't, and what's more I don't care. Three days ago, you didn't know any of that and you didn't care either." Steve sat back in the chair and chuckled.

"Well there you go. Taking on cases gives you the opportunity to learn things about the world you didn't know before." Tam drained the last of his beer and stood up a scowl crossing his face.

"You about ready? I think I have heard enough for one day," he growled. Steve took the last sip left in his bottle before he stood up. He smiled at Suko and handed her a ten dollar bill. She took it with both hands and bowed deeply.

"Come again soon, Mr. Cannon. I will pass on your greetings to my uncle and my husband." When Steve had returned the bow and turned around, Tam was already standing on the sidewalk. As Steve emerged into the heat, Tam pointed at one of the small newspaper stands in front of the restaurant.

"Looks like your gal, Rita has been busy." Steve pulled a dime from his pocket and slipped it into the slot on top of the metal box. He pulled out the paper, folded it under his arm and began to follow Tam as he walked to the Jeep a half block away.

JULY 4

STEVE LOOKED AT his watch. He had two hours before he was to pick up Remy and escort her to Bernie's barbecue. He spread Rita's article out on his desk in his narrow office. He placed the notebook with the police interviews beside it. From a bottom drawer he pulled out the three previous articles she had written on the murders. He started with the first article, printed the day after the first murder. He underlined several phrases and transferred two of them to his notebook. He read the second article even more carefully than the first, though there was little new information, most of the paragraphs were updates on the slow progress of the investigation, filled out with several long circuitous quotes from Samuels that all boiled down to the fact that he had no clue and didn't even have any idea where to look for one. The third article was the most interesting, coming as it did after Rita had interviewed Maggie Hannigan. Steve read over some of the verbatim quotes from Maggie several times. He rose from his desk and walked three steps to a bookshelf mounted on the far wall just above the record turntable. He selected a paperback volume and returned to the desk. He looked at the white unadorned cover. 'Nevada Southern University – 1963'. He flipped to the table of contents and then to the history department. He found the small black and white picture of Maggie Hannigan on the second page of the history section. He slowly read the short biography and smiled to himself as he neared the end. He picked up his notebook and made two entries. He settled back in his chair and read the latest story Rita had written. All three clues were laid out each with its' own paragraph. Rita had not wasted any time getting back in touch with Maggie. An hour later he had gone over all the names he had gathered off the evidence boards. They were four more entries in his notebook. He folded the articles carefully, keeping them in order and placing them next to his notebooks and the NSU handbook. The last thing he did was to retrieve the book that Maggie had given him from his bedroom. He placed that on his desk with the other materials and went to the shower.

An hour later, Steve opened the passenger door for Remy, as she stepped down onto the warm asphalt of the Casablanca Hotel parking lot. They walked on a wide path lined with multicolored flowers that led to the main driveway and into the hotel. They ascended a one story pedestrian bridge that spanned the four lane road and ended at two revolving doors leading into the main lobby. They joined several other hotel employees and guests as they crossed the gleaming marble tiled floors and spilled out into the courtyard. Bernie and Walter had set up tables on every available plot of ground and the smoke from four outdoor grills wafted toward the guests as they formed small conversational groups or claimed a spot at one of the eight person tables. Red, white and blue bunting hung from all the sides of all the buildings surrounding the expansive courtyard.

The first person Steve saw was Shelly Cointreau. The large black man was seated at one of the tables with his wife and their son. Steve walked up behind him and placed his hands on the big shoulders.

"Shelly, how you doing?" The man turned and half stood up as a large smile crossed his oval face.

"Big gun, good to see you." He clasped both of Steve's forearms and shook them playfully. He pushed his chair away from the table and reached down for his wife's hand. The slender light skinned woman stood up and smiled shyly at Steve.

"Steve Cannon, this my wife, Henrietta." Steve took the hand she offered and tipped his head forward and smiled.

"Good to meet you, Henrietta, I always wanted to meet the woman that tamed this guy." She smiled and waved him off.

"Hasn't happened yet, Mr. Cannon, I'll let you know when it does, but I wouldn't hold my breath." She smiled up at her husband as Steve turned and wrapped his arm around Remy's waist.

"Shelly and Henrietta, this is Remy DeMarche." Steve gave her a quick hug as she shook each extended hand in turn. As she patted Henrietta's hand in hers, she looked down at the table.

"And who is this?" The young boy in the starched white shirt and bright blue bow-tie, looked up at the strange woman and then at his mother, before his long-lashed eyes dropped to the table.

"Steven," he said in a quiet voice. Remy knelt down until her eyes were at the same level as the youngster.

"Well, Steven, would it be OK with you if Steve and I sat here at your table?" The boy's eager grin proceeded a big nod which was followed closely by a frown when he heard his father's voice.

"Steven. Answer Miss DeMarche." Steven looked up quickly.

"Yes, please, Miss DeMarche." Remy and Steve laughed as Steve pulled out chairs for them on the other side of the table. A waiter appeared and asked for a drink order as he picked up the empty glasses in front of the Cointreau family. Steve had just finished ordering when he saw a familiar tanned face bearing down on the group.

Tommy Carmino stopped on the far side of the table and smirked. He wore a powder blue suit and a light pink shirt. His only sartorial concession to the casual occasion was the lack of a tie, but he had substituted a light blue, silk cravet. He motioned with his drink toward Shelly and Henrietta.

"Good evening, Shelly, Mrs. Cointreau." He turned toward

Remy. "Miss DeMarche, how nice to see you." His smile thinned as he turned his gaze toward Steve. He held up his drink.

"Slick." Steve smiled.

"Tommy, how have you been?"

"Can't complain, Slick, and nobody would listen if I did, but I can't help but notice as I circulate around here," he swung his arm in a wide motion, "that it looks like a chapter meeting of the Former Employees of the Desert Inn Association. I expect to see Earl driving Miss Horvath around in a golf cart any minute, now." Tommy was gazing blankly at Steve, but Shelly squirmed uncomfortably in his chair. Tommy continued.

"Who else are you going to kipe?" Steve sat back and laughed.

"I don't know, Tommy, who you got?" Tommy smiled coldly as his eyes narrowed.

"I don't know, Slick, who do you want? How about Cal and Benny? Seems Jack Cathay has been putting a bug in their ear that maybe Bernie needs some floor help. Know anything about that?" Steve smiled and stretched his arm out on the back of Remy's chair who had turned and was engaging Shelly and Henrietta in conversation.

"Jack doesn't report to me, Tommy, and I wouldn't worry anyway, were I you. Everybody knows that the D.I. pays the best for casino help." Steve turned his gaze casually toward Shelly, before he looked back at the mobster. Tommy snorted and circled the table and sat down one chair away from Steve. He finished his drink and placed the glass on the table. He smiled and chuckled.

"Enough boring business talk, Cannon. How is your son doing? I heard he was in Marine boot camp." Steve nodded and took a sip of his newly arrived beer.

"He starts his next eight week phase in OCS next week. Should get leave the last of September." Tommy smiled.

"Just like his old man, right? Going to give 'em hell?" Steve shrugged.

"Don't know, Tommy, that's up to him and Uncle Sam." Tommy stood up and shook his empty glass.

"I gotta go get a refill, Slick, but a little birdie told me that they saw you hitting balls at the municipal range a few days ago. You going to start playing again?" Steve shrugged.

"Haven't decided. Just out for a little exercise, not a big deal." Tommy started to move away from the table.

"I hope you let me know if you do. I am always looking for easy money." Steve snorted and turned back to the conversation at the table as he watched Tommy disappear into the crowd that was milling around in front of one of the fountains. Shelly leaned back and spoke to Steve behind the two chairs between them.

"Damn, big gun, let me know before you bring guys like that over. He was shooting daggers at me the whole time."

"Story I heard, Shelly, was that you gave him a chance to match Bernie's offer. He's got no kick." The big man nodded.

"Yeah, but it don't pay to rub it in like that. You know?" Steve reached across behind Remy's chair and patted the big arm.

"Don't worry, Shel, you're safe here. Tommy wouldn't do anything to upset Bernie."

As if conjured, Bernie appeared at the table just behind Steven. He smiled at the little group, and then looked down at Steven.

"Steven, do you want a couple of hot dogs?" Steven looked at his father before he nodded energetically. Bernie looked at the rest of the group.

"I got steaks, hamburgers, chicken and hot dogs, plus salads, watermelons, cake, and the works. You need to get in line, before it is all gone, c'mon." Bernie swung his arm toward one of the grills and waited while Steve and Remy stood from their seats and followed the small family toward the line that had formed.

An hour later, Steve was sitting by himself, when Bernie came toward him with a plate of food. He put the plate on the table and sat down next to Steve.

"Where's Remy?" Steve indicated with his cigarette.

"She's over on the other side of the fountain with some of her girls. Shelly and Henrietta took Steven home. Are you just sitting down?" Bernie smiled as he cut into a piece of chicken and took a bite. When he had swallowed, he looked at Steve.

"Yeah. Walter ate earlier, now he is supervising the latecomers and those that want seconds." Bernie gestured with his fork in the general direction of the casino. "Got an earful from Jack this afternoon. He says the two of you think I need more help on the floor." Steve stretched and tapped the ash off his smoke into a paper plate before he replied.

"I don't want to see you doing all the work, Bern. There are a lot of pros in this town that would jump at the chance to work for you. I say load up the floor and keep the ones that work out the best. What do you have to lose?" Bernie shrugged as he chewed and swallowed a mouthful of potato salad.

"I told Jack to hire as many new guys as he thinks we needed to be covered on all the shifts. I figure the opening goes well, we are home free, but let me ask you a question. How much should we have in reserves on opening night?" Steve took a swig of beer and watched as a juggling clown walked by followed by a gaggle of kids.

"As much as you can raise, Bern. After the first week, take the excess to the bank and keep it there. Valley Bank will give you twenty-four hour access to the safe deposit boxes. Jack says that is what Tommy does. But my main worry is why you have no limit on blackjack and roulette?" Bernie put down his fork and took a sip of his beer.

"Funny, Skipper asked me the same thing. I hadn't really thought about it after somebody came up with the idea and now as I sit here, I don't remember if it was my idea or somebody else's." Bernie took a deep breath and looked out over the crowd. "What do you think?" Steve thought for a few seconds as he flipped a new pack of Pall Malls over repeatedly on the tablecloth. He turned to Bernie.

"I say, drop the no-limit for the opening except for baccarat. That will eliminate the need for extra security worries right out of the box. After a few weeks when we have had a chance to evaluate the level of action, introduce it into the private poker and black-jack rooms if we think it will increase play." Bernie smiled.

"I like that, that is a good plan." He hesitated for a second, then slapped his hand down on the table.

"I will put a million in cash out for the opening. After a week, you and Jack and I will decide how much stays here at all times and the rest goes into reserves down at the bank. Whatta' think?" Steve sat up straight.

"You sure, Bern? That is a lot of scratch." Bernie nodded his agreement.

"You're damn right it is. But there are elements in this town who would like to see us fail, and one slip up in not being covered would be all they would need to get the commission to put us out of business. The Gaming Control Board says seven hundred large, so they should be happy with a mil and the new limits." Steve looked up and saw Skipper coming toward the table as Bernie stood up and started stacking the empty plates. Skipper waved at Steve and then leaned across the table toward Bernie.

"I have been looking for you. The photographer from the Review-Journal is here. Wants some pictures of you, together with Jack, Remy, Milton, and whoever else we can get to stand still." Bernie moved with his hands full toward a waiter pushing a cart piled high with dirty plates and then turned back toward the table.

"Sure, Skip, let's go." Steve gestured to Skipper to get his attention.

"Nobody here from the Sun?" Skipper looked at Bernie quickly before he shook his head.

"Called them three times, finally someone called back late

yesterday. Said someone would be here." He looked at his watch. "Three hours late, now. The RJ guy's been here since the first people rolled in." Steve nodded thoughtfully as the Bernie and Skipper moved off toward the casino.

Two hours later, Steve switched on the desk lamp in his office. He opened the book that Maggie had lent him. He flipped to the back of the book until he came to the index. With the notebook open before him, he began to examine each name that appeared in the yellowed pages.

JULY 5

MISS PERONE SAT upright in the swivel chair behind her desk as she read the double spaced list on a piece of paper that Steve had just handed her. When she was finished, she looked up and smiled at the concerned face in front of her.

"Of course, Mr. Cannon, this will be easy." Her smile grew larger as the look of concern disappeared from Steve's face.

"Thank you, Miss Perone, I was afraid that it might be too much to accomplish in one day." Steffi waved dismissively.

"I will get in touch with all these people and set up the phone appointments. If we have to juggle Jack Cathay and Mr. Gold around a little, so be it." Steve tapped the desk twice as he stood up.

"Thanks, Miss Perone, let me know how you progress." Steve walked back into his office and shed his coat, crossing over to his desk, he picked up the phone and dialed a number from a small pink slip that Miss Perone had just given him. He waited for the connection to be made and for the three rings before the call was answered.

"Good morning, Mr. Stanwick. I was wondering if I could stop by your office in a few minutes and chat?" Steve looked at his watch when he heard the reply.

"I can be there in twenty minutes."

"Yes, I know the building. See you then." Steve put down the receiver and opened the top drawer of his desk and took out a new pack of Pall Malls and his notebook. He checked that he had a pencil as he re-crossed the hall into the reception area. Miss Perone was already on the phone as he bent over her desk and dashed off a quick note.

'back by ten'. He buzzed himself out and quickly descended the carpeted steps that led down to the lobby. He reached the Jeep and squinted at the sun as he rolled down the windows in the already hot interior.

Twenty minutes later, Steve stood outside the law offices of 'Stanwick, Shrader and Miller'. He walked slowly under the brick archway and into a courtyard that was filled with large ferns and other exotic plants as well as a gurgling fountain. He circled the fountain and entered a frameless door that was built into an entire wall of glass. His shoes sunk into the plush carpet as he walked the twenty feet to a high mahogany reception desk. One of the two women that were manning the area looked up at Steve expectantly.

"How may I help you, sir?" Her voice was calm and her demeanor was subdued but not unfriendly. Steve pursed his lips and nodded.

"My name is Steve Cannon. I am here to see Mr. Stanwick." She held his gaze for a long second before she picked up the phone in front of her and announced his name to the person on the other end. She glanced up quickly and pointed to two long plush divans that ran the length of the far wall.

"Mr. Stanwick's assistant will be with you shortly." Steve nodded and spun on his heels as he moved across the room and sat down. He had barely crossed his legs when a tall red headed woman strode quickly into the room from a large hallway to Steve's right. She stopped in front of Steve and looked him up and down as he rose from his seat.

"Mr. Cannon?" Steve nodded. The woman turned and indicated the hallway she had just appeared from.

"Come this way. Mr. Cannon."

Steve followed her to the big double doors. She pushed the door open and indicated that Steve should go in. Steve walked into another reception area that was only slightly smaller than the one he had just left. He saw Mr. Stanwick standing under an archway that lead into his office. Steve crossed the room, but neither man extended a hand. Mr. Stanwick kept eye contact with Steve as he turned and held out his hand toward the inner office. Steve nodded, walked across the threshold and sat down in a leather chair that was part of a small conference area in a corner of the office. The glass window looked out onto a private patio much like the one that Steve had walked through on his way to the front door. Benjamin Stanwick stood behind his chair and looked down at Steve.

"Well, Mr. Cannon, I assume you have something to tell me." Steve smiled thinly.

"Actually, Mr. Stanwick, I have several things to say, but I would prefer it if you would sit down." Stanwick's face reddened slightly as he sat down across from Steve. When he was seated, Steve leaned forward.

"What I hear from you, Mr. Stanwick, in the next ten minutes will decide how you and I go forward, or if we go forward." Stanwick stared straight into Steve's eyes and said nothing. Steve snickered and reached into his coat pocket and pulled out a sheet of paper. Steve placed the sheet containing eight names on the table and slid it slowly across until Stanwick reached out for it. Steve sat back while the page was studied. After ten seconds, Stanwick looked up quizzically.

"And, Mr. Cannon? What am I supposed to make of this?" Steve gazed evenly back at the lawyer.

"Two of those names are the victims. Do any of the others belong to you?" Stanwick looked down at the list briefly before he continued his blank stare.

"What do you mean by 'belong', Mr. Cannon?" Steve shook his head.

"Don't play coy. You know what I mean. How many of those names are LDS?" Stanwick did not change his expression.

"All of them. Where did you get…?" Steve interrupted.

"Out of the phone book." He secretly smiled as the blank gaze gave way to a look of confusion.

"I don't understand, and I don't have the…" Steve cut him off again.

"You better make the time, Mr. Stanwick or the two murders so far are just the beginning." Steve leaned forward and took the piece of paper from Stanwick's hand. He folded it lengthwise and put it back into his pocket as he gazed at the flustered look that came back from across the table.

"You see, Mr. Stanwick, all those last names are the same last names of some of the church members that took part in the Mountain Meadows Massacre. Now you just confirmed these are all LDS members, which makes it a pretty good bet that they are direct descendants of the perpetrators. My question to you is how much do you know about the connections if any, between the first two victims and any of the other names on this list." Stanwick sat back heavily in the chair. He raised his hands and then let them fall into his lap.

"I don't know how to answer that…." He shook his head. "Why are we talking about the Mountain Meadows Massacre?" Steve sat forward and spoke quickly and irritably.

"Because the murderer is talking about it. He left three clues that all tie in with the Danites and the massacre. So your daydream about the church not being involved is dead on arrival. But judging by the number of people from Salt Lake in town, something tells me that you already know that, and more besides." Steve stopped and waited. Stanwick rose from his chair slowly and walked to the center of the room. He stopped and turned back toward Steve. His neck was red, but his face was two shades whiter. He stammered as he began to speak.

"I..I…I need your help, Mr. Cannon." Steve stood up and jiggled the three Casablanca casino tokens in his front right pocket, as he coolly gazed at the man before him.

"Yes, Mr. Stanwick, you do, so let me make you a proposition. You hire me at my usual rate which is $200 per day plus expenses and if I solve these crimes, you pledge $10,000 of the church's money to help rebuild the monument in Mountain Meadows. And one more thing. If I get a whiff of double cross or any holding out, then the deal is off and I will hand you over to someone who will write a series of articles that will keep the church's dirty laundry on the front pages for months. Don't answer too quickly, Stanwick, take your time."

The two men stood still and stared at each other for thirty seconds before Stanwick turned and walked to his desk. He unlocked one of the drawers and pulled out a long black journal. He unscrewed the cap off a fountain pen and then looked up.

"Will a week of payment be enough, Mr. Cannon?" Steve shook his head. "Two weeks. I don't want to have to come all the way down here for that." Stanwick nodded and quickly wrote the check and walked back to the middle of the room. He handed the light green piece of paper to Steve. Steve did not look at it, but folded it and slipped it into his wallet.

"What now, Mr. Cannon?" Steve's eyes narrowed.

"I have a tight schedule on this case, Stanwick, so you and Amis Kinsley will be in my office at three sharp, tomorrow." Stanwick took a small step backward, his face reddening again.

"Kinsley? I don't have any control…" Steve interrupted as he took out his wallet and held out the check.

"If either one of you don't show, the deal is off. So I suggest you get on the phone to Salt Lake and put the pressure on." Stanwick nodded. Steve put the check in his front pants pocket and turned around. He strode quickly to the door. He opened it partway and turned back to Stanwick, who was still standing where he had left him.

"The cops aren't going to solve this for you, Stanwick. Make sure you convince Kinsley of that."

Steve left the door open and moved quickly out to the outer reception and slowed when he reached the atrium and heard the glass door close behind him. When he was on the street, he pulled the $2,800 check from his pocket. It was drawn on a bank account in the name of the Third Ward. He tucked it safely into his wallet. He pulled the new pack of smokes from his pocket and lit one as he walked. As he turned in the direction of the Jeep, he caught sight of a man who was standing across the street and who looked away quickly when Steve glanced in his direction. Steve walked the ten yards to the car and casually looked around as he opened the door and pivoted to enter. He smiled as he sat down. He recognized the man as a uniform cop. One that hung around Samuels and did his bidding. Steve sat for a few minutes smoking the cigarette. The cop had retreated to a bench at a bus stop a half block away. Steve waited until the city bus arrived and obscured the man from view. Steve started the Jeep and drove quickly to the corner and turned left before the bus pulled into traffic again.

Steve sat in his office and studied the schedule that Miss Perone had handed him on his way in. he slipped the one page document under the edge of his desk blotter. He pushed down the lever on the intercom.

"Yes, Mr. Cannon?"

"Miss Perone, please see if you can get Rita Malone on the line." Steve sat back in his chair and swiveled slowly back and forth. He was still lost in thought when the intercom came on.

"Miss Malone on one, Mr. Cannon."

"Thank you, Miss Perone." Steve punched the lit button just below the dial and held the receiver to his ear.

"Hello, Rita, how are you?"

"I am fine, Steve. I was expecting your call." Steve chuckled.

"Yes the article. I do want to cover that, but first, I must tell you that Remy, Miss Perone and I thoroughly enjoyed your show the other night. You and Bernie have a winner there."

"Thank you, Steve, but a lot of credit goes to Remy. She helped out a lot, and just having her around speaking French made Oscar feel more comfortable. But I am afraid it may be short lived. Oscar is homesick for Europe and more and more musicians are finding out that they are in the country and they are getting tons of offers, especially from L.A., so after the two months they signed up for, they are packing up and leaving." Steve sighed.

"That is too bad, Rita, what does Bernie say?"

"I don't think he knows yet, Remy and I just found out yesterday at the barbecue."

"Well, you're going to have to get some other show together." Rita laughed.

"Oh, I don't know, Steve, I'm an unknown quantity here, and working on the newspaper doesn't help when it comes to meeting other musicians."

"Well, Rita, I may be able to help. Give me a few days and I will get back to you on that."

"Sure, Steve, I would welcome that. I have caught the performing bug again, and I found out I miss it. But back to the article. I hope you aren't angry with me for publishing the clues you disclosed to Maggie." Steve scoffed.

"No, not at all. Any flak I get from Samuels will probably be worth the effect it will have and already has had on some of the people involved. In fact, I have another tidbit you can include in your next article. You have a pencil?"

"Yes, I do, shoot."

"Both of the victims are direct descendants of the main leaders of the Mormons involved in the Mountain Meadows Massacre." Steve waited as he heard the scratching of her pencil across the paper.

"How did you find that out?" Steve chuckled.

"Just old fashioned sleuthing. Reading what is right in front of me and looking past the obvious facts and looking in the opposite direction from where they lead."

"What does Stanwick have to say?"

"Not much. There are some other LDS elements in town and I get the feeling that he isn't too comfortable with them. I have a meeting with him and the head honcho of the visiting firemen tomorrow, so I will know more then. Have you had any other anonymous calls?"

"Not since the first murder."

"What did the caller say, exactly?"

"Only that if I wanted to know who was behind the murders, look at the church." Steve turned his chair and looked across at the main room tower a hundred yards away.

"That's all, huh? Old, young?"

"Mature man's voice, but not too old. I would guess late forties or early fifties."

"Well, I will be interested if you get more calls. I am a little worried for your safety, Rita. If anything looks out of place or suspicious, call me or Tam. I will alert him."

"Well, of course I will do that, Steve, but I don't think there is anything to worry about."

"I do, Rita, just be cautious."

"I will, Steve, goodbye." Steve hung up the phone and looked pensively at the receiver for several seconds. He crossed to the coat rack by the door and slipped on his sport coat as he entered the reception area.

"I am off, Miss Perone, I have two interviews and then I will be back."

"Very well, Mr. Cannon, I will see what I can do about contacting the last two names on the list."

Steve drove several miles toward Henderson on the Boulder Highway, before he turned down a narrow one lane road that lead to a jumble of industrial buildings that were off by themselves in the desert. He parked the Jeep in front of a chain link fence. He got out and turned his face away from the hot wind. He walked into the yard behind the fence and down a long row of heavy machinery, each one with the black and white logo which contained the name 'Pearce' and a small beehive. When he heard a piece of equipment start up in the row next to the one he was in, he walked between two yellow road graders and looked down the new row. Twenty feet in front of him, a back hoe shut down and a large man in a khaki shirt and blue jeans opened the cab door and swung easily to the ground. A silver hard hat was perched at an angle over his sun-reddened face that held an inquisitive smile.

"Can I help you?" Steve stood still and smiled as the man approached him. When the man was five feet away, Steve spoke.

"I am looking for Magnus Pearce Jr." The man stopped and removed his hard hat, turning it upside down as he peeled off his leather gloves and dropped them inside. He held out a pale hand. His arm was sunburned down to the wrist.

"That's me. What can I do for you?" Steve grimaced slightly.

"My name is Steve Cannon, and I need to ask you a few questions about the murder of your father, if you don't mind." Steve turned as he spoke and pointed to one of the buildings forty yards away. "Can we talk somewhere else?" Magnus nodded and walked quickly past Steve toward the low building.

Once inside, the man pointed to a glassed-in office on the far side of the room.

"Should be more comfortable in there." Steve walked behind him and sat on a low metal armed couch that was in front of the desk. Steve watched as the man looked briefly at a piece of paper on his desk before he sat down and gazed across at Steve.

"I'm sorry to bother you, Mr. Pearce, I only…"

"People call me 'Mike', Mr. Cannon." Steve nodded and continued. "I will try to be brief, Mike, but there are a few things I found in the police report I would like to check." A mild look of surprise, crossed Mike's face and he leaned forward.

"You're not from the police?" Steve shook his head as he retrieved his notebook from his coat pocket.

"No, I'm a private detective, though I sometimes work closely with the police." The look of surprise was now a scowl.

"Then someone hired you, Mr. Cannon." There was a five second pause as the two men locked their gaze across the desk.

"Yes, Mr. Pearce, but in this case I am not going to disclose the name of my client because one, it is usually my policy not to, and two, even if it wasn't my policy, it is not important at all to our discussion." Steve sat back and crossed his legs, his eyes not moving from Mike's face.

"Then in that case, Mr. Cannon, I am not inclined to answer any of your questions. I have had cops and people from the church in my hair for the last two weeks, I am tired of it." Steve tapped his pencil on top of the spiral notebook.

"And have the cops, or anyone from the church given you or your family any answers?" Mike sat back in his chair and sighed. He ran his hands through his hair and then grabbed the hard hat on the desk and threw it against the far wall. The gloves fell out as the helmet spun lazily around in the middle of the floor. Steve ignored the display, instead he spoke in a calm quiet voice as Mike Pearce stared silently at the top of his desk.

"The police are not equipped for a case of this type. They are used to scooping up suspects, quickly sifting through their statements and the physical evidence and making an arrest. These are the cases that get cold and then colder as the manpower is diverted to the new crimes, the crimes that are easy to solve. Just since your father was murdered, they have been two more unrelated homicides in the city. A month from now, they will be more and the newspapers will lose interest and once that happens, the boys from Salt Lake City will disappear too. I hate to tell you this, but, in my experience,

I am the only hope you have of finding out why your father died and who did it." Steve stopped and sat quietly. After twenty seconds, Mike's tearful eyes looked up at Steve.

"We built this company together, Mr. Cannon. I was looking forward to many more years working beside him before I retired and turned it over to my son, but now…" The words trailed away as Mike rose from the desk and stepping around it, bent over and picked the helmet and the gloves from the floor. He laid the gear down on an empty chair and returned to the desk.

"What kind of information can I give you, Mr. Cannon?" Steve slowly opened his notebook and braced it on his knee.

"The night your father was killed there was no one else in the house, was that normal?" Mike shook his head.

"No, not really. That weekend, my mother, my wife and I, had taken our eldest daughter up to Provo to let her see the BYU campus."

"Was that trip planned, or spur of the moment?" Mike shrugged.

"Some of both. My wife and I had been planning it for several weeks, but at the last minute, my mother decided to join us." Steve wrote quickly across a new page.

"The police say there was no sign of forced entry. Did your parents normally keep the doors locked?" Mike nodded.

"Always. Is that why one of the detectives said that maybe my father knew the person?" Steve shrugged.

"Perhaps. To your knowledge, does anyone else have the keys to the house?"

"Just my grandmother who lives next door." Steve looked casually around the office.

"There are several other construction companies as big as this in town. Any bad blood between yours and any of them?"

"Most of them ignore each other, and the ones that don't are friendly competitors. There is enough building going on to keep everybody happy."

"I need to get down some general biographical information

if you have a few more minutes." Mike shrugged and nodded, and for the next several minutes answered Steve's rapid fire string of questions.

Steve nodded and closed his notebook as he stood to go. He looked directly into the red rimmed eyes as he spoke.

"One more question, Mike. Are you aware of any of your ancestors being involved in the Mountain Meadows Massacre?" Mike shook his head slowly, as a frown spread across his face.

"No, Mr. Cannon, what are you trying to say?" Steve sighed.

"Mike, let put it to you this way. You, or your family at least, are LDS, and as such you have done the genealogy. Should be easy to find out." Mike stood up. He was two inches shorter than Steve, but stockier.

"I think you better leave, Mr. Cannon." Steve smiled thinly and turned toward the door. When he had pulled it open, he stopped and turned around.

"If you get to thinking at night, Mike, and you want to know the significance of what I just said, give me a call." Steve turned and crossed the bigger room and stepped out into the sunshine. He waited for a few seconds to see if perhaps Mike would think better of it and follow him. When the door to the office didn't open, Steve walked through the wire mesh gate and out to his car.

Steve drove down Boulder Highway a half a mile, turned onto Tropicana Avenue and headed back to Las Vegas. Twenty minutes later he parked in front of a two story split level house at the end of a cul-de-sac that held only two other homes. The sloped front yard was covered in little white stones that glittered with flecks of mica. A small forest of dwarf palm trees completed the outside décor. Steve walked up the winding red concrete walkway, stopping in front of a bright red door. The front door chimes rang out for several seconds after Steve pressed the button and stepped back on the covered porch. As the tones of the doorbell died away, he heard someone approaching the door. A blond-haired man stuck his head casually out the slight opening. Steve guessed he was around twenty-five. The man was bare-chested and wore a wet pair of surfer-style swim trunks. He looked at Steve with a blank expression.

"Hey man, whatever you are selling, we don't need any." He finished with a laugh that degenerated into a girlish giggle. Steve stepped forward and held up one of his cards.

"I'm not selling anything, at least not to you. I am here to see Mrs. Dame, is she at home?" The young man nodded and took the card.

"I'll go and ask her, wait here." Steve scoffed as he turned and looked at the other houses on the street as he waited. Several minutes later the door opened wider and the blonde man appeared once again in the opening. He pointed toward the back of the house.

"She's out by the pool. Through there." Steve walked into the white tiled foyer and turned as the man padded down the hall leaving wet foot prints on the stone floor. He descended the three steps that led to the sunken living room and crossed to the sliding glass doors that made up the whole southern wall of the room. Steve tested the nearest handle to see if it was locked. When the door slid open a few inches, Steve pushed it open several feet and stepped onto the pebbled stone patio, closing the glass behind him. He squinted from the glare off the swimming pool that was undulating gently from having just been disturbed. On the far side of the pool, Steve could see two bright green umbrellas and several chaise lounges, one of which held a woman that was staring at Steve from behind large dark sunglasses. He circled around the pool and stepped up onto the long, flat level that held the furniture. He stopped four feet from the chaise lounge. He put his hands in his pockets and looked down at the woman. She was wearing a black bathing suit and a white floppy hat. When she pushed her glasses down her nose and peered over them at Steve, he guessed her to be around forty-five years old. When she didn't speak, Steve stepped closer.

"I am sorry to disturb you, Mrs. Dame, but I have a few

questions concerning your husband's death." Mrs. Dame sat back in the chaise and pushed the glasses back in place.

"Suit yourself, Mr. Cannon, but I doubt if I can be of any help, even if I wanted to be, which I don't particularly."

"Is that so? And why might that be, Mrs. Dame?" Steve put a hard emphasis on her name. He heard the sliding glass door close behind him and turning, saw the young man come out to the pool with a can of beer in his hand. He walked around the far side of the pool, hopping quickly up onto the low diving board at the far side. He walked out to the end and sat down carefully, splashing his feet in the water. Steve turned back to Mrs. Dame.

"My husband and I didn't live together, Mr. Cannon, not for a long time. He stayed in his townhouse when he was in Las Vegas and he had a house in Carson City, where he spent most of his time."

"Quite a bit of real estate to keep up on a state senator's salary." Mrs. Dame smiled as she picked up a magazine from beside her seat.

"He was a smart investor, Mr. Cannon." She flipped absent-mindedly through the pages. Steve pulled the nearest chaise closer and sat down on the end of it.

"Anybody else live at the townhouse?" Mrs. Dame didn't slow her speed through the pages when she answered.

"You mean like a girlfriend or something along those lines?" Steve nodded as he watched the blonde man toss the empty beer can on a small patch of grass behind him just before he catapulted off the springy board, landing in the middle of the pool. A geyser of water fell on the pavement and Steve felt a few drops of the spray on his face.

"Girlfriend, maid, roommate."

"He used to have a maid, but I hadn't heard him mention her for several years. As to a girlfriend, don't know, don't care." She looked up as the blonde man emerged dripping on the far side of the pool.

"Eddie, would you be a dear, and get me an iced tea?" The man turned halfway toward her voice as he toweled off. He dropped the towel and disappeared behind the glass door. Steve listened to the pages of the magazine as they turned over.

"Was your husband active in the church?" She stopped flipping and looked over at Steve.

"Hardly. He was a jack Mormon at best, though he paraded it out when it suited him. He was from a big Mormon family in Utah, so he couldn't stray too far, though you wouldn't know it by the way he behaved when he thought nobody was watching."

"Any enemies aside from the usual a politician might have?" Steve heard Eddie coming up behind him in a noisy pair of flip flops. He put a tall glass of tea on the table next to Mrs. Dame, swept a surfing magazine off the same table and continued on, flopping down in the last chaise thirty feet away.

"Well, he wasn't easy to like, if that is what you are asking. He was arrogant and even worse, he was a bore." Steve nodded.

"Do you stand to inherit the whole estate?" Mrs. Dame pulled off her glasses and scowled.

"That is none of your business. I am tired of your questions. Eddie will show you out if you don't remember the way." Steve stood up, smiling.

"Eddie's the butler? I thought maybe he had a different job description." Steve turned and walked toward the house. When he reached the door, he turned around. Eddie was standing in front of Mrs. Dame. She was speaking to him and his head was turned looking at Steve.

When he got to his car, he looked at his watch and pulled out his notebook. He had just finished writing when he glanced in his rear view mirror and saw a silver and black car that had turned into the cul-de-sac, stop abruptly and back up when the driver saw Steve's car. Steve caught a quick glimpse of the man as the car accelerated around the corner and made a u-turn before speeding away. Whoever it was, he was wearing a suit and was not likely a cop.

When Steve arrived back at his office, he let himself in with his keys. He turned off the buzzer so that Miss Perone could get back in when she returned from lunch. He found three pink slips on his desk. He flipped through them quickly, selecting the last one. He dialed the number and sat back in his chair.

"Hello? Tam? How are you?"

"Better than you're going to be, I'm guessing." Steve chuckled.

"Well, don't be such a pessimist, Tam, what's got your goat?"

"Listen up, I don't have much time. Samuels had a big pow-wow with the chief this morning along with Agent Brady. Guess what the topic of conversation was?" Steve shook his head as a thin smile spread across his face.

"Let me guess. Samuels is all flustered because his precious clues got out, right?"

"Bingo."

"I wouldn't worry too much about that, Tam, that's business as usual for Samuels. If you don't have a clue, try to deflect that fact by pointing your finger at anybody that does." He heard Tam snort softly on the other end.

"This time the chief has the DA's ear."

"Larson? Are you sure?"

"Yep. Just heard two of the agents talking in the hall. Might be charges today or tomorrow." Steve pulled the book of yellow pages from his top drawer as he replied.

"I tell you what, Tam. Keep in touch, and if for some reason you can't get hold of me, leave any information with Miss Perone, OK?" There was a pause on the other end.

"That sounds ominous." Steve laughed.

"You don't think I am going to be a sitting duck for this guy, do you? And you best keep a low profile yourself where I am concerned. See you later, and thanks for the heads-up." Steve hung up the phone. His hand rested on the receiver for a few seconds as he thought. He opened up the bottom drawer and pulled out the 1911

Colt in the shoulder holster. He strapped it on and slipped into his jacket as he walked down the hall to the bathroom. In the mirror he adjusted the rig so that it was not noticeable under the pale gold sport coat. Back at his desk, he threw a few items into his gray canvas satchel, before he walked across the hall to Miss Perone's desk. He scribbled a short note, promising her that he would be in touch, before he locked the door behind him.

He walked across the shiny tile floor of the lobby and approached the front desk, where the day crew was busy setting up around the workmen who were still putting together the long curving mahogany counter. He caught the attention of a bellhop.

"Say, could you do me a favor and call a me a cab?" The young man looked quickly out the window, nodded and went behind the desk to where there were two temporary phones installed. He came back around a few minutes later.

"There is usually one there. Some of them think we are open already. One should be here in a few minutes."

"Thanks." Steve walked to the front doors, and stood just behind the large revolving glass. He pulled out his notebook and wrote a few lines and retraced his steps back to the bellhop.

"What time is Shelly Cointreau going to be here?" The bellhop looked at his watch.

"He has been coming in at two and he is usually here until midnight." Steve smiled to himself.

"Do me a favor, and give him this." Steve handed the small piece of paper and a five dollar bill to the man.

"Thank you, Mr. Cannon, I will." He pointed over Steve's shoulder. Steve turned as the yellow cab came to a stop outside the door. Steve turned and quickly swung through the revolving door and into the waiting cab.

"Downtown." Steve craned his neck back toward the parking lot as the cab moved down the palm tree lined driveway toward the intersection of the Strip and Flamingo Road. He did not see anything suspicious in the parking lot and no car followed as the cabbie pulled onto the Strip behind a city bus.

Steve had the cabbie circle the 400 block of Bridger street just off of Casino Center Boulevard twice before he told him to pull over. He leaned forward and pushed a twenty dollar bill over the front seat. As the cabbie grasped it, Steve held onto it for a few seconds until the man turned and looked into his eyes.

"There are two more of these for you if anybody that comes asking, walks away empty-handed." The cabbie nodded, as Steve let it go.

"Steve Cannon. I have an office in the new hotel where you picked me up. Check back in two weeks."

"You can count on me, mister." Steve grunted a reply as he surveyed the street one more time before he opened the passenger door and walked quickly across the sidewalk and down two cement steps and through a double glass door. He walked down a dark hall and knocked at the last door he came to. A middle aged woman opened it and smiled.

"Steve Cannon. I haven't seen you in a good long while." Steve smiled back and stepped inside as the woman moved to the side.

"Thanks, Sally, it has been awhile." Steve dropped his satchel on a chair by the door and looked around the room.

"Smaller digs, I see." Sally had moved to a door on the opposite side of the room.

"This was all we could get on short notice." Steve nodded.

"He in?" Sally nodded and put her finger to her lips as she slowly opened the door and peeked in.

"He's done with his phone call, you can go in. He has a meeting out on the Strip in an hour." Steve pushed gently by her.

"Thanks, Sally, I shouldn't be that long." Steve stood just inside the door until the man that sat behind the desk turned around. His face lit up instantly.

"Steve. What a surprise." The man reached across the desk and Steve stepped forward shaking the hand vigorously.

"Sam Wiser, how are you doing? I heard a month ago you were back in town but I have been too busy to stop by." The stocky ex-boxer smiled and pointed to the chair just behind Steve.

"I heard about Bernie's deal all the way out east and when someone told me the other day that you had an office there, I figured I would stop by, but here you are. You beat me to it." Steve sat down, catching the edge of the holster on the chair. As he adjusted it, he saw Sam looking at him pensively. Steve made his voice as casual as he could.

"So, Sam, how is Marvin Krattner? Still kicking loud about everything? And it's been two years. When you left, I remember you saying it was only for six months." Sam laughed and pushed an ashtray across the desk within easy reach of both of them.

"Yeah, Martin is fine. If anything, he is even bigger than the last time you saw him. It was one thing after the other back in New York. The horse racing syndicate, then the Celtics and the stock deal. Took that long to get all the legal wrangling put to bed so he could get things going here. Will probably be here for the next two years while he gets the new country club up and running. Did you need me while I was gone?" Steve lit one of the Pall Malls that he had just taken from his coat pocket. He used a big crystal lighter from Sam's desk to light up.

"Yes I did. You're back in the nick of time, I am going to need a good lawyer." Sam sat back, his craggy face grew serious.

"What fine mess are you in now?" Steve smiled, leaned forward and tapped the ash into the tray.

"Kind of an ongoing vendetta with a local cop. Normally, no big thing, but this guy is the head of the homicide division and doesn't like anyone else playing in his sand box, especially someone that knows what they are doing. Tam Polhaus made me privy to some of the hush hush info from the Mormon murder case, it hit the papers, and now Samuels sees it as his big opportunity." Sam pulled a big yellow pad over in front of him and retrieved a long pen from a double set just in front of Steve.

"What's your plan, Steve?" Steve shrugged.

"I am going to disappear for a while. I can't afford to spend the time it will take to fight this myself and still make headway on the case. That is where I need your help. Samuels hasn't been in town long enough to know which end is up, so he won't be too much of a problem for you, but the word is that the chief and Jim Larsen are involved as well." Sam listened and wrote a few notes, before he pulled a thin cigar from his breast pocket and stood up. He carried the lighter over to the window that gave a good view of the street. He lit the cigar and took a few puffs, before he turned back to Steve.

"Unless they got you on tape passing the info along, I don't think this is much more than a harassment case. Not being able to produce you will complicate things a little, but you and I have been through worse than this. Where you going to be?" Steve snuffed out the smoke and shook his head.

"I already have a list of places I can rotate in and out of. I can call you, and you can pass any messages through Bernie, or my secretary, Miss Perone." Sam nodded and sat back down at the desk, picking up the pen and looking across at Steve, he clamped the cigar in his teeth.

"So, let's hear the details."

An hour later, Steve threw a large leather valise into the yellow cab and locked his front door. No one had followed him from Sam's office and the street was deserted. He gave the cabbie instructions to take him back to the Casablanca. As he rode, he started making several lists in his notebook. He had made two calls from his house, one to Remy and one to Bernie. He would call Miss Perone when he was safely tucked away somewhere. He had the cab pull as close to the Jeep as he could. He stepped out and after opening the rear tailgate, he quickly transferred the valise to the Jeep. He followed the cab back out to the Strip and turned right onto Flamingo. He drove slowly in the curb lane and watched his rear view mirror constantly. When he hit the Boulder Highway, he turned right and a mile later, he pulled off the main highway and drove a hundred yards on the dirt apron, stopping in front of a garage. He parked under the fading sign: 'Vegas Trailer Supply'. He walked through the garage and out a small back door. He stopped for a few seconds and then moved to his left when he heard the sound of a hammer on metal coming from the other side of an Airstream trailer. He waited until the old man had finished his hammering and stood up. He glanced over at Steve and pointed with his hammer toward a group of small sheds beside the back of the garage. One of the shed doors was open. Steve nodded and returned to his car. He pulled slowly around the building and eased the Jeep into its' stall. There was not much room to spare on either side and Steve had to squeeze out of the drivers' door and inch his way along to the door. He swung the valise out of the back, locked the Jeep and slid the door shut. From a small pocket on the front of his satchel he took out a silver lock and slipped it into the rusty hasp on the garage door. He pocketed the key and walked toward the sound of the hammering. This time he did not wait for the man to stop work, but walked in front of him and when he had his attention, held up the five twenty dollar bills. The man nodded and pointed to his tool box three yards away. Steve tucked the bundle of bills under a screwdriver, nodded and walked back through the small door. He walked twenty yards to a diner that sat just off the highway. He ordered a cup of coffee and stepped into the phone booth that was connected to a long wooden porch that held several picnic tables. While he waited for the cab, he drank his coffee and watched the cars whiz by on their way to the lake or to Boulder City.

JULY 6

STEVE AWOKE BEFORE the sun was up and smoked a cigarette in the half-light. Even though he was three hundred yards away, he could hear the truck traffic whining down Highway 15. He dressed quickly and walked out to the sidewalk that ran the length of the three sides of the motor court. They were only two cars parked across the courtyard. Steve walked toward the small paved road and turned toward the highway. Forty yards later, he opened the door of the restaurant. He was the only patron, so he chose a booth that had a commanding view of the little group of ramshackle buildings ten miles south of the Strip. He swept both of the local papers off the counter as he walked by. Neither paper had a story on the murders, so Steve contented himself with the gambling news and the sports pages. As he finished his breakfast, he glanced at his watch. 7:30. He left a dollar on the table, replaced the papers on the counter and paid the man behind the register who also doubled as the cook and waiter. The sun was already making things warm outside as he walked the ten yards to the red and silver phone booth. He dialed the number for Gaudin Ford, turning so that his back was to the phone and he could see the highway. It took Duane a few minutes to come to the phone once Steve was connected.

"Duane, it's Steve. Is the car ready?"

"When can you be here?" Steve looked at his watch.

"No. Sooner, rather than later, is best."

"Fine. See you then." Steve hung up and stood outside of the booth for several minutes smoking a cigarette.

*

Steve drove the white 1960 Ford Falcon along Rainbow Boulevard as it snaked along the western edges of the city. He passed a wide strip of open desert before the road dipped into a wide wash area. Steve slowed and turned at a red mailbox and slowed even more as the rutted dirt track turned sharply to the right. Ahead he saw the black Pontiac. He pulled up beside the bigger car and smiled over at the driver. Steve pulled open the heavy passenger door and slid onto the leather of the front seat.

"You're late, I was getting worried." Steve smiled.

"Sorry, Bernie, Duane got hung up getting out of the shop." Bernie waved the reply off.

"No sweat, you're here. Give me the lowdown, you were pretty cryptic on the phone last night." Steve looked out the window where the dirt road wound lazily through a large stand of mesquite bushes.

"Let's take a walk down the road." He pointed and opened the door. Bernie climbed out the other side, joining him at the front of the car. Steve twisted the shoulder holster into a more comfortable position as they paced slowly away from the car.

"Samuels is pretty convinced that he can get me out of circulation for letting the clues get into the paper. But he will probably hit a stone wall with Hank Greenspun and Rita Malone. I just don't intend to sit in a jail cell while it all gets hashed out."

"Geez, how long you gonna have to be on the run, Steve?" Steve watched a small Chuckwalla lizard burrow quickly under a rock by the side of the road.

"I don't know Bernie. The faster I can solve this case the quicker it will all be over, but there is a lot of ground to cover. I will have to keep moving around, changing motels and cars every few days, but I talked to Tam this morning and they are still in the talking stage and they don't know I have gone to ground. Miss Perone and you, plus Remy and others all have the story straight, so when they do tumble to the fact that I have skiddadled, I will be several steps ahead of them. It isn't unusual for me to disappear into the desert for a few days, so they will be content with that for a while. Just make sure that you don't do anything that will give them cause to come down on you. I will call you every other day or so, and if we can keep the meetings to a minimum, we should all be OK." Bernie stopped and waited for Steve to turn around.

"Are you sure there isn't something else I can do here? From what you said last night, they will be at least two groups of guys always on the lookout for you. I would feel better if you cooled your heels in Palm Springs or somewhere." Steve laughed and rested a hand on his friends' shoulder.

"Listen to me, Bern. This is all going to work out. I am just sorry that I am leaving you in the lurch right before your opening, but I will make it up to you. I will keep in touch with you and you will know where I am at all times. If you want to do something, check in on Remy and Miss Perone every day and reassure them. The less contact I have, the better for all concerned. Will you do that for me?" Bernie nodded.

"Of course, I will." Steve smiled and turned back toward the car.

"Good."

*

Benjamin Stanwick's voice was not very pleasant when Steve made his request over the phone. Steve waited for the bishop to stop talking before he replied.

"This is my meeting, my call. So, take this down. There is a working man's bar at the corner of Decatur and Spring Mountain Road, can't miss it." Steve listened to the complaint.

"Then this will be a new experience for you. It's your

responsibility to get Kinsley there. It's ten o'clock, now. Be there no later than 11:30. If I am late, wait for me."

Steve hung up the phone without waiting for a reply. He made the short walk back to his room and stared down at the neat rows of papers he had spread over the bed.

The bar had just opened for business as Steve wheeled the car into a parking spot across the street. He watched the traffic increase on the wide street as the noon hour approached. Just before 11:30, he saw a car stop at the curb in front of the bar. It was silver and black and the same car that had backed quickly out of the cul de sac the day before. Benjamin Stanwick got out of the vehicle and looked up and down the street. He was joined by another man, taller, but about the same weight, and wearing a black suit. They were talking across the roof of the car. Steve rolled down his window in an attempt to hear what was being said. Though the voices were raised, Steve could not make out the conversation. The two men moved to the front door of the bar and continued their animated conversation for several more minutes before they disappeared inside. Steve watched all the cars that went by intently for a full ten minutes before he locked the car and after waiting for a lull in the traffic, he double-timed it across Decatur, slowing down on the sidewalk before he pulled open the door to the bar.

Even with the contrast of the bright light outside and the near darkness of the bar, Steve spotted the two men right away, sitting at a table as near to the entrance as possible. Most of the patrons were seated on stools in front of the long curved wooden bar and most glanced up when Steve opened the door, a few with lingering glances as Steve approached the table where Benjamin Stanwick and Amis Kinsley sat. Steve's smile was thin and his eyes were not friendly as he pulled a chair from an adjacent table and sat down. He stared at Amis Kinsley. Stanwick was the first to speak.

"Mr. Cannon, this is Mr. Kinsley, he is special..." Steve

interrupted. "I couldn't care less what his title is, I am more concerned with what his purpose here is." Steve continued staring. Kinsley, for his part, stared back.

"Well?" Kinsley broke eye contact and sat back in the chair, the skin on his face was smooth, pink and shiny. When he spoke, his voice was higher and more polished than his outward appearance would suggest.

"I represent the church's interest, Mr. Cannon." Steve scoffed.

"And I suppose that it takes thirteen guys in a cheap motel to get that job done, right?" Kinsley glanced irritably toward Stanwick, before his face composed and he gazed back at Steve.

"I like to make sure that all the bases are covered, Mr. Cannon."

"I am sure that you do, Kinsley, but you haven't said yet what the church's interest in this case is exactly." Kinsley shrugged.

"When the police and the newspapers frame events that portray the church in an unflattering light, we like to be on site to set the record straight." Steve nodded.

"So, you must be prescient then, Mr. Kinsley, as one of your advance elements showed up on June 19, the day of the first murder." Kinsley shrugged.

"Those three men were here on another matter." Steve smiled.

"Well, now I know there were three, my source was not too specific on that score, but that still doesn't wash as the first story only noted that Pearce was a prominent Mormon businessman, the Mormon murders business didn't start until the second one which occurred in the early hours of Sunday the 27th." Steve reached into his inside jacket pocket and retrieved his notebook. He took his time flipping through the pages until he found what he was looking for. "You and your whole contingent were in place on Thursday the 24th. Seems to me that you boys are a little sensitive, a little quick on the trigger, perhaps." Steve replaced his notebook and looked hard at the two stone faces across the table.

"I doubt either of you have ever played poker, but there comes a time in every game when it is time to throw all the cards on the table. Now, we might be at that point in the proceedings, or then again, maybe not. But in my experience, when I see people being less than forthcoming, I assume the worst. Especially when they start tailing me all over town." Steve eyes narrowed at Kinsley.

"I don't know what you are talking about, Mr. Cannon, why would we feel the need to 'tail' you, as you put it?"

"Well, then, I guess I won't be looking over my shoulder from now on. But just so we are clear, Mr. Kinsley, the next guy I catch shadowing me is going to pay the price." Kinsley smiled and folded his hands on his lap.

"Just make sure it's not the police, Mr. Cannon, before you do anything you might regret. My information is that they are most anxious to talk to you." Steve ignored the remark and looked over at Stanwick.

"You're pretty quiet, Mr. Stanwick. Can't talk when teacher is around?" Benjamin shifted uncomfortably in his chair.

"No, Mr. Cannon, I came hoping to hear more from you. We still have two unsolved murders and you still have my money." Steve snorted.

"Well, Mr. Stanwick, things are a little more complicated as our friend here has just pointed out, so I think in your case, patience will be a virtue. Unless of course you want to contribute some information to the general knowledge?" Kinsley shifted in his chair as both men waited for the reply. Stanwick's face started to color as he opened and closed his mouth. He took a deep breath through his nose, and straightened in his chair.

"I have told you everything I know, Mr. Cannon. What reason would I have to hire you if I knew more than you?" Steve chuckled.

"A lot of reasons, Stanwick. You might need me to do your dirty work for starters, or be the fall guy, or you might need someone to make yourself look good in Kinsley's report. Haven't met a client yet that comes across with the true gen right from the get go. Seems to be a genetic defect in the species. But since you are concerned about getting your money's worth, here's how things are looking so far for the church: Two elders are dead. Both have the same family names as two of the principals in the Mountain Meadows Massacre, and both bodies are surrounded by clues pointing to the Danites, though in this case they call themselves 'The Knights of Nauvoo'. As far as murder investigations goes, not much to see, but when it comes to the public and how they view the church, well, you be the judge." Steve looked hard at Kinsley.

"And as for you, I would worry less about what I am up to, and more about how this is going to play to the police. They are dimwitted, I grant you, but even a beginner would look in your direction with those facts."

Stanwick fidgeted in his seat and didn't speak further. Kinsley stood up and motioned to the seated man.

"Let's go." He looked over as Steve stood as well.

"You've had your, meeting, Mr. Cannon, and as I suspected, it was not productive." Steve snorted.

"Can't say the same from my side, Kinsley, but I am sorry if I was of no help. We seem to be at cross purposes in this deal, but as long as that is all it is, I just want to be left alone in my investigations." Steve looked over at Stanwick, who had just stood as well.

"I'm going to need to do some background work on the two victims. So, you need to open your genealogy files to me." Stanwick started to protest. Steve cut him off.

"Your other choice is to bring the material to me, but either way, I will call you in a day or two, so be ready."

Kinsley smiled as he let Stanwick pass in front of him as he headed for the door.

"There somewhere where I can reach you, Mr. Cannon?" Steve sneered as he started for the door himself.

"Don't bother, Mr. Kinsley, I will be in touch." Steve exited the door and stepped to his right as Amis Kinsley came out behind him and walked to the car, unlocking the passenger door for Stanwick, who silently got into the car and stared straight ahead. Kinsley gave Steve a last hard glance before he started the car and pulled away from the curb. Steve watched as the car made a left turn onto Flamingo and disappeared. He walked back across the street and passing his car, entered a rundown bodega. After buying a pack of Pall Malls, he watched through the grimy windows for several minutes until he was sure there was no one suspicious about. He crossed the lot to the car, cruised through the rows and then turned left onto Decatur, heading south toward Tropicana.

*

Steve sat on the spacious veranda and ate his hamburger. He was the only person sitting outside, but the weathered wood of the sloping roof over his head and the soft breeze made the space comfortable. From his perch, he could see the road that curved around the parking lot of the Rocking Horse Bar and led to Maggie Hannigan's place. Steve was halfway through his sandwich and fries when Murphy, the owner stepped out of the door and seeing Steve, came over and sat across from him.

"How you doing, Steve? I heard you wanted to see me." Steve looked into the deep brown eyes of Henrietta Wehrheim, affectionately known as 'Murphy', for some reason few people remembered.

"You still cook a good burger, Murphy." The woman laughed and her eyes twinkled.

"Burgers and beer. Keeps them coming back year after year." Steve smiled. He indicated the general direction of Maggies' house with a movement of his head.

"You have much truck with Maggie Hannigan?" Murphy looked to her right and shrugged.

"Used to be a regular for several months when she first bought the place ten years ago. Now the only time I hear from her is when she is complaining about the noise. Strange bird, if you ask me. Funny thing, though, she was in here a week or so ago, standing at the bar, drinking whiskey pretty seriously, if you know what I mean. Didn't say a word to anybody the whole time she was here. Not right to hide yourself away and get that antisocial." Steve nodded and wadded his napkin up, letting it drop into the red plastic basket.

"Remember what day, exactly?" Murphy gazed blankly across the porch at three horses that were tethered to one of the two hitching posts in front of the steps. She turned back to Steve.

"Yes. Yes, I do. It was the Saturday before last." Murphy rose from her seat. Steve rose as well. She reached out for the basket and the empty beer bottle.

"Don't be so much of a stranger, Steve, we still have loads of fun here on Saturday nights." Steve smiled.

"Yes, Murphy, I will have to revisit my youth one of these evenings." Murphy waved and walked back into the bar. Steve stepped off the end of the porch and walked slowly up the slope of the parking lot to the road. He paced himself up the asphalt as it snaked up the steep hill for a hundred yards. When he came to the cattle guard and the pipe gate he had broken a light sweat. He stepped on one of the lower bars and swung his leg over, straddling the gate for a second until he hopped down on the far side. He skirted the driveway and walked through the willows and past the well. He heard a noise from inside and announced himself as he climbed the two wooden steps, and stopped a few feet short of the open entrance protected by a screen door. He had only been standing there for a few seconds when Maggie appeared behind the screen. She looked at Steve for several beats before she spoke.

"I didn't expect to see you again. Back with more clues?" Steve smiled.

"Maybe, Maggie, may I come in?" Several more seconds elapsed before she swung the screen door open and moved to the side. Steve walked into the living room and stood behind one of the leather chairs. Maggie stood by the door with her arms folded. Steve gazed evenly across the room and waited for several beats before he spoke.

"I have to tell you something and then I have a few questions, if you don't mind." Maggie shrugged.

"Shoot."

"The cops are up in arms because Rita Malone printed the clues and their significance. Now, there is a good chance that Rita and her editor will stand on their principles and refuse to name their source, but there are plenty of clues to send them in your direction anyway. When and if that happens, I advise you to tell them the truth. I have a lawyer that will work on it from my end and I think he is the one who should handle it." He stopped as she considered the information.

"Alright, Mr. Cannon, if you think that is best. Is that all?" Steve shook his head, turned and walked toward a large display case in the corner.

"When did the Paiutes abandon their stone axes and take up the metal ones produced by the whites?" She unfolded her arms and gazed thoughtfully at the private detective.

"Around 1820, or 1825. They prized a particular one carried by the French trappers. They would grind them down until they were very thin and attach them to a longer handle. I didn't realize you have such an interest in the Paiutes." Steve pointed to the display case beside him.

"I don't, particularly. It's just that when I was here last, I noticed this middle shelf held two steel battle axes at one time, you can see where the missing one is outlined by the dust, and now there is only one." His finger traced the glass in front of the half empty shelf. He counted seven before she dropped her arms and walked to the cabinet, and turned toward Steve, who stepped back from the case.

"I returned it to its' owner, Mr. Cannon, it wasn't mine to keep."

"And who might that be, Maggie?" She smiled, but not warmly.

"Are you interrogating me, Mr. Cannon? Because I would rather not say, if you don't mind. Your opening statement proves that talking to you is not healthy." Steve snorted.

"As you wish, Maggie, but here is another one you can choose to answer or not. Why didn't you tell me that you were born and raised in the same small county in Arkansas that almost all the victims of the Mountain Meadows Massacre were from and that six of them are related to you?"

Maggie shook her head slowly. "You surprise me, Mr. Cannon, you would have made a hell of a researcher. How did you come up with that?" Steve moved forward and stood next to her, peering down at the bare place in the cabinet.

"Your hint of an accent, Maggie. When you join the Marines, you are thrown in with people from all over the country. Two guys in my unit were from Arkansas, so I just followed that hunch and here we are." Steve looked straight into the woman's eyes.

"Now I guess the question becomes: How motivated might you be to kill the descendants of the people that wiped out several relatives in your direct lineage and quite a few of their friends and loved ones?" He squinted at her blank expression, before he turned and walked to the door. He turned and looked back expectantly. When a long enough period had gone by for her answer, Steve shrugged.

"I have some free advice for you, Maggie. If you know anything at all about the murders, get yourself a lawyer and go to the police right now. If they come to you first, it will go harder on you, especially since people that live alone and are anti-social usually have a hard time with alibies." He stood with his hand on the screen handle for five more seconds before he pushed through the door and left.

*

Steve entered the corner drugstore on East Charleston Boulevard. He walked down the long aisle past the perfume counter and into one of the three phone booths at the back of the store. He had just dialed Tam's number when a beat cop walked into the front of the store and was looking around while he bought a pack of cigarettes. Steve waited until the cops' gaze was elsewhere before he turned his back to the store. Tam picked up on the fourth ring and put the phone down quickly and crossed his small office to close the door when he realized who was calling. Steve could hear something in Tam's voice that wasn't normally there.

"I'd rather not talk on these phones. Are you in town?"

"Yes. Let's meet tonight at the diner in North town. How about eleven?"

"Yes, see you then."

"Watch your back trail, Tam."

Tam hung up and Steve put another dime in the slot and dialed again. He turned toward the front of the store and noted that the cop had walked back out onto the street, but was still standing on the corner. Steve could just see his profile through the window as the cop took a smoke break.

"Hello Miss Perone, how are you this afternoon?"

"Yes, I am fine. I am driving a different car and after tonight I will be moving to a different motel."

"Well, 'exciting' isn't a word that leaps to my mind right away, Miss Perone, but it is out of the ordinary, I will give you that."

"Yes, I have my notebook out, shoot." Steve scribbled quickly as Steffi Perone read the messages he had received. When she was done, Steve turned back around and put the notebook in his coat pocket. The cop had moved away down the street.

"I am meeting Tam tonight, Miss Perone, and should have more to report to you tomorrow. If anyone asks where I am, I have gone hiking in the Mojave, and I didn't mention exactly where." He nodded his head as she replied.

"Unfortunately, Miss Perone, you are going to be in the direct line of fire on this deal, because the cops will assume that you and Remy are the most likely people to know where I am. I'm sorry about that. I have Sam Wiser working on it, and with any luck, he can shut it down quickly."

A few minutes later, Steve hung up and dialed the number for the Las Vegas Sun. When he was connected to Rita Malone, he put a quarter in the coin slot.

"Hi Rita, I only have a few minutes, so I will cut to the chase. How hard is it to get microfiche copies of daily newspapers from small towns in, say, Utah?" His brow furrowed as he listened to her answer.

"That sounds like it might take two or three days."

"Do small town papers keep all their back copies, like the Sun does?"

"Yeah, that might be the way to go. Thanks, Rita, I appreciate the information, if I need you to order some, I will let you know. Have you or Hank been contacted by anyone connected with the Mormon murder investigation?"

"Well check with him, and prepare yourself. They will want to know how those clues got into the paper. I have already warned Maggie Hannigan to tell the truth if asked, so if they start there, it might save you and Hank some grief. But that would take a level of noodle power I don't think they are capable of."

"You, too. I will be in touch, thanks." Steve hung up the phone and observed the activity in the store for several seconds before he left the phone booth and walked to the entrance, where he paused for a short spell. He bought a packet of Juicy Fruit gum and walked out onto the street.

Two hours later, Steve stood just inside the lobby doors of the Sahara Hotel. A large bus was parked in the porte-cochere and was disgorging a long line of tourists that were streaming past Steve and into the hotel. As the last stragglers stepped onto the red carpet just outside the doors, Steve saw the black limo ease slowly past him and stop. Steve moved outside and motioned to the doorman that he needn't open the door. Steve bent down and peered into the front cabin. He smiled when he saw the friendly black face. Shelly Cointreau smiled and jerked his head toward the backseat. Steve waved and reached for the back door. As he did so, he saw his face reflected in the tinted glass. As his hand closed on the handle the door swung toward him, being pushed from the inside. He smiled as Remy's face appeared. He took her hand as she slipped across the large backseat to make room. He quickly closed the door and buried his face in her hair and kissed her neck as she wrapped her arms around him.

*

Steve Cannon parked the white Falcon as far away from the nearest streetlight in the empty lot as he could. The only other car he could see was Tam's green Chevy Impala. Steve opened the door of the all-night diner and walked the full length of the spacious room to where Tam was sitting alone at a table for six. The detective gazed evenly at the newcomer as he approached the table. He pointed to the seat directly across from him and waited until Steve had sat down and the lone waitress had brought Steve a cup of coffee, refilled Tam's and retreated behind the counter across the room.

"Not good news. They issued a warrant for your arrest this afternoon. Samuels obtained permission to search your house and your office. He and his team are at your home right now. Hopefully, you have secured everything." Steve nodded.

"Yeah, two days ago, as much as I could. I better get with Sam Wiser tomorrow and see if he is making any progress. How were they able to get the warrant?" Tam tested the temperature of the coffee cup with his lip before he took a tentative sip. He replaced the cup in the saucer before he replied.

"They talked to Maggie Hannigan late this afternoon. She confirmed that you had brought the clues to her."

"She tell Samuels anything else?" Tam leaned in slightly and peered at Steve.

"No, why did you ask that?" Steve looked absently across the room.

"No particular reason. She knows a lot about the case, figured she might take the opportunity to tell Samuels what she knows." Steve decided to shift the subject away from the history professor. "So why do you still have a badge? I would figure that Samuels would have had your head on a spike by now." Tam snorted.

"Well, thank you very much for writing me off so colorfully. I am sure that Samuels suspects I was the source, but I think he is so excited about the prospect of locking you up, he is distracted. But so goes your fate, so goes mine, I hope that your lawyer is up to the task." Steve shrugged.

"Some of this will be the luck of the draw, but it isn't going to happen tomorrow. Meanwhile, I think that our best chance is to solve this case. Once the political heat is off, a guy like Larsen will forgive our little indiscretion." Steve smiled at Tam's sour expression. "C'mon, things aren't that bad." Tam's face darkened even more.

"Aren't they? I hope you have been making progress, because the task force certainly isn't." Steve sat back in his seat and sighed.

"I have been gathering some information, but none of it is clear cut and I have to be sure which direction is the right one to go in. We don't have the luxury of waiting for events to unfold in our favor. I have been putting pressure on the church guys, but so far they are playing hard to get. They don't care who did it, as long as it doesn't come back on them, but they know more than they are letting on." Tam took a big slurp of the coffee as he stood up.

"Well, that is why you get the big money. I'm leaving, I feel too exposed here." Steve chuckled as he rose, dropping a dollar bill on the table. He followed Tam toward the door. He waited until Tam had descended the steps and turned around in the lot.

"Sleep tight Tam, and don't worry, I will get you out of this mess." Tam shook his head and continued toward his car. Steve waited until Tam had driven away before he climbed into the Falcon and left.

JULY 7

IT WAS STILL dark when Steve packed his few belongings in the back of the Falcon. He had paid his motel bill the night before and now he would move his base a little west to the town of Goodsprings. He had in the past used the settlement as a jumping-off point for some of his longer desert hikes, so his appearance would be scant cause for curiosity. Las Vegas and its' doings held little interest for most of the residents, and a man on the run from the law was not likely to be a topic of conversation in the lone saloon.

An hour later, Steve drove through the nearly deserted streets of North Las Vegas. In a strip mall just off of the Boulder Highway he parked in front of a laundromat, the car facing toward a corner office space. He sipped on a cup of coffee he had bought at a gas station three blocks away. Steve opened a file folder that held several pieces of paper he had compiled from his own research and a page of his own handwritten notes. He was on his third cigarette when a car pulled into the parking space directly in front of the office. Steve waited until the occupant of the newer model car had unlocked the door and gone inside. When Steve arrived in the doorway, the man had his back to the front of the office and was twirling the black numbered dial on a wall safe. He was startled and jerked spasmodically when Steve spoke.

"A little early in the morning for banking, isn't it?" The man wheeled around, his eyes wide. He was in his early forties, thin, but not tall, Steve guessed just under 5 feet, six. His suit was not cheap, but fit him as if it came off the rack and he was in between regular sizes. The man moved self consciously away from the safe and leaned forward, his knuckles on the desk.

"I don't know who you are or what you want, but I am not open for business until nine." Steve smiled and moved closer to the desk and rested his hand on the back of one of the two chairs in front of him.

"Fine, by me, Mr. Jacoby, then I won't be taking you away from your business if you spend the next ten minutes answering a few questions I have." Wilmer Jacoby stared in frustration at the intruder.

"Answer your questions? Concerning what?" Steve moved in front of the chair and sat down.

"Questions concerning knowledge you may have about the recent Mormon murders." Steve watched the man's face closely as he spoke. He thought he saw a flash of fear in the black eyes.

"Look, I don't know who you are, but I have already been interviewed by the police." Steve flipped open the file and read from one of the pages.

"June 30, 2:45 pm, a detective named Alfson." Steve looked up at the flustered face. "I am not a cop, Mr. Jacoby, my name is Steve Cannon, I'm a private detective and let's just say that I am looking for things the police may have missed. I did a little digging, and I need you to explain yourself on one or two points. Now, I suggest you sit down and we can go through this rather quickly and you can get on with whatever you were doing in such a hurry when I walked in." Steve stared balefully at the face as it was slowly lowered to his level as the man sat down in the desk chair.

"That's more like it, Mr. Jacoby. Consider this the follow-up interview that the detectives should have done after the murder of Mr. Dame." Steve had his notebook in his hand and he was using the file folder as a support for writing. "You were a former assistant to Mr. Dame when he was a county commissioner and for two years when he was in the state senate, correct?" He spoke casually but deliberately.

Wilmer Jacoby sat back in the chair and crossed his arms. His speech was clipped.

"Yes, but I don't see the point." Steve pulled another page from the file. "You don't? Then suppose you tell me why the cops would bother to interview you about the murder of Magnus Pearce?" As Steve waited, he tapped his pencil on the file folder. Wilmer pursed his lips and looked down at the top of the desk. When he didn't answer, Steve sighed and read from the sheet of paper.

"Mr. Jacoby has had active lawsuits against Magnus Pearce and the Pearce Construction Company for the past seven years." Steve tapped the page with his pencil and looked expectantly across the desk. "I did a little more digging than the cops normally do, Mr. Jacoby and came up with the fact that Magnus Sr. thought you were responsible for two acts of arson and three acts of vandalism on company equipment." Jacoby shook his head.

"Pearce also thought everything that happened to him was my fault. If you did the research you said you did, then you know the police caught two juveniles breaking into the equipment yard, who also later confessed to vandalizing some of the machinery." Steve nodded his head.

"True enough, but that doesn't explain away the constant barrage of lawsuits, all of which have been dismissed over the years, the main one being rejected by the state court of appeals on…" Steve again consulted the file folder. He held up the paper. "On June 20, just days before Pearce is murdered. But that isn't the whole story is it, Mr. Jacoby? Or even the most interesting part. No, you and I both know the reason that the cops should have been at your door a week ago." Steve sat back and waited as the color rose in the cheeks of the man across from him. When he spoke, it was more of a rapid sputter.

"Hiram Dame was a friend and mentor to me, I resent your implications, Mr. Cannon…" Steve interrupted him.

"You were the third, but decidedly junior partner in a housing track deal," Steve consulted his file. "The Springhurst townhouse development off of Sahara. The other two partners were Pearce and Dame. When they cut you out of the profits and instead put the money into their next project which didn't include you, Dame mollified you by taking you with him to Carson City and by pretending to back you in your lawsuits against Pearce, and promising you your share out of the profits from the new project. But that didn't happen, did it? What did happen was that that Dame and Pearce sold the new venture, split the profits between them and then Dame pulled his support away from the lawsuits and fired you to boot." Steve sighed and held up the file.

"It's all here, Mr. Jacoby." Steve watched as Wilmer's shoulders slumped. Steve stood up. He looked down at the top of Wilmer Jacoby's head. "You need a good lawyer, Mr. Jacoby, and two airtight alibies for the nights in question. Anything you don't want to come to light about any of your other affairs, make sure you remove any evidence of them from your home and your office." Steve moved toward the door, opened it and paused just before he stepped onto the sidewalk. He looked back at Wilmer who had not moved a muscle since Steve had stood up.

"Another thing, Mr. Jacoby. If you have someone inside the church you trust, I would recommend that you seek them out. There is a rough element from Salt Lake City in town, and they are going to pay you a visit."

Steve drove the six blocks to the diner where he had met Tam the night before. This time there were at least twenty cars in the parking lot. Steve found an open space in the middle of a crowded row and scanned the lot for anything out of the ordinary. Satisfied, he walked up the short concrete steps and into the diner. He saw the person he was looking for in the corner at a small table. He moved through the crowded tables and stopped in front of Sam Wiser. Sam looked up from his paper and put a finger to his lips as he swiveled his head around. The diner was full of mostly working folks but the tables were close together. Steve jerked his head toward the door and turned as

Sam picked up his briefcase, rose from the table and followed him. Steve led him to where he had parked the car and unlocked the passenger door before he circled the back and climbed into the driver's seat. Sam lowered himself into the passenger seat and looked over at his client. Steve drummed his fingers on the steering wheel.

"Are you making any headway?" Sam nodded and looked out the windshield at a small whirlwind moving some paper trash in circles toward the chain link fence that bordered the lot.

"Some. But I was unable to prevail on DA Larsen to quash the warrant. He seems to think that if you come in of your own accord, that will be that." Steve scoffed.

"Samuels is salivating at that prospect. I don't plan on making him happy spending a week in the cells." Sam looked over at Steve.

"I doubt it will come to that." Steve shook his head.

"Trust me, Samuels will go to any length to get one over on me. What other developments are there?"

"I am going in front of the judge this afternoon to try and get the warrant vacated. They have pulled this Hannigan woman in for questioning and they are trying to get some kind of statement out of the Sun, but so far, Hank is stonewalling them. The fiction of you being in the desert will wear thin pretty quickly". Steve nodded and stared into the distance.

"While they still are looking at Maggie Hannigan, I will put a bug in Tam's ear. They should also be talking to a Mr. Wilmer Jacoby. He has the motive and the opportunity for both murders." Sam had pulled a small notebook from his briefcase and was writing the name down. He clicked his pen and replaced it in his pocket.

"That will help when I go before the judge. Maybe sway him a little that they should be concentrating on solving the case instead of worrying about their secrets."

"I am moving to another location later today. So, when you are asked where I am, you won't be lying when you tell them you have no idea." Sam laughed.

"Larsen didn't even bother, but thanks for the consideration. I assume a new car as well?" Steve nodded.

"Yeah, I have Duane lined up. That is where I am headed next." Sam sighed and nodded. He held his hand out across the bench seat. Steve looked into the lawyers' eyes as he shook it.

"Thanks, Sam. Do me a favor and leave a message with Miss Perone after you see the judge." Sam nodded.

"Will do. Wish me luck." He left the car and Steve watched as he walked four spaces over and got into a gold Mercedes. Steve waited until he had left the lot before he started the car and pulled in a slow circle around the perimeter on the way to the exit.

An hour later, Duane was in the agreed upon place when Steve pulled into the parking lot behind the convention center. This time Duane brought a dark blue Ford Ranchero. They quickly exchanged keys and Steve handed Duane five twenty dollar bills as well. They agreed on the new meeting place in five days' time and Steve drove the back way out to Desert Inn Road and then to the Strip. Forty minutes later he pulled into the motel just outside Gooodsprings. Since he was the only guest in the twelve room motor court he had his choice of rooms. He picked one in the corner of the horseshoe shaped building that had a back door that lead out to the desert. Steve pulled the Ranchero around behind the back and parked it just outside the room. He unloaded the valise and the cardboard box that held the materials he had worked up on the case. The room had a small writing desk in addition to a large chest of drawers. Steve spread the folders out on the top of the desk, sat down and began to write up the results of the last two days. When he was done he picked up the phone by the bed and dialed Tam's number.

"Can you talk?" Steve heard the door to Tam's office close before the detective replied.

"I am here. Hopefully you are not anywhere near any of your normal haunts, Samuels has every city cop beating the bushes for you."

"Don't worry on that score. New car since you last saw me and a new room even farther out of town than before. But I didn't call for that. What came out of the interview with Maggie Hannigan?"

"Not much. Samuels made sure she signed a statement swearing you gave her the information that she passed on to Rita Malone." Steve snorted.

"Get a pencil, I have some information you need to take down on her as well as Wilmer Jacoby."

"Why Jacoby?"

Steve took the next ten minutes detailing the information he had gathered on the two suspects. When he was done, he bid goodnight to Tam and decided to take a walk. Like most desert towns, the hub as it were, lay on either side of the main road, in this case Highway 161 which terminated in the town itself, before turning into a narrow secondary road that lead to most of the played out mines in the area. It was obvious as Steve walked toward the Pioneer Saloon in the center of town that the town had shrunk considerably in the hundred years of its' existence. Abandoned and crumbling buildings and foundations lay four blocks deep behind the main drag.

There were only three patrons in the bar when he swung the bottom of the dutch door open and stepped inside. Two he recognized, though only one acknowledged him. Steve sat on the far side of the U-shaped counter, the seats between himself and the others reserved for any other locals that might happen by. Behind the bar, a lanky man in his seventies disengaged himself from the conversation and straightened up, looking at Steve expectantly. It had been two years since Steve had last been in the saloon, but he was pretty sure the offerings hadn't changed much. Old Grand Dad and Seagrams Seven whiskey, J&B scotch, Coors, Olympia and Schlitz beer, plus a bottle of Smirnoff vodka that was reserved for one of the regulars but could be had for two dollars a shot if the owner wasn't around. Steve flashed a smile he hoped came off as friendly.

"Coors, please." The man nodded, turned and stooped in front of an ice drawer below the counter, pulling out the frosty bottle which he opened with a silver church key that hung on a leather cord from his apron. He pulled a napkin from a metal holder on the counter and set the beer down on top of it.

"Tab?" Steve smiled to himself as the conversation across the counter ceased. Steve looked up at the bartender and smiled.

"Yeah, why not?" He looked across at the expectant faces. "And while you are at it, let's put a round for everyone on it." The pleased murmuring was louder than before and as each patron received his free drink, he held it up in salute to Steve, who saluted back with the nearly empty Coors. He noticed that even though all three men had been drinking beer when he arrived, the generous shot glasses in front of them now held whiskey. Steve held up the empty beer bottle and twenty minutes later was sipping his third beer as two of the tipplers bid goodnight, nodding at Steve on the way out. Steve glanced at the only other person in the room beside the bartender. The cheery blue eyes above the full gray whiskers smiled as their owner left his seat and walked around the counter toward Steve. Steve swiveled on the stool and pointed questioningly toward a booth in the corner. The man nodded and slipped into the far side, while Steve ordered two more beers. Steve carried them over and sat them down in front of the shorter round man, sliding both of them across the table.

"Hi, Clancy, how you been?" The older man laughed and took a pull on the nearest long neck Coors before he answered.

"Good, how about you? I saw you when you pulled in today, didn't look like you were rigged for hiking and when you didn't stop by the store for provisions, I figured something else was up." Steve smiled and lit a Pall Mall, replacing the zippo lighter in his back pocket.

"Why does something have to be up? Can't a guy just come to town because he likes the scenery?" Clancy took another gulp of beer and chuckled into the brown bottle.

"Nope." He smiled happily across the narrow formica table at Steve. "All these old desert towns are good for, is hiding out." He laughed again and pulled out a small cloth bag and a sheaf of cigarette papers from the pocket of his shirt. Steve watched the rolling process for a short spell before he spoke.

"What you hiding from, Clancy?" The knurled fingers stopped and the blue eyes searched Steve's for a brief moment, before the beard began moving up and down in front of a laugh that rose from the man's belly.

"A vindictive wife and the U.S. Army." Steve leaned over the table and lit the homemade smoke for Clancy with his lighter before he settled back into the worn leather of the booth.

"I heard all about the wife, but what's this about the army?" Clancy shrugged.

"Got back from Korea, didn't feel like serving the last three months of my enlistment in a fly speck post in Texas, so I just took off." Steve tapped some ash into his empty beer bottle.

"You think they're still out there looking for you, Clancy?" Clancy laughed again, but not so heartily.

"Don't know, but I figure as long as I keep my nose clean I won't have to find out." Steve nodded thoughtfully at the logic. Clancy put his half empty second bottle of beer on the table and lowered his voice.

"Buy us both a shot of whiskey, and I will tell you something plenty interesting." Steve laughed and shook his head as he slid out of the booth and approached the counter. He returned a minute later with two shot glasses, so full he had to walk slowly back to the booth to keep from spilling the fiery liquid. They clinked the two glasses together carefully and each man took a large sip, leaving the glasses half full. Clancy licked his lips and after glancing quickly in the direction of the bartender, he leaned in closer to Steve.

"Two hours after you got here, black car with two hombres inside, stopped for a few minutes in front of the motel. They were discussing something and looking at the building. Well, after three minutes or so, they drove away toward the mountains. What do you make of that?" Steve worked his jaw muscles for a few seconds as he glanced casually around the room and past Clancy to the small section of the town he could see out the window.

"They come back through?" Clancy shook his head slowly.

"Nope, and there is no way back unless you take the Blue Jay Mine trail and who would do that if they had another choice, even if they had a four wheel drive. No, those boys are still up there." Steve nodded thoughtfully.

"They look like they could be Mormons?" Clancy's eyes lit up and he pointed a finger toward Steve's chest.

"That's exactly what they looked like. I couldn't put my finger on it, but by golly, you hit it right on the nose." Clancy's face had a concerned look as he leaned in closer.

"What do you think they are up to?" Steve sat back and took a small sip of the bourbon and shrugged.

"Don't know Clancy, could be anything." Clancy snorted softly and throwing his head back he downed the rest of his drink. The glass made a sharp noise as he put it down.

"My guess is, you do know, otherwise why would you ask me if they looked like Mormons?" Steve laughed.

"Saw them driving around looking lost on the way in, that's all. They were probably just deciding if they should get a room and they probably came back through here and you just didn't see them." Clancy shook his head slowly back and forth.

"I see every car coming and going, but have it your way. I was thinking that the only car that came through here in the last week was after you showed, and that was pretty peculiar. But have it your way." Clancy stood up and adjusted the suspenders on his shoulders. He looked down at Steve.

"Thanks for the drinks, Cannon. Stop by the store and see me before you leave." Steve held up his glass and smiled.

"Thanks, Clancy, I will." He watched as Clancy trudged across the street to his general store and antique emporium. Steve finished his drink and held up a twenty dollar bill so that the bartender could see it from his spot in the back. He laid it down under one of the empty beer bottles and walked out onto the sidewalk. He glanced casually up and down the street. He looked at his watch. 10:09. It seemed it was almost as warm as when the sun was up as Steve cut through a back street out of the glare of the three streetlights on his way back to the motel. When he arrived at the low yellow stucco building he came from the back and walked the long way around the horseshoe until he came to his front door. He turned it gently to make sure it was locked. He then walked to the corner of the building and stopped, peering around the corner to where the Ranchero was parked. Seeing nothing out of the ordinary, he opened the back door with his key. He switched on the light just inside the door before he stepped inside. Everything was just as he had left it. He pulled a flashlight from the valise and pulled the two blankets and both pillows off the bed. He carried them to the door and turned off the light. He slipped out the door and crossing the twenty feet to the car, he stood still for several minutes and listened. When he was satisfied that all was quiet, he pulled a rolled-up tarp from the back of the flat bed and tossed in the blankets and pillows. He unrolled the tarp on the ground and oriented it before he pulled it over the bed, hooking it in place with the grommet holes and the small hooks on the edge of the flat bed. On the side farthest from the motel he left several of the fasteners unsecured. He pulled back the edge of the tarp and climbed into the bed arranging the half folded blankets underneath him until he was comfortable. The radium hands on his watch said 10:40 when he pulled the tarp taut and fastened the grommet just above his head. Steve loosened the 1911 Colt in its' holster and rolled over on his side being careful not to move his feet off the blanket and make noise on the metal bottom of the bed.

JULY 8

IT WAS FOUR hours later when Steve heard a car approaching on the highway, but the sound died and Steve did not hear the engine as it cleared the motel and continued on into town like the two others had before it. He slipped the heavy Colt from his shoulder holster and eased off the safety. A few minutes later he heard the sound of a footfall on gravel and then nothing until the sound of whispering came from behind the car and in front of Steve's back door. He heard the jaws of a wrench being applied to the door knob and the metallic crunch of the door lock being crushed by the force of the turning tool. Steve moved silently to his knees and slipped the cover of the tarp back carefully. There was a flashlight sweeping his room. One of the intruders was in the room, the other was at the door with his back to Steve. Steve slowly hoisted himself up on the edge of the truck bed and dropped noiselessly to the ground. He took three silent steps toward the door, and as his foot hit the ground for the third time he brought the barrel of the gun swiftly down on the head of the man in front of him. The man fell forward without a sound, but his arms flailed out and cuffed his partner on the back of the leg. The startled man turned in a crouch and swept the beam toward the door. Steve smiled into the bright yellow light, his gun pointed at the man's stomach four feet away. He looked about as tall as Steve, but thinner. He wore a dark suit and tie and there was a small revolver tucked into his belt. Steve could see the wheels turning as the man backed up a step and looked first at his partner and then past Steve at the open door. Steve waggled the gun.

"Don't try it unless you want to give me an excuse to let loose on you." Steve had just barely finished when the cornered man made his charge. Before he reached the door, he had to sidestep his unconscious partner, Steve waited until he saw which direction the thug would take. Steve stepped to the side nearest the bed as the man attempted to sprint by. Steve tackled him against the dresser knocking the wind out of the assailant. Steve grabbed the man off the floor by the lapels and began to drag him from the small room. As he cleared the door, the man took a roundhouse swing at Steve. Steve stepped back and cracked the pistol across his jaw, turning the man half way around before he fell on top of his partner. Steve turned both men over and dragged them outside. He quickly frisked them and relieved them of their guns and their wallets. Steve unscrewed a garden hose from a faucet next to his door and with his pocket knife, began to slice the hose into long thin ribbons. He had just finished making a pile of the long strips when he heard a groan behind him. He stepped over the two prone bodies and entered the room, returning with an ice bucket full of cold water. He splashed the man he had just hit in the jaw with the pistol, full in the face and pulled him to his feet by his collar and shoved him against the stucco wall. He pressed the gun against the unshaven cheek.

"Now do what I say, or right now will be the best you feel for the next two weeks." He stepped back and pointed with the gun to the man's still unconscious partner.

"Pick him up and put him in the bed of the truck." He motioned with his head toward the Ranchero. The man shook his head groggily and rubbing his jaw, moved tentatively toward his partner, keeping his eyes warily on Steve. When he had pulled the unconscious man upwards by straddling him and placing his arms underneath the armpits, Steve moved to the back of the car and after folding back the tarp, he lowered the tailgate. It took several minutes to get the dead weight into the back of the truck. Steve waved the thug away and indicated that he should turn around.

"Get on your knees, put your hands behind you and flop on your belly." When the man had complied, Steve kneeled down with all his weight on the small of the man's back while he bound his wrists and arms with the rubber strips, tightening them with a short stick before tying off the knot. Steve walked backwards to the truck and tied the other man's hands and feet in the same fashion. He checked to make sure that the man was still breathing before he indicated that the conscious man should get to his feet.

"Get in the back and lay face down next to your partner." Steve held the gun on him as he turned and sat down on the lift gate before scooting himself onto the bed and turning, squeezed his body in next to his partner. Steve tied the mans' feet and legs with the last of the rubber strips. When he finished he leaned against the side of the car and pushed the pistol into view of the bound man.

"Now, listen up. Since you are a visitor to our fair state, I am going to give you a chance to see more of our beautiful scenery. Any moves on your part and I make sure you are buried out in the middle of nowhere. We understand each other?" Steve waited until the man grunted a reply, before he snapped the tarp cover back in place and closed the door of the motel room. He sat in the front seat of the car and folded a hundred dollars in twenties into a piece of paper he had written his name and room number on, securing it with a paper clip. He drove slowly around to the front of the motel and glancing up and down the deserted street to make sure no one was around, he slipped the cash into the mail slot that was beside the office door. He turned the car east and slowly drove out of town just as the sky began to lighten in front of him.

Steve turned a full 360 degree circle as he surveyed the flat desert that surrounded the isolated phone booth on Highway 267.

"Room 22."

After twelve rings the receiver was picked up. Steve waited for the other party to speak first.

"Who is this?" Steve smiled to himself..

"This is the guy who told you not to tail me anymore. Now you are going to pay the price just like I promised." There was a pause before Amis Kinsley spoke again.

"What do you want?"

"Information, Kinsley, and here is how I am going to get it. I have your two thugs tied up in the back of my car. You are going to drive out here alone and you are going to give me the information I want or I am going to take these two farther into the desert and give them just enough water to get them to the nearest settlement, which should take two or three days. But before I let them go, I am going to tell them that you refused to come out here and help them. Your choice is pretty clear cut, don't you think?"

"What guarantee do I have that you will let them go, or me for that matter, if I do what you say?"

"You don't, Kinsley and I think I should warn you that if I don't like what I hear, you are taking the hike with them."

"What makes you so sure that I won't show up with the cops?" Steve laughed.

"Go ahead and try. I will see you and them coming five miles away and then your buddies start walking. They should have plenty to say to the cops once they hit town, and I will make sure of it by telling the cops when and where they can find them."

"You got it all figured, don't you, Cannon?" Steve turned and checked the back of the Ranchero which was facing him from five feet away. When he didn't see any movement under the tarp he replied.

"Pretty much, Kinsley, pretty much. It was your choice to leave me alone or not, so now's the time to throw down the cards. Take down these directions and leave as soon as I hang up. I know exactly how long it should take and if you're late, all bets are off and they start walking." Steve gave Kinsley the directions in three short sentences and then hung up. He left the booth and pulled back the tarp. Both men were awake and conscious. He explained the situation.

"So, that's how it is boys. Either your fearless leader shows up and gives me what I want, or you're going to get the suntan of your young lives." Steve pulled a large canteen of water from under the front seat and gave both men several gulps. When they were done, he refastened the cover and drove toward the sun tinged mountains that lay just to the north

Steve stood in the shade of the pinion tree and swept the narrow valley and the winding road below him with the army surplus binoculars. He looked at his watch. Kinsley had only another fifteen minutes in which to arrive within the window of time that Steve had demanded. He glanced down at a small group of pinions just below him. Both thugs were laying quietly on their backs under two pinion trees. Neither one looked any too chipper after the long hike up to the shady spot. Steve was contemplating his next move if Kinsley failed to show, when he heard a car engine somewhere down the valley. The sound died away for several seconds before Steve saw the black and silver car negotiating the last hairpin turn three hundred yards below him. He waited until the car slowed and pulled into a wide gravel turnout where Steve had pounded in a wooden stake with a long piece of red plastic that fluttered in the wind, before he slid down the hill twenty yards to where the men lay. He pushed his pistol down into the back of his pants and looked over at the two thugs.

"You better pray that your boss doesn't pull a fast one. Unlikely anyone will ever know you are up here." When neither man replied, Steve looked down at the canteen at his waist. He lifted the canvas sling over his head and threw the water down at the feet of the man nearest him. He took one last look at the car below him before he stepped off the small ledge and began to wind his way through the pinion forest to the valley floor.

Kinsley was standing twenty feet from his car when Steve broke through the last stand of small trees and crossed the pavement in a slow walk. He stopped when he was thirty feet away and pulled the gun from his belt. He held it pointed in Kinsley's general direction. Kinsley took a small step backward, his eyes on the .45. Steve eyes narrowed as he moved to his left, forcing Kinsley to move farther away from his car to maintain the same distance from Steve. Kinsley held his arms out from his side.

"I am not armed, Mr. Cannon." Steve smirked, and moved two more steps so that Kinsley's eyes were blinking into the bright morning sun.

"Your kind never are, Kinsley." Steve stood gazing serenely at the man in front of him. Two minutes went by without either man saying anything. Kinsley began to fidget and pace around in small circles.

"What do you want?" Steve smiled and hitched the thumb of the hand not holding the gun into one of his belt loops.

"Actually, I've changed my mind. There isn't anything you can tell me that I don't already know or can't guess pretty quickly. No, Mr. Kinsley, I think you will do your time as an exile in the desert right beside your compatriots." Steve heard the sharp intake of breath from where he stood. Kinsley started to stammer as he replied, stopped himself and started again.

"I thought you were a reasonable man, Cannon. I have kept my side of the bargain." Steve smiled thinly, lifted up the pistol and rested it on his right shoulder.

"I'd like to think that you came all the way out here to save your guys, but like I said, I have changed my mind." Steve pointed with the pistol toward Kinsley's feet.

"Those shoes aren't especially suited for hiking through the desert. I suggest you keep to the road here. You might get lucky and there might be a car along before sunset, but folks around here aren't likely to pick up hitchhikers, especially ones wearing expensive suits." Steve let his words sink in before he turned and gestured to the large mountainside behind him.

"Now, both of your guys are tied up there somewhere on that mountain. They also have a half of canteen of water up there with them. So your choice here is pretty clear. Do you go up and find them and untie them, and the three of you make the trek, or do you just take the water and leave them there?" Kinsley unconsciously licked his lips as his eyes shifted toward his car ten feet away.

Steve pointed at the car and took two steps in that direction. "The keys go with me, Kinsley." Kinsley made a high pitched noise deep in his throat and held up his hand.

"Stop. Stop. I will tell you everything I know." Steve slowed his pace toward the car and pointed the gun at Kinsley as he came to a stop. He held out his hand. Kinsley looked down as he pulled the keys from his pocket. Steve indicated that he should throw them to him. Kinsley tossed them, the silver keys glinting in the sun as they sailed through the air and landed at Steve's feet. He didn't move to pick them up. Kinsley held up his hand and took a step toward Steve, but stopped when Steve held the gun level again. Kinsley held both hands out toward Steve and began speaking quickly in a low panicky voice.

"A year ago, there were two murders in Salt Lake City. The same code words and the same epitaphs. Then six months ago, another murder in Provo. The church was able to keep those three under wraps, but when they began happening in Las Vegas, well…." His voice trailed off. Steve regarded the man silently for a few seconds.

"So, who does the church suspect?" Kinsley looked around and shrugged.

"We think there is a group of apostates that have left the church and are trying to discredit it." Steve shook his head and snorted.

"You would. But do these supposed apostates have names?" Kinsley shook his head.

"We put a group of defiant polygamists in jail that were easily capable of the murders, but when the one in Provo happened, we had to let them go." Steve turned and pointed up the mountain.

"Let's go." He waited until Kinsley had started walking toward the road before he picked up the keys and followed. As soon as they left the road, Steve took the lead as they ascended the circuitous uphill route to the two men. Steve had to stop several times to let Kinsley catch up and then he had to wait even longer for him to catch his breath. When they reached the two pinions that were providing shade to the men, Steve stepped off to the side as Kinsley bent over with his hands on his knees, panting heavily. Kinsley straightened up and looked at Steve.

"Now what?" Steve turned his torso toward the south and pointed with the gun.

"I'm going that way." He turned back to the trio and threw the car keys in the dirt at Kinsley's feet. "You can do what you want." Kinsley bent down angrily and scooped up the keys. He pointed at the two men, one of whom was asleep.

"What about them?" Steve looked at the two as if it were the first time he had ever laid eyes on them. He smiled sardonically at Kinsley. Kinsley pointed again.

"They need medical help." Steve nodded.

"Quite possibly, yes, but that is no concern of mine. The way I see it, I am giving the three of you a huge break here, but any more guff or ingratitude and those keys will go with me." Kinsley looked as if he was about to say something, but instead glowered in Steve's direction. Steve turned to go, but paused and held the pistol up just before he shoved it down securely into the leather holster.

"If I see any of you in my way again, I will use this as it was intended to be used, instead of a club." Steve began to climb rapidly up the steep slope and in a few seconds had disappeared behind several large pinion trees.

*

Steve slid lower in the front seat of the Ranchero. He had filled the parking meter with several dimes and now he watched the traffic from the Police Center flow past him and on down the street. At a quarter to twelve, Tam's green Impala swept by. Steve pulled out quickly and caught up to him at the stop sign a hundred yards ahead. Tam took a left and then a right and Steve guessed he was heading to the steakhouse inside Binions' Horseshoe Club. Steve did not follow him into the parking lot, but continued on, turned left at the next street and parked at another meter in front of an auto repair shop. Steve fed the meter and then walked ten quick steps to the entrance of a narrow alleyway that lead to a private parking lot right beside the club. Steve stood outside a small glass door and busied himself lighting a cigarette until a dealer leaving his shift pushed through the door from the inside. Steve smiled thinly at the man and caught the door with his foot before it closed. He quickly walked down the long hall and into a wide corridor before anyone could question his presence. He slowed as he turned a corner and stepped between several banks of slot machines. He was passing in front of the bar when he heard his name being called. He stopped walking as if he meant to, and began patting his pockets as if he was searching for something while at the same time glancing in the direction the voice had come from. The caller spoke his name louder, and this time Steve looked up to see Benny Binion himself perched on a bar stool ten yards away. Steve smiled and walked to the edge of the green carpet, stopped, looked down, took a big step over the edge and then continued on toward Benny. When he got there, Benny was laughing.

"I saw what you did there, think that is pretty funny?" Steve laughed and turned to look back at the carpet five yards away. Benny was a convicted felon and had done time in the 50's, and subsequently he was barred from setting foot in his own casino. He held court and kept an eye on the operation from his reserved stool at the bar. Benny patted the shoulder of a man on the stool next to him and jerked his head toward the casino. When the man sauntered off, Benny indicated that Steve should sit next to him. Steve slid smoothly onto the stool and smiled at Benny.

"How you been, Benny?" The heavy set man with the round face smiled and turned to the bartender standing in front of him.

"Good, Steve, have a beer with me?" Steve nodded and swiveled his stool slightly as the cold bottle appeared in front of him along with a frosted glass. Steve tipped the glass and poured the pale beer as he smiled at Benny.

"Been winning?" Benny shook his head and gazed out at the casino floor.

"Bad streak lately. Got so I have to duck everybody. It's like they can smell the bad luck and they all want to play." Steve chuckled as he took a long sip of the beer.

"Don't worry Benny, it all comes back around eventually. But if I am truthful, I wish I had the time to get you over to Bernie's. I think I owe you a few hidings." Benny laughed and turned his stool all the way toward the bar and indicated that Steve should do the same. Benny bent his head over his beer and closer to Steve's right ear.

"Heard the cops are dragging the town for you. What did you do now?" Steve looked into the wise eyes and smiled.

"Just the job they should be doing. Same old story, Benny. You would think as many times as I am right about the things that go on in this town that I would get cut a little slack." Steve shrugged and finished his beer. He stood back from the stool and patted Benny on the shoulder.

"Got to go find somebody right now, Benny, thanks for the beer." Steve turned to go, but hesitated for a few seconds. "Needless to say, Benny, you didn't see me." Benny chortled as he watched Steve move away into the crowd.

Tam was sitting near the entrance to the restaurant that was just off the casino floor. Steve slid into the booth and sat with his back toward the door. Tam looked up from his meatloaf and shook his head slowly, before he cut another small slice of the meat and chewed it, gazing blankly at Steve. Steve smiled and took out his notebook. Tam swallowed and gestured toward the restaurant with his knife.

"I'm not the only cop who eats here, you know." Steve shrugged.

"I feel lucky today, how about you?" Tam made a weary open handed gesture. Steve looked closer at his friend.

"What's the matter with you today, Tam?" Tam frowned across the table and then shook his head.

"Of course, how could you know? There was another murder last night. I was up all hours, I just came here from the crime scene." Steve stopped flipping through the pages of his notebook and stared at the detective.

"Who?"

"Lamar Lee."

"The gaming commissioner?" Tam nodded as he chewed. Steve quickly turned to a new page and began to write. He waited until Tam swallowed and had taken a long draught of his beer.

"Time and particulars the same?" Tam nodded again.

"Coroner thinks between ten and midnight. Likely same weapon, same writing, but this time on a wall instead of the door, and the only other clue of any significance was a Polaroid picture of the Mountain Meadows site, and the monument. Probably real recent as it shows the monument half falling down." Steve sat back, sighed and looked at his notes.

"Well that's number six." Tam looked up quizzically from his plate.

"Six? What are you talking about?" Steve shrugged and gazed blankly at the detective.

"Just some information that Kinsley volunteered, that's all. Still haven't verified it, so forget I said anything." Tam leaned forward and pointed his finger across the table, forcing his voice lower as he began to speak.

"You listen to me. You got anything material, you let me know. That's our deal." Steve sat back thoughtfully for a few seconds.

"That how you see it, Tam? Seems to me you're forgetting that the only real progress in this case has been made by me, and the reward I get for that is that I have to go into hiding and sneak around. And in spite of that, I still come up with more angles than you guys." Steve had leaned forward and the two men's faces were only inches apart when Steve finished. For a long moment they glared at each other, before Tam shook his head and sat back in his seat. Steve flipped back through his notebook. He looked up and waited for Tam to make eye contact.

"How did things turn out with Maggie Hannigan and Wilmer Jacoby?" Tam finished the last of his beer before he looked back at Steve.

"Things haven't yet. We pulled Hannigan in, and aside from having no alibi that anyone can verify, it's being treated as coincidental that she is related to the Mountain Meadows victims. As for Jacoby, he has two airtight alibis and two real good lawyers, so unless you got more to add to that scenario, it looks like a stalemate." Tam paused and looked quickly around the room before he continued. "I figured when you sat down you had something big. Awful big chance you are taking just to say hello."

"Maybe, Tam, maybe not. I'm leaving for Utah this afternoon. I will call you if I need anything." Steve stared firmly across at the detective who was a little less comfortable than he had been a few minutes before. Steve glanced around the room as he slid out from the booth and stood up. He didn't look back as he moved toward the entrance and disappeared into the crowded casino.

*

Steffi Perone was irritated and elated at the same time when she picked up the phone and heard the voice of her boss.

"Mr. Cannon, I have been so worried. Where are you? Are you hurt?" Steve had to stifle a chuckle before he answered.

"No, Miss Perone, I am quite all right, thank you. I am on the highway to Salt Lake City, but more importantly, how are you?"

"I am fine, Mr. Cannon. The police were here most of yesterday. They searched the office and asked me the same questions over and over. Thankfully, I called Mr. Wiser as you suggested and once he came, they pretty much left me alone."

"I'm glad, Miss Perone, maybe you we should consider closing the office until this all blows over. It might be a couple more weeks. I don't want you to be under all this pressure for that long." Steve stopped talking when he heard her sharp intake of breath,

"Oh, no, Mr. Cannon, I could never do that. The phone needs to be answered and you have three more cases waiting to hear from you. Who is going to talk to these people?" Steve smiled to himself.

"Of course, Miss Perone, what was I thinking? You do what you think is best. I have complete confidence leaving you in charge."

"Mr. Gold has been here at least twice a day every day and he was here with me the whole time the police were here. He and Miss DeMarche even took me with them when they went to dinner last night." Steve leaned in toward the phone and held his palm over his ear as a big semi-truck pulled to a stop ten yards away.

"I will remember to thank them, Miss Perone." Steve had to raise his voice over the loud engine noise. "I have to get moving, Miss Perone, but I will try and call you tomorrow, hopefully from a hotel somewhere."

Steve hung up and looked around the truck stop that was just outside Cedar City. He was only seventeen miles from his destination: Parowan. But each mile he traveled off the interstate took him closer to a time that didn't exist anymore in most of the populated areas of the country. He drove the narrow two lane highway through the peach and cherry orchards and slowed when he approached Parowan's main street. He pulled into a Texaco station that was on the outskirts of the small town. He waited as a young boy and an old man approached from the building that was connected to the three bay garage. The boy's hands held a small squeegee and two red garage rags, one of them dripping soap suds onto the oil stained concrete. The man slowed as he approached the front of the car and glanced down at the license plate. He continued on toward the driver's side where Steve's window was rolled down. The man rested his left hand on the roof of the Ranchero and bent down slightly as he peered into the car at Steve. His face was lined and tanned, but friendly.

"Fill'er up, mister?" Steve nodded and pulled the door lever up slowly. The man realized that Steve was getting out and backed up several feet. The young boy pushed the long silver nozzle into the tank and then busied himself cleaning the windshield. Steve stretched as he casually glanced around the immediate area, smiling at the man when he turned his head in his direction. The man gestured toward the car.

"Drive all the way from Las Vegas today?" Steve turned slightly and glanced at the car himself.

"Yes. Yes, I did." The man considered the information as Steve moved out of the way of the boy as he came around to clean the back window. He stood on his tiptoes but could not reach more than a few inches of the flat glass. He looked at Steve and Steve smiled and nodded. The boy clamored quickly into the bed of the Ranchero and knelt down as he made long soapy passes on the green tinted glass. Steve turned back to the man when he heard him clear his throat.

"Need directions back to the interstate?" Steve shook his head.

"No, but if you could point me in the direction of a hotel or motel you recommend, that would be appreciated." The man rubbed his jaw and looked back at Steve with a slightly puzzled expression.

"Well back on the interstate", he indicated north with his arm, "there is a Holiday Inn, and back toward Cedar, there is...." Steve smiled and interrupted.

"I was thinking of staying in Parowan." The old man looked blankly at Steve for a few seconds before he turned and pointed up the street toward the center of town.

"There's the old hotel, of course, but..." he turned back to Steve. "Bathrooms are down the hall and there is no air conditioning, so..." Steve piped up again.

"That sounds perfect." He held his hand out toward the man.

"My name is Steve Cannon." He shook the man's hand firmly as the brown eyes searched his.

"Say, my wife is related to the Cannons over to Panquitch, are you headed there?" Steve chuckled mostly to himself and shook his head.

"No, no relation...Mr?..." The man grinned self-consciously and dropped Steve's hand.

"Gleamer, Harold Gleamer." Steve turned and nodded at the young boy who had hopped out of the other side of the truck bed and was busy hoisting the heavy nozzle with both hands in an attempt to replace it on the hook.

"He yours?" The man peered around Steve at the boy and waited until he had successfully hung up the nozzle before he replied.

"Yep. Roy, my middle daughter's youngest." Steve dug into his pocket and pulled out a quarter, holding it up so that Roy could see it. The young child looked expectantly at his grandfather who nodded back. Roy came slowly around the back of the car and stopped three feet away. Steve bent over at the waist and dropped the coin into the small outstretched hand. The child replied shyly and bent his head after speaking, his short blond hair catching the late afternoon sun.

"Thank you." Steve smiled and straightened up. Harold Gleamer was pointing toward the building.

"Let's go inside and call Miss Beatrice to see if she has room. There are only four suites that she rents out." Steve fell in behind Harold and Roy as the trio marched into the narrow room. Steve spun the postcard display while he half-listened to the conversation coming from behind the desk. He looked up when he heard his name being called. Harold had his hand over the large black receiver and an expectant look on his face as he repeated himself.

"Miss Beatrice would like to know how many nights you will be staying." Steve thought for a second.

"Four." Harold turned back to the phone and repeated the number. A few seconds later he hung up the phone and smiled up at Steve who was now leaning on the counter.

"The rooms aren't much to write home about, but Beatrice is one of the best cooks in the county. Makes a good breakfast." Steve grinned and straightened up.

"Sounds fine, Harold. Let me ask you a question you may know the answer to." Steve waited until Harold nodded.

"The old newspaper closed in 1960. Do you know where the papers' archives might be located?" The older man looked down at the wooden desk top with a bewildered expression on his face. When he spoke, it was if he was talking to himself.

"I bet Miss Purcells down at the library would know." He looked back up at Steve. "Should I call her?" Steve leaned forward again, his hands clasped and his arms on the counter.

"No, that won't be necessary, Harold. It's getting late. I will wander over there tomorrow." Harold nodded.

"Just ask Miss Beatrice, she will direct you. You have some kind of business here?" Steve pulled two rolls of orange lifesavers from a small rack at his elbow.

"I haven't paid you for the gas, Mr. Gleamer, all I have are twenties, will that be OK?"

"Sure, sure, that will be fine." Harold looked out the window to where Roy was talking to an older kid who had just ridden up on a bike. He leaned over and rapped on the glass to get the youngster's attention. When Roy looked in his direction, Harold swung his arm back toward the inside of the building. Roy appeared in the doorway three seconds later. Harold pointed to Steve.

"Ride into town with Mr. Cannon, here, and show him where the hotel is, and if he wants, show him the library too." Before Steve could protest, the boy had nodded to his grandfather, skipped between the two gas pumps and was already swinging open the passenger door of the Ranchero. Steve took his change and the brown bag from Harold's hand.

"That's quite a long way just for him to have to turn around and come back." Steve moved the bag through the air in a compact motion tracing the route. Harold shook his head as he came out from behind the counter.

"He'll just walk across the street to his mother's dress shop. She will be closing soon and he will walk home with her." Steve moved toward the door.

"Thanks Harold. I will stop by and see you before I leave if I don't run into you sooner." Harold stood in the doorway and waved as Steve opened the driver's door and climbed in. He looked over at Roy as he pulled the waxy blue string on the Lifesavers and peeled the paper away from the first orange candy. He held it out to the young boy who expertly separated the top one from its' neighbor and popped it into his mouth. His thin arm returned to the door rest which was only a few inches below his head. He smiled up at Steve while he leaned forward and pointed over the dashboard toward the tree lined street.

"That way." Steve smiled and sucked on one of the tart candies as he eased the car away from the gas station and pointed it toward the small burg.

"What grade are you in, Roy." Steve looked down at the small serious expression.

"I am in second grade, Mr. Cannon." Steve nodded.

"So, you must be seven years old, right?" The blonde head shook with even a more serious expression.

"No. I'm six."

"Well, you must be pretty smart." The head shook again as Roy leaned forward and pointed out the windshield.

"No, I just started early. There is the hotel. If we turn here, I will show you the library." Steve made a slow wide left hand turn onto a street narrower than the main one. The tree branches from both sides reached for each other across the space, shutting off most of the sunlight. A cool breeze came through the open windows. After two blocks, Steve slowed to a stop as they both gazed up at the pale beige edifice of natural stone. Roy pointed at the front door.

"Miss Purcells is nice. She will let you take more books out than you are supposed to, if you always bring them back on time." Steve smiled.

"Thanks for showing me that, Roy. Which way to your mothers' shop?" Roy twisted in the seat, stretched his arm as high as it would go and pointed back over the seat in the direction they had just come. Steve backed the car up in front of the library and turned back toward the main street. He pulled into a parking space in front of a high curb and watched as Roy pushed the heavy door open and clamored out. Steve held out the open roll of lifesavers. Roy smiled as he leaned back into the car. A few seconds and a wave later, Steve watched the glass door of the shop close behind him.

Steve made a U-turn across the wide main street and parked in front of the hotel. He swung his valise out of the truck bed and walked across the wide sidewalk and under a short arbor that covered the front door. He stepped inside and onto a large red oriental rug. There were several overstuffed chairs grouped in front of a white fireplace and a small desk just set out from the side of a staircase, that appeared to be the place for check-in. Steve set his valise down in front of the table and rang a little silver bell that sat next to an avocado green telephone. When several minutes went by and no one appeared, Steve wandered over to the window and watched the small parade of local people going about their business. Presently, he heard a small noise behind him and turned around. A tall thin woman with wispy gray hair was standing in front of the desk peering down at the valise. Steve cleared his throat and the woman let out a small yelp as she put her hand to her throat, leaning back on the table with her other hand for support.

"Oh my gosh, you almost gave me a heart attack!" Steve smiled and waited as the older woman composed herself. She shook her head and straightened up, smiling at Steve. She wore a long plain pale blue dress, and her skin though wrinkled, was tanned and healthy looking. Steve guessed she was in her early 70's.

"You must be Miss Beatrice." Steve smiled and advanced a few steps toward the woman and stopped. She smiled graciously.

"Yes, I am, and you must be Mr. Cannon." Steve dipped his head and smiled.

"Well follow me, Mr. Cannon. If you are not local, I always insist you see the room first before we do the formalities." She walked to the staircase and began to slowly ascend the steps. Steve let her get halfway up before he followed. At the landing, she turned left and walked down a long hallway, stopping at the last door on the left. As Steve made the turn, she pointed to the door just in front of him.

"That is the bathroom, Mr. Cannon. This room is the farthest one away, and though there are only two other guests at present, you won't be disturbed in here." She pointed to the door she had just opened as she stepped back, clasping her hands in front of her to let Steve enter. Steve ducked under the low doorframe and walked into the middle of the room. The room was dominated by a large feather bed in a brass frame. There was a chest of drawers along the wall and a small table by the bed which held a copy of the 'Book of Mormon'. Above and behind the bed was a large window covered with several layers of white gauzy curtains. Steve shrugged to himself as he turned to face Miss Beatrice who held up a long, thin finger.

"I serve breakfast, Mr. Cannon, but not lunch or dinner. There will be no smoking in the hotel and no drinking." Steve nodded as she turned toward the stairs.

"Of course, Miss Beatrice, whatever you say."

A half hour later, Steve opened the valise on top of the bed and began to unpack. He placed his .45 under several shirts in the top drawer of the chest. When he opened the closet, he discovered a chair which he pulled over next to the bed. When he was done, he looked at his watch. It was nearly six o'clock. Steve walked down the hall to the bathroom and washed up. Back in his room, he changed into a fresh shirt before he locked the door and descended the stairs to the parlor. He didn't see Miss Beatrice anywhere as he opened the door and stepped out onto the sidewalk. He looked casually up and down the street ignoring the police car that was parked right next to the Ranchero. The cop was sitting quietly in the front seat and Steve could feel his watchful eyes. Steve made a decision and smiled over at the cop as he walked toward the car. The driver window was down and Steve bent over at the waist.

"Good evening, officer. My name is Steve Cannon. I'm staying at Miss Beatrice's hotel just there." He pointed back toward the hotel without turning around, before he extended his hand toward the window. The cop didn't respond, but looked at Steve from behind his mirrored glasses. He stared at Steve for several seconds before he spoke.

"You got business here or are you just passing through?" Steve straightened up and stretched his back. He looked down at the officer.

"Oh, mostly passing through, officer. I thought I might spend a couple of days exploring the area." The cops' lips moved in a funny fashion as he thought.

"So, you drove straight here from Las Vegas to just look around for a few days and see the sights?" Steve shrugged his shoulders as casually as he could.

"Pretty much." The lips twitched again.

"So, you've explored St. George, Cedar City, Hatch and all the rest and now it is our turn, right?" Steve was regretting his choice of strategy, but he smiled down at the cop.

"Parents brought me through here as a kid, and I always thought it might be a great place to come and spend a little time. A little change of pace from the city." The cop was distracted as the radio crackled on. The cop listened for a few seconds and then started his engine. He looked up at Steve as he shifted into reverse.

"We don't like folks from the city think they can come here and break our rules, so watch yourself." Steve smiled benignly as the cruiser backed into the middle of main street and moved away in the direction of the Texaco station. Steve looked across the street at the only diner he had seen so far. He thought better of it and climbed into his car. He pulled out and slowly drove down the street in the opposite direction from the one that the cop had taken.

Twenty minutes later, Steve pulled off the interstate and parked in the gravel lot of the Holiday Inn. Next to the motel was a state package liquor store. Steve steeled himself for the complicated process of obtaining an alcoholic drink in Utah. He entered the store and approached the counter. He pulled out his Nevada drivers' license and held it out for the clerk. The middle-aged man took it from Steve, examined it, and entered the particulars in a large book that lay open behind the counter. He handed it back to Steve and then stood to one side so Steve could see the paltry offerings. The only scotch that was visible was Cutty Sark. Steve sighed and indicated the bright green bottle. The man retrieved it from the shelf and held it out to Steve. Steve nodded.

"One or two?" Steve slipped his license back into his wallet.

"Two."

The man disappeared into a back room, returning several

minutes later with two small brown cardboard boxes which he placed by the register. He rang them up slowly and accepted Steve's twenty dollar bill. He placed the change on top of the boxes and slid a journal with lined pages across the counter. Steve signed his name just below the last one that had been entered. He picked up the change and slid it into his pocket. The man stacked one of the boxes on top of the other and carried them over to a small window that was a pass through into the hotel.

Steve walked into the lobby and followed the sound of laughter to the lounge. There were several traveling businessmen at the bar drinking in a group. The bartender who was reading a newspaper ambled over and took the two boxes from the window and placed them on a counter behind the bar. He turned and looked at Steve. Steve pointed to a row of short glasses behind the man.

"Neat." The bartender nodded. He opened one of the boxes and pulled out a small flat jar with a screw top lid. He poured all two ounces into one of the glasses. He turned toward Steve.

"Name?"

"Cannon" He wrote the name on the other box and placed the glass in front of Steve. Steve slid a silver dollar across the bar and picked up the glass and a cocktail napkin. He walked to the back of the lounge to the last table. The space was separated from the restaurant by a low wooden panel. One of the waitresses from the other side came to the table as Steve was lighting a Pall Mall.

"Can I get something for you sir?" Steve smiled.

"Can I get dinner and still sit here?" The young girl smiled.

"Of course. I will bring a menu." The waitress walked away toward the bar.

A half hour later, Steve sat back in the comfortable chair and finished his second scotch and third cigarette while he gazed into the fireplace twenty feet away. When the noise from the bar increased, he stubbed out the Pall Mall and made his way out a side door to the parking lot. He passed only one other car on his way back to

Parowan. Just before he reached the hotel, he discovered a narrow alleyway that led to a parking area just behind the historic building. Steve pulled his car in as far as it would go. He walked back out the alley and looking back, was pleased that the Ranchero could not be seen from the main street. There was no one about when he entered the drawing room that was dimly lit by two table lamps. He ascended the creaking stairs and paused on the landing when he heard the sound of voices coming from the other end of the hallway. He continued on to his room, locking the door behind him.

JULY 9

STEVE BENT OVER his copy of the Cedar City Times as he ignored the frequent stares from the other end of the breakfast table. The table had ten places and the three at the far end were occupied by a couple and a single man. From the small bits of conversation that Steve heard from time to time, the man was some sort of traveling farm implements salesman and the couple were on their way from Salt Lake to Arizona to visit their daughter. They were already there when Steve had walked into the sunny dining room ten minutes before. His cheery good morning had been met with almost imperceptible nods and even after Miss Beatrice had breezed in from the kitchen with fresh coffee for Steve and had made the introductions, the atmosphere had not improved. Miss Beatrice sensed the lack of simpatico and instead of her usual practice of placing large platters of eggs, potatoes, toast, biscuits and sausage within reach of everyone, she offered each new dish to Steve first, before she proceeded to line them up in the middle of the table. Steve had just finished the paper when Miss Beatrice sat down across from him. When her intention of starting a general conversation became obvious, the other three guests excused themselves and returned to their rooms. Steve smiled at Miss Beatrice over his coffee cup.

"I'm afraid that I am not good for business, Miss Beatrice." Miss Beatrice laughed softly and held up her glass of orange juice.

"I think the smell of coffee brewing alerted them to your

presence, Mr. Cannon. Just as I make sure that travelers such as yourself see the room first, I also make sure that my LDS guests know that I will make certain all my guests have what they need to make their stay as comfortable as I can make it."

"Well, I can certainly vouch for that, Miss Beatrice. That was the best night's sleep I have had in quite some time." Miss Beatrice picked up a platter of fried eggs and slid two onto Steve's plate.

"Glad to hear it, Mr. Cannon." She peered closely at Steve as he sprinkled pepper on the sunny side up eggs. "I don't normally pry into the affairs of my guests, Mr. Cannon, but you are not the typical tourist that glides through on the way to somewhere else, and you can expect that most people around here will react to that, and unfortunately, most of the time it will not be in a friendly way." Steve nodded as he swallowed a bite from his plate.

"Yes, Miss Beatrice, I have already had that experience with the local constabulary." Miss Beatrice scoffed.

"Darren Wiggins. I went to school with his grandmother, hooligans all of them. Was one of the worst things this county ever did, pinning badges on him and his brother. They just lord it over everybody. You steer clear of them. But if worst comes to worst, you tell me. I know ways to make them toe the line." Miss Beatrice's voice was more strident that it had been just minutes before. Steve sat back and sipped from his coffee cup.

"With a little luck, Miss Beatrice, I can wrap up my business here in a couple of days." Miss Beatrice had grown quiet since her outburst and seemed rather chagrined. Though Steve knew she was dying to know what 'business' that might be, she nodded and smiled politely in reply. Steve placed his napkin next to his plate and stood up.

"I will probably be gone all day, Miss Beatrice." She stood and began clearing the dishes. Their eyes met as Steve was pushing his chair back under the table.

"I hope you don't get the wrong idea, Mr. Cannon, this is a good town full of good people. They just get a little skittish when outsiders come around." Steve handed Miss Beatrice his plate.

"I am sure you are right, Miss Beatrice. Hopefully I will see you this evening." Steve did not return to his room, but walked out the front door and stood in the sun for a few minutes before he clutched his canvas satchel under his arm and turned down the leafy side street.

*

The musty smell of books washed over Steve as he opened one side of the big double doors at the top of the ten stone steps. He stood for several seconds just inside the door, and not seeing anyone, he walked down a long row of stacks to where several tables sat under a large stained glass window. He was gazing at the biblical scene when he heard the quick click of a woman's heels behind him. He turned around as a petite woman with dark brown hair swept up in a small beehive emerged from one of the stacks with several books in her arms. She stopped, pushed her black rimmed glasses higher on her nose and looked pleasantly at Steve.

"May I help you?" Steve walked half the distance between them and stopped.

"You are Miss Purcells, I presume?" The young woman whom he guessed to be in her mid-twenties, laughed softly.

"You are not from around here, how did you know that?" It was Steve's turn to laugh.

"Harold Gleamer's grandson, Roy, told me. My name is Steve Cannon." Miss Purcells smiled when she heard Roy's name and stepped up to the table in front of her and spread the books in her arms out on the surface. She moved toward Steve and held out her hand. Steve met her halfway and shook it gently, as he looked intently into her eyes.

"I need your help, Miss Purcells." She took a step back and her expression matched Steve's serious tone.

"Of course, Mr. Cannon, I will do what I can." Steve pointed to several cabinets against the wall under the windows that held drawers that were long and narrow.

"Harold Gleamer thought you might be housing the archives of the Parowan Times." Miss Purcells glanced quickly at the same drawers.

"Yes, Mr. Cannon, Robert Mitchell, the owner and editor, entrusted them to me before he retired. Do you have specific dates in mind?" Steve shook his head.

"I don't suppose they are on microfiche, are they?" He could see from the disappointed expression that crossed her face that his job was going to be harder than he thought. As she replied in the negative he knew he had to come to a quick decision on whether he could take her into his confidence or not. He held up the canvas satchel as he pulled out one of the chairs next to him and indicated that she should sit down. When they were both seated across the table from each other, Steve pulled out two of his notebooks from the satchel. He held one up and riffled the pages before he spoke.

"I am a private detective from Las Vegas, Miss Purcells, and as you can see, I have spent many hours looking into what I am about to tell you." He could tell from the earnest look in the young woman's eyes that she was intrigued.

"There have been three murders in Las Vegas in the last month, and the only connection between the victims that I can uncover is that they are all around the same age and they all grew up in this little community." Steve slipped a thick piece of paper from the satchel and handed it across the table to Miss Purcells.

"Those are the three names, Miss Purcells. Do you recognize them?" She nodded slowly as she read them and then looked up shaking her head.

"These are certainly family names from this area, Mr. Cannon, but as I am sure you are aware, families around here are very large and I can't say that I have ever heard these names, exactly."

"That makes sense, Miss Purcells, as they are all in their early fifties and most likely left here at an early age." Steve leaned across the table, his voice took on a tone of urgency.

"I think something happened here that is the motivation for someone to kill them. They would have graduated from high school in 1932, so if I could see the editions from say, 1928 until 1935, I think that might be a good place to start, don't you?" Miss Purcells nodded and rose from the table.

"I will bring them out for you, Mr. Cannon. Some of them, especially those from before the war are beginning to dry out, so I must ask you to handle them carefully."

"Of course, Miss Purcells."

As Steve begin his search, Miss Purcells covered the table with two foot high stacks of the old papers. The Saturday edition which was the longest, was only twelve pages long and most of the weekly ones were considerably shorter. After four hours, Steve had dozens of references to the three names and all but one was from the sports pages. He was also receiving an education in the political and social underpinnings of the small community and the handful of families who stood for election year after year, the offices almost handed down from generation to generation. There were few stories that featured crimes that rose above low level physical disputes, though there had been a bank robbery in Cedar City in 1934, where the culprits were apprehended a day later just outside Parowan. It was when Steve decided to go back over all the editions from the five year span, that he found an ongoing story that at first intrigued him from a detective's point of view and then played on his mind as he took a break and drove toward the Holiday Inn on the interstate. He had not seen one phone booth in the whole town of Parowan and the only phone theoretically available to him was in Miss Beatrice's drawing room and was too public.

The straight road shimmered with heat mirages as Steve drove at a leisurely pace away from Parowan. The story concerned a young man of seventeen, Garret Dawkins, who went missing for several weeks in the summer of 1932. He was eventually found dead outside a campground thirty miles from home. The conclusion of the authorities was that he had run away and had somehow fallen to his death while hiking. What had intrigued Steve as he had followed along by reading each new story in the sequence was that at almost every turn, there was evidence given to the paper by his family and friends that disputed almost all the major conclusions of the investigation. No one had ventured the opinion that he had run away until after his body was found. He was not the outdoor type at all, and when Steve went back and looked, the only other time his name was in the paper was for winning a spelling bee in eighth grade. Almost as reflex, Steve had jotted notes as he read the drama that played out over forty editions of the paper. He had a full list of names, most of whom were long dead based on their ages quoted in the paper, but as Steve parked in the gravel lot, he figured there might be enough people still around to satisfy his growing curiosity. The lobby of the Holiday Inn was nearly deserted when Steve chose the roomier of the three phone booths and sat down on the narrow stool and pulled out his notebook. His dropped three quarters into the slot and dialed his first number.

"Gem?" He was surprised that he reached her so quickly.

"Steve, I was hoping I would hear from you today. Where are you calling from?"

"A Holiday Inn just outside Parowan. It is the only private phone for miles. How is the hotel progressing?"

"I think everything is fine, at least what I have seen. I haven't seen Bernie since Wednesday night, but I am sure he has a million things to do. Are you coming back soon?" Steve rubbed his forehead and sighed.

"I don't know, Gem. I haven't talked to Sam Wiser or Tam yet, so I don't know how things stand. I hope to wrap up things here which haven't been as productive as I thought so far, but other than that, I can't predict when I will be able to show my face back in Las Vegas. If this continues, I am going to have to kidnap you and we can hide away somewhere." Gem's voice had a soft purr to it when she replied.

"I will drop everything right now, just say the word, mister." Steve laughed.

"Don't tempt me, Gem." Steve and Remy talked for ten more minutes before his quarters ran out and Remy was called away from the phone. Steve walked to the front desk and changed two dollar bills for quarters. His next call was to Sam Wiser, who was out. Steve made an appointment with Sally to call him at one o'clock the next day. After a short conversation with Miss Perone and a quick lunch at the bar, Steve headed back to Parowan.

The newspapers were still where Steve had left them. Miss Purcells was busy with other library patrons when he walked past the front desk, so he separated the editions detailing the disappearance of the young boy from the others. He was studying the pictures of some of the principals involved when Roy appeared across the table. He was wearing red shorts, a striped t-shirt, high topped black tennis shoes and an oversized baseball glove that hung from his belt. Steve smiled.

"Hi Roy, how are you today?" Roy smiled shyly.

"Hello, Mr. Cannon, what are you doing?" Roy fingered the yellowed pages of the newspaper in front of him.

"I am reading about some of the things that happened here many years ago." The young boy nodded his head and looked down at the newspaper in front of Steve. He walked around the table and peered over Steve's shoulder. He placed a short thin finger on the page.

"That is my great aunt, Delma." Steve leaned forward and looked at the grainy black and white photo. The caption read: 'Delma Givens, friend'. Steve turned and looked at the young boy who was leaning against the table and curling his legs around the chair next to Steve.

"Does she live around here, Roy?" Roy nodded as he straightened up and walked toward the end of the table.

"She lives two houses down from Grandpa Harold. I have to go get my books, goodbye."

"Goodbye, Roy," Steve replied as he gazed at the picture. Delma Givens' name appeared in several of the articles and Steve had the impression that she was considered the closest person to the deceased boy. She had also been the 1932 homecoming queen. The homecoming king that year was Hiram Dame.

*

Steve walked through the front door of the hotel just after three-thirty. He heard voices coming from the dining room and when he appeared in the doorway, the conversation between Miss Beatrice and the farm equipment salesman stopped. Steve smiled and said hello. Miss Beatrice stood up.

"Can I get you some lemonade, Mr. Cannon? It is almost ninety degrees out there today."

"Yes, Miss Beatrice, that would hit the spot." He smiled at the salesman who stared back blankly, stood up abruptly and left the table. Miss Beatrice appeared several seconds later with a large pitcher of lemonade and three glasses. She looked around at the mostly empty dining room with a confused look on her face. When she looked at Steve, he shrugged.

"Where is Mr. Scruggins, Mr. Cannon?"

"I guess he remembered something he had to do, Miss Beatrice." She frowned as she put the tray on the table.

"I am going to have a word with him, Mr. Cannon, I can't abide rudeness." Steve sat down wearily.

"Don't say anything on my account, Miss Beatrice. He will be back, I probably won't." Miss Beatrice made a face and filled two glasses with lemonade. She handed one to Steve and then sat back in her chair so that she was in the line of fire from an oscillating fan that sat on the break front. Steve took a long sip of the cool, sweet liquid.

"This is very good lemonade, Miss Beatrice." She smiled

"Thank you, Mr. Cannon. What has kept you so busy today?" Steve sat back in the chair to avoid the rush of air that came his way every five seconds.

"I am glad you asked, Miss Beatrice, because I stumbled across something interesting at the library this afternoon and I thought you might help me to understand it."

"Did you ask my niece, Miss Purcell, Mr. Cannon? If she didn't have the answer, I am sure I would be of no help." Steve smiled.

"This all happened before she was born, Miss Beatrice. Do you remember the case of the missing boy, Garret Dawkins?" He stopped talking to gauge her reaction. Her expression didn't change.

"Of course, Mr. Cannon, I was working at the post office back in those days. No one in this town who lived through it will ever forget it. But why would it interest you? Is that why you are here?" Steve made the same calculation that he made earlier in the day when he had stood in front of Miss Purcells.

"Let me answer that, Miss Beatrice, by asking you a question. There have been six murders of men from this town in the last year and a half. Three in Las Vegas in just the last three weeks. Yet, if I go by the local papers I have read since I have been here there is no mention of them. Why is that, Miss Beatrice?" The woman across the table regarded Steve for several seconds before she replied.

"That isn't how things are handled here, Mr. Cannon. The newspaper would be the last place the murders would be mentioned." Steve took a slow sip of the lemonade.

"Do you believe the story that Garret Dawkins ran away from home and fell to his death while hiking in the mountains?" Steve sensed a reaction in the way that the unexpected question was framed. A vague tenseness crossed the kindly face, but only for an instant.

"It doesn't matter what I think about what happened thirty years ago, but there are plenty of people in this town that are going to resent the asking." Steve decided to change tactics. He reached for his satchel which he had placed on the floor by his chair. He pulled out a notebook and pencil. Miss Beatrice watched quietly while he flipped to a page near the back.

"Magnus Pearce, Hiram Dame, Lamar Lee. What are the other three names, Miss Beatrice?" Steve waited with his pencil poised. He could see that Miss Beatrice was doing her own calculations of trust. After a full minute of silence, Miss Beatrice looked down at her hands that were folded in her lap. Her voice was quiet.

"Donald Hatch, Leslie Hamblin, and Cornelius Spencer." Steve wrote quickly so that he wouldn't have to ask her to repeat the names.

"What year did they all graduate from Parowan High School, Miss Beatrice?" She looked up with a wistful look.

"1932." As Steve wrote the number in his book, he hoped that Miss Purcell would remember to leave all the papers where he had left them.

"I imagine, Miss Beatrice, that you remember this group of young men pretty well, am I correct?"

"Yes, Mr. Cannon, you are correct. And to answer your next questions: Yes, they were all very good friends, they were always together. They were on the football team and they were the whole basketball team, the one that almost won the state championship that year." Steve gazed steadily at the proud face.

"But there is one name missing, isn't there, Miss Beatrice?" Steve reached into his satchel again and pulled out the list of LDS members that he had shown to Stanwick the day he visited him in his office. He smoothed it out on the plastic table cloth before he held it out to Miss Beatrice. She looked at him for several seconds before she took it from his hand. The paper shook a little as she laid it down in front of her. She let out a small sigh before she replied.

"Terence Leavitt." Steve wrote the name down and took the

paper from her hand when she held it out. Steve let several seconds slip by before he spoke again. He tried to make his voice as gentle and as matter of fact as he could manage.

"Do you know Delma Givens, Miss Beatrice?" Miss Beatrice nodded and poured herself another glass of the lemonade.

"She is Delma Wiggins, now, Mr. Cannon." Steve's expression was one of surprise in spite of himself. Miss Beatrice sensed she had the initiative and leaned forward, her voice was huskier now.

"Yes, exactly, Mr. Cannon. You see I am right now, don't you? This town is no different than any other in the world. There are things that are ours and ours alone and like everyone else we will fight for the right to handle those things our own way." Steve sat back in the chair and looked Miss Beatrice in the eyes.

"Normally, I would agree with that, Miss Beatrice, but not when there are lives at stake and a serial killer on the loose. I appreciate what you have told me so far, and I don't want to distress you any more than I already have. Unless you have anything else you want to tell me, we will leave it here for now."

"I am worried for you, Mr. Cannon, if you keep asking these kinds of questions. I don't know who would be behind these killings, and as I sit here, I swear to you that nobody else in this town knows either." Steve stood from the table. He bent over to pick up his satchel. He paused and looked down at the older woman.

"They might not know who is doing the killing, Miss Beatrice, but I am sure more than one person in this town knows why." He walked toward the stairs and then stopped. He turned around as Miss Beatrice looked up at him quizzically.

"One more question, Miss Beatrice. The year that Garret Dawkins died, 1932, who was the bishop here then?"

"Why, Harold Gleamer, Mr. Cannon."

*

The desk clerk at the Holiday Inn greeted Steve as if he were a regular as he passed by the front desk on his way to the lounge. There was not a soul to be seen as Steve slapped three dollar bills on the top of the bar. He decided to forego the liquor ritual, the exact decision the draconian process was designed to encourage. Quarters in hand, Steve strode to his favorite phone booth.

Tam was home when Steve's call came through, and Steve could tell that Tam was somewhat surprised to hear his voice.

"Cannon? Where the hell are you?"

"Parowan, Tam, Utah."

"I know where Parowan is, wise guy. I meant more why are you there?" Steve shook his head.

"Listen to me closely, Tam, and take some of this down." He heard a groan from the other end.

"I come home to get away from all this crap and then you call."

"Well, Tam this 'crap' as you call it, actually has some substance, so if you don't mind, pay attention."

"Fine, shoot."

"I got the info from Amis Kinsley that there have been in fact six Mormon murders all together." Tam interrupted.

"Funny thing, I haven't seen him around for a couple of days, he's usually under our feet all the time."

"Well, he and a few of his guys are probably a little worse for wear."

"I'm not even going to ask."

"Back to the business at hand, Tam. All six of these guys are from this little one horse burg I am in right now. They all graduated together, football, basketball, the whole nine yards." Steve repeated each name twice for Tam.

"What am I supposed to do with this?" Steve shook his head even more impatiently.

"I told you that, so I can tell you this. There is one more name. Terence Leavitt. He is the last name and the only one of these guys that is still alive. I am convinced he is the next target for our killer.

He is an attorney in Las Vegas. I have heard his name, and I think he does the legal end on big land deals. You need to get police protection on him as soon as possible." There was a long pause on Tam's end.

"And how am I supposed to do that? Stand up in morning roll call and say: Here is how Steve Cannon thinks we should be planning our day?" Tam chuckled at his little joke. Steve took deep breaths and waited.

"Cannon? You still there?" When Steve spoke, his voice was low and icy.

"You better think of something, because I am going to call him right now and after that I am going to call his law partner and tell him the same thing. So unless you want to get to get hung out to dry if he turns up dead, I suggest you quit making jokes and start acting like a policeman." Steve slammed the receiver down and headed to the bar. He reloaded his collection of quarters and cooled down before he returned to the phone booth. Terence Leavitt was called to the phone by his wife.

"Who is this?"

"Mr. Leavitt, this is Steve Cannon and I would like.." Leavitt interrupted.

"I don't know who you are, Mr. Cannon, and I don't take calls like this at home. If you have legitimate business than call my office tomor...." Steve cut him off.

"How many funerals have you been to recently, Mr. Leavitt?" He heard a sharp intake of breath. He continued before he could be interrupted. "Unless you want your wife and family to attend yours in the near future, I suggest you listen to what I have to say." Steve stopped and waited. A few seconds went by.

"I am listening, Mr. Cannon."

"You are the last of the Mohicans, Mr. Leavitt. You are also the last man that knows the real reason that the other six murders were committed. Now, whatever transpired, you have no doubt by this point in your life rationalized your part in it and think you are safe.

But I assure you that whoever has killed your friends has found you guilty, if only by association."

"Why should I believe you?"

"Because I am in Parowan right now. Do you want me to describe the hotel and what Miss Beatrice served for breakfast this morning? What happened to Garret Dawkins, Mr. Leavitt?"

"What? Why are you asking me?" Steve cut him off again.

"Because I suspect you are the last person alive who truly does know what did happen. But even without your statement, Mr. Leavitt, I will get to the bottom of this. I just hope for your sake that I figure it out quickly enough." Steve waited through a full ten seconds of silence. Steve's voice was weary when he spoke again.

"Last piece of advice, Mr. Leavitt. Tell at least two other people what I have said to you tonight and go to the police tomorrow and ask for protection. Ask to see Detective Polhaus. If you have something to say to me, leave me a message at the Parowan Hotel."

Steve clicked off and walked back through the lobby and out into the parking lot. He smoked two cigarettes as he leaned back against the Ranchero. The half phase moon cast long thin shadows in the cherry orchard behind the parking lot.

JULY 10

STEVE DELIBERATELY APPEARED in the dining room later than the previous morning. All the dishes had been cleared except for his place setting at the far end of the table. He picked up the Cedar City paper from the break front and was skimming through it when Miss Beatrice came in from the kitchen. She smiled when she saw Steve and turning back, returned a few seconds later with the coffee pot. She poured some into his cup and placed the pot on top of a coaster. She chuckled as she sat down across from Steve.

"Since you are the only one here, I can leave the pot out. To tell you the truth, Mr. Cannon, I have always liked the smell of coffee, even though I was twenty years old before I first smelled any. I have been told it tastes bitter and if you don't drink it when you are young, you never develop a taste for it, is that true, Mr. Cannon?" Steve smiled over the cup.

"Yes, it is true, Miss Beatrice, and also true of a few other things that come to mind. But I have to say, for never drinking any, you make a fine cup." Miss Beatrice smiled, and stood up.

"I will bring your breakfast right out. Eggs over soft?" Steve replied as she disappeared through the door.

"Yes, please."

A few minutes later as Steve was finishing his meal, he noticed a worried expression coming from across the table.

"Miss Beatrice, what's wrong?" Miss Beatrice shook her head.

"I was wondering about tomorrow, Mr. Cannon, what will you do?" Steve smiled to himself as he placed his knife and fork at an angle on the bone china.

"Don't worry, Miss Beatrice, I think I will return to Las Vegas tonight and come back on Monday if that is all right with you." He held up his hand. "I know, Miss Beatrice, I will make sure I buy gas and everything else I need today." As she cleared the dishes from the table, Steve wondered how many times he had heard tourists complain about being stranded in some town in Utah on Sundays.

He looked at his watch. He needed another two hours in the library. He walked out the front door and stood on the sidewalk. Across the street, in front of the diner, he saw Darren Wiggins and another cop talking to two other men. One of the men saw Steve and said something to Darren. They all turned and looked in his direction. Steve stared back casually for several seconds before he moved off toward the library.

Three hours later, he pulled into the Texaco station. On his way into the building, he was met halfway by a young man who wore a pair of coveralls and a baseball cap.

"Fill 'er up, Mister?" Steve smiled and turned toward the car.

"Yes, please and could you check the oil as well?" Seeing nobody else in the building, Steve followed the man back to his car.

"Harold Gleamer around today?" The man glanced up from his position under the hood.

"No, not today. This is his day over at the church." Steve leaned closer so that he could see the dipstick before the man wiped it clean.

"Which way is that?" The man looked up quickly before he plunged the stick back into the small tube on the side of the engine. He straightened and made small motions with his hands before he spoke. His expression was one of exasperation.

"Well… Mister..you can't exactly go…" Steve smiled benignly and held up his hand.

"That's OK, I know what you are trying to say, and I understand." The man's face showed immense relief, before it broke into a grin.

"But how about I call him over to the church and he can come outside and meet you?" Steve fell in behind the man as he headed toward the building.

Harold Gleamer was standing just outside the neat red and white brick building when Steve pulled to the curb and parked his car. He walked the fifty yards on the narrow concrete pathway that cut through the closely mown, well-watered lawn. The closer he got to Harold the more worried the elderly man looked. Steve tried to disarm him by stopping and smiling. He swung his arm in a half circle.

"This is a beautiful building you have here, Mr. Gleamer." He stepped forward and held out his hand. Harold looked a little more at ease as he grasped Steve's hand and smiled.

"Yes, Mr. Cannon, we take great pride in it." There was an awkward pause as Steve put his hands in his pockets and looked evenly at Harold who was shifting his weight back and forth.

"Somewhere we could talk privately, Mr. Gleamer?" Harold took a deep breath.

"Harold, please, Mr. Cannon, and may I call you Steve?" He pointed toward the front of the church. "Follow me." Steve followed him through the wide white doors into an expansive foyer. Harold opened a side door and stood aside to let Steve enter the room. Steve walked in and looked around as Harold closed the door behind them. The whole room was made of a light cherry wood and was filled with bookshelves, most of them containing volumes that looked to Steve to be very old. Harold motioned to an oval wooden table and six chairs in the middle of the room. Steve pulled one of the chairs out, laying his satchel on the one next to it. Steve cleared his throat when he saw that Harold had made himself comfortable across from him.

"I don't want to keep you too long from your duties, Harold, I just have a few questions I think you might be able to answer." Harold nodded almost imperceptively, his eyes were intent upon Steve's face.

"What kind of kid was Garret Dawkins, Harold?" Harold's expression didn't change and for a moment Steve thought that perhaps he hadn't heard the question. Harold cleared his throat, but his voice was slightly restricted when he spoke.

"Garret was a good kid, Steve, obedient, very smart." Harold shook his head and looked down at his hands clasped on the table in front of him. "It is a very sad and tragic story, Steve, which I am sure you know if you are asking." Steve waited a few seconds before he asked the next question.

"How did he get along with the other kids?" Harold still stared at his hands.

"There were difficulties…kids are kids..and.." Harold's voice trailed off as he looked up at Steve. Steve decided to try a different angle.

"How many kids graduated from the high school in 1932?" Harold took a deep breath and looked up at the intricately inlaid ceiling.

"The most we have ever graduated is twenty-two, so it couldn't have been more than that, I would say eighteen or nineteen. If it is important to you, I can check the records."

"No, that won't be necessary." Steve drummed his fingers lightly on the table top. "I am curious, Harold, why you haven't asked me yet why I am asking all these questions about things that happened over thirty years ago?" Steve studied the wrinkled face in front of him. Harold sat back and slid his arms off the table dropping his hands into his lap.

"I know why, Mr. Cannon, the whole town knows why. You think the death of Garret and the recent murders of his classmates are related."

"Don't you, Mr. Gleamer?" Harold traced a forefinger along the smooth edge of the table.

"I don't know, I don't see how." Steve willed his voice to be as casual as he could when he spoke again.

"Well, perhaps I can help you make the connection. Garret Dawkins was studious, didn't play sports and his best friend was Delma Givens, the most popular girl in the class. Now we were all young once and if we try, we can remember how things were then. Emotions run high, others that are different than we are come in for ridicule and abuse. Now, you were the bishop back then, and though I don't know a whole lot about your religion, I grew up with a lot of Mormon kids and you would have been in charge of the many youth groups and in a town this size, you would have likely been present on every outing, every picnic, every dance. You said there were difficulties, Mr. Gleamer, what kind of difficulties?" Harold swallowed hard and looked down at his hands.

"Fights, bullying….if you went to school with members of the church, Mr. Cannon, then you know that around eighth grade is a very difficult time for them when they start seminary. Some drop out then. That is when Garret quit coming. Most everyone was relived, but I saw later that it was a mistake and only made Garret's differences more apparent." For several long seconds neither man spoke. Steve shifted in his chair and wrote in his notebook. Harold Gleamer sat quietly. Steve flipped to a new page and looked up, waiting for Harold to make eye contact.

"The last night that anybody remembers seeing Garret was a Saturday night and there was a dance at the high school, right?"

"Yes, it was the last dance of the year. The graduation ceremony was the following Friday night."

"Did you see Garret at the dance, Harold?" Harold shook his head.

"He wasn't in church the next day either. His father and step mother always made sure he attended even though he was not interested anymore." Steve flipped back several pages in his notebook.

"I don't find much mention of his parents and the Dawkins name isn't in any of the papers that I have read. Is the family still in the area?"

"No, Mr. Cannon, they are living in Arizona, just the other side of the Arizona strip. They moved away the same year that Garret died." Steve snorted softly as he recorded the information.

"You said stepmother, Mr. Gleamer, where was Garrets' mother?" Harold squirmed uncomfortably in the hard, wooden chair. He shook his head as he spoke.

"There was a scandal, Mr. Cannon. She left town with another man when Garret was three years old."

"Remember the man's last name?" It was becoming harder and harder for Harold to answer the questions as his reply was barely above a whisper.

"Robbins." Steve made a point of snapping shut the notebook after he had written down the name.

"Do you have any questions for me, Mr. Gleamer?" Harold looked up and gazed at Steve but dropped his eyes as he spoke.

"I've heard you are a private detective with a bit of a reputation where you come from. I guess I am curious as to who has hired you?" Steve took several seconds to let his eyes wander around the room. When he looked back at Harold, he was staring intently at Steve.

"That is confidential, Harold, but suffice it to say, you would be very surprised if you knew."

Steve stood to leave but stopped.

"Harold, have you ever heard the words: 'Knights of Nauvoo'?" The sudden change of expression on the older man's face compelled Steve to sit down again. Harold shook his head slowly from side to side with a half-smile on his lips.

"I haven't heard that for over forty years. That was what they used to call themselves when they ran around town as a gang, getting into mischief. 'The Knights of Nauvoo'." Harold chuckled to himself in a private reverie. Steve stood again.

"I have taken enough of your time, Harold. I appreciate you answering my questions. I hope I haven't caused you too much trouble." Harold waved weakly and returned to his private thoughts. Steve stood for a few seconds looking down at the gray hair and shaggy eyebrows.

He was half way down the pathway when he saw the police car parked behind the Ranchero. Darren Wiggens was leaning on Steve's car with his arms crossed. Steve walked to within ten feet of the cop and stopped, folding his arms across his chest as well. He could see his own reflection doubled in the mirrored lenses.

"Is there a problem officer?" Steve's voice was low and menacing. Darren smiled.

"Quite a few actually, now that you're asking." Steve snorted.

"Well, unless any of them involve breaking the law, I don't see why we are having this little meeting." Darren stood from the car and dropped his hands, his right one coming to rest on the butt of his pistol.

"All your questions about things that don't concern you has got most of the town uneasy. I think it would be best for all concerned if you left." Steve chuckled.

"Well, Darren, you get your wish. The last place I want to be is in a Mormon town on Sunday, so I am leaving here this evening." He walked past the officer and around the front of the car. He paused with the door open.

"Oh yeah. I will be back bright and early on Monday morning." He smiled widely as he bent over to get into the car.

*

Sam Wiser's voice held an edge of excitement. Steve sat in the Holiday Inn phone booth and sipped a coke through a straw.

"All done, Steve. I got Jim Larsen to withdraw the warrant this morning. You can resume your normal activities." Steve snorted.

"I never stopped, Sam, but at least now it will be a little less inconvenient. How were you able to swing that?"

"A little luck never hurts, Steve. The last victim, Lee, being a Gaming Commissioner, brought the feds into it. Wade being a state legislator had them moving in that direction already, but the Lee murder tore it, for sure. They reviewed the case, and the evidence, and they came to the conclusion that Samuels was running it all wrong. When I heard that, I got with Larsen and he convinced the judge that your little indiscretion was not detrimental to the case. And there you are." Steve shook his head in wonder.

"Well, I'll be. Good work, Sam, I knew you would get it done, just faster than I thought."

"Well, that is all well and good, Steve, but I think Larsen is the one you should thank. He went out on the limb. By the way, he wants you to go see him when you get back in town."

"I am coming back this afternoon, I will grab a bite to eat and then hit the road. Maybe I can catch up with him tomorrow. I will stop by your office later this week and settle my bill." Sam chuckled.

"How about just buy me lunch at the Copper Cart?"

"That too, my friend, but that is one bill I look forward to paying." Steve rang off and then wandered over to the restaurant. He sat down, and smiled at the same waitress that had served him since he arrived. He had just ordered and had just lit a cigarette when he saw the waitress coming toward him followed closely by an older woman. The older woman stopped as the waitress approached the table and smiled weakly at Steve. She seemed nervous and she stuttered slightly as she spoke.

"Mr...Cannon, this is my aunt Delma" She cupped her elbow and held her hand up near her chin and turned slightly toward the woman. "She would like to speak with you if you have the time." Steve rose almost unconsciously from the table as the waitress indicated that Delma should step forward. She smiled quickly up at Steve as she stopped beside her niece. Her shoulder length brown hair was streaked with gray and her face was smooth with just a few lines on the forehead of her handsome face. She held her purse tightly in front of her. Steve snuffed out his cigarette before he pulled out a chair and waited until she had seated herself.

"Would you like some lunch, Mrs. Wiggins?" She looked at her niece and shook her head no. Steve caught the niece's eye.

"Hold that lunch for me as well, and maybe bring us two lemonades." The waitress nodded and hesitated while she looked down at her aunt. Delma looked up and gave her a small wave as she moved away from the table. Steve settled back in his chair and waited for a few seconds before he spoke.

"Forgive me, Mrs. Wiggins but I am surprised to see you." Delma was staring at the center of the table but she nodded in reply, before she fastened her blue eyes on Steve.

"I can't tell you why, but I had to come. There is a part of me that has been waiting all these years for something to happen and maybe now it has." Her voice trailed off and an anxious look came into her eyes as she again looked down at her purse. Steve sat with his hands folded in his lap. He didn't move his head as he watched Delma's niece coming toward the table with the lemonades. She paused for a second to look down at her aunt before she left the table. His voice was quiet and even when he spoke.

"Miss Wiggins, what can you tell me about the death of Garret Dawkins? Were you there?" Delma looked up at the low wall beside the table and shook her head slowly before she looked again at Steve.

"No, Mr. Cannon, I wasn't, but I know what happened."

"How do you know, Mrs. Wiggins?" Delma straightened in her chair and Steve could sense that she was revisiting a decision she had already made. Her voice was tighter and flatter when she replied.

"Terence Leavitt told me the night he said goodbye, and left town."

"I know this is painful, Mrs. Wiggins, but what did he tell you?" Delma's eyes were clear and focused when she looked at Steve, as if she had struggled over the biggest hurdle. Her normal voice returned.

"Hiram Dame killed him in a fit of jealousy, the rest of them were there and they helped hide Garrett's body." Delma looked down, but Steve saw the tear forming before she did. He pulled his kerchief from his pocket and held it out to her. She nodded her head and took it from him. Steve waited for several minutes until she sniffled and lifted up her head.

"I know you must think poorly of me, Mr. Cannon, going to church every Sunday and keeping this a secret for thirty years."

"That is not my place, Mrs. Wiggins. But tell me why it was Terence that told you and not Hiram." She lifted the kerchief and daubed her eyes again.

"Hiram and I had gone steady since ninth grade, but I loved Terence, and now my silence has probably killed him, the same as Garret." She stifled a small sob and looked away out toward the rest of the tables. Steve leaned forward and spoke softly.

"No, Mrs. Wiggins, I spoke with Terence yesterday. He is alive and well." When she turned and looked into his eyes, Steve could see even more tears, but her eyes searched his face for confirmation of what she had just heard.

"Alive?"

"Yes, Mrs. Wiggins, alive and well." She dropped her gaze and nodded, and Steve felt that a small reprieve from the pain had come and just as quickly had gone. Delma stood slowly from the table and turned to go, but paused, and Steve saw the pain clearly through the blue eyes.

"If I had said something years ago, Mr. Cannon, would things be much different than they are now?" Steve stood up and placed his hand gently on the thin shoulder.

"None of us can know those things, Mrs. Wiggins. There are probably more than a few people in this town who could ask themselves the same question." Delma looked into Steve's eyes for several seconds before she nodded and turned toward the door. Her niece met her halfway and put her arm around her as they walked past the front desk and out the door together.

Steve sat back and opened a new pack of Pall Malls, and smoked two while he finished the lemonade and stared into space. Ten minutes later, he was driving down the interstate toward Las Vegas. As soon as the Utah state line was behind him, he pulled into the first road tavern he came to. Two beers later, he was back on the road, the long, thin, blue edge of the Spring Mountains dividing the earth and the sky in front of him.

*

Steve waded through what was left of his material possessions in the dim dusky light. He stepped around a jumble of empty drawers from his bedroom bureau and snapped on the living room light. All four rooms of the house had been emptied into several piles in the room he was standing in. Silverware and dishes littered the carpet. The door to his safe had been forced open and it lay on its' back blocking the way into the kitchen. Broken glass and the contents of the bottles were spread across the kitchen floor. Steve retrieved a towel from one of the piles and laid it down over part of the kitchen floor so that he could reach the phone on the wall. He dialed a number, spoke for a few moments, then hung up and stood in the gravel of his driveway smoking a cigarette until he saw the black and white police car crest the small hill and slow before it turned down the slope and stopped in front of him.

JULY 11

STEVE SAT WITH Remy next to the pool. A large white umbrella shielded them from the hot ten o'clock sun. Steve watched two golfers drive by as they played the second hole of the Desert Inn golf course, the bright sunlight glinting off the chrome of their clubs. He pondered Remy's question for a few more seconds before he answered.

"I can't worry about the state of the house right now. I need to get a few things done today, before I head back into Utah tomorrow. One of my priorities is to meet with Bernie and see if I can't make up for some of the time I have missed. I have a meeting at three with Jim Larsen and Tam, so I guess the house will have to wait until I get back from Utah."

"I want to help, Steve, just tell me when." Steve smiled at her earnest look as he pulled the champagne bottle from the ice bucket and topped off both of their glasses.

"I know you do, Gem, and I appreciate it more than you know. I've shown you the Polaroids I took when the police were there last night. Pretty big job." Remy sipped her champagne.

"It will go quicker than you think. I would go over and do it myself, but you need to be there to see what can be salvaged." Steve nodded and stared blankly across the course.

"What do you hope to find by going back to Utah, Steve?" He

sighed and took a small sip of the wine. He looked at Remy and twisted his lips into a grimace.

"Some clue as to who the killer is. The answer is there. I am sure of it."

"But if the whole town knew about it, it could be anybody." Steve considered the statement for a few moments.

"I don't know, Gem. It isn't as if the whole town knew the story, it is more a case of not wanting to know. Those seven boys were the best the town had ever produced. It was almost as if some sort of silent bargain was struck. As far as I can tell, none of them has ever gone back and their contact with their families has been almost non-existent." He shook his head and looked down at the pebbled concrete. "If somebody who lives there was the killer, I just feel in my gut that they would have acted long before this." They finished their champagne in silence and twenty minutes later they drove together to the Casablanca Hotel.

Steve found Bernie in his suite, two doors down from the one Jack Cathay occupied. Bernie's face held a happy look of surprise when he opened the door and saw Steve standing in front of him.

"Man, are you a sight for sore eyes. Get in here and tell me everything. I will get us some drinks."

Steve walked into the spacious suite and looked around. It was furnished much like Bernie's townhome out in the valley, except there was a large balcony which looked down over the courtyard, the pool, and the tennis courts. He leaned against the railing as Bernie brought out two glasses of scotch. They moved into the shade and looked out over the sprawling property.

"So, tell me how things went in Utah." Steve shook his head and looked at his watch.

"It's eleven o'clock, now. I have to be in Jim Larsen's office at three. I bet if we start now, we can get a lot done. I still have to go back up there tomorrow. I'll give you the highlights on the way down to the casino floor." Bernie clicked Steve's glass and swallowed the rest of his scotch.

"Good idea. I have everything that I need you to help me with, ready to go." Steve followed Bernie out of the suite and the two men strolled past the front desk on their way out to the courtyard and the casino building beyond.

*

Jim Larsen looked through the small stack of papers that Steve had placed on the desk in front of him. He set them aside when he was done and read the pages of Steve's notebook that Steve had indicated with paper clips. When he was done, he sat back in his chair and looked across at the two detectives sitting in front of him. His gaze fell upon Steve.

"So, you are convinced that the killer of our three victims here is the same one that killed three more in Utah, and it is all connected to the death of…." Jim leaned over his desk toward the piece of paper on the top of the stack. "Garret Dawkins, back in 1932?" Steve held the Assistant District Attorney's gaze.

"Yes, sir. It is the only common denominator that links the six men and their involvement was confirmed by a source in Utah." Larsen nodded, and looked at Tam.

"Have you looked at this evidence, Detective Polhaus, and do you concur?" Tam cleared his throat.

"Yes, Mr. Larsen, I have and I think it fits most of the facts we have been able to uncover, which admittedly is not very much." Larsen harrumphed as he pointed to the tall stack of files on the side of his desk.

"I would say that is an understatement, detective. There is an awful lot of man hours in those files and precious little that actually pertains to what really happened, as Cannon, here, tells it. But, let's move on. What is the next step?" Steve cleared his throat and looked quickly at Tam, before he spoke.

"I need to go back to Parowan and get some leads from my sources there. We have the motive, now, we need to connect it to someone that has used that motivation to commit six murders." Jim Larsen shook his head.

"But the next likely victim is here in Las Vegas and we have to presume that the killer is as well." Steve nodded agreement.

"But all we are reduced to here is waiting for the killer to strike and hoping the security we have thrown up around Leavitt is enough. I am convinced that even if no one in Utah knows who is doing this, they have information that will lead us to that person." Jim rotated his chair back and forth slowly as he contemplated Steve's words. After a few seconds, he leaned forward.

"OK. I will give you two days there to come up with something. But in the meantime, the FBI and the state police will conduct their parallel investigations, so don't be surprised if you have company where you are going."

"I appreciate the head start, but any overt presence of outside law enforcement will do more damage than good. They are extremely wary of strangers and they close ranks very quickly." Jim nodded.

"Understood, Steve. Two days. Now what else do you have?" Steve reached in his pocket and extracted an envelope that he handed across the desk to Jim Larsen. Jim removed the packet of pictures and flipped through them, looking at each one for several seconds. He sighed, looked up and then handed them to Tam Polhaus when he reached for them. As Tam glanced through them quickly, Jim pointed at them.

"I see your point, Steve, that is clearly outside a proper search protocol. What would you like me to do at this point?" Steve took the pictures from Tam and put them back into his pocket.

"Sam Wiser is going before the judge tomorrow and filing a complaint against Samuels. It would be helpful if you could file a friend of the court brief and I want my guns back." Jim raised his eyebrows as he considered the request.

"That may be premature. Let's wait and see what the judge says. I can file my own charges from this office, which I will do if my investigation warrants it. Meanwhile, I will make sure that Samuels personally returns your guns by this evening." Steve smiled and stood up.

"Thank you, Jim, I appreciate your help. I will be in my office until six." He looked over at Tam.

"You coming?" Tam got wearily to his feet.

"This involve a meal?" Steve laughed and rolled his eyes in Jim Larsen's direction. He looked at his watch.

"If Bernie still has his canteen open it does." Tam grumbled something under his breath as he followed Steve out through the outer reception area and down the marble steps. Steve waited for Tam to pull behind him before he left the parking lot for the twenty minute drive to the Casablanca.

For the second time that day, Steve parked in the lot that now extended all along the property bordering the Strip. Bernie was busy with Milton in another part of the hotel, but Steve spied Walter behind the steam tables in the canteen.

"Walter is there anything left to eat in here?" Walter took two steps to his right and pulled the silver top off a large metal tray, the escaping steam obscuring the thin man for a few seconds.

"Bernie's famous pot roast, potatoes and vegetables, but we can cook up anything you want. The American café is open for business as of yesterday." He gestured over his shoulder toward the court-yard. Steve pointed at the tray when Tam nodded his approval. They carried their plates over to a quiet part of the canteen that was now teeming with hotel staff, dealers and cocktail waitresses, as well as the last remnants of the huge construction crew Milton had assembled. After several minutes, Tam looked up from his food.

"I was thinking on the way over here, what if you're all wrong about this Utah business and the killer is not even connected to the ones in Utah and has an entirely different motive?" Steve put his fork down and stared across the room for a few seconds before he turned back to the red face of his dining companion.

"Then the worst that will happen is that we have protected the wrong man. But I bet every poker pot I will win from here on out that somebody connected to or who knows about the killing of Garret Dawkins is behind these murders." Tam's look was still skeptical, so Steve spoke lower but with more emphasis on each word. "I think we should be looking for someone that is new to town. If he is from here, it is unlikely that he would start in Salt Lake and Provo. I also think he is the anonymous caller to Rita Malone, so her description is male, late forties, early fifties, and I think we can add to that description, Caucasian. He also has some major beef with the church. My guess is that he doesn't have a job, he saved up to come here, and that might explain the fact that there are nine months between the Utah murders and ours." Steve was mildly surprised when Tam took out his notebook and recorded the items that Steve had listed. Steve continued.

"If you guys have the manpower, I think that it would be productive to concentrate on the transient housing, the flop houses and the cheaper apartments. I wouldn't check the ones that the dealers and cocktail waitresses live in out by the Strip, until last. Our guy is probably the type who is more comfortable downtown, he would feel too out of place on the Strip." Tam wrote down the last observations, stretched, then yawned.

"That's it for me. I haven't slept but six hours in the last two days. The line-up has changed. Samuels is under the Feds and is working for Brady and Molini, mostly to keep an eye on him and limit any damage he might do. I am in charge of the department's resources, and with Samuels out of the way, I can deploy quite a few bodies to canvass downtown." Steve nodded in agreement.

"My job is to go back to Utah and come up with a name and a description." Tam pulled a toothpick from his shirt pocket. Steve stopped and looked at the small piece of wood.

"That been used before?" Tam took it out of his mouth and peered at it.

"Yeah. Why? I just unwrapped it at breakfast, it is still good." Steve shook his head and stood up from the table.

"I have to go up and see what kind of shambles Samuels made of my office, though I am sure that Miss Perone has it all back ship shape already. I will call you from Utah if I learn anything worth reporting." Tam stood up with him and pointed over Steve's shoulder. Steve turned and saw Bernie and Milton Swanson coming toward them from the direction of the steam tables. Bernie smiled and held out his hand to Tam.

"How ya doing, Tam? You're almost a regular around here." Steve saw Bernie's face light up in the usual manner when he had an idea. He gestured toward Tam with a roll of blueprints. "You play poker, Tam?" Tam shrugged his shoulders and grimaced.

"A little I guess, why?" Bernie laughed.

"Because after all this craziness is over, I am going to have a big poker night at Foxy's to celebrate. I want you to come." He turned to Steve. "And I want you to get him up for it." Steve snorted and jerked his thumb toward Tam.

"I have trouble getting him to do his job right, let alone protect him from those sharks that circle around your games." He smiled at Tam, who waved him off good naturedly. Tam stepped away from the table.

"I have to run. Thanks for the meal and call me." He pointed to Steve, waved at Bernie and Milton and headed for the front entrance. Steve watched him go before he sat down next to Bernie and Milton who already had the plans out and were deep in discussion. He waited until there was a natural lull in the conversation.

"So, Bernie, how close are we here?" Bernie sat back and looked at Milton and sighed.

"Well the last ten percent takes ninety percent of the time, or so my partner here keeps telling me." He indicated Milton with a red pencil he then replaced behind his ear. Milton nodded and looked at Steve.

"Just finish work right now. Bernie wants the rooms to be spot on before the first guests arrive which will be next Saturday at noon, just after the ribbon cutting ceremony. We figure that is more important and if we miss the deadline on the last little bits on the casino and the card rooms, the guests will tend to overlook that more." He looked across at Bernie as he continued. "But I think it will be all done and in perfect order by the time the curtain goes up." Bernie tagged on to the sentiment.

"And several of the entertainers are already staying in their suites and are busy rehearsing, so it's all coming together." Steve nodded his head.

"Every time I come in here, it is almost a miracle compared to the last time I have seen it. You make a good team. Hopefully there will be another opportunity for you guys to work together on a new project." Steve stood up and was about to leave when he saw a look on Bernie's face that usually meant something was up and he was deciding whether he was going to mention it or not. Steve sat down and looked at Bernie for several seconds as he decided. When he spoke, Bernie used his serious voice, that one that usually made Steve tense his jaw muscles to keep from laughing.

"Steve, I know you have a lot on your mind with the Mormon murders and everything, so bear with me here for a moment. You are going to get a letter sometime this week from the gaming commission." The look that crossed Steve's face made Bernie sit up in his chair and hold up his hand. "I know, but you just have to bear with me here. We have a whole month to reply, so there is plenty of time to talk about this after you wrap up your case and before the opening. I just want to make sure that you don't throw it away when you see it." Bernie's voice trailed off at the end and he adopted his little hurt puppy face that he thought was his secret weapon when he wanted to make an unpopular point. Steve shook his head as he stood up.

"That is good timing on your part, Bern, because you are right, I have got a lot on mind at the moment and even though the cops aren't looking to put me away, my house is a little messy, and I have nowhere to live at the moment, so we will table this for now. I only have one question: Is this something I should get Sam Wiser on?" Bernie shook his head in an exaggerated fashion.

"Oh no, no, Steve, this can all wait until later. Then you can decide how you want to go forward." Steve's eyes narrowed as he gazed down at his friend of sixteen years.

"You're up to something, I can feel it, but I have to go." He patted Milton on the shoulder as he passed by, Bernie called out to him as he left.

"See ya, Steve, good luck." Steve snorted to himself as he approached the exit that lead to the courtyard.

*

Steve was sorting through the pink call slips that he found on his desk when the door buzzer sounded. He walked into the hallway and peered at the door through the reception area. Agent Molini was standing at the door holding a cardboard box. As Steve started toward the door, he saw a gray fedora peeking out from behind the pudgy FBI agent. He shook his head as he leaned over Miss Perone's desk and pressed the buzzer that opened the heavy glass door. Agent Molini walked through and stood in front of Steve. His face had an irritated look, which grew stronger when he looked behind him and saw Samuels still standing out in the concourse, the door clicking shut in front of him. He turned back to Steve.

"What a pain this guy is. Hit the button again." Steve shook his head as he repeated the action.

"Don't I know it." He straightened up as Samuels walked into the room and stood on the other side of Molini. He was carrying four long objects wrapped in brown paper and he was looking around the room in an obvious ploy to avoid eye contact with Steve. Steve circled around Molini and stood squarely in front of the Detective. He held his arms out at the waist.

"Give those to me, Samuels," he growled. Samuels turned around and laid them on the long couch, glared at Molini and walked to the front door. He was reaching for the doorknob, when he realized that he had to be buzzed out.

"Forget something, Samuels?" Steve stood in the middle of the room with his hands on his hips. Samuels turned and with a sneering look, pointed to the desk.

"Let me out of here." Steve snorted.

"Asking favors are we now, Samuels? You think you can destroy a man's home and then expect civil behavior? Let me tell you something, little man. You will pay for that." Molini made a grunting sound. Steve didn't take his eyes off the tiny detective, as Molini moved into his vision blocking out his view of Samuels.

"Take it easy, Steve, no threats, OK?" Steve didn't reply but took a step sideways so that he could once again see Samuels.

"You have been lucky so far, I am usually slow to anger, but that is all over. If you know what is good for you, you'll stay out of my sight." Samuels looked down at Steve's balled fists and took a step backward bumping up against the door. Steve smiled with narrowed eyes as he crossed behind Molini and pressed the button as Samuels turned and pushed several times at the door, which finally yielded on the fourth push. Steve watched the raincoat and the gray fedora disappear around the corner. He turned back to Molini.

"I don't envy you your job, that's for sure." Molini handed the box to Steve and pushed his hat back on his head.

"Luckily, I don't have to have much truck with him. Just my bad luck, I was standing by the water cooler when the DA came looking for someone to make sure Samuels did what he was supposed to do." Steve pointed over his shoulder toward his office.

"How about a drink?" When Molini turned and looked out toward the concourse, Steve continued. "Don't worry about him, he can't get into too much trouble out there. Let him cool his heels for a while." Steve snorted in the direction that Samuels had disappeared, before he turned and led the agent back across the hall.

Agent Molini squirmed his ample posterior into the chair in front of Steve's desk. Steve handed him a short glass with a finger of scotch in the bottom. Steve held his glass in the air.

"Here's to catching this guy, and soon." Molini drank half of the contents of his glass and then balanced it on his knee.

"What I don't get is how he wasn't able to come up with the fact that these guys were all from the same town and graduated from the same high school for god's sake. Plus, he had those church guys under his feet all day long and he never bothered to question them and find out about the other murders." Steve swiveled his chair back and forth and shrugged.

"That's what I have been trying to tell you and Brady and anybody who would listen all the way back to when Sorelli killed Tam's wife. The guy is incompetent." Steve shook his head in disgust and looked down into his glass, swirling the golden liquid, before he took another sip. He looked over at the FBI agent.

"Now that you guys are on board, we might be able to make some headway here. I am going back to Utah tomorrow and I will be in touch with Tam with any new info I get. I gave him the rundown this afternoon, so check with him. Do me a favor and make sure that the police protection around Terence Leavitt and his family is beefed up. Samuels was not too happy to be told what to do there, and I am always suspicious where he is concerned." With a little effort, Molini extricated himself from the chair and placed his glass on top of the desk.

"I gotta go. Hopefully when I drop Samuels off downtown, he will be out of my hair for good." He paused and turned around his large frame filling the doorway.

"Agent Brady is counting on you to get us something we can work on down here." Steve had stood and now followed the agent out to the reception area. He pressed the button when Molini was in front of the door.

"I'll see what I can do." He watched as Samuels appeared from the end of the concourse and intercepted Molini as he started down the stairs. Shaking his head, he crossed back into his office.

JULY 12

STEVE SLOWED DOWN as the red Jeep passed the Texaco station on the outskirts of Parowan. Though it was half past nine, the lights were not on, and he could see no one inside. Two blocks later, Steve slowed even more as he entered the center of town. In the four blocks he had traveled he had only seen one person out and about. He eased the Jeep down the narrow alley behind the hotel, parking it where he had parked the Ranchero two days before. He walked to the front of the hotel and glanced across the street at the diner. The stools that were visible through the large plate glass window were empty. Steve turned and entered the hotel, walking through the drawing room where he dropped his valise and continued into the dining room. It wasn't the fact that it was empty that impressed Steve at first, but there were no food smells coming from the kitchen. He swung open the big door that separated the two rooms and glanced around, letting the door swing closed on the empty room as he backtracked and picked up his valise on the way to the stairs.

Ten minutes later he was descending the last three steps of the stairway when he saw Miss Beatrice coming through the front door. Something in her face when she looked up and saw Steve made him stop cold.

"Miss Beatrice, is everything all right?" She was wearing a hat and she had a pair of black gloves on and she was carrying an empty dish in her hand. She didn't reply but just shook her head as she walked into the dining room. When Steve followed her in, the door was just swinging shut behind her as she made her way into the kitchen. Steve decided not to follow, but sat down in the chair that was his accustomed place at the table. After a few minutes, she came slowly back into the room. She gazed at Steve as she reached up, pulling two long hat pins from her hair, and carefully removing her hat, she laid it on the sideboard. She smoothed her dress and clasped her hands together in front of her and for several seconds looked at Steve with a very apprehensive expression. When she spoke, her voice was hoarse with pain.

"Delma Wiggins hanged herself in the family barn yesterday evening." Steve sat back in the chair as his breath, no longer under his control escaped his lungs. He shook his head as he took three deep breaths and struggled to recover.

"I am very sorry to hear that, Miss Beatrice. I spoke with her briefly, Saturday evening on my way out of town." He stopped when he saw the queer look on Miss Beatrice's face. "What's wrong, Miss Beatrice?" She leaned forward and supported herself on the back of one of the dining chairs.

"That is just it, Mr. Cannon, her niece has told several people that she drove her to the Holiday Inn and that after she spoke with you, she was even more despondent than before. Her son and I daresay others in this town, are blaming you, I'm afraid." Steve spoke carefully and gently.

"Did her niece say that it was her idea and that I had no idea who she was or what she wanted until her niece brought her to my table?" Miss Beatrice nodded in agreement but the look on her face did not change.

"Yes, Mr. Cannon, but I am afraid that small fact has been forgotten. People are angry that you have come to town and all this gets dredged up again," Steve sat back and pursed his lips as he contemplated her words. When he spoke, his voice was flatter and his eyes were not as friendly.

"Kill the messenger, is that right, Miss Beatrice?" She started to shake her head in disagreement when Steve continued. "This whole town stands by and abides a murder of a young man, whether in hot blood or cold, for over thirty years out of some misplaced loyalty to a group of favored sons. Then when they start turning up murdered, nobody has anything to say on the subject. Am I right so far, Miss Beatrice?" Steve didn't wait for an answer before he went on. "I come here and start asking questions, and now everyone is righteously indignant?" Steve shook his head disgustedly as he pulled his notebook out of his back pocket and retrieved a pen from his satchel.

"Mr. Cannon, I wish I was more successful in getting you to see our side of things." Steve's look when he glanced up, stopped her and she fell quiet. For a few seconds, there was silence, until Steve turned over a fresh page.

"I am going to ask you a few questions, Miss Beatrice and the quicker I get answers to these questions, the quicker I leave town. If you don't know the answers, I suggest you get whoever does over here in a hurry." He stared into her eyes until she nodded. He took a deep breath and tried to make the tone of his voice as reasonable as possible.

"Garret Dawkins' mother left town under some sort of scandalous cloud. What was it?" Miss Beatrice wrung her hands and looked down at the white plastic tablecloth.

"It's all very complicated, Mr. Cannon. I…" Steve interrupted.

"I know this is hard, Miss Beatrice, but the sooner the facts are out, the sooner that we can stop the dying." He stopped and waited as he saw that she was turning over something in her mind.

"Polygamists." Her lower lip trembled slightly as she slowly pulled the chair out and sat down. She put her head into her hands for a few seconds before she found her resolve and looked up.

"The Dawkins family were polygamists, Mr. Cannon. The whole town knew, but they mostly kept to themselves and were good neighbors, so they weren't bothered much. All that changed when the church found out. Our elders were given the choice: Banish them or face expulsion. The banishment terms were very specific. There were four wives and four children. Garret had an older brother, but Garret's mother had to choose. She had to leave one of her children behind with Garret's father and the one wife that was allowed to stay in town. She chose to take her older son and leave the younger one." She stopped and looked down at her hands folded in her lap. Steve had been writing as she was talking, and now he waited a few seconds before he asked his next question.

"What was his name, Miss Beatrice?"

"Calvin. Calvin Dawkins, Mr. Cannon."

"And where did the two of them go?" Miss Beatrice sighed and shook her head sadly.

"I don't know. Mr. Cannon, and I don't know if anyone in town knows. The church wanted it that way." Steve made a small irritated sound in his throat.

"How about Harold Gleamer?"

Miss Beatrice nodded, but for a few seconds was silent.

"Yes, Mr. Cannon, if anyone knows, it would be Harold."

Steve nodded and snapped his notebook shut. He and Miss Beatrice looked at each other across the table for several moments, before he slowly stood up and left the room, returning to the drawing room several minutes later carrying his valise. She was standing in front of the picture window when she heard Steve and turned around.

"Can you give me directions to Harold Gleamers' house, Miss Beatrice?"

*

Steve parked the Jeep in front of the neat brick house three blocks from the downtown area. He stood beside the car for a few seconds casually scouting the neighborhood. There were few houses on the street and most were separated by large parcels of land that held horse corrals and truck gardens. He stood back four feet from the door after he knocked on the freshly painted wood, and looked up and down both sides of the street. A young woman opened the door. Steve guessed her to be in her late twenties. She had long brown hair and brown eyes that smiled shyly at Steve.

"You must be Mr. Cannon." She held out her hand. "I am Rachel, Roy's mother. You look just like the way my son described you." Steve looked around as she spoke. He was feeling a little exposed on the front porch. She sensed his uneasiness and stepped to the side. "Would you like to come in, Mr. Cannon? My father is home." Steve nodded and followed the young woman into the compact living room which held two small couches and two arm chairs. Rachel paused before a long hallway. "Can I get you some lemonade or homemade root beer?" Steve shook his head.

"No thank you, Rachel." He settled into one of the arm chairs as she disappeared down the hall. A few seconds later, Roy came around the corner and jumped onto the couch next to Steve. Steve smiled at the young boy, who was dressed as he had last seen him except for a different shirt and no baseball glove.

"How are you today, Roy." The young boy curled his legs underneath himself and shook his head.

"Can't go outside today at all." Steve smiled.

"Maybe tomorrow, Roy." The young boy turned his head toward the hallway as Harold Gleamer walked slowly into the room. He sat in the arm chair across from Steve, but didn't look at him directly. Instead his eyes wandered to his grandson. He indicated the back of the house with a small sideways jerk of his head. Roy sighed and unfolded himself off the couch and skipped out of sight down the hall. Steve spoke first.

"I was sorry to hear about Delma Wiggins, Harold. I met her just briefly, and she seemed to be a soul in torment." Harold looked over at Steve for the first time since he entered the room. He looked ready to say something, but changed his mind, preferring to shake his head while looking down at his shoes. Steve waited a few minutes and when it didn't look like Harold was going to volunteer anything on his own, he decided to start the conversation himself.

"When Calvin Dawkins and his mother were banished, where did they go?" Harold looked up and replied quietly.

"Manti. I sent them to Manti."

"Why Manti?" Harold Gleamer looked at the scarred hard wood floor at his feet. He spoke without looking up.

"That is where the church told me to send them." He looked up at Steve and seeing a lack of understanding in his intent expression, he looked down at the floor and continued.

"The church moved strongly against the polygamists right around then. There had been some national publicity and it was easy to sanction the ones who were open about it. Those that refused to go, were excommunicated or they left the church on their own and formed secretive colonies in New Mexico and Arizona." Steve wrote quickly in his notebook.

"Tell me about Calvin Dawkins."

"He was three years older than Garret. Stronger, too. Always looked out for his younger brother. If the church had allowed me to send Garret away with his brother and his mother, all of this would have never happened."

"Why didn't they trust your judgement in the matter, Harold." The old man looked over at Steve and shook his head.

"They had to make an example. Make sure everyone knew what the penalties were for disobeying the church." He ran his hands through his coarse gray hair. "Maybe, they were right. As far as I know, there haven't been any polygamists in Parowan since the day I put those two on the bus." Steve sat back in the chair and took a deep breath as neither man spoke for several minutes. The first one to speak was Harold.

"I knew when I read about the murders in Las Vegas that this day would come and come with a vengeance. The minute I saw your license plate and you climbed out of your car, I realized our day of reckoning was upon us." Steve nodded as Harold turned in his chair and indicated the front door. "The sooner you go, the better for everybody, including yourself." Steve stood and looked down at the thin man in front of him. When he couldn't think of anything to say, he crossed to the front door and opened it.

"Goodbye, Harold, and tell Roy goodbye for me." He left Harold Gleamer staring at the floor as he walked the ten yards to the red Jeep.

*

Tam sounded relaxed when he answered the phone call from the Holiday Inn on Interstate 15.

"You sound like you're working hard." Tam laughed, and for the first time in several days, Steve did not hear his office door being closed.

"Well, it's amazing how pleasant life gets around here, when Samuels isn't running the show. I got everybody out canvassing the downtown area looking for leads, but that is going to wear thin pretty soon, probably by this afternoon, and then I will have to come up with something else."

"Get your pencil ready, Tam, here it is. See what information you can come up with on a 'Calvin Dawkins', probably out of Manti, Utah."

"Manti? Never heard of it. Where's that?"

"That is where I'm heading from here and it's about three hours away, so I can't stand around chatting with you all day. Pass it along to Brady and Molini. They might have something on the federal level. White male, 54 or 55 years old. I will call you tonight or tomorrow if I find out anything worth reporting in Manti. Got it?" Tam answered in the affirmative and as Steve hung up the phone the first sign of trouble walked through the front door of the hotel carrying a baseball bat. The heavyset man in levis and a work shirt spotted Steve as he turned to leave the phone booth. He spun around and pushed through the double glass doors that led to the parking lot. Steve walked casually toward the door, passing the wide-eyed desk clerk.

The morning haze had burned off as Steve stepped into the middle of the dusty parking lot. The man that had spied Steve in the lobby was leaning on a car parked next to the Jeep along with another man. Across the lot and on Steve's left was a pick-up truck with two more men beside it, one carrying a three foot piece of pipe and the other a short handled shovel. Steve's eyes narrowed as both groups walked slowly and menacingly toward him. He waited until they stopped five yards away on each side. Steve grinned at each group in turn.

"Well, you boys didn't have to form a welcoming committee just for me. A couple of days late wouldn't you say?" Steve nudged the Colt .45 on his side forward with his left arm underneath his sport coat. The one with the pipe took a step toward Steve as he slapped the gray steel in his left hand.

"You got a real smart mouth for a guy that is about to get his ass whipped." Steve took a quick step forward.

"Am I?" The unexpected move made all the assailants back up and before they could regroup, a black pick-up truck drove off the interstate and slid to a stop in the gravel twenty yards away. The passenger door opened and Steve recognized Darren Wiggens in civilian clothes. The driver moved quickly around the front of the truck and joined him. Steve saw the family resemblance and grinned once again.

"Well, boys, the cops here, have just saved you." He stopped talking as he saw the wild look in Darren's eyes as the off-duty cop made a rush toward Steve from the front of the truck. Steve drew the Colt smoothly from the shoulder holster, the hammer cocked, it's front sight centered between Darren's eyes. The younger man skidded to a stop just inside the circle of attackers. Steve was not smiling when he addressed the cop.

"This is ready to go, so no false moves." He glanced quickly to his right and then to his left to make sure that his words had the intended effect. For a few seconds, everybody froze. Steve continued.

"If you want a piece of me, Darren, that's fine, but if this is a gang-up, then some of you are going to die." He could tell by the look in Darren's eyes that he had never had a gun pointed at him before.

"I put the gun away, Darren and you get the first swing. But I have to warn you. You better make sure it counts, because if I get up off the ground, one of us is going to the hospital." Steve swept the weapon quickly right to left, making both groups back away several feet. Steve swung the weapon back to Darren's forehead.

"What's it going to be, Darren?" Darren shifted his eyes to his group of companions on either side of him before he looked back down the barrel. When he didn't speak, Steve continued.

"I can hold these sights on you all day if you want, but maybe you better consider this: Tomorrow or the next day, there are going to be state police and at least one FBI agent from Las Vegas here and they won't be as polite as I am when they ask their questions. I am sorry about your mother, but there is a serial killer loose and you need to remember that you are a sworn officer of the law." Steve waited a few seconds to let his words settle. "What's it going to be, Darren?", Steve repeated while Darren's mouth twitched as he mulled over his options. His brother was hissing something into his ear that Steve couldn't hear. The group on Steve's right was edging closer. Steve was just about to swing the gun in their direction when Darren took a step back and held out his hands.

"Back off everybody. I don't want to go to jail and lose my job over this." He spat on the ground in front of Steve. "He ain't worth it." Steve took two steps to his right and waggled the gun to move the two men who were blocking his route to the Jeep out of the way.

They moved apart from each other and Steve quickly moved into the breach, turning and holding all six of the men at gunpoint. He rested the pistol on his shoulder and looked at the brothers.

"Maybe the two of you should direct some of that anger where it might do some good. I'm no expert, but your mother did not strike me as somebody who was about to take her own life. Open an investigation and get some law enforcement from Salt Lake involved."

He slowly opened the door of the Jeep and climbed in without holstering the semi-automatic .45. He kept his eye on the group in the side mirror as he started up the car. Instead of reverse, he eased it into low drive and punched the gas, crossing the five yards of pavement before his tires dug into the soft dirt of the cherry orchard. He spun the wheel and bumped onto a hard pack dirt road that ran behind the Holiday Inn. When he had cleared the building, he pulled back onto the tarmac and sawed the wheel quickly as he swung onto the highway. He slowed briefly and looked into his rear-view mirror. No one was following. He pulled his canteen into his lap and unscrewed the cold metal top. He took two long gulps of the sweet water before he took the speedometer up to eighty.

*

Two and a half hours later, Steve crested a hill on Highway 89. From twelve miles away, he could see the Manti temple shining brightly white in the midday sun. The temple was over seventy-five years old and dominated the small town from the prominent bluff upon which it sat. Steve drove slowly down the main street, before swinging into a parking space in front of a small blue sign: Police.

Steve walked through the front door and stood under a large ceiling fan. There was no one behind the counter and the three desks behind it were all empty as well. Steve was about to leave when a large man in khakis emerged from a backroom and stopped halfway to the counter when he saw Steve. His eyes swept Steve up and down as he laid a piece of paper he had been carrying onto the desk beside him.

"Can I help you?" Steve took two steps forward and stood in front of the counter.

"My name is Steve Cannon, I am a private detective and I am investigating three murders in Las Vegas and by association three other connected ones in Utah. I have the cooperation of the Las Vegas District Attorney as well as the FBI." The man interrupted him as he sat back against the edge of the desk and folded his arms. His dark brows were knitted in his broad face.

"How does that concern me?" Steve met the hard gaze for several seconds before he spoke quietly, but firmly.

"Because I think the killer comes from here." The man scoffed as he stood up and pointed out the window behind Steve.

"I don't think so, mister. There hasn't been a murder in this town since the 1880's." Steve shrugged and used the same tone of voice.

"I would like to think I have your cooperation voluntarily, chief. I am talking to the Chief of Police, right?" The man dropped his casual attitude and straightened.

"Yes, I am the Chief of Police and that sounded like a threat to me." Steve smiled thinly and leaned casually against the counter as he plucked a pack of Juicy Fruit from his shirt pocket, unwrapping the gum as he gazed out the window. He turned halfway back to the chief.

"Not a threat, chief, just a friendly warning of what's coming your way. I gave the lead detective on this case a name this morning. Now, when he shares that name with the FBI, how long do you think it will take them to drive here from Salt Lake?" Steve wadded up the gum wrapper into a little ball that he sent sailing into a wastebasket at the Chief's feet. He could see the wheels turning behind the frown, so he decided to offer more encouragement.

"This person of interest is no longer here and if I get the

information I need, neither will I, and the whole Fed circus will likely pass you by." Steve stood up and held out his hands impatiently.

"That would suit me just fine. What do you want?" Steve took out his notebook and a pencil and leaned on the counter as he flipped to a new page.

"The name is Calvin Dawkins. What do you know about him?" The chief, who had resumed his position against the desk straightened up and walked to a file cabinet against the wall. He pulled out a file from the second drawer down, walked back to the counter and dropped it in front of Steve.

"That is what I got on him, until 1950, the year he went to state prison."

"What did he go up for?"

"He broke into the house of one of the elders. Tied up his wife and pistol whipped the man." Steve wrote in his notebook.

"Got a picture?" The Chief opened the file and flipped quickly to the back, turning it, so Steve could see the 5x6 black and white photo.

"He was thirty-eight years old when this was taken." Steve looked at the strong features and the piercing dark eyes. He turned the file back around and pushed it toward the cop.

"You have the facilities to get this picture down to Las Vegas?" The Chief's look of contempt was the only answer that Steve received as the chief slipped the picture from the file and walked around the corner, disappearing down a hallway. For the next ten minutes, Steve studied the file. When the chief returned several minutes later, Steve had filled six pages with notes.

"When did he get out?" The chief took the file and put it on the desk behind him.

"Never did. They sent him to the state hospital in Provo. Still there as far as I know."

"His mother still alive?" The expression that crossed the cop's face told Steve she was.

"Can't give out that kind of information." Steve straightened and looked the Chief in the eye.

"The more information I gather here, the less likely the feds are going to bother you. I am not going to say it again." Steve turned to go, when the Chief made a noise in his throat. Steve turned as the Chief was bent over his desk writing something on a small piece of paper that he now held out to Steve. Steve walked over and took it from his hand. He looked up at the Chief as he pushed the paper down into his shirt pocket.

"I will make my report to the FBI from Provo." Steve snapped a small salute toward the Chief as he turned and headed for the door. When he looked back, the Chief was looking on impassively.

Steve drove up and down the four block main street three times looking for a phone booth, before he gave up and parked in front of the drugstore. He waited in the front of the store for five minutes before the single pay phone in the back near the stools and counter of the soda fountain was free. Steve dropped two quarters into the slot and waited while the call was connected.

"Tam, this is Steve. What have you been able to find out?" Steve held the phone cradled against his face and the notebook above his head, pressed against the glass of the booth. He started to write as Tam spoke.

"Released? When?" He wrote down the date.

"I just got most of that from the local Police Chief, except he doesn't know he has been released. No contact with police since 1964?" Steve stopped writing and replaced the notebook in his pocket. He waited until Tam had finished his reply.

"Get with Agents Brady and Molini. See if they can get the FBI in Salt Lake to interview his doctors in Provo. It would be a wasted trip for me, I had to work too hard to get the information I got from the Chief, I doubt they would talk to me. Did you get the picture from the Chief?"

"Yeah, it is fifteen years old. I am going to see if I can get a recent one." Steve hung up a few minutes later, then inserted several more quarters.

"Hello, Sally, is Sam available?" Steve waited and watched the seats at the fountain filling up with late afternoon shoppers. His attention was drawn back to the phone by the cheerful sound of his lawyers' voice.

"Sam. How are you doing?"

"Yes, I am out of town, but I hope to be back tomorrow, by midday. Let's have lunch at the Copper Cart, if you aren't booked."

"Twelve-thirty is fine. But between now and then, do me a favor and check with your contacts at the Gaming Commission and find out why they might be sending me a letter. Can you do that?"

"Swell, and Sam? Do you want cash or a check to settle my bill?" Steve chuckled at the reply and hung up the phone. He gathered several pairs of eyes as he left the booth and walked past the lunch counter and down the long aisle that led to the front of the store.

*

The small white frame house was not hard to find amid the logical grid system that typified most every town in Utah. Five minutes after he parked in front, he was sitting in a small parlor across from Maddie Robbins, the mother of Garret and Calvin Dawkins. Though she was the same age as Miss Beatrice, she appeared much older physically. Steve had told her his name and where he was from, and she had shown him into her parlor and as he sat and looked across at her, she had yet to utter a word. Steve gazed intently now as she seemed on the verge of saying something. When she did, her voice was softer than her appearance would suggest.

"Is this about Calvin, Mr. Cannon?" Steve nodded as he pulled out his notebook and laid it on the table. Maddie Robbins looked at the curled edges of the nearly full book before she looked up with a pensive look.

"What has he done?" Steve shook his head slowly.

"I don't know for sure if he has done anything, Mrs. Robbins. I need to locate him and ask him a few questions." Steve waited as she took in the information. The ticking of the clock on the wall was the only sound for nearly a minute.

"I don't know where he is, Mr. Cannon. I haven't seen him since he began refusing my visits to the hospital five years ago." Steve nodded.

"Mrs. Robbins. Do you mind if I ask you a few questions about your sons?" A slightly confused expression crossed her face for a second before she replied.

"About Garret?" Steve nodded assent.

"Yes, about Garret, Mrs. Robbins." She sat back a little in her chair and the expression on her face suggested to Steve that he could proceed.

"How often did you see Garret after you and Calvin left Parowan?" There was a long pause and Steve could not tell from her expression if she was having trouble with the memory or if she couldn't remember.

"Only once. Two years after I left, I had a friend drive me back to Parowan and I waited outside his school and watched him walk home. They told me that if I ever tried to see him again, they would take Calvin from me." Steve took his time writing in the notebook.

"Did Calvin ever see Garret again?" She nodded her head quickly.

"As soon as he could drive, he would take a friends' car down there at least once a month."

"So that would be when? 1928, 1929?" Maddie nodded.

"When Garret was in High School, Calvin would take him fishing at Panquitch."

"I get the impression that both of your boys were very smart. Can you tell me about that?"

"I don't know what you want me to say, Mr. Cannon. Yes, they were both very smart boys. But Garret was more sensitive and weak. Calvin was every bit as smart, but he was a rough and tumble kid and very headstrong. Calvin saw Garret's weakness and always wanted to protect him." Steve paused before he asked his next question.

"A notation in his police file from the time Garret disappeared suggested that Calvin had to be restrained and put under house arrest during the investigation, is that true?" From the change of expression, Steve knew his questions were pushing Maddie into an uncomfortable area.

"They didn't want him underfoot while they looked for Garret." Steve didn't write in the notebook and didn't drop his gaze before he asked his next question and as he did so, he tried to keep his voice as gentle as he could.

"Isn't it true, Mrs. Robbins, that the police put him jail briefly, because he believed that Garret had met with foul play and he thought he knew who the perpetrator or perpetrators were?" There was a long silence as Maddie Robbins gazed at her hands in her lap. Her voice was half as loud as it had been before.

"Calvin always thought the boys from Parowan killed Garret and made it look like an accident. Even before Garret died, he had several run-ins with them. The Chief of Police showed up here one day a year before Garret disappeared and told me and my husband that if Calvin showed up in Parowan again, he would be arrested." Steve decided to change directions.

"Why did you leave Parowan with Calvin instead of your youngest, Garret?" For the first time in the conversation, Steve say a flash of defiance in the light brown eyes. By the time she replied, the spark was gone.

"Calvin was the most disruptive child in the compound. It was my ex-husband Gerald Dawkin's decision. The church let him decide." Steve looked around the small neat home.

"Where is your husband, Mrs. Robbins?"

"Harold died two years ago, Mr. Cannon." Steve nodded and wrote the information down.

"How did Calvin turn from a smart young boy into a man who

would terrorize and pistol whip a church elder, Mrs. Robbins?" Steve and the older woman looked at each other for a brief moment and Steve thought he saw some of the same pain behind the old eyes that he had seen two days before in Delma Wiggens. She looked down and shook her head.

"After Garret died, he let everything go. He couldn't finish anything he started. He tried several colleges and he couldn't hold a job. The longest one he had was in the oil fields in Wyoming, but he was always in trouble, getting into fights and drinking. He spent six months in jail in Rock Springs when he got into a fight over another man's wife. He moved back here and lived with my husband and I for a while after the war, but he would drive into Wyoming to drink on weekends. He became more outspoken against the church and would sometimes disrupt the services or town events. They decided when he was in prison that he needed to be in the state hospital in Provo. They let him out in early 1964. I haven't seen or heard anything of him since."

Steve was quiet for a few minutes after he finished writing her comments in his notebook.

"Do you know anyone, anyone at all, that Calvin might go to for help. Friends, family, people he may have worked with?" Maddie shook her head and looked up at Steve. He could tell from her expression that she wanted to ask him something. He waited until she was ready.

"You have come a long way to ask your questions, Mr. Cannon. Something has happened and I wish you would tell me." Steve sighed and sat back in his chair as he considered the worried face in front of him.

"I guess I should begin by telling you that Delma Givens committed suicide late Sunday night." A small gasp from Maddie caused him to stop momentarily. He nodded to confirm what he had just said before he continued. "In the one brief conversation I had with her in Parowan, she confirmed that Garret was indeed killed by

Hiram Dame and that the rest of the gang helped him to cover up the crime." Steve stopped and slid his kerchief across the table as Maddie broke down. After several minutes, she composed herself and raised her face from the white cloth. Steve shifted uncomfortably in his seat.

"There is more, Mrs. Robbins. Do you want me to continue?" He grimaced when she nodded.

"Six of the seven men who were involved in the murder of your son have themselves been murdered." Maddie's eyes stared blankly at the table for several seconds before they focused and she looked up at Steve. He guessed what was coming next.

"When?", she asked weakly.

"The first one occurred two months after Calvin was released from Provo." He stopped and let the information sink in. He was surprised when after several seconds of rocking gently in her chair, Maddie Robbins got up and left the room. Steve read over his notes for the few minutes she was gone. When she returned, she held a small cardboard box that she placed on her lap when she sat back down. Steve could see that the box held photographs as she quietly sorted through them. When she was done, she set the box on a table behind her and slid three photographs across the table to Steve. He turned them over and set them side-by-side. Two were taken in the hospital and Maddie was in the first one. In one he looked older and bigger, his hair was slightly thinning and Steve thought he saw a little gray around the ears. He held that one up to his mother.

"Is this the most recent of the three?" She leaned forward and looked at it carefully, before nodding her head.

"May I keep these for a while Mrs. Robbins? I will mail them back to you in the next few days."

"Yes, Mr. Cannon." Steve placed the photos in his shirt pocket.

"Thank you, Mrs. Robbins, is there anything you would like to ask me?" She nodded her head slowly and Steve noted the sadness in her eyes.

"What is going to happen to him, Mr. Cannon?" Steve folded his notebook carefully and put it into his shirt pocket next to the pictures as he replied.

"The authorities will look for him and when they find him, they will question him about the murders. If he has done nothing wrong, everything will be alright, Mrs. Robbins." He saw the same flash in her eyes that he had seen earlier.

"But that's not what you think will happen, is it, Mr. Cannon?" Steve stood slowly from the table and looked down at the expectant face.

"No, Mrs. Robbins, I don't think that is what will happen. I hope I am wrong for your sake, but Calvin looks like the most likely suspect now." He placed one of his cards on the table, and pointed to it as he replaced his wallet. "Thank you for your help. Call me if you need to ask me something, or just to talk." He moved toward the door and stopped only when he heard her clear her throat.

"Mr. Cannon, I told his doctor that they should never let him out of there." Steve nodded and opened the front door. He left Maddie Robbins sitting at the dining table sorting through the small box of photographs.

Two hours later, Steve drove past the Holiday Inn on the interstate. He looked in the direction of Parowan, the peach orchards tinged in burnished gold as the sun slipped behind the southern Utah mountains. It was nearly ten o'clock when he parked the car in front of Remy's house.

JULY 13

TAM POLHAUS WAS still tying his tie when he opened his front door at ten minutes before six. He stood to one side as Steve walked into the middle of the living room and watched as Tam closed the door and continued tying the blue striped cloth in the hall mirror.

"You're up early, I didn't expect you back until noon." Steve sat down wearily on a long couch.

"Didn't see the point in staying in Utah, once I got all the information there was to get. At least from my end." Steve looked around the tidy living room. "Where's Lisa?" Tam turned and lifted his suitcoat from the wooden rack by the door as he gazed down at the private detective.

"At camp, for the next ten days." Steve nodded absentmindedly as he pulled his notebook from inside his sport coat.

"I thought I might buy you breakfast somewhere and we could go over some of this." Steve held up the book. Tam nodded and picked up a small leather briefcase from a table next to Steve.

"How about Foxys? It's halfway for both of us. I am assuming you will be heading to your office?" Steve shrugged.

"Maybe. I want to check in with Terence Leavitt soon. What's the set-up on his protection?" He stood as Tam opened the door and gestured toward the outside. He turned when he reached the porch and waited until Tam had locked the door. Tam stood and gazed at the man in front of him before he replied.

"Put together a volunteer roster of uniform and plainclothes guys that wanted some overtime. Filled in the gaps with myself and two other detectives. Two guys there after dark, at least one guy during daylight hours, sometimes two. The shift cops drive by every couple of hours and make a circuit around the neighborhood. Nothing, so far." Steve nodded as he turned and headed toward the Jeep parked at the curb. He waited until Tam had opened the garage and backed his Chevy Impala into the street in front of him, he pulled behind the big Chevy and let Tam lead the way to the deli.

Steve was surprised to see Walter behind the counter when he and Tam took a table by the door. When Walter brought two cups of coffee to the table, Steve pointed to the empty chair beside Tam.

"We're the only ones in here this early, sit down and have a cup with us." Walter smiled as he pulled out the chair and sat down.

"Already had two cups, but I can sit for a few minutes. Haven't seen you for a while, have you been out of town?" Tam flashed a quick grin across the table toward Steve. Steve nodded and shrugged.

"Yes, you could say that, but I am more interested in why you are here and not over at the Casablanca?" Walter smiled and pointed at the heavy-set man that had just come through the swinging doors that led to the kitchen.

"Bernie wants me to make sure Rocco is checked out on everything before the opening of the hotel on Saturday. He will take over the day-to-day running of the store. Bernie and I will show up from time to time until we can hire another manager to replace Rocco." Steve watched as Rocco began to distribute the salt and pepper shakers to all the tables.

"Almost the end of an era, without Bernie in here. Are you sure you have enough help over at the hotel? With all Bernie's got on his plate, you should make sure that you have experienced people you can rely on." Walter nodded his agreement.

"Yeah, Bernie is a little worried about that too, with four restaurants in the hotel, plus room and food service at the pool, but the run-throughs have worked pretty well. Just like you did in the casinos, I decided to hire extra sous chefs and waiters for the opening and keep the ones that fit in the best." Walter looked up as a buzzer went off in the kitchen and indicated to Rocco that he would check on it.

"Well it's been swell chewing the fat with you guys, but duty calls." Steve waved a farewell as Walter strode toward the kitchen. Steve turned to Tam and indicated with his coffee cup.

"So, what do you have on our guy?" Tam tugged his briefcase up onto the table and pulled out several sheets of paper, sorted quickly through them, selected one and held it up.

"This is what Molini got from the Salt Lake FBI guys who went out to the hospital. It's not much, but they should be getting a court order today to open all the files. Steve read the two paragraphs quickly and then handed the sheet back to the detective.

"No known associates, no visitors other than his mother and not even her for the last four years of his confinement. They say why they let him out?" Tam snorted into his coffee cup.

"Governors' wife made mental health her pet project when he was elected. Raised a stink about the overcrowding in the hospital at Provo. Our boy was in the second wave they released, but here is something that is not yet in the official report." Tam leaned in closer. "One of the agents told Molini that he was approached by one of the doctors who showed up when he got wind that they were there inquiring about Dawkins. Evidently this guy had opposed Calvin's release. Anyway, he tells the agent that Dawkins was always going on about how the church ordered the killing of his brother and that he knew the group of Danites personally that did the dirty deed and that he was going to make sure they suffered accordingly." Steve sat back in his chair and crossed his arms.

"Did the doctor indicate that all this was in the files?" Tam shrugged and turned in his seat toward the table behind him, picking up an ashtray and putting it between the two of them.

"Who knows. You would think from what he said that would be in the files. We should know soon enough." Tam took out a pack of menthol cigarettes and held out his hand. Steve passed his zippo lighter across to him. Steve drummed his fingers on the table deep in thought. When Tam handed the lighter back, Steve pulled a cigarette from his pack and lit it, peering at Tam through the blue-white smoke.

"I'm going to check on Leavitt this morning. My hunch is our guy is definitely here and I get the feeling that he is one of those killers who thinks he has nothing to lose, so he will try to complete his mission, no matter how much protection we throw up around Leavitt. But do me a favor, and pull the stolen car reports for the last month. One of the pictures I saw at his mother house had him sitting in a souped up '49 Ford. I got the impression from her, that he was driving at an early age. Might be nothing, but it might be a lead." Tam nodded.

"We have checked almost all the flop houses and cheap motels in the downtown area. I switched some of the guys to the ones out on Boulder Highway, and if that comes up zilch, I guess we check Henderson." Steve nodded absentmindedly before he quickly looked up and gestured at Tam with the hand holding the cigarette.

"When you get back to your office, stick some pins in all three murder scenes and Leavitt's house. Draw three concentric circles around the group, each one an inch bigger than the last and put some guys on any motels or trailer parks or anything that might be a short term rental inside the circles. Start with Leavitt's house and work outward. Our guy is nothing if he's not smart and I think it is safe to say he has done his homework and is probably close by, figuring out his move as we speak. Does Leavitt go to his office every day?"

"Yeah, whoever is on duty calls a squad car to follow him down there, while they keep watch on the wife and kids. He has hired a security firm that has put a guard in his office whenever he is there." Steve pulled out the three photos that he was given by Maddie Robbins.

"Take these two downtown to the lab and get them duplicated and pass them out to your guys as quickly as you can. I will show this one to the guard at his office and then you can have it as well." Tam slipped the photos into his briefcase. He looked up at Steve and made a sucking sound with his teeth. Steve looked up from slipping the photo into his notebook and looked questioningly at the detective.

"What?" Tam shook his head and sighed.

"Lot been going on since you been on the lam. Had a visit from Jack Cathay two days ago. He just appeared in my office. Evidently, he went to Tommy Carmino and they both went to Tommys' boss and Jack was able to convince them both and by extension, the guys in Cleveland and Florida that because Sorelli whacked Nash Brannock, it is still open business. The upshot is that they formed a little unit of hoods that are now, as we speak, crisscrossing this great nation of ours, looking for one Angelo Sorelli. And get this: They report directly to Jack." Steve sat back and sighed.

"And what happens when they find him?" Tam shrugged.

"Didn't get that far in the conversation, but knowing Jack, it is unlikely that he will let someone else do the honors."

"Yeah, that would be my guess too. When I get a chance, I will talk to him." They both stood up as Steve slipped two dollar bills under his saucer. Steve pulled a small piece of paper from his shirt pocket and held it up for Tam. Tam leaned over and squinted. Steve pointed to the address.

"This is Leavitt's address. This is in the Royal Crest Ranchero subdivision, right?" Tam straightened up.

"Yeah, just a couple blocks off Maryland Parkway on Carriage Lane. You going there now?" Steve shoved the paper back into his pocket.

"I thought I would drive around the area and follow him to his office. See what he has to say. When I spoke with him briefly on the phone, he was not too forthcoming and tried to come off like he didn't know who or what I was referring to. That always intrigues me." Tam laughed over his shoulder as they headed toward the door.

"Well, in that case, I am glad he has protection."

*

Steve could already feel the warmth building inside the Jeep as he looked at the large ranch style house from fifty yards away, midway around a curve in the street that put him just out of sight of the two cops who were almost through with their night shift. He had driven all through the upscale neighborhood and had seen nothing out of the ordinary. Now as he watched, he saw the garage door open automatically and a tall man in a gray three-piece suit come out from between two cars, bending over to pick up a newspaper from the middle of the driveway. The man gave a short wave toward the cops as he retreated back into the garage. Two minutes later, a long white '65 Ford station wagon backed slowly down the driveway and into the street. From farther down the road out of Steve's sight, a black and white police car came around the corner and drove by the Ford, going past Steve's position and stopping at the corner. As it went past, Steve gave the high sign to the officer in the passenger seat whose name was Gateson and was well known to Steve. He waited until the Ford with the black and white following had both gone around the corner, before he pulled across the street halfway into a driveway, backed up and drove slowly after them. When he turned onto Maryland Parkway, they were a hundred yards ahead. He hung back watching the traffic, paying particular attention to any cars that came within forty yards of the white station wagon.

Steve parked across the street from the office building that Leavitt shared with Clifford Jones' firm. There was a security guard pacing outside the front door as Terence Leavitt walked from his car, keys in hand. Steve spent a few watchful minutes in his car smoking before he locked the Jeep and walked across the deserted street. He stood on the walkway just outside the office and caught the eye of the security guard. The guard unlocked the door from his side and opened it two inches.

"Who are you?"

"My name is Steve Cannon, and I am working with the police on the case that concerns Mr. Leavitt." The man shook his head.

"Nothing doin'. My orders are nobody comes in before business hours." Steve looked at his watch.

"It is after 8:30 now. What time do you consider business hours?"

"9:00." Steve grumbled as he took out his wallet and slipped his card into the small opening.

"Take that to Mr. Leavitt. I need to talk to him." The guard looked briefly at the card and then locked the door before he left. Steve waited for a full five minutes before the guard returned and unlocked the door, holding it halfway open as Steve turned sideways and walked through. He waited until the guard had relocked the door and turned toward Steve. Steve held out the photograph at arms-length until the guard took it into his hand. As he was examining it, Steve spoke.

"This is the guy you need to look out for. He might look a little older than the picture, but he is probably six foot one or two, close to my height. If you see him..." Steve was interrupted by someone clearing his throat from several feet behind the two men. Steve turned and saw Terence Leavitt. He turned back to the guard, took the photo from his hand and held it up in front of his chin.

"I was just showing your man here, a picture of an old friend of yours." The green eyes that were at the same level as Steve's held a menacing look as they glanced away from Steve and briefly took in the photo.

"Who is that?" Steve turned the photo around in a gesture as if he was checking to see that he had the right one. He displayed it again to both men.

"Why, that is your old nemesis, Calvin Dawkins. You remember him, don't you, Mr. Leavitt? As far as I can tell, he was the one person in the whole town of Parowan that stood up to you and your cronies. Well, the bad news for you, as I am sure you already know, is that he was released from the state mental hospital almost two years ago, and has spent most of his free time tracking down and killing everybody that was involved in the murder of his younger brother, Garret." Steve glanced in the direction of the security guard. "You want me to continue, or should we have our little talk in your office?" Leavitt's neck was beginning to turn red and he started to say something, but stopped and turned toward the open door of his office. Steve smiled thinly as he walked through, stopping in the middle of the spacious room and waiting until Leavitt had joined him and closed the door. Steve looked around the office and chose a chair on the far wall that sat alongside two others. His had a low table next to it. Leavitt stood still in the middle of the room.

"Stand if you want, Leavitt, but it won't change any of the information I have, so you might as well make yourself comfortable." When Leavitt didn't budge, Steve shrugged and crossed his legs, frowning at the malevolent look on the face of the man peering down at him.

"Relax, Leavitt. We both know you were involved in the death of Garret Dawkins. The only other person that knows for sure and could have testified to it, died under suspicious circumstances on Saturday night or early Sunday morning. So that only leaves Dawkins. Who is convinced that you helped kill his brother, which sad to say, is the same as knowing it as far as you are concerned. Do you get my drift?" Leavitt put his hands in his pockets and continued glaring down at Steve. Steve made a wry face and snapped his fingers.

"Oh, and I almost forgot the goons that say they represent the interests of the church. Now, one school of thought might hold that I am in effect just an unwitting bird dog for them. They follow me around and take out anyone that looks like they can shed some light on this deal, and make the church look bad. In that case, I guess we would have to count them and that makes two good reasons why you should adopt a more courteous attitude." Steve stared coldly at the lawyer as he pulled a pack of cigarettes out and kept his gaze steady on the reddening face as he pulled out his lighter and prepared to light it. Leavitt made a noise in his throat that indicated he was about to object when Steve shook his finger and cut him off.

"Attitude, Leavitt, attitude." He smiled thinly as he lit the cigarette, taking a deep inhalation and letting the gray smoke stream out into the middle of the room. Leavitt retreated to the door and pressed a switch that turned on a fan, as air began to blow from the vent just above Steve's head. He sat down on a dark brown leather couch that filled most of the space on the wall opposite Steve. Steve sat quietly waiting for Leavitt to speak. When he didn't, Steve shrugged and tapped a bit of ash onto the table, before looking over at the lawyer.

"Unless, of course, we are all wrong about this and something happened to the tight little confederacy the seven of you had, and what, Mr. Leavitt? Murder among murderers? Maybe Dawkins is just a poor misguided sap who can't hold a job and is adrift in the world, nothing more than that." Leavitt snorted softly.

"You must think you are pretty smart, Mr. Cannon." Steve shook his head and interrupted.

"No, Mr. Leavitt, just persistent." When it was apparent that Leavitt had nothing further to say, Steve continued. "You know how they catch lions that terrorize the local villages in Africa, Terence? They tether a live goat just outside the village and then hide themselves. Now, all the goat knows is that he isn't where he should be, which is back in the herd with all the other goats, so he bleats continuously in an effort to bring the herd to him. Of course, the lion eventually hears the goat, and well, Mr. Leavitt, as they say, that is that." Steve stood up and looked across at the couch. "I guess my only advice to you, Leavitt, is try to keep the bleating down, if you know what's good for you." Steve crossed the room and opened the door, startling the security guard who was just outside. Steve grinned at the man and held out his cigarette. When he made a move like he was going to drop it on the carpet, the guard carefully took it from between his fingers. Steve smirked toward Terence Leavitt who was now standing in the doorway, before he turned his back and walked through the door and out onto the sidewalk.

He was halfway across the street when he saw Agent Molini standing by the red Jeep. Steve quickly jogged the rest of the way and stopped a few feet away from the FBI agent. He smiled at the irony of the two of them working in tandem when he thought back over a year ago to their first meeting. Molini grinned and pointed across the street.

"Gateson told me he thought I could find you here. You talk to Leavitt?" Steve moved his shoulders in a noncommittal way.

"That's about all that happened. He is playing it extremely close to the chest. But let me ask you something. How come he is still going about his business? Wouldn't it be safer and easier for all concerned if you just took Leavitt and his family to some place out of town until we can get a line on this guy?" Molini chewed determinedly on a piece of gum and was shaking his head before Steve finished his last sentence.

"That was Agent Brady's recommendation from the get go, but he got overruled by the brass. You aren't going to want to hear this, but nobody in the bureau is convinced that you are right about Dawkins. If it wasn't for Tam, there would no protection at all for Leavitt, and his chief is getting pressure from the governor and the church guys as it is." Steve shook his head in disgust.

"Sometimes I wonder why I bother. Instead of looking at my theories like a three-dollar bill, why don't they sit down with Amis Kinsley and the church guys and figure out what their motives are?" Steve yanked open the door of the Jeep. Before he got in, he pointed across the street where a man and a woman were walking in the door to Leavitt's office.

"If he thinks one underpaid security guard is going to protect him from Dawkins or the church guys, we will all know the answer soon enough." Steve started the engine and waved to Molini as the pudgy agent walked back toward his car. Steve drove for three blocks, parked his car and walked half a block to the clothing store; Ronzonis'. Two hours later, he filled the back of the Jeep with several pairs of pants, shirts, three pairs of shoes and two new sport coats. He slipped one of the new coats on before he drove away toward the Strip and the Casablanca.

*

Miss Perone was at the open door of his office when Steve was still ten steps away. Steve smiled warmly back at the equally large smile on his secretary's face.

"Good morning, Mr. Cannon, I was hoping you were coming back today." Steve dropped his canvas satchel on the chair and sat down beside it.

"I was actually here for a few hours on Sunday, Miss Perone. Everything looked ship-shape, hopefully Samuels didn't create too much of a mess for you." Miss Perone smiled impishly.

"Not at all, Mr. Cannon, I wouldn't let him in. I called Mr. Wiser and told Mr. Samuels through the speaker there, that he wasn't to come in until Mr. Wiser got here and said it was alright. Mr. Gold, came and persuaded Mr. Samuels and the two policemen with him to wait downstairs until Mr. Wiser arrived. By the time, Mr. Samuels came in, he spent so much of his time arguing with Mr. Wiser and Mr. Gold, that he hardly looked around at all." Steve chuckled as Steffi Perone ended her story.

"I couldn't have wished for it to turn out any better, Miss Perone, remind me to thank Bernie when I see him." Miss Perone had just handed Steve several phone messages when he saw Jack Cathay standing outside the door. He got Miss Perone's attention and she buzzed him in. Steve jerked his head toward the inner office before turning and leading the way. He closed the door behind the portly man. Steve crossed to his desk and shoved an ashtray and a cigarette box close to the side where Jack now sat in one of the wing chairs.

"So, Jack, how is it going?" Jack flipped open the top of the small box and extracted a cigarette. He tapped it on top of the table a few times and lit it with his lighter.

"OK, I guess. Everything under my control is ready to go for the opening. After we both talked to him, Bernie has hired more than enough casino help and enough for everywhere else from what I hear, so…" Jack shrugged and took a deep draw on his cigarette. Steve sat back and swiveled his chair slowly back and forth.

"I heard that you and Tommy and Tommy's boss had a little pow-wow, care to fill me in?" Jack nodded and tapped the smoke quickly on the edge of the ashtray.

"Figured you have a lot on your plate right now, thought I would leave it 'til later." Steve looked at his watch.

"I got lunch with my lawyer in twenty minutes, should be plenty of time to cover the highlights."

"Sure. Well, I got this bright idea after the fiasco with Jimmy Rossini over at the Stardust last spring. I point out to Tommy that Nash was technically under our umbrella, at least that's how some of the people back east would see it, and that it was our responsibility to protect him, even when he made dumb-ass moves, which we all know he certainly did. Tommy didn't see it that way, but decided to take it to his boss, who saw it my way. So now there is a little dedicated team of wise guys that are scouring both sides of the border looking for Sorelli. And there you have it." Jack held out his hands, palms up as he finished. Steve continued to swivel the chair back and forth for several seconds before he spoke.

"What is the protocol when they locate him?" Jack took a short drag on the cigarette and squinted at Steve.

"Don't know exactly. Kind of out of our hands at this point, but I got the strong impression that when they find him, they are going to help themselves to whatever he's got going on, at which point he becomes so much extra baggage that will be disposed of. One of the Florida affiliations is interested in the drug end of things for seventy cents on the dollar, assuming that is still his game. You don't have a problem with all this, right?" Steve shrugged.

"Saves us the effort, is how I see it. When he was doing the fake land deal with Nash, I was trying to get Tommy involved, so I guess better late than never. When I heard it from Tam, I guess I was concerned that you were using them as bird dogs so you could take another crack at him, that's all." Jack stubbed out the smoke and stood up.

"I gotta admit, that was part of my reason for taking it to Tommy, but since I'm not a part of that organization anymore, like I say, it's out of my hands and maybe that's for the best." He walked to the door and opened it partway before he continued.

"That's not to say that I wouldn't jump at the chance to take him out if those guys tree him around here." Their eyes met for a brief second before Jack walked back into the reception area.

When Steve heard the front door close, he buzzed Miss Perone on the intercom.

"Miss Perone, I am leaving for lunch with Mr. Wiser. Please call Rita Malone and find out what would be a good time for us to talk this afternoon?" After her affirmative reply, he adjusted the shoulder rig under his sport coat and closed the office door behind him.

Sam Wiser was already seated at one of the banquettes and chatting with Jack Dennison when Steve appeared at the maître d' station inside the Copper Cart restaurant. He pointed in their direction and followed the tuxedoed man over to the table. Jack stood up and took the menus from the maître d' and shook Steve's hand.

"Good to see you, Steve. I was just telling Sam here, that it was a nice surprise to see his name in the reservation book. Kinda like old times." Steve patted Jack's arm and smiled down at Sam.

"Yes, we did spend a lot of time in here in the old days. It was the only place I could ever get Bernie to come to. Are you coming to the opening?" Jack nodded as he handed them both the menus.

"Of course, Bernie called me himself. Wouldn't miss it." He looked up as a large party arrived and after a quick wink in their direction, he left the table. Steve slipped into the booth so that he was facing Sam. He pointed to Sam's drink.

"That looks like good scotch, and since I have been in the land of the dry throats for the better part of last week and part of this, and since my personal supply is spread all over my kitchen floor, I sure look forward to a stiff drink." He pointed down at the drink when the waiter approached the table with glasses of water.

"Two more of those, please, as quick as you can." He looked up at Sam.

"How did our day in court against Samuels go?" Sam grimaced and took a healthy sip of the scotch.

"Not so well. The judge was unsympathetic and hung his ruling on the fact that there was an active warrant out on you when Samuels tossed your place, but all is not lost, because the scuttlebutt is that Samuels has been suspended. Seems Larson has been investigating him for several months, something I hear you already know about, and he included the overzealous search as part of the package, so in a way, we got the result we were looking for, just, as it usually seems to happen in these cases, not the way we planned." Steve nodded and smiled as the waiter put down two drinks in front of Steve and another round in front of Sam. Steve took a drink and let it slide slowly down his throat.

"So, suspended. Temporarily, or permanently?" Steve held out his hands. Sam shrugged.

"The Feds are going to investigate and then we'll see. In my experience, we shouldn't hold our breath, as the benefit of the doubt will always be on his side." Steve sat back and enjoyed the scotch. Sam reached into his briefcase and pulled out several papers. He looked curiously at Steve before he placed them in the middle of the table. Steve ignored the papers, but frowned at his lawyer. Sam cleared his throat.

"I don't quite know any other way to tell you this, but you own three points in the Casablanca." Steve put down the empty scotch glass and leaned in toward Sam.

"I just heard you say that I own three points in the Casablanca. How could that be possible?" Sam shrugged.

"You tell me. It is all there in black and white. You're listed right there along with Bernie and the rest of the investors." Sam pointed to the papers. Steve picked them up and skimmed them quickly. He put them down and picked up the second scotch, emptying half the glass. He looked across at Sam. Sam reached across the table and patted Steve's wrist.

"This is something you and Bernie need to work out between the two of you. If at the end of that discussion, you are still an owner, then I need to sit down with you and Bernie and make sure all the paperwork is in order. There are a lot of issues involved apart from the Gaming Commission."

Steve nodded absentmindedly as the waiter approached the table to take their lunch order.

It was just after one-thirty when Steve appeared in front of his office door and Miss Perone buzzed him in. She handed him a pink slip.

"Rita Malone says any time after two, today, Mr. Cannon." He nodded and replied as he started for his office.

"Thank you, Miss Perone. Could you find out where Mr. Gold is right now?" He walked into his office and sat down behind the desk and carefully read the three pages that Sam had given him. He had just finished when Miss Perone came on the intercom.

"Mr. Cannon, Mr. Gold is in his office on the casino floor."

"Thank you, Miss Perone." Steve folded the papers lengthwise and slipped them into his inside coat pocket as he crossed the hallway. Five minutes later, he made his way across the main casino floor to a small staircase that led to a suite of offices that looked out over the spacious casino. Bernie had neglected to hire any personal staff, so the reception area was empty as Steve walked over to the door of Bernie's private office. Bernie was sitting behind several stacks of papers and a wooden rack filled with newly minted Casablanca casino chips. Steven rapped lightly on the door sill. Bernie looked up, and smiling, waved him in. It was the first time that Steve had seen Bernie's office and as he looked around the cramped space that held a desk as it's only piece of furniture, Steve laughed.

"Is not having any furniture part of your plan to keep people out?" Bernie stood up and came around the desk, pointing to a double door.

"Right this way." He opened the doors and stepped back. Steve walked to the opening and looked into the room that was three times the size of the space he was standing in. There were three felt covered tables and the walls were covered with some of Bernie's Las Vegas memorabilia. Steve shook his head as he turned around.

"You've recreated the back room at Foxy's." Bernie moved in front of him and into the room.

"Come in, sit down and have a drink. You are the first person in here outside of Milton." Steve chose a table and sat down. Bernie returned from a wooden bar that was built into one wall. He put two beers on coasters in front of their chairs. Steve held up the beer stein when Bernie sat down.

"Here's to you, Bernie." Steve took a big sip, while Bernie waited until Steve had replaced the thick glass on the coaster before he drank.

"So, Bernie, time for a little talk." Bernie paused with the glass still an inch from his lip. His face went blank as he sat the beer down without taking a sip. Steve pulled the papers from his coat and laid them on the table.

"I had Sam Wiser make some discrete inquiries at the Gaming Commission. Want to guess what he found out?" Bernie sighed deeply and held up his hands.

"Let me explain." Steve smiled.

"That's why I am here, Bern." Bernie stood up and began pacing back and forth in back of his chair for a few seconds before he stopped and leaned on the dark polished wood.

"Here it is. You told me not to front you the $50,000 G's for a piece of the land deal, but I went ahead and did it anyway. Norman Kaye included it in the escrow deal if anybody ever needs to check. Anyway, that 50 large turned into four hundred grand including payback of the loan, when Clifford Jones and I sat down with the investors and valued the deal. By Clifford's calculation, you got three points and change in the Casablanca. Was going to tell you, but kept putting it off, so I understand if you're sore. But try and look at it from my point of view, Steve. You have to start looking to the future, you and Remy have to build a life together." Bernie's eyes shone as he remembered another good point. "Don't forget, it was your idea to buy the land and hold Jay Sarno's feet to the fire, and make him pay through the nose to get it back. I just did what you told me, that has to be worth something, maybe even more than three points." Steve held up his hand as he was worried that Bernie was running out of breath and could collapse at any second.

"OK, Bern, what's done is done, and I would be an ungrateful lout if I didn't say thank you. So thank you, my friend, and I will reward your friendship by telling you a little secret. More than once since that deal for the land closed, I have wished that I had gone in with you, so as far as I am concerned, we are square with each other. But now, I feel a little guilty that I haven't done more to get the Casablanca ready for the opening." It was Bernie's turn to stop the conversation.

"Your contribution has been huge, are you kidding. Look, I know you do what you love and I don't ever want to be the cause of you stopping. I am just happy that you took an office here and I know that you are close by and I can run things by you." Bernie stopped talking and the two friends looked at each other for several seconds without speaking. Steve held the glass of beer up. Bernie moved in front of the chair and hoisted his as well. They clinked them together and smiled.

They were interrupted by Milton Swanson's voice as he entered the outer office and not seeing Bernie, called out.

"In here, Milton." Milton came through the door and winked at Bernie when he saw Steve sitting there. Bernie moved to the door to greet him.

"All done?" Milton nodded. Bernie turned and pointed to the table. "Great, have a beer with us." Milton nodded his agreement and pulled out a chair next to Steve.

"How are you Milton? Still burning the midnight oil?" Milton chuckled up at Bernie as he accepted the glass of beer.

"Yep, Steve, still a lot to do." Bernie sat down and looked across at Steve.

"Well, since this is a day for coming clean, Milton has just completed a little job for me." Steve looked from one to the other as Milton cleared his throat and spoke.

"I took one of my foreman and six of my guys over to your house yesterday and this morning. Repaired all the damage and got rid of everything that was broken or wrecked." Steve looked over at Bernie.

'You're kidding. How did you think to do that?" Bernie shrugged.

"I just had the idea, right after you showed me the pictures of the mess. Some of Milton's guys are still here until the weekend when they fly back to Chicago after the opening and there isn't much left for a lot of them to do, so I thought…" Steve stood up and was shaking Milton's hand as he looked at Bernie.

"Thank you Milton, that was above the call of duty. Bernie, I don't know what to say in the face of your generosity sometimes." Bernie waved dismissively.

"How many times did you help me out for no money and no questions asked? Irving Glassman?, Desmond Rooney? You are always there for me, the least I could do." Milton cleared his throat again.

"We saved as much of the furniture as we could, but there isn't a lot left. Your personal things we put in several boxes. You can decide if any of it is worth keeping." Steve stood up.

"I have to go make a phone call." He shook Milton's hand again. "Thank you Milton, let me know if there is anything I can do for you." He shook his head at Bernie. Bernie waved him off again. Steve pointed to the papers on the table.

"Can I have Sam Wiser get together with Clifford and go over the paperwork?"

"By all means, Steve. I will alert Clifford that Sam will be calling him." Steve nodded, looked silently at Bernie for a few seconds and still shaking his head, he left the office.

*

Rita Malone was glad to hear from Steve when she picked up the phone.

"I was worried when you didn't call, but Miss Perone assured me that you were alright and would be back in touch. Do you have any news? I need to write an article soon, or I'll go crazy." Steve chuckled.

"Yes, Rita, there is quite a bit of news and I am going to need your help to catch this guy." Steve spent the next forty-five minutes leading Rita through the maze of information he gathered in Utah. Near the end of the conversation, Rita asked a few questions.

"Can you help me get clearer on just how Amis Kinsley and his henchmen are wrapped up in this?"

"They're being very secretive and don't share any information even with the police, but I think they knew what the score was from the first murder in Salt Lake City. I even think they worked out who was doing the killing and why. Don't forget, they started all this with all their secrecy when they dealt with the polygamy problem. They got Calvin Dawkins railroaded into the state hospital, but they never counted on the governors' wife and her crusade setting the wheels in motion to free Dawkins. Once he was on the loose they have been trying to contain the situation for their own ends and playing catch-up every step of the way. If they had come clean and come across with everything they knew from the beginning, a lot of this bloodshed could have been avoided." He waited for her next question as the sound of her pencil scratching across the paper came through the line.

"Terence Leavitt. Do you think it is worth my time to try and interview him?" Steve thought for a moment before he answered.

"Well, I think you have to try, if only for a no comment for your article, but I think he figures that by stonewalling, nobody can link him to the original crime in '32. What he doesn't get, is that is the least of his problems. But by not broadcasting it, he is avoiding showing up on Kinsley's radar, at least for the time being. I guess it is your call on that."

"Last question, Steve. Do I characterize Delma Wiggens' death as a suicide, possible suicide, or what?"

"If you're asking me what I think it is, I think that it is a highly suspicious death, and you can quote me that I talked to her less than twenty-four hours before she died and while she was distraught, I don't think she was despondent enough to kill herself. But it is hard to know why people do what they do sometimes."

"Thanks, Steve I want to get on this right away. I think it would be best as a two-part article, with the first part in tomorrow's paper, what do you think?"

"I am not the person to ask about things like that, but I will say, that for purposes of putting some pressure on Dawkins, sooner is better than later." Steve wrapped up the conversation and was just hanging up the phone when Miss Perone entered the office and closed the door. She crossed over to Steve's desk, bent over at the waist and started whispering.

"Mr. Polhaus came in ten minutes ago when you were on the phone and Mr. Carmino just came in and wants to see you. What shall I do?" Steve sat back in his chair and chuckled.

"Well, Miss Perone, give me five minutes and then you send them in together. How about that?" Steffi Perone straightened up with a perplexed frown, before turning toward the door.

"Well if you say so, Mr. Cannon. They don't seem too happy to be in each other's company out in the reception area, but I will hold all your calls." Steve smiled to himself as he left his desk and walked across his office to the built-in bookcase. He pulled down a solid panel revealing two crystal decanters filled with scotch and whiskey and six crystal glasses. He brought three of the glasses back to the desk and then returned for the two decanters. He opened a drawer just below the panel and removed a mahogany cigar chest and brought it to his desk, placing it next to the large crystal ashtray and his cigarette box. He walked to the door and opened it just as Tommy was approaching from the reception room. Tam was behind him and neither looked happy. Steve held the door open wide as he smiled at the two men.

"Gentlemen, come in." Steve held his arm out indicating the room behind him, and closing the door when both men had entered. Tommy Carmino went immediately to the chair sitting squarely in front of the desk and sat down. Steve winked at Tam and gestured to the chair on the far side of the desk. When Tam had sat down, Steve moved between the two men and filled each of their glasses with drink. Tam's with Jack Daniels, and Tommy's with scotch. He picked up the humidor and held it out under Tommy's nose. Tommy shrugged a little and nodded as he lifted one of the Cuban cigars to his nose. Tam leaned over and peered into the box and hesitated.

"Come on, Tam, have one, it won't kill you." Tam snorted and picked one up.

"Not worried about that, just don't want to get used to expensive cigars." Tommy shook his head.

"Just like a cop, always looking a gift horse in the mouth." Tam busied himself with lighting the cigar and didn't reply. Steve filled his glass from the scotch decanter and sat behind the desk holding one of the cigars in his other hand. He waited until Tommy Carmino was done lighting his cigar before Steve took the lighter from him and lit his. He sat back smiling at his two visitors as he exhaled the smoke from his first puff.

"Well, this is a cozy group, don't you think?" Tommy removed the cigar from his mouth and took a sip of his scotch.

"Why all the party favors, Cannon? You taking a page out of my book?" Steve held out his hands and smiled.

"As you just said, Tommy, don't scrutinize a free horse. Can't I just have two of my friends around for booze and cigars, for no particular reason?" Tommy snorted.

"Nice try, Slick. We both show up here unannounced and you act like it's old home week." He shook his head and looked over at Tam. Tam grimaced and pretended to look at the book collection. Steve leaned forward and gestured with his cigar.

"As it happens, Tommy, I think the three of us have a little business we can discuss that concerns us all. Then it's your turn to tell me what's on your mind and then Tam here and myself have a case we are working on together we need to go over." Tommy held out his hands and shook his head with a frustrated smirk.

"I'm all ears." Steve smiled thinly across the table at the mobster and swiveled slowly in his chair.

"So, Jack tells me that we now have some help in hunting down Angelo Sorelli. What can you tell us about that?" Tommy looked from Steve to Tam and back again and held out his hands in mock supplication.

"What don't you understand?" Steve shook his head.

"No, Tommy. I want to hear from you how all this was settled." He stopped and stared intently across the table. Tommy shrugged and took a puff on his cigar and glanced out the window at the room tower across the courtyard before he spoke.

"Jack comes in to my office four days ago with this crazy notion that somehow our organization has some responsibility for protecting Nash Brannock, because the group he was a part of at the Dunes was sponsored in part by us, if you know what I mean. I tell him to get outta town, Nash soiled his own nest and good riddance as far as I was concerned. But one of the secrets of good leadership is to know what is your call and what isn't." Tommy pointed his cigar at Steve and used it to punctuate the words of his next sentence. "You should take a lesson, Slick. You might not find yourself in so much conflict with others." He didn't wait for a reply, but continued. "So I make Jack get up and we go to my boss, who listens to his story, thinks it over and the next day comes in and tells me that Jack is right. Getting soft is what I think, but that is neither here nor there. I put in a call back east and: presto! A whole group of guys are now combing the sticks for the scumbag as we speak. Waste of resources if you ask me, but obviously, nobody did." He stopped talking and looked at Tam before he continued. "So, you got a problem with that?" He looked back at Steve before Tam could reply. Steve shook his head.

"Not really, Tommy, just curious how it all came down and what happens when they catch him, that's all." Tommy shook his head and leaned forward to tap the ash from his cigar.

"What do you think is going to happen, Slick? A free trip to Disneyland?" He looked at both of them in turn. "What is with you guys? You want him to say he's sorry or something?" Steve laughed and waved his hand in a dismissive manner.

"No, Tommy, it's nothing like that. In fact, we would be more worried that you wouldn't whack him, it's just that Jack gave Tam the impression that this unnamed group of hoods answer to Jack.

We don't want to see Jack get hurt, that's all." Tommy shook his head slowly.

"Well, isn't that sweet of you guys. You guys kill me, you really do. But since you ask, yeah, it's true that they report every week to Jack and give him the picture. That was the one condition that my boss gave Jack. That way, any screw-ups fall on his head, not ours, and since he isn't part of the organization any more, we're clear. We get credit for not letting somebody get away with whacking one of our own. We got it wrapped up any way it goes." Tommy held up his hands and smiled, swiveling his head in turn toward both men. Steve took a quick puff on the cigar and looked over at Tam.

"You have any other questions for Tommy?" Tam frowned at the mobster, but shook his head.

"No, I'm clear." Steve looked over at Tommy.

"Me too, Tommy, thanks for clearing that up for us. Now what can I do for you?" Tommy picked up his glass and moved it around in a circle indicating the hotel at large as he spoke.

"I hear that you got four points in this place. Is that true?" Steve glanced at Tam who was sitting with a perplexed look on his face. Steve smiled across at Tommy.

"Yeah, as it turns out I do, except it's only three." He drummed his fingers on the green blotter as the two men gazed at each other across the table. Tommy spoke first, his eyes narrowing.

"I guess the question I have, is when you were going to tell me and how long have you been partners in this deal with Bernie?" Steve rolled the cigar in his mouth several times before he took a small puff and exhaled.

"I just found out today, probably same as you. I had Sam Wiser make some inquiries over at the commission. I confirmed it with Bernie less than an hour ago. But to answer your question, I would have told you when I got around to it." Tommy smirked.

"Well, lucky for me, Slick, I hear everything that goes on in this town." Steve smiled.

"I am sure you do, Tommy, but what is it to you? You got your own deal with Bernie, you don't see me kicking about that." Tommy moved his cigar around in the ashtray, shaking his head to himself.

"Not the same, Slick. You know the understanding I have with Bernie and where this is all heading in a couple of years. I just want to know who I am getting in bed with when the time comes, that's all." Steve snorted.

"How many points you got in the Desert Inn, Tommy? How many in the Stardust or the Dunes, huh?" Steve smiled at Tommy and then at Tam before he took a deep inhalation of the cigar. A few seconds later he exhaled and spoke again.

"Nothing to say, now, Tommy? You know what your problem is, Tommy?" Steve held the cigar out across the desk and copied Tommy as he emphasized each word he spoke. "You're one of those guys who think sixty/forty to you is a fair deal." Tommy sat back in his chair and hooked his thumb into the watch pocket of the light gray vest he wore under the charcoal suit.

"You have to pay for information, Slick. It's too valuable to be left lying around so any goofball can bend over and pick it up. I don't have a problem throwing in with you, especially if it makes Bernie happy, even though you know squat about how to run a casino, much less a hotel, but I'm not going anywhere and play second fiddle." Steve gazed back intently.

"Bernie know that, Tommy? Cause to tell you the truth, it is all the same to me. I didn't ask for the points, they were Bernie's idea, like you said, Tommy, it makes him happy." Tommy stood up, laying the cigar in the ashtray.

"Well, Slick, I think we are clear, here. You want that I should repeat all this in front of Bernie, let me know, and the three of us will have a little sit-down." He glared down at Steve. Steve swiveled his chair to the side and stood up, looking Tommy in the eye.

"Be a waste of Bernie's time. I think you are right. I think we are clear here." Steve smiled as Tommy turned and walked out of the office. He sat down and looked across at Tam who was shaking his head. Steve laughed.

"Cheer up, Tam, that was nothing. You always seem to have an opinion on my relationship with Tommy Carmino, I thought this might be a perfect opportunity for you to see how it works." Tam looked down at his cigar that he had neglected and that had gone out several minutes ago. He reached over and tossed it into the ashtray. He looked up at Steve and smiled thinly.

"You got a lot of guts, I give you that. I never heard of anyone challenging Tommy Carmino and walking away feeling good about it." Steve laughed.

"Just a game we play, Tam. The trick to Tommy is getting him to believe that you have something or know something he doesn't. Then his bark is worse than his bite. You're lucky, you have the law and all that entails backing you up. Out here, to work effectively in this town, you have to be able to dance with guys like Tommy." Steve stood up and walked over to the window. He watched the glass elevator that Milton had designed move quickly up to the fifth floor before it stopped. He turned and looked at Tam.

"But truth be told, Tam, and if you repeat it, I'll deny it, I like and admire Tommy. He is good at what he does and does it with a certain style, that you have to admit, is his alone." Tam snorted and finished his drink.

"Yeah, swell. The mob is just a bunch of family men teddy bears. I want to go home and be with my daughter, so can we get on with why I am here?" Steve sat back down behind his desk and pulled out his notebook.

"I assume you have more information from the FBI guys in Utah?" Tam nodded as he opened his briefcase and pulled out several typewritten sheets. He balanced the briefcase on his knee while he scanned the sheets.

"Calvin Dawkins was released on a kind of parole, meaning he had to report once a month to the authorities and he had a social worker or someone he had to tell where he was living and where he was working, those kinds of things. Two months after his release, they never see him again. He next shows up on the radar when an associate of his is picked up in Idaho in a stolen car that he swears he got from Dawkins. Evidently, Dawkins works construction, and that is how this guy knew him. Guy says that Dawkins needed more cash than the job paid and was boosting cars and selling them to his co-workers. The next time the authorities hear his name is when a doctor who worked at the state hospital is found murdered. The place had been ransacked and a lot of patient records had been destroyed. The housekeeper came up with a description of a guy that had been hanging around and it fit Dawkins to a 't', and they found some of his records half burned in the fireplace next to the body. Provo police picked him up with two other guys in a stolen car eight months ago, but let him go when he gave them a false name. The guy who was driving, gave up his real name several days later, but it was too late, nobody has seen him since." Steve wrote for several minutes before he looked across at Tam.

"So, the stolen car angle might be one way to go after all. What did you come up with on that?" Tam pulled some handwritten notes from the briefcase. He held them up to Steve.

"I got with the stolen car detail and went over every boosted car case in the last year. Not much jumped out, until I started sticking pins in the map, and there is a little group that has occurred in the last two months and they are all clustered around where the concentric circles you had me draw intersect. I have two teams of guys out canvassing the area now. One guy covered the trailer parks and apartments two days ago, but I got them digging deeper." He handed a sheet of paper to Steve. "There are the VIN numbers plus make and model." Steve glanced at them briefly and then laid them aside.

"What do the auto theft guys say about how he may be disposing of the cars? It's unlikely he knows enough people here to sell them, he must have a chop shop or someone he unloads them on as soon as he takes them." Tam nodded.

"They got some of their guys rousting the known fences and anyone that might be tempted to branch out into stolen cars. A lot of footwork involved, could take some time." Steve sat back in the chair and sighed.

"Yeah, it always does. Do all the shift guys have a picture of Dawkins?" Tam nodded. "Any activity around Leavitt?" Tam shook his head.

"Nothing to report in that regard. The chief is complaining about the overtime, that's all."

Steve drummed on the arms of his chair as he gazed at Tam. He sat up abruptly.

"What's the name of that cop? The one who retired a few years ago, worked in auto theft. Gil, something. Greek guy." Tam thought for a second, then snapped his fingers.

"Pappas, Gil Pappas." Steve nodded and took out his notebook.

"Yeah, that's the guy. I used to run into him down at the Golden Nugget. He fancied himself a poker player, but after a few thrashings from the sharks down there and at Binions, he went back to black-jack. Seemed like a good guy, and he knew every angle in this town when it came to anything stolen with tires on it. I think I'll look him up, he might give us a new angle." Tam shrugged and stood up.

"I'm glad you're volunteering, I've got too much to do as it is. Keeping twelve guys in the field and efficiently deployed, takes all my time. Let me know what you find out, and the same goes for me. Thanks for the cigar." Tam hesitated by the door. "You are moving up in the world, Stevie boy. Just remember where you come from." Tam held up his hand in the shape of a gun and made a clicking noise with his tongue before he turned and left the office.

*

Steve held the door open for Remy as they entered his house. Their footsteps echoed across the wooden floor and off the bare walls. They stood in the foyer and took in the bleak scene. For a few seconds, neither of them said anything. Remy was the first to break the silence.

"I'm sorry, Steve, I thought there would be more that could be saved." Steve stepped forward and ran the toe of his shoe across the scarred wood where the living room carpet had once been.

"I didn't." They walked into the small office where Steve's record collection sat on the floor in the corner. The contents of his missing desk were in four boxes stacked against the wall. It was the same in the other rooms and besides his bed and the dinette set, the safe that had been in the closet was the only large item left. Remy touched Steve's arm lightly.

"Do you have a tape measure, Steve?" Steve nodded and headed for the front door.

"The garage was the only room they didn't destroy. In too much of a hurry to bother breaking the locks, I guess." Steve went outside and opened the locks and slid the door back. He smiled at the Corvette as he moved to his workbench and retrieved a tape measure and an old wooden yardstick. He closed and locked the garage and handed both to Remy when he reappeared in the living room.

"Here you go, Gem, what are you going to do?" Remy smiled and reached behind Steve, playfully pulling his notebook from his back pocket and handing it to him.

"Tear out a few pages and let me borrow your pencil. I am going to take a few measurements for the new drapes and carpet. You give me an idea of the type of furniture you like and I will check the stores in town and see what I can come up with." Steve cast his eyes around the small living room, before he looked back at Remy.

"Maybe I ought to consider selling and buying something else. Maybe Bernie's right, maybe I should live out in the valley by him." He looked at the deep brown eyes that were searching his face from three feet away. Remy moved to him and placed her hands on either side of his chest. She smiled up at him.

"Would you be happy out there?" Steve looked down at the beautiful face and the same old lightheaded feeling came over him.

"I would be happy if you were there with me." It was his turn to search the face that now held a questioning look.

"What do you mean, Steve?" He clasped both of her hands in his as he leaned down and kissed her lips gently before he spoke.

"I know we both agreed to take it slow and it hasn't even been a year since Nash died, but maybe buying a place together would be the next best step." Remy laid her head on Steve's chest for a few seconds before she replied in a quiet voice.

"That is too big a step for me, Steve. I still don't know who that person was that lived with Nash for six years, and I need time to put all that in its' place." She leaned her head back and looked into his eyes. "I love you and I want us always to be together, but I am not ready, Steve, not yet."

Steve forced a smile and sighed. He kissed her forehead and held her out in front of him.

"The last thing I want to do is push you, Gem. You can take all the time that you want. But they are going to want the house back soon, aren't they?" Gem shook her head.

"The boss at the Dunes that replaced Nash has five kids and he and his wife are building a house out in the valley, so the kids can go to the new Valley High school. They have offered me good terms and with what Bernie is paying me, I can afford to buy it." As she spoke she moved a few feet away, folding her arms as she looked at the floor for a few seconds before she looked back up at Steve. His voice was as quiet as hers had been when he spoke.

"I see. I didn't know you had made a decision about that." They looked at each other quietly for another few seconds.

"I didn't either until just a few minutes ago." Steve nodded slowly.

"You know, Gem, I will help you, if that is what you want."

"I know you will, Steve, and if it came to that, I would, but this is something I feel that I need to do on my own, without having to worry about how someone else is feeling. Do you see that?" Steve nodded.

"I just want to make you happy, Gem. Bernie said something today that made sense. He said I need to pay more attention to the future. I thought about it a little, and you know what I discovered?" Remy shook her head slightly as she gazed into his eyes from two feet away.

"I found out, Gem, that there isn't one without you."

JULY 14

STEVE PICKED UP the phone on his desk when the clock on the wall across from him said a little after seven in the morning. He dialed the number for Pearce Construction. A few minutes later he locked the door of the office behind him, descended the stairway and pushed through the front doors of the Casablanca. A few of the front door staff was on duty and Steve looked around for Shelly Cointreau as he crossed the pedestrian bridge, but didn't see him. He pulled into the light morning traffic on the Strip and headed north toward Desert Inn Road.

Steve parked the Jeep on the hard baked ground and watched as a large crane swung a wrecking ball against the pink stucco that had once been the Las Vegas Downs racetrack. He got out of the car and walked toward a group of men that had taken shelter from the wind and were huddled behind a road grader looking at blueprints. Steve smiled to himself when he saw that Mike Pearce was part of the group. They all turned with puzzled expressions when they were aware of Steve's presence. All except Mike Pearce, who frowned and shook his head. Steve stopped several feet away from the group, his hands in his pockets. He looked directly at Mike.

"Got a few minutes?" Mike looked at a smaller man by his elbow and handed him the blueprint he had been holding in his hand.

"I'll be back in a minute. Don't do anything until I say so." He moved toward Steve as Steve turned and they walked back halfway to the Jeep and just out of earshot of the other men who busied themselves opening their thermos bottles and pouring coffee. Mike stopped and crossed his arms.

"Make it quick, Cannon, this pile of junk has to be out of here and the site clean by this time tomorrow." Steve smiled thinly and nodded.

"Yeah, I imagine, Krattner is a tough nut to work for all right." Mike Pearce snorted.

"How would you know about that?" Steve turned away and cupped his hands around his lighter to shut out the wind while he lit a Pall Mall. He turned back and smiled.

"News spreads fast, at least among the right people. You got the contract to build the clubhouse?" Mike stared at Steve for a few seconds.

"No. Just the demo of the old horse track and then we build the wall around this place. Krattner has his own architects for the golf course and the clubhouse. Don't know who won the bid to build those." Steve nodded and let the wind pull the smoke from his mouth. He took a picture of Calvin Dawkins from inside his sport coat and held it up in front of Pearce. Pearce looked at it for a brief moment.

"So?" Steve put it back in his pocket.

"So how long did he work for you? You do recognize him, right?" Mike nodded.

"Yeah. So what?" Steve's eyes narrowed as both their heads turned toward a big section of the grandstand as it crashed into the desert, a large cloud of dust rising from the debris, the wind sweeping it away toward the Convention Center. Steve turned back to the burly man.

"So, I don't know what he told you his name is, but his real one is Calvin Dawkins." Mike scoffed.

"And I suppose that should mean something to me, Mr. Cannon?" Steve shook his head and replied nonchalantly.

"Maybe not, but this will. He was born in Parowan Utah, two years before your father." Steve watched as the expression on Mike's face went from a frown to a blank stare before the anger twisted his lips into a sneer.

"What are you trying to tell me, Cannon?" Steve took a puff from the cigarette before he replied with a slight shrug of his shoulders.

"I don't believe I'm trying to tell you anything in particular, Mr. Pearce, mostly looking for answers to questions, myself." Steve ground out the cigarette beneath his toe and pulled out his note-book, turning it at an angle so that his body shielded the paper from the wind. He looked up at Mike.

"Dates and times." Mike shook his head.

"He was hired in early June. Said his name was Billy Collins. One of the guys had worked with him on a road crew in Utah and vouched for him. Not much of a worker as far as that goes, but he kept his mouth shut and did what he was told which is almost as good. Quit three weeks later, right around the end of the month. Haven't seen him since. Now, your turn." Steve could feel Mike's stare as he finished writing the information down in the notebook. Steve looked up with a neutral expression.

"He's probably the one who killed your father." Steve kept his expression the same as several others washed over Mike Pearce's face in a rapid sequence. It was a few seconds before he could speak. When he did, his voice was a low growl.

"How do you know this?" Steve shrugged.

"I said probably. I have spent most of my time since the last time I saw you in your office gathering information in Utah. I believe he is responsible for at least seven murders, and when I found out he worked construction…" Steve gestured to the area in which they were standing. "Here I am. Now what I need from you is any paper-work you have on him. Most of it is phony, I'm sure, but there may be something in there I can use." Mike sighed deeply and turned away looking out at the empty track and the pile of rubble. When he turned back, Steve could see a tear track on the dirty cheek.

"Go down to the yard and talk to Monica. I'll tell her you are coming." The large man walked quickly away without looking back at Steve. Steve watched him join his crew before he turned himself and walked toward the Jeep. He was only ten feet away when he saw a flash from a glass surface three hundred yards away in a vacant lot across Joe E. Brown Drive, the road that snaked around the racetrack property. Steve increased his pace and was able to retrieve his binoculars from the glovebox in time to see two men get into a dark blue panel truck. One was holding a pair of binoculars. Steve started the Jeep and mashed on the gas, sending a swirl of dust up behind him as he headed straight for the truck. He figured the occupants must have seen the maneuver, as the truck bucked into the air when it hit the curb of the service road that lead to the back of the Convention Center. It was fifteen seconds later when Steve drove at a high rate of speed past the same spot. A few seconds after that, he rounded the curve that bordered the front of the Center and slowed. He looked in all directions and even made the circuit around the spaceship shaped building again, but did not see any sign of the blue truck. He looked down at the binoculars next to him on the seat and wished he had tried to get the plate number, instead of trying to catch up with them. He stopped in front of the building and walked into the cool interior. He called Tam from the long line of phone booths on the south wall of the lobby, and gave him the alias that Dawkins was using. He stood for several minutes smoking a cigarette behind the dark glass. When the red Jeep, parked all by itself at the curb, didn't draw any further attention, Steve crushed out a smoke in an ashtray by the door and left.

It was a little past eight-thirty when he walked through the glass doors of Foxy's. He went straight to the large double doors behind the counter and knocked twice. He opened the door when he heard a response from the other side. As he pulled the door shut behind him, he spied Bernie sitting at one of the green felt covered tables, poring over some of the advertising tear sheets for the Hotel. He looked up and smiled when he saw Steve.

"You're a little late, which is not like you." Bernie shoved out one of the chairs next to him with his foot. "When you called last night and said we should meet here for breakfast, I figured it was also a chance to concentrate on some of the things I still have to do, without getting interrupted every five minutes. I think I will keep this a secret and hole up here when things get too hectic at the hotel. How you doin'?" Steve sat down and picked up the cup of coffee that Bernie had poured while he was talking and slid across the table to Steve's side. He took a quick sip before he answered.

"Pretty, well, Bern, a little on pins and needles with this case. Got a serial killer still loose and precious little to go on." Bernie shook his head sadly.

"Man, I was scared when they had that warrant out for you, that could have turned out bad for everybody, but I got a good feeling that you will come up with this guy soon. How did your house look?" Steve snorted.

"Empty. Empty in more ways than one." Bernie frowned as he watched Steve's eyes glaze over for a few seconds.

"Wanna talk about it?" Steve's eyes focused again on his friend.

"No, Bernie, not right now." Bernie nodded thoughtfully and rose to help the waiter that was coming through the door with several plates of food. When the dishes were on the table in front of the two men and the waiter had retreated back into the restaurant, Steve waited until Bernie looked up from his plate before he spoke.

"Tommy Carmino dropped by late yesterday." Bernie smiled over a forkful of fried egg.

"Oh, yeah? What was on his mind? Must have been something, he doesn't leave the Desert Inn unless it is important."

"He had just found out about my interest in the Casablanca, and he was a little perturbed about the implications, if you know what I mean." Bernie frowned across his coffee cup as he brought it to his lips.

"No, I don't know what you mean. I don't see how it is any concern of his. What did he say?" Steve shrugged.

"To tell you, the truth, I don't remember word for word, I was just waiting for him to leave so I could talk to Tam about the case, but the gist is that he seems to think the two of us are in some kind of competition to be partners with you." Steve held out his hands and shrugged. Bernie snorted.

"That means I can expect a call from that direction. I thought I was clear on the plan. All his profits from Carmino Lighting and what he gets if and when he gets a chance to cash out his share in the D.I., go into the pot. I match it and we add as many other investors as we need and we buy or build a hotel, when the time is right. He knows that." Bernie shook his head and turned his attention to his eggs and toast. Neither man spoke for a few minutes, until Bernie slid his plate into the middle of the table and looked over at Steve.

"Since we are on the subject, I think I should tell you how I'm going to handle my share of the Casablanca." Steve stopped eating and sat back with his cup and smiled across at Bernie.

"Sure, Bern, I'll listen."

"I own sixty-two percent of the Casablanca. The roughly three and a half percent that you own, will pay dividends depending on the profit picture. My financial guy says that if you let them ride, in two years' time you could own five or six percent, maybe more. I am going to give Remy, Walter, and Jack one percent a year until they own three percent each. If Skipper sticks around, he will get the same, as will your son, Mike if he decides to come aboard. Walter has been with me since 1952, it will make a swell retirement plan for him. And Remy. Well you know the story there. What a godsend. She is so good at what she does, now I am afraid that someone is going to hire her away."

"I wouldn't worry about that, Bernie, Remy is the most loyal person I know after you." Bernie waved dismissively, but continued.

"I want you to know, and I will tell Walter, Remy, and Jack as well, that at any time, if anyone wants to cash out, I will buy back their share at the last quarter's valuation. Just so you know." Steve nodded.

"That's very generous Bernie, but I don't think you're going to get anybody taking you up on it for quite a while."

"That's fine. I hope everybody I love is along for the ride for a long time to come. All that is separate from any partnership I have in the future with Tommy. When the time comes, I may have to sell a big chunk of the Casablanca to swing it, but that is the commitment I have made. I will explain all of this to him again, when he calls, meanwhile, if he brings it up to you again, you can give him chapter and verse as well."

"That's fine with me, Bern, after you talk with him, I don't expect that we will hear about it again. But on to another subject. What do you need me to do for the big opening on Saturday?" Bernie looked around and shrugged.

"Nothing special. Just put on your tux and be there. The governor is cutting the ribbon at noon and there will be the usual rush at the tables." Steve nodded.

"I have already talked to Jack and I will be there with him to monitor the action, at least until the next morning, if it winds down." Bernie smiled and held up his hand.

"Subject number two. What should I do about Rita? Has Remy talked to you about it yet? Oscar Aleman and Stephane Grappelli are out of here the middle of August."

"Remy and I had a conversation last week and I got in touch with Buck Monari. I gave him her album, told him what the story was and he promised to come up with something in the next two weeks. He is going to put a group together that will showcase her voice. He might even front it himself, depending on who he decides to go with. He is looking for guys that can make the long term commitment, so you have a show you can count on." Bernie nodded.

"That's good, Steve, I am glad to hear it. I feel kinda bad since I got her involved and now the plug is getting pulled.

"That's OK, Bern, she understands how this business works. I think she will like the new arrangement." Steve stood up.

"I have taken enough of your time today, Bernie. If you think of anything else I can do, call Miss Perone and let me know." Bernie stood up and followed Steve to the door. He waited until Steve turned back to say goodbye.

"Don't forget, Steve, I would love to make you and Remy a sweet deal on one of my condos out in the valley." Steve smiled wistfully.

"I haven't forgotten, Bernie. Maybe someday that ship will come in." Steve left Bernie with a perplexed look on his face as he made his way out of the restaurant.

*

Steve stood in the doorway of the Stardust Golf Club card room. Though it was only eleven o'clock, the room was almost full. He looked over the crowd and saw several faces he recognized. He tugged on the sleeve of a waiter that was coming out of the room with a silver tray that held several empty drink glasses.

"Could you point out Gil Pappas to me, please?" The waiter nodded and indicated a table near the window that overlooked the eighteenth green.

"The gentlemen in the red shirt, that is Mr. Pappas."

"Thanks." Steve remembered the face as soon as he was pointed out. He strolled casually through the tables and waited until there was break in the game. He stepped forward.

"Mr. Pappas?" The tanned face under the thick mane of silver hair looked up, the light gray eyes part of the kind expression that greeted Steve.

"That's me. Who wants to know?" Steve extended his hand.

"My name is Steve Cannon, you probably don't remember, but…" The man who was still seated interrupted.

"Of course, I remember you. You're that poker playing private detective that is friends with Polhaus. Yeah, sure, no introductions needed. What can I do you for? You want to play a few hands of gin?" Steve smiled and shook his head, turning to smile at the other men sitting at the table who were all expressing their agreement.

"No, maybe give me a raincheck on that. I need your professional advice." A mild look of surprise crossed Gil's face.

"Now, that is something I haven't heard in a long while." He looked down at the cards that were being scooped up for another hand.

"Count me out on this one, guys. I will be back in a few minutes." He stood up and nodded toward the door.

"There is another bar across the hall. Nobody usually in there. We can talk." Steve nodded to the table and followed Gil out of the card room and through a double door that led to a cozy bar. The only other person in the room was a bartender who stood from his stool when he spotted Gil Pappas. Pappas walked halfway to the bar and turned around.

"You want a drink?" Steve smiled and walked over to the bar.

"Let me buy you one, Gil, after all, I am the one dragging you away from your game." Gil waved Steve off, and signaled to the bartender.

'Nonsense. I need the break and besides, I need to burn off my $150.00 tab for this month." Steve smiled and pointed to the handle that poured the draught version of Coors beer when the bartender looked his way. They carried their beers over to a table by the window that was as far away from the bar as they could get. Gil indicated the bartender with a slight movement of his head as they sat down.

"If this is too cozy for you, we can go outside." Steve shook his head and held up his beer.

"Thanks for the beer, Gil." They both took large pulls on the pale yellow liquid, before Steve put his on the paper coaster in front of him. He waited until Gil had finished before he spoke.

"Here's the deal, Gil. I need some information on a guy I'm trying to track. He's the guy I suspect is behind the Mormon murders, and I have reason to believe he is boosting cars and selling them to finance his stay in our fair city." He quit talking and took another smaller drink from the large stein. Gils' look was intense as he leaned in toward Steve.

"How can I help?" Steve lowered his voice slightly.

"If some guy who is new to town and might not know what he is about, wants to do business in stolen cars or parts, who would deal with him?" Gil sat back.

"That is a very good question, because the guy you describe isn't likely to get anywhere with the established guys. They are too spooked to deal with anyone they don't know. Now, I have been retired for three years so I may not be up to date on all the goings on, but I've kept my hand in a little bit, so I think I can help." Gil pulled a score card and a short green pencil out of a glass cup on the table and tore off a piece of the thin cardboard. He wrote for several seconds and pushed the scrap across to Steve. Steve picked it up and then looked quizzically at Gil.

"Never heard of this place." Gil smiled.

"This guy was always my ace in the hole. He has dealt with these lowlifes for over twenty years, all the time feeding me information and they were never the wiser. You know any specifics, like make, model, anything like that?" Steve nodded and pulled the list of car thefts in the area that Tam had mentioned. He handed it to Gil. Gil nodded as he read the list.

"A Ford man. Well, that will make it easier. This guy will definitely know where these cars are and more importantly, where they came from." Steve took the sheet back and grimaced.

"Why will he talk to me?" Gil chuckled.

"You're right, normally, he wouldn't, but you have to use the right 'open sesame'." Gil pulled his wallet out and took a card from the back and handed it to Steve. Steve held it up. It was the Greek flag on one side, and a black scorpion on the other. Steve's face held a questioning expression when he looked back at Gil. Gil shrugged and smiled.

"A little game we developed when I was on the force. Snitch gives us information, he gets one of those. He collects enough of them he gets special dispensation if he is unfortunate enough to find himself in the stir. Show him that. If he isn't convinced, have him call this number." Gil pulled the scrap of scorecard back to his side of the table and wrote a phone number on the other side. He handed it back to Steve and watched as Steve slipped it into his pocket.

"So, you think you got a line on this Mormon killer guy?" Steve nodded.

"Maybe. But let me ask you something Gil. When you were working cases, did you ever get the feeling that someone was dogging your every move and bad things were happening behind you wherever you happened to go?" Gil shrugged with a small grimace.

"Yeah, once or twice. That's a not a good feeling. Who you got on your trail?"

"I can't say, but I got a pretty good idea." Steve stood up and looked down at the tanned open face.

"You've been a big help, Gil, thanks for the beer and the information. I will circle back when this is all over and tell you how it went. But watch yourself. If I'm being bird-dogged, at least they don't know who I was talking to in here. Don't do anything to tip them off, OK?"

"Thanks for the warning and good luck, Cannon." Steve smiled as he turned toward the door. He made his way through the vestibule, stopping just short of the front door. He peered up and down the street. When he was satisfied that nothing was obviously amiss, he made his way quickly to the Jeep.

*

Tams' eyes lit up when Steve filled his open doorway. He rose from his desk and stretched his back.

"Just in time to buy me lunch." Steve shook his head.

"Maybe later, you and I have a little errand to run." Steve looked around at the office which was more crowded with files than normal. "Can't you wrangle a bigger office? You're running the whole show, after all." Tam snorted as he lifted his sport coat from the hook behind the door.

"I'm a public service worker, my friend, no money for big fancy offices and a personal secretary like some people I know." Steve smiled as he backed out of the office to let Tam go by.

"That gonna be your new theme song? You think because I have a few points in Bernie's joint, I'm rich? Nobody's standing in line to give me a gold watch and a fat pension when I hit fifty-five." Tam waved dismissively.

"Not enough to live on, Stevie boy. My accountant figures I have to save half of every paycheck from here on out if I want to quit at sixty-five." Steve shook his head as he held open the glass door for Tam.

"Gil Pappas seems to be doing OK." Tam turned around, eyes narrowing from the glare of the sun.

"Pappas invested in real estate from the get go. At least that's the story he tells." Steve raised an eyebrow as the two men looked at each other. After a few seconds, Steve pointed across the street toward the diner.

"Don't need a car, we are going to take a little walk." Tam shrugged and fell in behind Steve, the two men standing shoulder to shoulder as they waited for the traffic to clear. Steve jerked his thumb toward the motel three quarters of a block away.

"You seen Amis Kinsley or any of his boys lately?" Tam looked down the street.

"That where we're going?" Steve nodded as they stepped off the curb and walked quickly across the street. Steve stopped just in front of the diner.

"Yeah, that's where we're going. Somebody is keeping pretty close tabs on me and since it was his guys last time, we need to stamp his passport." Tam nodded as they headed down the wide sidewalk toward the motel.

Steve snorted to himself as they turned off the street and approached the motel office. The same man as before, in the same position as before, and with the same bored expression on his face, watched the two detectives as they swung open the door to the lobby. Steve smiled widely at the man.

"You seemed so disappointed last time that I wasn't a cop, so I brought you the genuine article." He jerked his thumb at Tam who was standing just over his right shoulder. The man sneered and took the foot he was leaning on, off the desk chair, turned around and tossed the motel register onto the low counter in front of Steve.

"Been gone for three days. Didn't leave a forwarding address, no cards or letters for you." The man smiled widely back at Steve. Steve leafed casually through the register.

"How'd he pay?" The man didn't change his expression.

"Don't have to tell you that." Tam stepped forward and pinned the man's wrist to the counter as he reached for the register. His face contorted in pain, and Steve could see the man was trying hard not to cry out. Tam leaned over and hissed in his ear.

"How did he pay for the rooms?" Tam leaned more of his weight on the thin wrist. The man held up his free hand in an act of surrender.

"OK, OK, I will get it for you." Tam released his grip and the man staggered backwards, a hurt look on his face as he rubbed his left wrist. After a few seconds he bent over and pulled open a small drawer. He picked up a sheaf of checks that were fastened with a paperclip and sorted through them with his good hand while he pressed them to his chest. He pulled one out and laid it on the counter in front of Steve. Steve held it up so that Tam could read it over his shoulder. Tam read out loud.

"Intermountain Interfaith Council. Salt Lake City." Steve handed the check back to the man and took his notebook from his coat pocket. He wrote the name down and motioned to Tam that they were going to go. He stopped after Tam had walked back outside and looked back at the man who was still rubbing his wrist.

"Ice. I think that's the ticket." Steve joined Tam, who was busy lighting a cigarette. He clapped a hand on the detective's shoulder and pointed down the street.

"Lunch on me. Get your strength back." Steve smiled to himself as he led the way back through the driveway and onto the sidewalk. When they were seated in their usual booth in the diner, Steve grinned across the table at his friend.

"Been awhile since I've seen you get rough with a guy." Tam shrugged as he looked over the one page plastic menu.

"Guy's always flouting the law. Always has a bad attitude. Rents out rooms to hopheads and hookers. Surprised the Mormon guys could stay there." Steve nodded.

"If they're Mormon." He caught Tam's eye as he glanced up from the menu.

"What did you mean by that?" Steve laid the menu down and took a sip of the ice water in front of him.

"My guess is that when you run a check on that organization, it will turn out to be some phony front for Amis and his goons. They might be church guys or they might just be muscle the church hires to do their dirty work." Tam pointed to the meatloaf on the menu when the waitress came to the table. Steve ordered a grilled cheese sandwich. Tam sat back in the booth after she left.

"I don't get it. Those guys have been under our feet since this thing started. They were always clear who they were representing."

Steve looked out the yellow curtains that hung from a brass rod and covered half of the window,

"The way I see it Tam, a lot of big organizations are the same when they decide the rules that everyone else plays by, don't apply to them. Take a guy like Tommy. He's got muscle and everybody knows it, he doesn't make any bones about it, in fact he counts on it. The church has to at least make a show of legitimacy, but they still have to find a way to get the job done. That is why Stanwick is so afraid of Amis and his henchmen. If there is no such thing as Danites, these guys can certainly fill the bill until the real thing comes along."

"So why do you think they pulled up stakes?" Steve waited until the waitress put down the two plates of food and returned quickly with the glasses of beer before he replied.

"They somehow got the word from Utah that Calvin Dawkins is the killer. Which now means that he is in just as much danger as Leavitt. Two guys with binoculars were very interested in what I was doing this morning, when I was talking to Pearce out by the race track. We are going to have to start covering our tracks a little more and quit being so obvious." They ate their lunch in silence. As they were finishing their beers, Tam leaned in a little closer.

"So, Gil Pappas any help?" Steve nodded as he pulled a pack of cigarettes from his front shirt pocket.

"Well, he answered my questions and gave me a lead that looks promising, so yeah, it was worth the effort." They stood up and walked to the front. Steve paid the bill while Tam took a tooth-pick from a small glass by the register and walked outside. When Steve joined him on the sidewalk, Tam pointed to something just behind Steve.

"Just like déjà vu. There's another article by Rita." Steve held out his hand and snapped his fingers twice. Tam dug into his pocket and slapped a quarter into Steve's hand. Steve folded the papers under his arm as they jogged across the street. He handed one of the copies to Tam just before he started moving toward the Jeep.

"Read it over, Tam. When I get a lead on where Dawkins is selling the cars, I will let you know." Tam waved absentmindedly as he started reading the first part of the front page article.

*

The address Gil Pappas had given Steve was north of the Nellis Air Force base, just off the interstate. Steve drove down the narrow asphalt and came over the top of a small rise. Off to his right was a large car junkyard that easily covered five acres of desert. Steve drove through an opening in the chain link fence and parked in front of a ramshackle house that was connected to several sheds. There were deer antlers nailed above each door and several of the sheds had only strips of tarpaper for their outer walls. Steve waited for a few seconds before he opened the car door, in case the place was guarded by any unfriendly dogs. When none appeared, he crossed in front of the Jeep and knocked on the main door. He knocked two more times before the door creaked open on its' rusty hinges. A craggy faced man in his late sixties peered at Steve from beneath gray bushy eyebrows.

"Make and model?" Steve looked down at the scrap of paper that Gil had scribbled on.

"Everett Turner?"

"Yeah, that's the name. Make and model." Steve shook his head in slight frustration.

"Make and model of what?" The craggy face held an equally frustrated look.

"You gotta tell me the make and model of the parts you are looking for, so I will know if I got the car in the yard or not." Steve waved the small piece of paper and shook his head.

"Don't need parts. I need information." The man started to close the door as he spoke.

"Don't sell information, check with the library." Steve was not fast enough with his foot to prevent the door from closing. He knocked hard on the door three or four more times to no avail. He walked around the side of the house where he saw the man through one of the side windows. Steve knocked on the window and held up the card that Gil had given him. Everett Turner pointed toward the front door. Steve waited impatiently for it to open again. When it did, Everett held out his hand.

"You don't look like a cop." Steve ignored the hand and stepped into the space just behind the door to avoid having the door shut in his face again.

"I'm not. You have a place where we can talk?" The man turned and looked around the small room that had been converted into an office. He pointed to two desk chairs that sat in front of an old door across two sawhorses that served as a makeshift desk. Steve pulled out his notebook and his list of stolen cars as he sat down. He slid one of his business cards across the table and waited while the older man studied it. When he was done, Steve cleared his throat.

"What I need from you, Mr. Turner, is information about a person who might be new in town trying to unload stolen cars." Turner held out his hand and pointed to the small card that Pappas had given Steve. Steve slid it across the table. Everett stuffed it down into his front pocket and smiled thinly.

"Haven't seen one of these in a while. Hope they still work." Steve ignored the remark but pointed to his notebook, Turner shrugged.

"Why do you want to know?" Steve tapped his pencil pensively on the top of the metal spirals.

"Because that person may be responsible for several murders." Everett's eyes widened.

"He could be the Mormon murderer?" Steve glanced over at the latest edition of the Sun lying on the corner of the desk.

"Maybe. Maybe not. Either way I need to locate him. Here is a list of stolen cars we think he may be trying to unload." Everett read the list carefully before he handed it back to Steve. He gazed at Steve for several seconds before he spoke.

"Guy came by yesterday, driving one of the cars on your list.

Said he had another one that is also on the list. Wanted me to buy both of them. Didn't know him, so I passed."

"Did you get his name?" The man shook his head and reached across the table and pulled a small piece of paper out of a cigar box and handed it to Steve.

"No, but he left that number." Steve looked at the number which had a North Las Vegas prefix.

"Can you describe him?" Everett moved his shoulders noncommittedly and looked around the room before he looked back at Steve.

"Seems like this information is pretty important to you." Steve stared blankly at the man in front of him. Everett leaned forward and tapped Steve's knee.

"Fifty bucks." Steve's eyes narrowed.

"Forty." When several seconds passed without any reply, Steve stood to go. Everett held up his hand.

"OK, forty." Steve took out his wallet before he sat back down. He pulled out two twenty dollar bills and held them up. When Turner reached for them, Steve moved them out of reach and shook his head.

"Description first." Everett sat back in his chair and shrugged his shoulders,

"Tall, like you, dark hair, kinda wild looking eyes." Steve pulled the picture he had shown Pearce from the inside pocket of his sport coat. He held it up. He could tell by the look in Turner's eyes that the man who had come into the junkyard the day before was Calvin Dawkins. Steve stood up, dropped the bills on the table, then put the photo and his notebook away.

"He shows up again, you call whatever cop you know best, and stay out of his way." Everett nodded as he reached over and picked up the paper. Steve glanced out the window to the road before he opened the door. He drove out of the gate and took a right, driving for a half mile before he spun the Jeep in a U-turn and drove back the way he had just come. He did not see another car until he was almost to the freeway. He drove south to a liquor store that sat away from the frontage road but that provided easy access on and off the interstate. The proprietor was waiting on a customer when Steve came through the door. Steve held his hand up to his ear as if he were holding a phone, the man behind the counter pointed toward the back. Steve walked down the long aisle to the wooden phone booth. He pulled the accordion doors shut and dialed Tam.

"Tam. I got a lead on Dawkins. Here is the phone number I got from Pappas' guy." Steve repeated it into the phone and waited until Tam had copied it down and read it back to him. "If you get an address on that, take a couple of your guys and check it out. If you want me there, let me know."

"What are the chances he will still be there?"

"You tell me. The word I got was that he stopped by this guy's junkyard yesterday and is probably still waiting for a call. So far, he doesn't have any reason to dig in deeper, though I am sure that Rita's article will spook him quite a bit."

"Let me see if I can connect an address to this number, then go from there."

"Fine. Keep me posted." Steve left the booth and walked out to his car. He sat in the front seat with the passenger door open and read the article that Rita had written. It was two parts as she had said, the second part was due out in the Thursday edition. Though she named Calvin Dawkins as a leading suspect in the Mormon murders, she concentrated on the background story of the church and its' long history with polygamy. The last part of the article wove in the story of Garret Dawkins, his disappearance and death, along with the recent events in Parowan and Manti. Steve winced a few times when he read passages that implicated the church and he thought he could see Hank Greenspuns' fine hand in some of the sentiments that were expressed. When he was finished reading, he separated the article from the rest of the paper. As he deposited the remains of the Sun into a trash barrel, he saw the blue panel truck passing with traffic on the opposite side of the interstate. Both occupants were looking at Steve as it drove by sixty yards away. The front seat passenger was Amis Kinsley. Steve jumped into the Jeep and wheeled it around crossing the two lanes of the interstate on his side and bouncing quickly over the soft sand median that separated the two directions of travel. There was no traffic in sight coming from behind him as the front wheels gripped the tarmac and he coaxed the Jeep up to speed. The panel truck was a half mile ahead of him and the occupants had most likely seen Steve's maneuver as it began to accelerate as well and careened off the interstate onto an exit the led to a housing development in North Las Vegas. By the time Steve had taken the same exit and cruised into the housing development, the truck was nowhere to be seen. For the next half hour, Steve crisscrossed the residential streets, but came up empty.

It was after three-thirty when Steve parked in front of the Casablanca. He smiled as he walked toward the front entrance. Shelly Cointreau was standing in the late afternoon sun, his hands on his hips as he addressed a group of doormen and car runners that were standing in the shade of the portico. Steve gave Shelly the high sign and received an acknowledging nod in return as he paused and listened to Shelly informing his troops of his expectations for their performance at the upcoming grand opening. The coldness of the air conditioning felt good to Steve for once as he made his way through the lobby and up the marble staircase to his office.

Steve could see that there was someone waiting for him in the reception area, but it wasn't until Miss Perone pressed the button from her side and Steve stepped through the open door that he recognized the back of Benjamin Stanwick. Steve winked at Steffi Perone as he moved in front of the chair and stared down at the startled bishop.

"Mr. Stanwick. What brings you here?" Steve laughed sardonically and pointed toward the doorway that led to his office. "Shall we?" He took two steps back to allow Stanwick the room to rise from the chair. Steve noted that there was a different expression on his face, one he had not seen before, one that lacked his usual confidence, and bluster. Steve followed him into the office and waited until he chose one of the two wing chairs to sit in. Steve walked slowly behind his desk and dropped into his chair. Steve decided a preemptive statement might be the best course.

"You're probably wondering what your money has bought you, so if you have the time, I will give you the full report, right up until ten minutes ago." Steve paused when he saw the expression on Stanwick's face. Stanwick leaned forward and his voice was hoarse and carried more than a hint of urgency, his brow glowed from perspiration.

"You have to tell me what I need to do. Kinsley is threatening me, and I can't get anyone to listen to me…" Steve held up his hand and then motioned for Stanwick to sit back in his chair.

"Hold on. Let's slow down a little and start from the beginning. The last time I saw you, you and Kinsley were as tight as Laurel and Hardy. Why the big rift all of a sudden?" Stanwick shook his head back and forth several times and leaned forward again.

"He's gone crazy. Won't listen to me, won't take my calls. He just appeared in my office last night and told me that if I said one more thing to anyone about the case, he would kill me." Steve swiveled the chair slowly back and forth as he contemplated the frightened man in front of him.

"Know where he is?" Steve kept his voice as casual as he could. Stanwick looked up incredulously.

"Know where he is? He was in my office threatening me last night. Isn't that enough?" Steve shrugged and still kept a calm cool demeanor.

"Checked the motel across from the police station, they're gone. Thought you might know where they went, that's all." Stanwick sat back in the chair, shaking his head angrily.

"I don't know where he is, but you're missing the point. I need to go somewhere where he doesn't know where I am." Steve shrugged.

"Maybe. What's the church say? You tried them yet?" Stanwick slumped in the chair and stared back at Steve.

"You're not going to help me are you?" Steve sat forward in the chair and his tone was a little flatter and a little more direct when he spoke.

"Not much I can do if I don't have any information to go on. Kinsley and his minions are following me everywhere I go. So let me tell you the facts of life as they relate to you." Steve waited for a few moments until he was sure that Stanwick was listening. "You came here asking me to help you prove the church wasn't responsible for the Mormon murders and you withheld information while the whole time you were in cahoots with Kinsley, playing both sides against the middle. Now, Kinsley has found out for sure who is behind the murders and you are on the wrong side of the street. You're just a guy who knows too much and has outlived his usefulness. No, your big mistake was coming to me. Most PI's I know would have taken your money, strung you along for a while and then cut you loose, none the wiser. Kinsley figured out early on that I might actually get somewhere they couldn't get themselves, and now I am in a race to find Calvin Dawkins before they do." Steve stopped and let his words sink in. When he saw the resigned look cross Stanwick's face, he continued.

"Here's the best advice I have. Skip town and skip quick. If you trust the church to play you straight, go there, otherwise, go far away and burrow in deep. If you feel lucky, try the police, but I don't think they are up to the job and I wouldn't trust their motivation were I you."

Stanwick stood up, his face red and his fists balled. "I should have never come to you in the first place. If anything happens to me, Cannon, it will be on your head." Steve stood up and shook his head slowly and sadly at the stocky man.

"No, it won't, Mr. Stanwick, no it won't." He watched the back of the bishop as he headed for the door. "Funny isn't it, Bishop, how the more we push sometimes, the less we end up with."

Steve's words stopped just as the door closed. Steve picked up the phone and dialed quickly.

"Tam? Get anything yet?" Steve listened for several seconds.

"Check the motel?" Steve nodded into the phone.

"Yeah, he's being careful. When he didn't get a call from Everett, he scrammed and set up shop somewhere else. But we have him on the move, if we keep the pressure on, he will make a mistake or get flushed out into the open. Now is the time to beef up the patrols on Leavitt. An undercover car patrolling the immediate neighborhood to back up the stakeout guys might be the best way to accomplish that. I will even volunteer for a few shifts if you need me." Steve listened to Tam for a few minutes.

"Another thing. See if you can spare a few shifts to keep an eye on Benjamin Stanwick. He was just in here. Amis Kinsley has been threatening him, and if he doesn't take my advice and leave town quick, he will need the protection. Looks like we have two psycho killers to watch out for. Was the motel inside the concentric circles you drew on the map?" Steve nodded as Tam replied.

"Then I think you should concentrate your manpower on the flophouses and fleabag motels in that area. I will go down and scout around myself when I get the chance." Steve looked up as Miss Perone appeared at the door.

"Hold on a minute, Tam." Steve put his hand over the receiver and nodded at Miss Perone.

"Mr. Cannon, Hank Greenspun is in the outer office. Can you see him?" Steve uncovered the receiver.

"Yes, Miss Perone. Give me a minute and then show him in." Steve returned to the conversation with Tam and hung up several seconds later. He was just starting for the door when it opened, and Hank walked in briskly, stopping quickly and extending his hand.

"Steve, sorry to barge in like this. If this is a bad time, I can come back tomorrow." Steve smiled and shook the firm hand.

"Nonsense, Hank. I always have time, sit down." Steve pointed to the chair that sat squarely in front of his desk. He looked at the clock.

"It's almost five, Hank, you want a drink?" Hank waved toward the door.

"No, thanks, Steve, I was farther out on the Strip and I wanted to see the Casablanca for myself. I have a meeting downtown in an hour, so I won't be here long." Steve nodded and smiled and waited while the older man made himself comfortable in the chair. Hank folded his hands on a crossed knee and gazed at Steve.

"Several things I wanted to cover with you, Steve. Firstly, I was surprised to hear that you are an owner here." Steve smiled and shrugged.

"Why surprised, Hank?" Hank kept a serious but benign look on his face as he continued.

"It's just that you are on the board of Carmino Lighting, and now this. I guess I always saw you as separate from this side of things, if you know what I mean." Steve nodded.

"Yeah, Hank, I think I do. But I see it as more of a progression. This town is changing and I have been around gambling longer than you have, and I had no interest before, but now…?" Steve held up his arms and indicated the hotel in general. "What's not to like? Bernie is squeaky clean and gets the Good Housekeeping Seal of Approval from the Gaming Control Board all the way up to the governor." Hank was nodding as Steve spoke, but held up his hand when Steve stopped.

"I know what you are saying, Steve and most of that is true, but these guys rarely change their spots and frankly, guys like Tommy Carmino are the not the best business partners out there."

"I agree, Hank, but like I said, the wild card is Bernie. I know the relationship those two men have and trust me when I tell you,

Tommy Carmino will be a different man when he is partners with Bernie." Hank sat back in his chair and sighed as he lifted his hands off of his knees.

"Enough said, Steve, I just wanted to let you know how I see things." Steve chuckled.

"I appreciate that, Hank, but I think that I could have guessed that one." Both men looked at each other for a brief moment before they both chuckled wryly.

"Somewhat on the same subject, Steve, what do you know about Jay Sarno and the money invested at Caesars Palace?"

"Probably not much more than yourself, Hank. I know there is union money involved, and I only know that because some of Milton Swanson's people have hired on over there and the word is that Jay yells Hoffas' name whenever he needs to win an argument with his partners. Plus, I heard a little about who may be running the casino, and if that info is correct, he is headed for trouble there as well. Looks like he will be getting it from all sides. I have known Nate Jacobsen for several years, not well, but well enough to know that Jay has overspent and overbuilt and he might have trouble delivering the returns that some of the money people might be expecting." Hank nodded.

"So, you know who has been tapped to run the casino?"

"Yes, a guy named Jerry Zarowitz, a bookmaker from back east. According to Nate, this guy came along with some investment money from Florida and against Nate's advice, Sarno was desperate for more money and agreed to let Zarowitz run the casino." Hank shook his head.

"You saying Jay is likely to get skimmed?" Steve shrugged.

"Yeah, probably. At least that is Nate's suspicion, but Jay has a funny notion that gambling is not going to be the big breadwinner over there. Figures he can make good money off the food, rooms and entertainment." Steve smiled at the expression that came to him from across the desk. "Yeah, I know, I couldn't figure it either, but the funny thing is, I mentioned it to Bernie and he didn't think it was such a crazy idea, maybe a little early in the game, but after thinking about it for a while, I don't know. Jay can be prickly and crazy as a jaybird, forgive the pun, and I sometimes wonder about his ability to focus for very long, but you can't deny the excitement he has generated for his property. Bernie counts himself lucky that he is opening a year ahead of Caesars, I don't think we would want to compete head on with that circus." Hank smiled and pointed a finger toward Steve.

"I have interviewed him twice for the paper, and I think your observations are pretty spot on. What I think are crackpot ideas he comes up with, everyone I mention them too, thinks they are great, so maybe times are changing in this town, or at least the in the tastes of the people who come here to have fun. Which reminds me. I have been hearing a little more about corporations being able to own casinos. There is a perfect example of a former crackpot idea that is now being seriously considered. I remember you talking about it at least two years ago, and now, some worthy people other than the Clifford Joneses' of the world are talking about it too."

"Yes, but until the governor gets behind it and maybe a few new faces appear on the Gaming Commission, I don't think it is going anywhere very quickly." Hank glanced at his watch, frowned and leaned a little more forward in his chair. His voice took on a more serious tone.

"You read Rita's article today?" Steve nodded as Hank continued. "Caused a big stir, I can tell you. The Governor has called twice just this afternoon, and the church is threatening to sue. The meeting I am going to later? Our lawyers. Funny how the murders and catching this guy are not the top priority of many people other than you. The church is particularly upset about the polygamy angle, they're crying foul. So, one of the questions I need to ask you, because I know I will be asked it in the next hour is this: How solid is the ground underneath us on this one?" Hank stopped and waited for a reply. Steve thought for a few seconds and spoke carefully.

"I spent almost four days in Southern Utah talking to the principals involved. I'm not saying that the polygamy material came easy, in fact, it was very hard for those people to give out that kind of information to an outsider, but it's one of those things that has been suppressed for so long that it just boils over when the lid is raised. I am sure you know exactly what I am talking about. There are several people that can corroborate what I told Rita and what appeared in her articles. I can give you a list of names, other than the ones that Rita cited if you would like them." When Hank indicated by a gesture that it was not necessary, Steve continued. "The church's obsession with secrecy is what set off this whole chain of events in the first place. We all know the stories and the rumors, and I think it is pretty common knowledge inside and outside the region that there are small communities of polygamists all over Utah, always have been, probably always will be. At issue here is how far the church is prepared to go to protect their image." Steve stopped when he saw Hank's eyes narrow and his strong jaw tighten. When he spoke, it was through teeth that were partially clenched.

"Are you saying what I think you're saying?" Steve shrugged, but his look was as grave as the publishers'.

"This is what I am saying: The group of guys that was camped out in the motel across from Police headquarters are bad actors and they are either part of the church security system or have been hired as mercenaries. I don't have to tell you what their job is here, you have been the victim of their tactics the same as me. Now they are threatening one of the Bishops, and they are trailing me, hoping that I will lead them to Dawkins. The church will no doubt deny that they have any connection to Kinsley and his gang, but you and I and the police know differently. Things have moved in an uglier direction where the church is concerned. I think all of us need to be extra careful from here on out." Hank stood up and offered his hand across the desk.

"I think you are right, Steve. I am sorry I have to run if I am going to make that meeting. Can I call you if I need clarification on some points?" Steve smiled and looked at his watch.

"Sure, Hank, I'll be here for the next two hours at least. Feel free to call if you need to."

Steve watched the editor and publisher of the Sun, leave the office and walk into the reception area. He sat back down in the chair and lit a cigarette. He felt the .45 tucked snuggly under his arm as he leaned the chair back and propped his feet up on the desk.

JULY 15

STEVE'S ALARM CLOCK woke him at one a.m. He quickly dressed and stepped out into the warm, dark night. He steered the Jeep toward downtown, and when he reached Fremont Street, he began to make long sweeps below the rows of the brightly lit casinos as he prowled the numbered streets that lay inside the concentric circles of Tam's map. He had the most recent descriptions of cars stolen from the area taped to his dashboard as he tried to keep his speed up enough to not arouse suspicions but slow enough to check out most of the cars he could see parked on the streets or in the narrow alleys behind the small older houses. He was making a last pass on eighth avenue before heading toward Stewart Street on the other side of Fremont when he saw the rotating lights of a police cruiser, a half block ahead. He pulled to the curb twenty yards back and parked the Jeep. He recognized Officer Gateson who was standing on the sidewalk talking to a lady of the evening. Steve walked nonchalantly toward the couple and stopped ten feet away. When the prostitute looked over at him, Gateson turned around.

"Hey, Cannon, what are you doing down here this time of night?" He was smiling as he turned back to the woman indicating that she should stay put as the interview was not over. Steve walked up and stood near the police car.

"Just out prowling around for our suspect. Have you seen

anything?" Gateson shook his head and turned back to the woman who was trying to use the conversation as an excuse to slink away.

"Hey, come back over here, you and I are not done talking." Steve put a hand on Gateson's arm.

"Let me talk to her for a minute." Steve walked the fifteen feet to where the woman stood and held out the photo of Calvin as he smiled at the sallow face under the red dyed bangs.

"You see this guy anywhere around here?" He lowered his voice. "I'll put in a good word with Gateson here, if you take a look." The woman crossed her arms and looked skeptically at Steve for a few seconds before she reluctantly leaned closer to view the picture. Steve held it up so that the streetlight illuminated it. The prostitute huffed.

"Yeah. Looks like the guy that roughed up my roommate two nights ago." Steve held the picture closer to her face.

"You sure?" She looked again and nodded.

"He wanted me at first, but there was something about him I didn't like, so he walked to the corner and picked up Debbie." Steve pulled out a pack of Pall Malls and held one out to her.

"What's your name, Miss?" She accepted the smoke and the light that followed, squinting at Steve as she straightened up.

"Sally." Steve smiled.

"Well, Sally, can you tell me where I can find Debbie?" Sally took a deep drag and turned her head and eyes toward Gateson as she exhaled. Steve nodded slightly.

"Just between you and me." She turned her torso so that her back was to Gateson who was ten feet away.

"She's usually on fifth between Stewart and Fremont. Spends time in the bar at the Mint too, if they're real busy and not watching." Steve nodded and spoke quietly.

"What does she look like?"

"Shorter than me, round face, black hair. She's wearing a green dress tonight." Steve tossed his cigarette on the ground and stubbed it out with the toe of his shoe.

"Wait here." Steve walked over to where Gateson was leaning on the car and talking on the radio. He paused when Steve approached the car.

"Cut her some slack tonight?" Steve jerked his head toward Sally who was busy watching a car cruise by. Gateson's brow furrowed.

"She come across with some information?" Steve nodded.

"Yeah, she gave me a pretty good lead." Gateson shrugged and stood upright.

"Get along Sally. I'm going to dinner and when I get back out here in an hour, I don't want to see you the rest of the night. Got it?" Sally tossed her head and moved quickly toward the corner, her high heels clicking on the concrete. When she had moved out of the arc of the light from the streetlamp, Steve turned back to Gateson.

"Thanks. You want to help me work on this? You know how cranky Tam can get when he gets hauled out of bed." Gateson looked down at the radio in his hand. He reached inside the cruiser and replaced the handset onto its' hook.

"Got two more calls that have stacked up just while you have been here. Shouldn't take long though, so why don't you go ahead. Where are you going to be?" Steve looked at his watch.

"Let's meet outside the Mint Hotel in an hour. If I don't see you, I'll figure you got caught up in something and I will roust Tam." Gateson nodded as he circled around the front of the car.

"Be careful. All the crazies are out tonight." Steve smiled and waved and watched as the police car moved quickly to the corner and disappeared in the same direction that Sally had taken. Steve turned left at the first corner he came to and then turned right onto fifth, crossing Fremont two blocks later. As soon as the bright neon of the downtown casinos faded in his rearview, he slowed and began to methodically check every car and pedestrian on the two block section between Fremont and Stewart. He had just made a U-turn at Stewart and was heading back when he saw a short woman in a green dress step out onto the sidewalk from a rundown two story hotel. There were two men with her and the trio stopped to light cigarettes before they turned and walked toward downtown. Steve passed them and parked halfway down the next block. He could see the back of the Mint a hundred yards away. He locked the Jeep and began walking back toward the group. He stopped on the corner and watched as they came to the corner opposite and began to cross toward Steve. When they were twenty feet away, Steve waved expansively and called out to the young woman.

"Debbie. How are you?" The trio stopped still in the street for a few seconds, before one of the men motioned to the others to stay where they were before he turned and took two steps toward Steve. The man was not much taller than 5'6' and pudgy. He wore a light brown fedora with a green hatband and an off-white linen suit that was one size too small. He pointed at the private detective.

"Who are the hell are you? You need something, you talk to me." Steve's brow furrowed and his face darkened.

"I wasn't talking to you and I need to talk with the lady here without your two cents." Steve took two steps to the edge of the curb, but didn't step into the street. The man stepped toward Steve menacingly and puffed up his chest. Steve looked impassively into the man's bloodshot eyes as he shot his left fist into the soft flesh just above the man's belt. As the man's stale breath blew from his lungs, Steve chopped a quick right down onto an exposed cheekbone as the man began to bend over from the first blow. He crumpled into the street, his fedora rolling to the curb. Steve stepped around him and looked hard at the second man as he walked toward the couple still standing in the middle of the street. The man, a Caucasian in his mid-fifties turned and ran, not looking back until he was a half block away. Steve watched him until he disappeared around the corner before he turned to the woman who was looking at the unconscious man lying on his back, his arms stretched out. Steve pulled out a pack of cigarettes and offered one as he jerked his head toward the prostrate man.

"He your boyfriend?" The woman took the cigarette and sneered.

"You know what he is, and you just got me into a whole lot of trouble, mister. And how do you know my name? I have never seen you before, I would've remembered." She reached across and took Steve's hand in hers, pulling the hand and the cigarette it was holding up to her face and lighting the one that dangled carelessly from her lips. Steve shrugged and looked down at the pimp.

"He's likely to be out for a while. Let me buy you a drink at the Mint." He pointed over his shoulder toward Fremont Street. Debbie twisted around and looked past Steve at the body in the street. She looked back and shrugged.

"Why not?" She walked by Steve and stepped up on the curb. "Just don't be surprised if they kick us both out of there." Steve caught up with her and chuckled.

"Don't worry, Debbie, they won't kick us out."

Ten minutes later they were ensconced in a booth at the back of the large bar. Steve tossed a new pack of cigarettes on the table between them.

"Help yourself. You want to eat something?" Even in the dim light of the bar, he could see the dark needle marks and the long red streaks on both of her arms. She picked up the pack of cigarettes and shook her head. Steve shrugged.

"Suit yourself." He waited until she had lit one of the cigarettes, watching while the rest of the pack disappeared into her purse. The cocktail waitress put down a scotch in front of Steve and two large vodkas in front of Debbie. She took the tumbler in her hand and poured the double down her throat, her eyes glassing over for several seconds before she wiped her mouth with the back of her hand and refocused. Steve cleared his throat.

"Here is the price of admission, Debbie. I need to know everything you can remember about the guy who beat you up two nights ago." She picked up the second tumbler and paused just before she drank half of its' contents.

"What guy?" Steve grimaced and tossed Calvin's picture on the table between them. At the same time, he signaled the waitress to bring Debbie another round.

"This guy." She glanced down with a pouty look on her face.

"Who told you about him." She repeated the drinking ritual after she spoke. Steve waited until she looked across the table at him.

"Sally. She was there when he picked you up. How about it?" She shrugged as she looked up at the waitress as two more vodka doubles were placed in front of her. She smiled at Steve.

"I am wasting valuable time sitting here with you." Steve reached into his back pocket for his wallet and pulled out three twenty dollar bills. He held them up.

"There're yours for something I can use." She drank her third drink, her eyes shining across at Steve before she spoke.

"Yeah, sure that's the guy. He was bad, but not as bad as some." Steve pulled out his notebook.

"He tell you his name?" She shook her head as she raised a glass to her lips. Steve tapped his notebook with his pencil and waited.

"Where did you take him? Your place or his?" She held up the empty glass toward Steve and waggled it as she spoke.

"His." Steve shook his head.

"Nothing doin' sister. You tell me what I want to know, you can buy your own." The pouty look returned as Steve pointed the pencil at her.

"Where did he take you?"

"Some house over on Stewart."

"Where on Stewart?"

"I don't remember. It was white, I think." Steve sat back in the booth and gazed at the woman for several seconds.

"Think you could pick it out again?" Debbie shrugged casually.

"Maybe." Steve held up the three bills.

"Take maybe ten minutes and I will add another one of these. You can be in here throwing those back in no time." He pointed at the empty glasses as Debbie grimaced and slid out of the booth and looked down at Steve.

"What if I can't remember?" Steve dropped several bills on the table and smiled.

"Oh, I think you will."

There were two white houses on the section of Stewart that Debbie said was where he had taken her. Steve pulled to the curb and looked over at Debbie.

"So, what was the set-up? He have the whole house to himself?" Debbie stared blankly through the windshield for several seconds as Steve repeated the question.

"No. We went down a side path and into a room at the back of the house. There was a garden or something like that back there." Steve nodded and swung the Jeep around toward Fremont Street. A few minutes later, Steve pulled up in front of the Mint Hotel. He held out the eighty bucks. Debbie took the bills from his hand and quickly stuffed them into her padded bra. She looked anxiously around for a few seconds before she opened the door and stepped onto the curb. Steve leaned over and looked up at the dyed black hair that was backlit by the bright yellow lights on the front of the casino.

"You want to ditch that pimp for good, call Tam Polhaus down at the police station, I will let him know that you might call." Debbie closed the door of the Jeep without replying. Steve watched as she moved into the crowd and was gone. He waited for ten minutes and was just about to leave when he saw a police cruiser pull up behind him. He adjusted his rearview mirror until Gateson's face came into view. He got out and walked back to the black and white. Gateson was just getting off the radio when Steve appeared at the window.

"Find out anything?" Steve nodded as he monitored the traffic that was moving by just inches away.

"She showed me where he may have taken her." Gateson nodded.

"You have been busy." He pointed at the Jeep. "You can't leave that here, pull around and park it in the lot in back. I will follow you." Steve jogged quickly back to the Jeep and five minutes later he was standing in the lot smoking a cigarette when Gateson called him over to the car. He pointed to the radio handset in his hand and lifted his finger from the send button.

"You want Tam or some other back-up?" Steve shook his head.

"No, it will take too long to get Tam out here, and too many people will queer the deal. Let's just you and I go." Gateson nodded and relayed the information back to the dispatcher. Steve let himself into the passenger door of the police cruiser and Gateson pulled out of the lot and turned right. He looked over at Steve.

"Let's come in from the Mesquite Street side, won't be as obvious."

Steve motioned for Gateson to pull over when they reached the block on Stewart. Steve pointed toward the two houses that were three buildings apart.

"That first one looks like a single family dwelling and there doesn't seem to be a walkway on the right side. Move down closer to the other white one." Gateson eased the cruiser forward twenty yards and stopped. There was a light on that illuminated the front porch and a little of the front yard. From where they sat, the two men could see the concrete pathway as it branched off from the sidewalk that came off the street and lead to the front door. The two men contemplated the scene silently for several moments. Steve cleared his throat.

"How do you want to play this? You want to call for backup?" Gateson shrugged.

"Naw, I don't think so. We should be able to suss the guy out if he is there. How would Tam do it?" Steve snorted.

"He would send me in there to smoke him out. If he doesn't see the uniform, he might not run, at least not right away. I am going up the alley and see whatever there is to see. You sit tight, I'll be back in ten minutes."

Steve walked to the corner and strolled across the street thirty yards in front of the cruiser. He moved quickly out of the cone of light that illuminated the street corner when he reached the other side, slowing his pace as he moved into the shadows and toward the dark alleyway. The white house was four houses in, and Steve walked slowly on the uneven surface of the deep ruts, stopping every ten steps or so, as he swiveled his head and listened. When he reached the house, he was facing a seven foot high fence of smooth boards with a gate in the middle. Steve pulled slowly on a small peg that hung off the gate on a thin cord. The gate latch released and the gate came open several inches. Steve took a deep breath and slipped the Colt .45 from its' holster. He held it up in front of his face as he pulled the wooden slats open just enough with his left hand to allow him to turn sideways and slip in. Steve took a quick step to his right as he pulled the gate closed silently behind him. He stood still and listened for any sounds that might come from the house. The twenty yards between himself and the house was pitch black, the white clap-boards a pale white in the darkness. Steve moved his foot to the left and felt around until his toe scraped across the edge of a cement walkway. He chose to walk beside it in the dirt to make as little noise as possible. Ten yards in front of him was a side building that looked to him like a workshop or large garden shed. Steve stepped carefully across the sidewalk and approached using the shed as cover from anyone that might be observing from the house. There was a window on the side where Steve now stood listening for any sounds, but it was covered in a curtain. Steve pressed his ear to the side of the rough wooden boards and listened. Hearing nothing, he took two long steps around the corner of the building, his hand finding the door knob as he came to a stop. The knob turned noiselessly in his hand and only one of the hinges squeaked slightly as he pushed the door half open. He held his pistol up in front of his face with two hands as he took a step inside the door and another one quickly to his right, extending the pistol and swinging it slowly back and forth. There was a skylight in one half of the peaked roof and though it was covered in dirt and dead leaves it still provided enough light for Steve to make out the workbench along the far wall under the window and a drill press covered with a piece of canvas in the middle of the floor.

"Freeze right there." The door had swung open and hit Steve on the back of his leg as he heard the command from over his left shoulder. Steve held up his hands, letting the pistol fall down in front of his hand, his index finger all the way through the trigger guard. The gruff voice spoke again.

"Turn around slow and no quick moves or I pull both these triggers." Steve turned around in a big circle, stepping backward two small steps at the same time. He looked down into the eyes of a thin man that Steve guessed to be near eighty years old. The double-barreled shotgun he held up with both hands was nearly as long as he was tall. He wore a thin coat over his pajama bottoms and his feet were clad with a pair of step-in slippers. He was standing just outside the open door and had both barrels pointed at Steve's face. In the dim light, the man's bald head bobbed just above the stock of the shotgun.

"Who the hell are you and what are you doing creeping around on my property?" Steve tried to force a casual smile as he spoke evenly.

"Are you the homeowner?" The barrels shook menacingly.

"I'm asking the questions here." Steve nodded his head quickly.

"My name is Steve Cannon and I'm looking for the guy who rents that back room there." The man backed up two steps and motioned for Steve to step out of the building. Steve turned to his right as he came through the doorway, keeping his hands high in an attempt to keep the gun from view. The man stepped closer and pressed the barrels against Steve's chest.

"I'm calling the cops." Steve gestured toward the front of the house with his left hand.

"Don't have to. There's one sitting in his car on the other side of the street." As the man began to turn in the direction that Steve indicated, his head jerked backwards, and the barrels fell heavily against Steve's chest. Two bright flashes had erupted from beside the house followed by the deafening sounds of a .45 being fired from an enclosed space. Steve heard the second bullet as it whizzed by his left ear and hit the fence ten yards behind him. He reached out and held the small man as he crumpled toward the ground. He took the shotgun from his hands and felt for a pulse as he scanned the area in front of him for signs of the attacker. There was a feeble but steady throb in the thin wrist and a large hole in the man's upper chest. Steve re-gripped his handgun and began to move quickly toward the sound of footsteps running away from him in the dark. As he crossed into the arc of light from the porchlight he met Gateson who was coming down the path.

"You see anyone run past here?" Gateson had his service revolver out and was looking up and down the street.

"No, but I heard somebody going that way, just as I got to this side of the street." Steve grabbed the officer's arm and pointed down the walkway that lead to the backyard.

"Homeowner shot and down back by the shed. You call an ambulance, I am going after the shooter." Steve pivoted as he finished speaking and jumped over the short hedge in front of him, sprinting diagonally across several lawns before he hit the street, his arms pumping him toward the only streetlight he could see two blocks ahead.

Three minutes later, Steve slipped the Colt .45 into its' holster as he ran toward the last block of buildings before Fremont Street. He had seen two quick flashes of the man he was pursuing. The last one was in the half light of a gas station and the denim jeans and red flannel shirt gave Steve hope that he could trail him into the teeming crowds that were now only a hundred yards away. His lungs were burning as he turned the corner onto Fremont Street coming out between the Four Queens and the Golden Nugget Casinos. He looked quickly both ways up and down the sidewalk, stepping up onto a newspaper machine to see over the heads of the milling crowds. He was just lowering himself to the pavement when he saw someone darting between the cars piled bumper to bumper in the traffic jam that never ended on the brightly lit street. Steve saw the red flannel shirt disappear into the front of the Fremont Hotel as he dodged between the honking cars and leapt the last four feet onto the sidewalk in front of the street front casino. As soon as he entered the casino he turned right and ran up two courses of red carpeted stairs, turning left at the top and crossing quickly to the railing of the small mezzanine. As he ascended the stairs he had asked himself where in the casino he would run if he wanted to escape detection. His eyes swung to the long lines of slot machines and several seconds later he spied Calvin Dawkins moving rapidly through the crowd, looking back nervously over his shoulder every few feet. Steve moved his gaze ahead of the escaping man and spied his destination. At the far end of the slot machine banks, a dimly lit hallway sat beside one of the casino bars. Steve knew it lead to the back parking lot that the hotel shared with Binions' Horseshoe club next door. Steve was on the move almost as soon as he saw Calvin's plan. He sprinted to the end of the mezzanine and down the two fights of steps on the far end of the casino, racing along the edge of the dice pits as he sought to dodge through the sparser crowds and make up ground on the longer route. He had just entered the corresponding hallway on his side of the casino when he found his way blocked by two burly security guards. Steve skidded to a stop on the slick carpet five yards in front of the nearest guard who stood blocking the door to the parking lot with his hands on his hips.

"Where are you going in such a big hurry?" Steve started walking toward the door as he replied.

"I'm chasing a murder suspect and instead of blocking the way, you can help me find him." The first guard was starting to reply when the second guard grabbed his arm and pointed at Steve.

"Which way was he heading?" Steve pointed to his left as he pushed by the guard and through the double doors.

"He was heading for the parking lot door on the other side by the slots. He is wearing a red flannel shirt and dungarees." The smaller second guard turned back toward the casino.

"I will go that way." Steve motioned to the remaining guard to follow him as he walked briskly into the dimly lit parking lot. He climbed up onto a low concrete wall and began to scan the section of the lot in front of the opposite door fifty yards away. The second guard popped out of the far door and waved at Steve as he began jogging down the long row of cars just in front of him. Steve jumped down and pointed to the right side of the lot.

"Start there and get down to the end of the row as quick as you can." Steve started at a fast trot down the middle of the row right in front of him. He swiveled his head and dropped onto his stomach two or three times to make sure that Dawkins had not gone to ground and was hiding under one of the cars.

Ten minutes later, the three men met and looked back at the hundred yards of cars between them and the back of the Fremont Hotel. The smaller guard spat on the ground.

"He could be a mile away by now." Steve nodded grimly.

"Let's split up and search on the way back in. Thanks for the effort." Steve chose a different row on the way back into the hotel and when he had exited empty-handed onto Fremont Street, he stopped just inside the casino that was open to the sidewalk and smoked a cigarette as he watched the crowds move by. He dropped the butt into a silver ashtray by the door and turned right and started up the street toward the Mint.

*

Steve saw Tam's Chevy Impala when he parked in the near deserted police parking lot near the doors of the justice center. Gateson and

Tam were conferring in the booking area when Steve came around the corner. Tam turned narrowed eyes toward the detective.

"Well, if it isn't the one man circus." Tam made a big show of looking around in the area behind Steve and the underground parking lot beyond before he turned back to the two men.

"Well? Where is he?" He held out his hands and gestured questioningly. Steve snorted and turned to Gateson.

"How's the old guy?" Gateson shrugged.

"Touch and go. The bullet took out part of his right lung, but the doc says he is a pretty tough old bird, gives him 50/50." Steve turned to Tam.

"Get as many guys as you can muster to flood downtown. Red flannel shirt, blue dungarees. Unless I miss my guess, he will not stray far from there and he now has no place to stay. I'm going to get something to eat and then I'm heading back there myself. You turn his room yet?" Tam smiled as he bent down to pick up a small paper cup filled with coffee.

"On my way. Join me when you are done with your R&R. Looks like he's graduated from hatchets to guns. Bad luck you didn't get him." Steve smiled back as he turned to leave.

"Good luck his aim was off the two inches it was, or me and the old guy would be sharing the same cold slab downstairs." He didn't wait for a reply, but walked back up the ramp and out into the gray dawn. The lights of the diner were just coming on as he strolled across the quiet street.

It was just after ten when Miss Perone buzzed him into the office. His body felt like lead as he dropped into the chair behind his desk. He pulled an envelope from his pocket and spread the contents out onto the green blotter. There were twenty Polaroid photos that Tam had taken of articles he had removed from Dawkins' room. Steve picked up one from the line and switched on his desk lamp. He studied the picture of the Paiute hatchet for several seconds before he dropped it back into the rest of the pile. He leaned the chair back and put his feet up on the edge of his desk. A few minutes later, light snoring was the only sound coming from the room.

*

There was no sound in the room as Steve stared down at the picture of the hatchet. It lay on the small coffee table between his chair and the one that Maggie Hannigan sat in. He looked back up at the fearful expression on the woman's face.

"Now's the time, Maggie." He reached into his coat pocket and took his time retrieving his notebook and pencil. Maggie stood up and walked the four steps to the window. She stood holding herself and watching the willows sway back and forth in the hot wind before she spoke, her voice low and muted.

"He came to a lecture I gave down at the library. He stayed behind to ask me some questions about the history of the Mormon church. Then he began showing up and sitting in my classes at NSU. After a few times we went for coffee." Her voice trailed off and she didn't speak for a few seconds. "I am such a fool. We were supposed to meet for lunch several weeks later. I came back here when he didn't show, and that is when I saw the hatchet was missing. It was only after the second murder that I suspected the truth." Steve sat motionless in the chair, his pencil poised above the blank page. For several minutes no one spoke. Steve tried to keep his voice emotionless when he finally spoke.

"Why didn't you say something? You had plenty of opportunity." Maggie turned from the window and their eyes locked for several seconds.

"I was afraid. The night the Sun article came out about the clues, he called me and made vile threats. He has called me twice since, always with the same threats." Steve wrote quickly in his notebook.

"When was the last time he called?"

"Three nights ago."

"What did he say?"

"I told you. He threatened that if he heard about me talking to anyone about the case, he would use the hatchet on me." She turned and started to walk toward the door, but instead collapsed into the chair beside her, holding her head in her hands and staring at the floor.

"Maggie. I need to ask you some more questions." When she didn't reply, he sighed and started anyway.

"Do you have a picture of him?" Maggie shook her head.

"Did you ever see where he lived?" Again, he received the same negative gesture.

"Ever see him with anyone?" This time there was a pause, and as Steve was about to ask the question again, she held her head up and looked at him, her features obscured by the bright backlighting of the window.

"Once, he asked me to drive him someplace. Before we got there, he changed his mind and convinced me to let him use my car. I waited at a Denny's while he went on alone. He came back a half hour later, but he wouldn't tell me where he'd been." Steve wrote quickly and looked up.

"Which Denny's?

"The one on Spring Mountain Road, just the other side of the interstate." Maggie walked past Steve and stopped in front of the cabinets.

"There is something else I need to show you, Mr. Cannon." Steve rose and stood beside his chair. Maggie stepped to one side and pointed at the cabinet. Steve took two steps forward and peered through the dusty glass. There was an empty space where the second hatchet had once rested. Steve looked questioningly at the older woman.

"Yesterday morning. I was out back weeding the garden. I must have left the front door open." Steve's eyes narrowed as he looked at his watch.

"Yesterday morning? Are you sure it didn't happen today?" She shook her head.

"It was in there yesterday morning when I got up. By ten thirty, it was gone." Steve looked quickly around the room.

"Where is your telephone?" Maggie pointed to the black instrument on top of one of the smaller cabinets. Steve picked up the receiver and rapidly dialed a number.

"Come on. Come on," he implored impatiently as the rings went unanswered. He was just about to hang up when he heard the receiver being lifted on the other end.

"Tam. Listen carefully. Get a unit over to Benjamin Stanwick's house and one to his office as soon as you can. If there is no answer, break in. I am out in the valley, I will try and meet you there." Steve hung up the phone and stared at Maggie. She backed up a step and shook her head imploringly.

"I'm sorry, Mr. Cannon." Steve scoffed as he headed for the door.

"You need a good lawyer, lady. As far as I can see, you are an accessory before as well as after the fact, and there at least three people that should be alive right now that aren't." He banged the screen door behind him as he ran to the Jeep.

The number of police cars parked haphazardly told Steve all he needed to know as he turned the corner onto the quiet street where Benjamin Stanwick lived. He parked two houses away and walked across the lawn to where Tam was speaking with a uniformed cop. Tam gestured to the cop when he saw Steve.

"Officer Lincoln, here, says he saw Stanwick go in at eight last night. He and his partner were across the street until they were relieved at midnight. Molini has tracked down the relief shift and they saw nothing unusual at all." Steve gestured toward the house. Tam nodded.

"Yep. 'Knights of Nauvoo'." Steve shook his head and before he could say anything, Tam nodded his head again.

"Sure. Go ahead. Samuels is cooling his heels at home some-where. Coroner is on his way. Tell me what you think." Steve turned and walked into the large split level house. He found Stanwick sprawled across the floor in his spacious study. A large pool of coagu-lated blood spread out across the white carpet from under the body. The words, 'Knights of Nauvoo' were scrawled across the wall behind the desk. Whomever had done it, had taken the time to remove a large picture before they left the bloody clue. When Steve had seen everything he needed to see, he walked down the long sidewalk and whistled to Tam when he saw the detective walking toward the cor-oners' car. Tam turned and retraced his steps back across the lawn, Steve met him halfway and looked around as he did so to make sure they were out of earshot of the gathering crowd of investigators. Steve gestured toward Tam's cigarette and used it to light one of his own when Tam handed it over. He took a deep puff and looked out of the corner of his eye at the round cheeks flushed from the heat. Tam held out his hands.

"What?" Steve's face held a small sardonic half smile.

"Notice some things in particular when you were in there?" Tam took a drag on his own smoke and nodded. Steve nodded back.

"Not our boy." Tam turned his head slightly and looked at the coroner and his assistants who were preparing to enter the house.

"Who then?" Steve waited until Tam had turned back to face him, before he spoke.

"My money's on Amis Kinsley and his little pack of rats." Tam's eyes narrowed and he took a step toward Steve, lowering his voice as the coroner passed him as he traversed the sidewalk that lead to the house.

"Say, what spooked you enough to call me in the first place?" Steve dropped the butt of the Pall Mall into the grass and stepped on it with his right foot.

"I was at Maggie Hannigan's when she came across with the fact that the second Paiute hatchet had been stolen from its' case yesterday. Only one reason someone would do that this late in the game. Somebody wants to make it look like Dawkins has expanded his list of victims." Tam shook his head.

"And you think Kinsley?" Steve nodded.

"Perfect cover and he has been threatening Stanwick for the past week. As far as I can tell, Stanwick is the only person who was privy to who Kinsley is and who he is working for. I tried to warn him early on that he was playing a dangerous game, but..." Steve's words trailed off as he looked back toward the house. Tam spoke with an impatient tone.

"Now what?" What else you got?" Steve stepped back and chuckled.

"Hold on, Tam, this is no time to get all flustered. We have to split our resources, because now we got two boogie men to worry about. Maggie came across with a piece of info that might be something, might not. You going back to your office?" Tam looked around and shrugged.

"Might as well. Nothing for me to do here." Steve was already walking toward the Jeep as he spoke.

"Meet you there in fifteen minutes."

Steve was tracing the large street map in Tam's office with his finger when the detective walked in and joined him.

"What you got?" Steve placed his finger on Spring Mountain Road just on the other side of the freeway.

"Dawkins took Maggie to the Denny's right here. He then took her car and was gone for thirty minutes, give or take." Steve stopped when he heard the sharp inhalation beside his left ear.

"What? Maggie and Dawkins? Since when?" Steve continued to trace several streets adjacent to the freeway.

"I'll fill you in on the way over there. I figure this area right here." He pointed to a cluster of small streets that held warehouses and small industrial businesses. Tam leaned closer and peered at the map.

"Rough area. A lot of chop shop activity and some real shady characters. Lot of ex-cons seem to live around there or so the probation guys tell me." Steve smiled.

"Perfect. Let's check it out." Steve saw something in Tam's face and he noted the detectives' sudden lack of enthusiasm.

The area they drove through as soon as they crossed under the interstate was one that most Las Vegans never saw. Full of dilapidated buildings, some of them deserted, small ramshackle houses were mixed in along with a few historic adobes. The open stretches of desert in between the buildings were littered with trash and cast-off furniture. Tam pointed to a long low building that was sun-bleached clapboard on top of an ancient foundation. The building had settled into the soft soil on one side and it listed to the north.

"Pull over here." Steve rolled the Jeep to the curb, cut the engine and waited for Tam to speak.

"There's a machine shop in there, or that is what the owner claims. More like a clearing house for stolen cars and other merchandise that's waiting for a fence. Guys' name is Calveras Esperanto. Did time in San Quentin and up north. Kind of the big wig in this neighborhood. If Dawkins has contacts here, this guy knows it. Nothing happens around here that he doesn't initiate or OK." Steve shrugged and started to open the car door.

"Let's go talk to him." Tam grabbed Steve's arm and stopped him.

"Can't. He's off limits. He got tired of being stopped and questioned, so he hired a big time lawyer, Herbert Milligan, out of LA. He's got the police commission and the chief, everybody, afraid to say boo to him. If anybody wants to talk to him, they have to go through the DA's office and there better be a good reason or they won't even bother calling his attorney." Steve settled back into the seat and frowned.

"He's a felon on parole, right? Any cop anywhere has the right to stop and search him and his property or did I hear wrong?" Tam shrugged his shoulders and cocked his head to one side as he looked over at the building.

"What can I tell you? Sometimes things don't go according to Hoyle." Steve shook his head and drummed his fingers on the steering wheel.

"Well, those rules don't apply to me." Tam shook his head.

"No dice. We have been made a least three times since we came through the underpass. And even if I am just waiting in the car, the result will be a whole lot of trouble for everybody." Tam smiled and leaned back into the seat.

"I just brought you over here as a point of interest." He winked at Steve. Steve nodded and started up the Jeep. He made a U-turn in the middle of the street and three minutes later they were on the other side of the interstate. Tam pointed to a patrol car that was parked in front of a 7-Eleven.

"Drop me off there. I will get a ride back to the station with those guys." Steve pulled into the small lot and parked next to the black and white car. Tam climbed out and then leaned over and looked back in at Steve.

"Give it a few hours at least. Tomorrow would be better, but you decide. Remember, you are on your own in there." Steve nodded and backed the Jeep out onto Spring Mountain Road. Four blocks later, he turned right onto the Strip and slowed down as the Casablanca came into view, three sets of spotlights were playing across the five story room tower in the twilight.

*

As soon as all the lights on the Strip had been ablaze for an hour, Steve left the Casablanca parking lot and retraced his steps of two hours before. Most of the streetlights were out as he parked in the same spot where Tam had pointed out the headquarters of Calveras Esperanto. Steve reached into his glove box and retrieved his snub-nosed hammerless .38 revolver. He slipped it into his waist-band and adjusted it until it sat comfortably in the small of his back. When he turned to open the drivers' door, he was startled to see two men standing twenty feet away in the middle of the street. Steve casually stepped out of the Jeep, and turned his back for a few seconds to lock the car. When he turned back around, the two men were now only ten feet away and they had separated themselves and were now fifteen apart from one another. Steve took two deliberate steps toward the nearest one, the one whose features he could see the clearest in the faint light from a streetlight on the corner. The man was shorter than Steve, but wiry, with muscular arms and a tattoo that ran from his wrist all the way to the hairline behind his ear. When he opened his mouth, the man's grin showed a gap where two front teeth once were.

"You lost mister?" Steve turned his head slightly to the left so that he could just make out the other man in his peripheral vision. He shrugged.

"No, I think I have the right place. Mr. Esperanto around?" The man who had spoken to him, chuckled and looked over at his companion, before he looked back at Steve.

"If'n he was, he would have no truck with a cop." Steve took another step forward and pointed at the man.

"I'm no cop, and if he wants to keep this little Shangri La of his in one piece, he would do well to meet with me." Steve's step forward had unnerved the man, and now he glanced over toward the figure looming just off Steve's left shoulder before he took a step backward. The man then pointed at Steve.

"You wait right here." He turned his head and spoke to the other man. "You watch him, make sure he doesn't pull anything." He backed away into the darkness as he finished speaking. Steve watched him go before he turned and walked the four steps back to the Jeep, keeping his watch dog in view as he did so. He leaned up against the car and pulled out a pack of Pall Malls. He sized up the man that was now was only ten feet away through the orange flare of the match.

This man was huge, easily three inches taller than Steve and looked to be a native American. His impassive black eyes looked back at Steve's with little interest. After the light from the match died away, Steve ignored him. Steve had finished his cigarette and was reaching for another when he heard the sound of footsteps approaching from the direction the first man had taken. This time, the figure appeared and stopped just inside the dim circle of light, his shaved head and the ruby earring in his ear catching the pale illumination. His face was rugged and craggy and Steve was forced to squint into the darkness to make out more of the figure. Just before the man spoke, Steve realized that he recognized the face from the newspapers. Several years back, Esperanto had been relieved of his position as the head of the biggest outlaw motorcycle gang in Nevada. He had been the victim of an informer among the membership and had gone to prison in northern Nevada for three years. Shortly after he was released, most of the gang scattered, leaving behind several mysteriously dead members. The voice Steve heard had a soft southern drawl.

"I hear somebody that's not a cop wants to talk with me." He spat on the ground and brought a small cigar that Steve hadn't noticed before to his lips. Steve leaned back against the Jeep and folded his arms.

"I'm a private detective, Mr. Esperanto, looking for a serial killer." The corners of the man's mouth turned down as he nodded.

"Serial killer? In this nice neighborhood?" He held out his arms to indicate the immediate surroundings as soft laughter from the first man floated out of the darkness behind him. Steve ignored the remark but used the opportunity to slip the photo of Dawkins out of his back pocket. He held it out to the Indian who was five feet away. The Indian looked over for the nod from his boss before he took three steps closer to Steve and took the picture from his hand. He then crossed over to Esperanto and held it up for him to see before Esperanto took it from his hand. He looked at Steve and held the picture up so that someone standing behind him could see it.

"Nobody we have ever seen, right?" There was a murmur of accord from the darkness. Esperanto let the picture fall from his hand to the ground before he shrugged at Steve.

"There you go, party over." He was turning to leave as Steve spoke, his voice hard and several decibels louder than normal.

"No, it's not, unless you want to see this whole place crawling with Feds when you wake up tomorrow." The man had stepped from the light, but now turned and stepped back in, his black eyes narrowed and focused on Steve's face.

"And just what would cause something like that to happen?" Steve sensed the anger that was boiling just below the surface.

"Because he killed two public officials and the FBI is hunting for him. He has had dealings with someone here and may be even hiding out here. Perhaps you don't know everything that goes on around here after all. You would be doing yourself a favor." Esperanto glared at Steve for a few seconds.

"How you figure that?" Steve took a deep breath.

"Helping to capture a major criminal like Dawkins could go a long ways in taking the heat off you and your confederates." Esperanto shrugged.

"Nobody can just walk in any time they choose as it stands now, why do I need to stick my neck out?"

"Because the Feds are a whole different kettle of fish, Calveras. They don't care what little arrangement you have with local law enforcement, they will shut you and all your operations down." Steve walked slowly to within three feet of the criminal and picked up the photo of Dawkins. He put it into his coat pocket and brought out one of his cards with the same hand. He held it out to Esperanto. For a few seconds the two men looked at each other across the small distance. Esperanto's face broke into a half grin as he took the card from Steve's hand.

"Never hurts to check. If I find out anything, I'll let you know." Steve's expression was deadpan as he replied.

"Make it soon." He spoke to the man's back as he disappeared into the night. When he turned, the big Indian was also gone. The sweep of the headlights revealed only empty streets as Steve made the same U-turn and rolled slowly toward the interstate.

JULY 16

STEVE HAD BEEN in his office for three hours when Miss Perone used her key to let herself in the door just before nine o'clock. She dropped her things quickly onto her desk when she saw that all the lights were on and that Steve's door was open. She crossed through the hallway and rapped softly on the doorframe. Steve looked up from his work and smiled.

"Miss Perone, it is good to see you. How are you this morning?" Steffi Perone crossed over to the desk and sat in the chair and looked down at Steve's desk.

"I am fine this morning, Mr. Cannon, when did you get here?" Steve looked at his watch.

"A little after six, Miss Perone, there was a lot I wanted to catch up on. I want to be prepared when I meet with Mr. Gold this morning." Miss Perone nodded gravely.

"Certainly, Mr. Cannon, is there anything I can do to help you? Have you had coffee yet?" Steve smiled and leaned back into the chair stretching his arms forward and stifling a yawn.

"I made a pot a couple of hours ago and there are probably one or two cups left. I think I have everything I need, but in a little while I will need to go over some things with you to make sure I haven't overlooked something." Miss Perone nodded as she stood to leave.

"Of course, Mr. Cannon, and if you have a few minutes, perhaps we could go over some of the phone messages from the last two days." Steve nodded just before she turned toward the door. When she was gone, he picked up Thursday's edition of the Sun paper and settled in to read Rita Malone's article for the second time. Rita reiterated parts of the first article but went into greater depth when she described the response of the church to the murders and included several quotes from many of the church officials in response to her probing questions. The unmistakable impression that one took away from the articles was that the church was actively impeding the investigations and did not have an adequate explanation for the presence of Amis Kingsley and his large contingent of followers. Next to the article was a long sidebar detailing the Mountain Meadows Massacre and the manner in which the churches' position on the event had changed over the years. Steve guessed that today or tomorrow there would be a third part after the murder of Benjamin Stanwick, although the police had made no official statement that they considered it to be another in the long line of 'Mormon Murders'. Steve looked at his watch, and pressed down the lever on his intercom.

"Miss Perone, I have to leave now to meet with Mr. Gold. I should be back by ten thirty."

Bernie was sitting at one of the green felt covered gaming tables in the large room just off his office, when Steve knocked on the door. He was carrying a thick file folder that held most of the written material he had collected since the hotel construction had begun. He sat down in a chair that was in front of a place setting that was already held a cup and saucer. Bernie poured coffee into the cup as he greeted him.

"Right on time, Steve, how you feeling this morning? You must have gone through the ringer in the last few days, with another murder and all that." Steve smiled and waved his hand casually.

"Just more of the same, Bernie, I'm pretty much used to it by now, but let's talk about the grand opening. I have had two conversations in the last day and a half with Jack Cathay and we have double-checked everything on the casino side, including the extra security that will start to come on shift at noon today. Jack got Tommy Carmino to lend us five of his top guys, so along with Jack, any con artists won't have a chance. We figure the big crush will hit around sundown tomorrow, so we have it scheduled that three quarters of our security guys will be on the clock then." Bernie nodded as he shifted a few papers from one pile to another. He looked up as he sat back in his chair.

"Thanks for the update. Tommy called me bright and early this morning to make sure that I know that his guys are only for the weekend and not to be stolen away." Both men chuckled as Bernie continued. "The only big change you need to be aware of is the parade. Pete Fountain and several groups of Dixieland musicians are going to start at the Tropicana at eleven. That whole New Orleans Mardi Gras parade party will wind back and forth up the Strip and pick up the governors' limo just before they get to our parking lot. My thought was that maybe we should mix in some of the security people to make sure everything goes smoothly, what do you think?" Steve nodded as he sipped on his coffee.

"I think that is a good idea. I'll get with Jack and we can recruit maybe ten guys that would rather be outside than be cooped up their whole shift. Give them all tambourines and let them loose." Bernie smiled as he lifted his coffee cup in mock salute.

"That should work, swell. The cages have been running smoothly and everybody seems to know what their jobs are, thanks to Jack and all those hours that were put in with the dealers and the pit bosses. I can't think of anything else on your side. My only real problem is juggling some of the entertainers who all want to be part of the opening. I am sure that Remy filled you in on that. I just need to smooth a few ruffled feathers and unless something else rears its' ugly head, I think we are on track. Let's go down and take a last tour of the casino and get some breakfast." Steve nodded as they both rose from the table.

It was nearly eleven when Miss Perone buzzed Steve through the door. Steve had just sat down at his desk when Steffi Perone's voice came over the intercom.

"Yes, Miss Perone?"

"There is a man on the line that insists on talking with you, but won't give me his name. He says he is your friend from Shangri La." Steve snorted and pressed down the lever.

"That's Ok, Miss Perone, I will take the call." The phone buzzed once and Steve picked up the receiver.

"Mr. Esperanto, I presume?"

"Yeah, it is, but better no names, you never know who is listening."

"I assume you didn't call to see if I got home all right last night." There was a snort on the other end.

"I checked like I said I would. Turns out you were right, one of the guys here has been doing car business with this Dawkins character and I got it from another source that he is living around here too, so I think we may be able to do some business along those lines." Steve pulled out his notebook and a pencil from his desk drawer.

"I'm listening."

"Thing is, Cannon, I don't want no Fed beef, so you are going to have produce one of them in the flesh or the deals' off."

"An FBI agent work?"

"Yeah, Cannon, that's a start, but we gotta do this my way and the way I say, got it?"

"As I said before, I'm still listening."

"OK, here is how it goes down. We have to meet somewhere out of the way, I can't be seen with the heat. You have to bring this FBI guy or someone higher than that who can give me assurances that if I turn over this guy, I get peace and quiet and no Fed interference. Think you can swing that?"

"Tell me when and where, we will be there."

"You know that little dirt road that winds off the Strip and goes through the old El Rancho property?"

"Yeah, I do."

"Meet me behind the burned out wind mill at one o'clock." Steve looked at his watch.

"I'll be there."

"One more thing, Cannon. Just you and the FBI agent and make sure he brings his badge," Steve shook his head as the line went dead. He pushed down the buttons on the phone and dialed Tam's number.

"Tam, is Molini around?"

"Yeah, do me a favor. Tell him to stay put until I get there, and tell him to eat something now because we have an errand to run." Steve quickly filled in Miss Perone on his way out of the door. Twenty minutes later he was locking the car in the parking lot of the Police Station. He stepped into the coolness of the shadow of the large building and walked through the revolving door into the rotunda. Tam was standing by the vending machines talking to one of the dispatchers. When he saw Steve, he pointed across the large space toward the far doors.

"Molini is in the offices down that hall." Steve fell in behind the detective as they pushed through two heavy wooden swinging doors and entered the Federal side of the building. They found Agent Molini sitting with Agent Brady and Jim Larson in one of the open conference rooms. They stopped their conversation as the two men joined them. Steve smiled at Jim Larson who was in the process of putting several papers into his briefcase and preparing to leave.

"You might want to stick around here for a while, Jim. I would like your opinion on something." Jim shrugged and sat back down. Steve walked to the front of the room and put a foot up on one of the metal folding chairs. He looked out at the four men as he outlined the events of the morning and the previous evening. When he was done, he straightened up and waited for a reaction. Agent Brady was the first to speak.

"Never heard of the arrangement you are talking about." He turned to Jim Larsen, who shrugged and shook his head. Steve looked over at Tam who cleared his throat.

"That's because it's informal. The city attorney and the commissioners got tired of the constant claims of harassment and that was the accommodation they came to." Brady looked over at Larsen.

"That has to be one of the most cock-eyed things I have ever heard." He then turned back to Steve.

"And you're proposing that we agree to the same thing just on the off chance we catch this guy?" Steve chuckled and put his hand in his pockets.

"No, I'm suggesting we let Mr. Esperanto think we are agreeing to the same arrangement. When was the last time either of you went in there to question anyone or serve a warrant?" The two FBI agents looked at each other blankly.

"See what I mean? What have we got to lose? He gets an agreement with an expiration date and we get our best chance to corner Dawkins." The four other men in the room looked at each other, before Jim Larsen spoke up.

"I think it is worth a shot. I think the best way to get this done is for Steve and Agent Molini and myself to make this meeting and convince this Mr. Esperanto to cooperate." He looked at each head nod in turn before he turned to Steve.

"Sound alright to you?" Steve nodded.

"He might take some convincing, but I have an idea about how we can skin this cat." He looked at his watch.

"It's twelve thirty now, we should get going." He tagged Tam on the arm as the other men filed out of the office.

"I plan on acting on whatever we find out with Molini right away. You OK with that?"

"Yeah, under the circumstances, I think that is best. I got a meeting in an hour with the chief and he wants to divert most of my manpower to running down Amis Kinsley before the public gets wind that another group of murderers is on the loose."

"I guess you have to do what you have to do, Tam. I can't be concerned with Amis right now, but keep me posted. I will be busy at the Casablanca all day tomorrow with the opening, so find me there if you need me." The two men parted in the same spot they had met a half hour earlier. Steve followed Larsen and Molini out to the plaza where Jim pointed to his car several yards away.

"We can take my car, if you like." Steve shook his head.

"Better if we take the Jeep. He knows my car and will be a little more comfortable." Without waiting for a reply, he led them toward his parking space. As they drove down Las Vegas Boulevard toward the Strip, Steve went over as many details as he could remember about the man they were about to meet.

*

Calveras Esperanto was standing alone beside his truck when Steve came slowly around the corner. He had picked his way through what was left of the El Rancho after the suspicious fire four years before. Now as he slowed to a stop twenty yards away from the ex-convict, he suddenly felt he was closer to Dawkins then he had at any time since he sat in his mother's front parlor in Manti.

Calveras watched with a stone face as the three men approached him, stopping ten feet away. He leaned back on the red Chevy pick-up and smiled cynically at the three men. When Steve was closer, he saw that there was an older man sitting in the passenger seat. Calveras gestured with a nod of his head.

"Well, Cannon, who do we have here?" Steve indicated the men beside him with a casual wave of his hand.

"FBI Agent Molini and Assistant District Attorney, Jim Larsen." Esperanto looked at both men in turn.

"Cannon, here, fill you in on what I need?" Jim Larsen stepped forward two steps and put his hands in his pockets and began to talk in an unhurried manner.

"Mr. Cannon was very specific where your demands are concerned, Mr. Esperanto, but I fear you may have gotten a little ahead of yourself here." Esperantos' face darkened and his lips curled into a sneer. He squinted at Steve.

"I thought I was clear how this was going to go down." Steve smiled thinly and shrugged.

"You wanted someone here that can provide the kind of assurance you want." Steve pointed at Jim's back. "Well, here he is." Before Esperanto could reply, Jim Larsen cut in.

"You have already indicated that you have knowledge of an important case that involves law enforcement at the highest level. So, the way I see it, Mr. Esperanto, there is no reason why I can't order Agent Molini here to arrest you right now as a material witness, and then you can get a lawyer and we will get warrants and we will see what we will see. I would like to avoid that turn of events, myself." Larsen stopped talking and looked directly at the criminal. Esperanto was twisting a braided leather cord in his hands. He looked menacingly at Steve.

"You double crosser. You better hope our paths don't cross again." Larsen held up his hand before Steve could reply.

"Threats in front of a Federal officer is not going to help your situation, Mr. Esperanto, so why don't we see if we can put together a deal that lets everybody go home happy." Esperanto's eyes reluctantly slid off Steve's face as he turned toward the assistant DA.

"I'm listening." Jim smiled broadly.

"Very simple, Mr. Esperanto. You give us all the information you have gathered on the whereabouts and the activities of Calvin Dawkins, and I give you my word that we will not pursue any criminal activity we may uncover in our investigations." There was a pause of several minutes as Calveras Esperanto leaned forward and spoke in low Spanish to the man in the truck. In response to one of Esperantos' questions, the man leaned forward and fastened his gray eyes on Larsen, before he sat back and nodded his head. A few seconds later, Esperanto stepped off the running board and turned back to Larsen and Steve.

"Ok, you got a deal, but on one condition. No one in there is to know where this information came from. If I can have that assurance, we have a deal." Jim turned and looked at Steve and Agent Molini before he turned back to Esperanto and held out his hand.

"Deal."

Esperanto motioned them over to the hood of the truck and spread a home drawn map out onto the hot metal.

"This is the building that he is hiding in. The best way in is through this little alley, but it is hidden and if you go that way, everyone will know that someone has squealed. So, go through the machine shops in front." He looked at his watch. "No one will be around working until after dark, so it would be better in the day time." Steve stepped forward and looked at the map, his brow furrowed as he stared into the black eyes two feet away.

"You see him yourself?" Esperanto shook his head slowly.

"No. But he is there. Hasn't moved since yesterday. He is trying to convince the guy who owns the shop to buy one last car so he can get away to some other place." Steve stepped back and looked at Jim.

"I think we move now. I will take us back to the Strip. Molini can call for a black and white to come pick you up. Molini and I will take my car." He turned toward Esperanto. "How much time you need to cover yourself?" Esperanto shook his head.

"Everyone thinks I have gone to LA for the weekend to see my mother, which I just might do, that way I won't have to deal with all the commotion." Steve snorted and turned to Molini.

"Gentlemen, I think we go." Steve's two companions answered by moving quickly to the Jeep and clamoring in. Steve turned to Jim Larsen as he waited for the dust cloud to settle as Esperanto slid his truck in a wide arc back toward the Strip.

"You think he is on the up and up?" Jim looked out the window and shook his head.

"I don't have a good feel for it, what do you think?" Steve put the Jeep in low and eased it down the rutted trail.

"I don't see an angle where it would be in his best interest to lie. I think he wants to keep a low profile and someone harboring a guy like Dawkins is too much heat. I got that feeling when I met with him last night. He's not stupid enough to send an FBI agent into a set-up." Steve glanced in the rear view mirror when Molini snorted at the last part of his comment, just as he pulled into a dusty strip mall off the Strip. Molini pointed to a phone booth and Steve pulled the Jeep up beside it. Jim and Steve waited while the FBI agent called the station. He returned quickly and pointed down the street.

"There is a black and white two blocks away. Should be here in a couple minutes." Jim Larsen got out of the front seat and looked back in at Steve.

"Go ahead. I will wait here for the squad car. Good hunting." Steve nodded as Molini replaced Jim in the front seat. As they pulled back onto the street and headed for Spring Mountain Road, Steve tapped Molini on the arm.

"What are you carrying?" Molini frowned at the question and looked out the side window as a large patch of empty desert went by the window.

"Short barrel .357 magnum." Steve smiled as he turned onto the road and headed for the freeway underpass.

"That FBI issue, Agent Molini? I thought they modernized and were all carrying semi-autos by now." Molini shrugged.

"Some do, I'm sure. Never trusted them myself. Give me a good old fashioned wheel gun when the chips are down." Steve slowed and pointed to a row of warehouses directly in front of them. He pulled to the curb and held out the map that Esperanto had drawn. He pointed to one of the streets on the edge of the paper.

"That's where we are right now. The little village of criminals starts there." He pointed out the window to the warehouses. His finger traced a circuitous route to the building that held an 'X' on the map and was on Pioneer Road. "I say we park here." He tapped a small street a half block away. "There were a lot of cars that were being worked on parked along this curb when I was here last. The Jeep may look too new, but it is our best bet." He handed the map to Molini who slipped it inside his suit coat. Steve pulled away from the curb and drove slowly through the streets in an attempt to garner as little attention as possible. When they reached the area Steve had selected, they picked a space between two cars that were older models but did not appear abandoned. Steve locked the Jeep and looked across at Molini.

"Whoever sees us from here on in, will make us quick, so I suggest we move fast." Molini nodded as they walked across a dirt driveway and turned into a narrow path that wound between the buildings. After a few feet, they crossed an overgrown yard that housed several old wrecked cars and turned up the alleyway that Esperanto had mentioned. Steve stopped and nodded at the sagging wooden building in front of them. The rusty metal door had a chain wrapped around the handle, but did not appear to be locked. Molini turned his back toward the building and kept an eye on the street while Steve carefully unwound the chain, letting it drop noiselessly onto the ground. He gave the sliding door a tentative shove and with just a few squeaks it opened far enough to allow Steve to enter, though Steve had to slide it a little further on the track to give Molini enough room to squeeze into the dark interior that smelled of oil and solvent. They paused for a few moments to let their eyes grow accustomed to the small amount of light that came in through two small grimy windows. They found themselves in a series of interconnected rooms, some large spaces, other smaller, but all were filled with cars and car parts. There was one room that was set up to be a paint booth and another that held several engines swinging on hoists. They took turns covering each other as they moved from the protection of one wall toward another. After a few minutes they came to a large room that had six open doorways leading to rooms in several different directions. Molini leaned against a low workbench and pointed across the sixty foot expanse.

"I'll take the rooms that lead out that way, you take these three here." Steve peered around him at the dark openings. He looked at his watch.

"We meet back here in five minutes exactly." He held the watch face up so that Molini could compare the time with his. Molini nodded and moved cautiously across the oil stained floor toward the far wall. When he reached it, he waved at Steve and disappeared through the first door. Steve turned and holding his .45 in front of him stepped through the door at an angle, hugging the wall in the pitch black space. He held his breath for a few seconds and listened. Hearing nothing, he made his way slowly to the far wall and another door beyond. Just before he reached his destination, his shin collided with a hard object. He reached down and felt for the obstruction and realized his leg had struck the edge of a bed. He dropped down low and squinted his eyes in an attempt to see the rest of the details of the room. It was then that he realized there was a different smell in this room, and a few seconds later he knew what it was. Honed by months in the jungle during World War II, he recognized the faint odor that lingered in the space where a human had just been. He turned his attention to the opening four feet away that led to another room. From where he knelt, all he knew about it was that from the ambient light that turned the opening gray instead of black, it must have a window. He covered the small distance as quietly as he could. He leaned against the edge of the doorway and peered in. At first, it looked like all the other rooms he had just gone through, except there was a little more light and he could make out several partial car bodies that looked like they had been cut into pieces with some sort of torch. There was something else there, and as Steve held his breath, he heard it. The shallow breathing of another human being. He dropped quietly to the floor and looked under the car bodies but could see nothing. He knew he had to make a decision in the next few seconds or risk Molini coming into the room unawares. Six feet away he saw an old refrigerator against the wall. Almost instinctively, he crept forward rapidly and pushed his back up against the cool refuge of the white metal. As he moved, he thought he heard a sound from the other end of the room. He held the gun up next to his face. He took a deep breath.

"Give it up, Dawkins, it is all over." There was no answer for several seconds. When the voice came, it sounded deep and anguished to Steve's ears.

"Who are you?" Steve saw his white knuckles out of the corner of his eye and deliberately loosened his grip on the pistol.

"My name is Steve Cannon and I have been tracking you for almost three weeks now. There is nothing left to prove, so let's do this quietly." The voice scoffed.

"Oh there is plenty left to prove, Cannon. One of the scum that killed my brother is still alive and the church hasn't even begun to pay for what they do." Steve judged the voice to be coming from a distance of about fifteen feet. He took a deep breath and holding the pistol in front of him at eye level, he swung his body around the edge of the refrigerator. Even in the low light, he could see Calvin Dawkins standing with his back against the wall in the far corner of the room. The white dot on the back of Steve's front sight rested squarely between the black, anger-filled eyes. Steve took in the details of the scene quickly. Dawkins was dressed in the same clothes from the night before and was holding something waist high in front of him. When Steve was able to glance down, he saw it was a large hunting knife. He took a step forward, peering around the pistol sight at the serial killer. For a few seconds the two antagonists stared into each other's eyes. Dawkins' face held a small smile. Steve spread his legs a little and shifted his weight to his good leg. When he spoke, his voice was low and the pace of his speech unhurried.

"I was in Manti, last week, Calvin. I spent some time with your mother. She told me how bad it was for you, and she told me all about the things that happened in Parowan." At first, the only answer he received was the point of the knife being extended several more inches toward him. Dawkins' lips curled into a sneer.

"You wasted your time. None of that matters anymore. I took care of the past." He laughed softly to himself. "Know what? None of those devils even knew why they were dying. I made Dame suffer the most. He was always the ringleader, always the guy calling the shots. Well, good Mormon boy that he was, I don't think he is calling the shots where he is now, do you?" Steve replied quickly to cover any noise when he saw Molini emerge from the darkness, moving very slowly toward the opening five feet left of where Dawkins was waving the knife toward Steve.

"Time to give yourself up, Dawkins. You're lucky. They will probably send you back to the same hospital they let you out of." Molini was just on the other side of the door, but couldn't see Dawkins from his angle inside the adjoining room. Steve wanted to signal Molini to stay where he was, but he was so close to Dawkins, he could only look at Molini out of the corner of his eye. Dawkins made a menacing gesture toward Steve with the knife.

"Not going back there. If you're going to shoot me, you better do it now." Steve lowered the gun slowly and carefully slipped it back into the holster.

"No, Calvin, I am not going to shoot you. But I am going to have to take that knife away from you." Steve crouched into a fighters' stance and took two steps to his left, his senses alert to any forward movement that Dawkins might make. Dawkins countered Steve's move by taking a step to his left, blocking Steve's view of Molini. Steve was making preparations to rush the killer, when Molini began moving through the opening. Dawkins spun around at the small noise Molini made when his arm scraped against the concrete door sill. Dawkins took in the scene in an instant and wheeling back around he looked Steve in the eyes as he plunged the knife into his own throat. Steve and Molini reached the dying man at the same time, Steve pressing his hand over the jagged wound as they lowered him to the floor. Molini stripped off his jacket and Steve pressed even harder in a vain attempt to staunch the bleeding. He looked up at Molini.

"Get out of here and find a phone. Get an ambulance. I'll do what I can here." Molini quickly left the room through the same door that Steve had entered. Steve pushed with his legs and bore down as hard as he could on the wadded-up coat. As he had many times in the war, he stared into the bloodshot eyes and watched as the light in them grew dim and then was gone. He sat back on his haunches and covered Calvin Dawkins face with Molini's blood stained light blue suit coat.

*

Tam Polhaus sighed and pushed the piece of paper across the desk toward Steve. He watched as Steve scrawled his name across the bottom before he took it back from the private detective and frowned at the document skeptically.

"You know this better gibe pretty closely to Molini's statement, right?" Steve shrugged and pulled a new pack of Pall Malls from inside his coat pocket. He took his time unwrapping the pack and lighting one of the cigarettes before he spoke.

"Now why would you think for even one minute that it wouldn't." Tam snorted as he read over the statement one more time.

"Because I've been doing this for a while, and sensationalized cases like this one have all the powers-to-be up in arms, so they get looked at like a three dollar bill. Nobody is going to be happy with this outcome, kinda anticlimactic, don't you think?" Steve smiled thinly at his friend.

"Could'a shot him between the eyes while he was holding a knife, would that have made you happier?" Tam ignored the attempt at humor and picked up the phone, asking for Agent Brady when he was connected. While he waited for the senior FBI agent to come to the phone he regarded Steve with a cool expression.

"Don't forget your friend Samuels. He may have stepped in it himself, but he has plenty of ears he can whisper into on the police commission and in the DA's office." Steve sat back in the chair and shook his head disgustedly.

"Well, unfortunately for him, they will have to crucify a federal agent as well. Not my blood all over Molini's jacket." Tam held up his hand as Brady's voice crackled over the phone. He listened for a few seconds before he replied.

"Yeah, I got his statement right here. You want me to send it along with him?" Tam nodded and hung up. He folded his hands in front of him on the desk and cocked his head toward the door.

"Brady's waiting to interview you and it sounds like Jim Larsen will be there as well." Steve stood up and snubbed out his cigarette in Tam's small tray that was piled high with butts. He was halfway to the door when Tam called him back and handed him the statement.

"They're in room 201, the other side of the rotunda. Good luck." Steve snorted to himself as he swung the door closed behind him and headed toward the wide round entryway.

An hour and a half later, he pushed through the revolving door into the warm, windy late afternoon. He was almost to his car when he saw the red Cadillac bearing down on him. Steve stopped and watched as the car came on as if it were going to hit him, swerving at the last minute and screeching to a stop right beside him. Tommy Carmino's grinning countenance beamed up at him from the bright white leather upholstery.

"Hey, Caped Crusader. How about I buy you a drink?" Steve hesitated for a few seconds, shrugged, opened the wide heavy door and sank down into the soft seat. The radio was playing a Mantovani tune. As soon as the door thudded shut, Tommy rocketed the car to the entrance of the lot and squealed the tires around the sharp corner. When the car straightened out, it headed toward Fremont Street.

Tommy and Steve had taken barely ten steps inside the Mint casino before they were approached by two men. The smaller of the two stepped in front of Tommy. He lips held a tight smile, but his eyes were earnestly fastened onto Tommy's face.

"Tommy. How long you going to be here? If you stay more than twenty minutes, I gotta go tell the boss, and he ain't gonna like having to come down here." Tommy snorted and continued toward the long bar on the far side of the casino.

"Well, Mitchell, why don't you go somewhere way out of my sight and keep your eyes on your watch?" Steve stepped around Mitchell and continued with Tommy to the bar. Tommy stepped up and snapped his fingers at the bar supervisor who was standing at the end of the bar watching the forty or so patrons filling the stools in front of him. When the supervisor made eye contact, Tommy held up his hands in a questioning gesture.

"Private booth." The older man nodded and gestured for Tommy and Steve to follow him. He moved to the end of the bar and pointed to a swinging door.

"Doris will take care of you." Steve nodded at the man as Tommy swept by and was already pointing out which booth he wanted when Steve cleared the swinging door. Doris was dressed in a black one piece uniform that reminded Steve of a playboy bunny outfit. He nodded at her after Tommy ordered a scotch on the rocks.

"The same, only neat." He settled back into the soft comfortable chair and watched as Tommy pulled out two Cuban cigars, handing one to Steve.

"I would throw you a little party, Slick, but this will have to do on such short notice." Steve chuckled ironically and borrowed Tommy's clipper to snip the end before he danced the flame from his zippo in front of the aromatic cigar. Doris returned quickly with the drinks and Tommy sent her off with a hundred dollar bill and a wink. The two men savored the first sips of their drink.

"Well, Slick, you made quite a name for yourself, today. All the kings' horses and all the kings' men, but Steve Cannon comes through and shows 'em all how's it done." Steve frowned toward his companion.

"What do you care, Tommy? Nothing that happens to the normal people in this town ever seems to affect you." Tommy smiled benevolently over his glass.

"Don't get all riled up, Slick, I was just joking. But I'm serious, this town owes you a debt of gratitude."

"Didn't know you cared so much, Tommy." Tommy took a large sip of the scotch, holding it in his mouth for a moment before he swallowed and spoke.

"Don't a whole lot, Slick, what's a few less Mormons in a town crawling with them? From where I sit, they got a sloppy organization and deserve their troubles." Steve's eyes narrowed.

"Speaking of that, Tommy, how about using your connections to beat the bushes and see if you can come up with the whereabouts of their little wrecking crew?" Tommy pursed his lips and looked down at his cigar as he rolled it gently between his fingers.

"That an official request, Slick, or just an idle comment?" Steve shrugged.

"Would be doing your civic duty, Tommy, that's all. Why should I have all the fun." Tommy leaned forward.

"I think you are forgetting that my head tracker works with you, now." Steve persisted.

"Oh, I'm sure you have replaced him. You need to keep tabs on too many people and their comings and goings, but if you don't want to, don't." Steve finished the last finger of scotch in his glass and signaled to Doris to bring another. Tommy held up his hand.

"Not that I don't want to, Slick. I just don't see the need. The cops are pretending the bishop got it from Dawkins, who, thanks to you, is now conveniently deceased, so what's the problem? That little band of Indians will probably slither away soon, if they aren't gone already." Steve made a downward gesture with his mouth.

"Maybe, Tommy, maybe not." He watched as Doris put another round on the table and put the two empty glasses on a tray she carried. He held the glass up toward Tommy.

"Salud." He finished the two fingers in one go. He set the glass down on the table and looked evenly at the gangster. For the first time, in several hours, he felt calm and focused.

"You didn't get into your car and track me all the way downtown to talk about the suicide of a serial killer, so what's on your mind?" Steve settled back in the soft black leather as Tommy signaled Doris for another round. Tommy leaned back and spread his arms out along the back of the booth. His thin, light gray suit was accompanied by a lavender shirt and a cream colored tie. He drummed his fingers lightly as he smiled across at Steve.

"Oh, just a little thought I got recently. Want to hear about it?" Steve accepted his third glass of scotch from Doris as he shrugged his ambivalence. Tommy smiled broadly and continued.

"I hear you are pals with Jay Sarno, right?" Steve took a large sip of the golden liquid.

"No. You heard wrong. Jay just has a bee in his bonnet because he knows I was involved in Bernie beating him out on the land deal and he thinks I can persuade Sinatra to dump the Sands and work his room." Tommy waved dismissively and continued.

"The point is, Slick, you know quite a lot about what's going on over there and don't pretend you don't. So I need your advice." Steve stopped his glass halfway to his mouth. He shook his head and pointed at Tommy with the index finger on the hand that was holding the glass.

"You want advice from me?" He drew the words out with a long space between each one. Again, Tommy ignored the remark and continued, taking his arms down and folding them in front of him on the table.

"So, Slick, my boss has a chance to take over the casino at Caesars Palace. The question that has been put to me and that I now put to you, is this: Should we do this or pass?" Tommy sat back and took another sizeable gulp of the scotch as he stared intently at Steve. Steve shook his head and looked over at the other empty booths beside them. He looked down at his watch.

"Say, Tommy, we been here for quite a while. Shouldn't we continue this soiree somewhere else?" Tommy's smile was replaced by a look of irritation. He shook his head and reached to his left, grabbing a handful of the slick black curtains beside him. With a quick jerk he spun them on the circular pole around the booth until the two men were completely out of sight of the rest of the room. He glared across the table at Steve.

"They have to find us first. Now quit stalling and tell me what I need to know." Steve sighed and sat back in the booth, turning his glass back and forth in half circles on the shiny surface of the table. He looked up at Tommy and spoke in a low voice.

"In my opinion? No. Jay is a great promoter and has some good ideas. Ideas that might well change the way everybody in this town does things, but I don't think he is the right person to run that resort." Tommy's eyebrows arched as he waited for more.

"Jay operates by screaming and refusing to proceed unless he gets his way. He's burnt through almost all the money that Hoffa fronted him and he is not even halfway done. At this point it might not even happen. He's still trying to perfect his glass brick that he insists is going to be the main theme in almost all the walls over there. So, even the best run casino is not going to do you guys any good if the place closes down around you." Steve stopped and waited for the gangster's reaction. When Tommy seemed lost in his thoughts while he stared down at his drink, Steve asked a question of his own.

"If the deal goes ahead, will you run it yourself?" Tommy looked up and shrugged.

"Naw, don't think so. Last thing I want is another casino skim job tied to my tail." He sighed and sat back again. "We caught a group of guys in Florida trying to pull a fast one on what's left of Lucky's gang and one of the guys is Zarowitz's boss who very kindly offered up the casino in Caesars as a way of apologizing. Boss was just curious, that's all." Steve shook his head and finished his drink.

"Gee, Tommy, happy to help. You about ready to go?" Steve stood up and moved the curtain halfway back. Before Tommy could reply, the curtain was jerked back even further and Steve found himself face-to-face with Mitchell. He was accompanied by another, older, taller man in a black suit who patted Mitchell on the shoulder, indicating he should move out of the way. Tommy stood up and hitched up his pants as he pulled another hundred dollar bill from the roll in his pocket, dropping it onto the table. He looked disdainfully at the older man.

"You got a problem, Mickey?" The older man's posture stiffened as he pointed a short stubby finger at Tommy.

"It's you that's got the problem, Tommy. They hear about this back east, your boss ain't going to be real happy." Tommy smirked and shouldered past Mitchell who had to step back quickly and brace himself against the wall to keep from falling over backwards. Tommy stopped in the middle of the small space and looked back at Mickey as he rolled his eyes around the room.

"Why don't you Irish schmucks stay in Jersey running bingo games and shortchanging little old ladies in your laundromats?" He indicated the general direction of the east coast with his thumb. He jerked his head at Steve and turned his back on the two gangsters. Steve smiled politely at Mickey as he walked through one half of the swinging door that was being held open by Doris. Steve caught up with Tommy on the sidewalk in front of the entrance. Tommy's expansive mood had faded. He motioned with his cigar at the bright lights on the Mint's marquee above his head.

"Look at this dump. Where do these guys get off anyways?" He pointed to the wide opening that led right off the street into the slot machines and scoffed derisively. "Penny slots. And he's got the nerve to talk to me?" Tommy turned and stomped off toward his car. Steve laughed to himself as he followed and waited on the curb for the Caddys' automatic top to refasten itself, before he swung open the door and joined the unamused gangster for the ride back to the Justice Center.

Steve pulled down the shade as he drove into the last of the sun setting the edge of the Spring mountains aglow in a fiery orange. He was feeling no effect from the scotch as he thought back over the days' events. Everybody was acting as if it was all over, as if Benjamin Stanwick's death could be chalked up to Dawkins and his homicidal rampage. Even Assistant DA Larsen had downplayed the urgency of tracking down Amis and his gang. Only Tam had backed him up when he insisted that the task force be kept together and that Larsen and the Chief start putting the pressure back onto the church. They had all agreed in the end, but Steve noted a general lack of enthusiasm as well as the foul smell of political influence in the room and he was skeptical that any real efforts would be made and that in a few days' time the task force would cease to exist. He was still mulling over his next move when he turned off the narrow asphalt road into Remy's driveway. He was not surprised to see her car parked in front of the door. Everything that could be done in preparation for the opening of the Casablanca had been done, and Steve looked forward to a relaxing evening before all the hoopla that would swirl around them tomorrow.

JULY 17

STEVE FOUND BERNIE in his office at six o'clock the next morning. They spent several minutes with their coffee cups looking down on the expansive inside patio areas, all of which could be seen from the windows that covered the east wall of the room.

Bernie sighed softly as he watched Walter instructing some of the staff on the precise location of the two dozen green and white umbrellas that graced the outdoor seating area of the largest restaurant.

"Somehow, I never really believed that this day would ever actually come." Steve looked down with a look of surprise.

"Are you kidding? I never had a doubt. To me it was an article of faith, and now, there it is." He gestured toward the five story tower that glowed a burnished yellow in the soft morning light. Bernie shook his head slowly.

"I always thought that it would be a close thing, you know? But five days after I decided to do it, I had to turn away guys who wanted to put up money. For a kid that arrived in Chicago with no family, no friends and no money, that was a reality that took some getting used to."

Steve smiled to himself.

"Well, Bern, I would say that you have done all right." They watched the sun pull itself slowly over the rim of Sunrise Mountain before they went their separate ways.

At noon, Steve was standing on the mezzanine that overlooked the large octagon shaped casino with Jack Cathay when a wall of noise built from the front of the hotel and reached their ears just before large crowds began streaming past the security guards, filling every available place at the gaming tables in a few minutes' time. The procession, led by Pete Fountain, included most of the musicians and showgirls employed at the hotel and had started just outside of the Tropicana Hotel, but by the time they had reached the Casablanca, the governor and several thousand excited tourists and locals had joined them. Now the crowd dispersed to all the corners of the new hotel, throwing up a happy din that echoed off the two foot thick stucco walls and the glass chandeliers.

After a few minutes, Jack and Steve split up. Steve ascended the back stairs and crept through the catwalks checking each position for lines of sight, while Jack prowled the casino floor as he watched the action in all of the four money cages in turn. After an hour, Steve was called to the store level where the open air bazaar that Bernie had designed was receiving more attention from the visitors than expected. Steve marshalled an extra ten security guards from other parts of the hotel and stationed one at the entrance to each of the stores that were built in the style of large stalls and were open to the central patio. When he had the guards controlling the number of people that could be in a store at any one time, he made a circuit of all three showrooms where the entertainment had kicked off as if it were already dark.

At four o'clock, Steve and Jack met Bernie in the main cage to supervise the counting and get an inkling of the take to that point. Steve and Bernie watched nervously as Jack collected the tally sheets that runners had brought from the other cages. He sat down at a small table and cranked away on a ten-key machine for several minutes. He tore off the thin roll of paper and motioned with his head to Steve and Bernie to follow him out of the cage. Just outside the cage, Bernie opened a narrow elevator with one of the keys he carried in his pocket on a large ring. The three men squeezed into the tight confines and were all relieved when the thirty second ride was over and they were able to sprawl comfortably around one of Bernie's tables with drinks in hand. After a large gulp of scotch, Jack cleared his throat.

"Well, gentlemen," he began in his deep gravelly voice, "We are $240,00 to the good." He handed the small slip of paper to Steve who read it and then passed it on to Bernie. Bernie laid it on the table in front of him and looked over at Jack.

"Pretty unusual, wouldn't you say? The house margins are running higher than I've ever seen." Jack took another sip of his drink and shook his head.

"You can throw all that out the window on opening night. None of the players play their normal games. Got a big winner at every table? They will all double down until they go bust. Even the toughest guys out there will be off their game. Let's hope they just keep it up for a while and give us a cushion. I've only had to throw one shark out of here so far, so that tells me the bad guys are waiting to hit us later this week." Steve nodded his assent.

"The staff should be seasoned by then if the play keeps up at this pace. So far everywhere I have been, things are running smooth, how about you?" Jack shrugged.

"A few of the dealers we hired from downtown are a little slow, not used to the big crowds, but I got Benny giving them more breaks and letting the older hands work another half shift, so that should smooth out soon." Steve stood up and finished off his drink. He smiled down at Bernie.

"If you need me, I will be in 'Rick's Café and Cabaret'." He glanced down at his watch. "If I hurry, I can catch the last half of Remy's show." Bernie waved to him as he headed toward the door.

"See you back here at midnight. We will take the count again, and then turn it over to the night crew."

It took Steve almost ten minutes to work his way through the celebrating crowds before he arrived at the bank of doors that led to the showroom. There were a hundred people standing outside that had been unable to get in, parting grudgingly as Steve worked his way up to the head maître d'. He recognized the man from the Sahara Hotel where he had worked for many years.

"Ray, I didn't know you hired on here." Ray nodded as he shook his head and finger at the same time toward two couples that were trying to get by his podium. Three security guards stationed in front of the doors gently turned them back toward the crowd.

"Yeah, Bernie's been after me for months. Dead end where I was. Maybe I can move up in this joint. You want in?" Steve nodded. Ray turned to one of the security guards.

"Take this guy over to the side entrance." He smiled at Steve. "Good luck. It's standing room only and they are already going to do two more shows tonight." Steve smiled back and clapped the man on the shoulder as he followed the security guard through a velvet rope and alongside the large showroom. Twenty yards later, another guard opened a locked door for Steve and he stepped into the showroom. The wave of sound from the stage and the crowd washed over him as he took in the sight of every aisle between the tables jammed with cheering people. One of the numbers had just ended and Steve took the opportunity to quickly cross down a sloping aisle to the side of the stage, nodding to the security guard as he ascended the four steps that took him to the backstage area. From his vantage point he could see the six or seven groups in both wings waiting to come on. Remy had put together a show that unfolded in three parts and used several scenes from the movie 'Casablanca' as the basis for the production numbers. She had previewed it for the press four days before and the enthusiastic reviews had made it the hottest ticket in town. He caught the eye of one of the stage managers who pointed to an almost hidden set of wooden steps that led up toward the first bank of lights that were turning from green to blue to magenta as Steve took the staircase two steps at a time.

Remy DeMarche was standing on a small platform that hung just inside the folds of the main curtain. From where she stood she could see the whole stage and the two men working the lights in a booth twenty feet away. She looked down and smiled at Steve as he stepped up onto the platform. Below on the stage a young singer dressed as a French waitress sang a soft ballad. On either side of the backstage, the dancers and singers were assembling for the 'Le Marseillaise' number that had already become one of the highlights of the show. Steve put his arm around Remy's shoulders and whispered in her ear.

"How you holding up, Gem?" She had to arch her neck to answer back as the music and the crowds' cheering swelled when several dancers swept onto the stage.

"Fine, so far. What are you doing here?" Steve smiled and shrugged.

"Everything is under control in the casino, I thought I might just see the show as you see it." Remy laughed softly and leaned back against Steve's chest as the first strains of the French anthem rose up to them followed by a loud burst of applause from the audience.

JULY 17

STEVE DROVE THE short trip back to Remy's house in half the normal time. Remy had elected to stay the night in the hotel as her last show would end at two a.m. Bernie had insisted that Steve go home and just past twelve thirty, he climbed the circular staircase toward the bedroom.

When the phone buzzed loudly from the night stand, Steve was unsure where he was for several seconds. When he was aware that the phone required his attention, he sat up groggily in the large bed and pulled the instrument to his face, cradling it under his chin.

"Hello?" His voice was cracked and full of sleep.

"Steve. This is Hank Greenspun. I need your help. I need it now." Steve sat up straighter and then slipped off the bed as he rubbed his forehead.

"Hank, what's the matter? What's going…" The publisher cut him off, his voice becoming thin with anguish.

"They got Rita, Steve. They got her and you have to help me get her back…" This time Steve did the interrupting.

"They got her? Who has her? How do you know this?" He could hear Hank taking big gulps of air before he was able to reply.

"Amis. Amis Kinsley has her, he just called me five minutes ago. If I don't give him what he wants, they are going to kill her. They're only giving me five hours, Steve. What do I do?" Steve picked up his watch from the nightstand and held the fading radium hands up to his face before he replied.

"Calm down, Hank, we'll get her back. Take a deep breath and tell me slowly exactly what he said." A few seconds later the normally low tones of the publisher came back over the line.

"I have to write a story retracting all the things that were said about the church since the murders started. I have to bring it to them and prove it to them."

"Did they tell you where to go?" Steve could hear the anguish creeping back into the husky voice.

"No. They said they would call me in two hours and tell me where. They said I had to be ready by then." Steve pressed his fingertips against his eyes as he cleared his head of the last of the sleep and began to think.

"Hank. Where are you right now?"

"At the paper." Steve interjected.

"Good. How soon before the next edition comes off the press?"

"Two and a half hours, why?" Steve tightened his grip on the phone and spoke as slowly and clearly as he could.

"Listen to me, Hank. You are going to have to stop the run right now. Start writing the retraction and put it on the front page with as big a headline as you can. I will be there in twenty minutes." He spoke the last sentence over protests coming from the publisher.

"I can't do that Steve. Not enough time." Steve cut him off.

"Start writing now, Hank, I want to see it finished when I get there." Steve hung up the phone and begun scooping up his clothes from the bench at the foot of the bed as he raced down the staircase.

Steve rattled the door impatiently as an elderly watchman fumbled with his keys as he slowly made his way to the front door of the Sun building.

"You have to have per…" Steve pushed by the guard without acknowledgement as he took the steps three at a time, turning at the top and jogging to the editors' desk at the end of the long bay filled with desks. Hank was staring down at something on his desk when Steve crossed the threshold of his office. Hank held up the two single-spaced pieces of paper.

"This is it, Steve. They are setting it up down in the basement as we speak." Steve took the pages from the shorter man's hands and read it quickly, dropping the first sheet onto the floor when he was done with it. He looked up at Hank Greenspun.

"Looks good to me. But let's hope it passes muster with Amis." Hank sat down and shook his head.

"Murray says he can have it in an hour and a half. Will that be enough time?" Steve looked at his watch and made several swift calculations.

"Depends on where you have to go, Hank. That much time suggests it is somewhere out of town, but let's hope not. When is he going to call back?" Hank looked at his watch.

"In an hour and forty minutes." Steve grimaced.

"No way to speed up the process?" Hank shook his head glumly.

"No. I don't know how Murray and his crew are going to pull it off in the time he says, but God, let's pray he makes it." Steve nodded at the sentiment.

"I assume you are to come alone and no cops?" Hank nodded as Steve continued.

"Once we find out where it is you are supposed to go, I want you to stall them for a little more time, so that I can get there before you." Hank shook his head.

"No, Steve, they'll see you and then they will…" Hank could not bring himself to finish his sentence. Steve stood up and leaned forward on the desk, waiting until the editor looked up at him. His voice was low pitched and firm.

"Listen to me, Hank and hear what I am telling you. Amis is going to kill Rita no matter what you say or do, unless I get to him first. Do you understand that?" The two men looked deeply into each other's eyes before Hank dropped his gaze to the desktop and replied, his voice just above a whisper.

"Yes. I understand that. You are right." Steve sat back into his chair and crossed his legs as he gazed across the desk.

"We need to relax and stay calm, Hank. I think I have a pretty good idea of the general area we will be going." Hank pointed to a cabinet on the wall next to Steve.

"Drink?" Steve shook his head.

"Not for me, but you might benefit from a short one." Hank nodded and retrieved the bottle of bourbon from the cabinet and poured a small amount into a paper cup.

Steve was watching Murray hurrying up the aisle toward Hank's office with the damp paper in his hands when the phone rang on Hank's desk. Steve held his hand up and the index finger on his other hand across his lips as Hank picked up the receiver. Murray stopped outside the door and slumped down into one of the chairs in Hank's makeshift waiting room. Steve moved quietly around the desk and leaned over as Hank held the phone as far away from his ear as he could manage and still hear the voice on the other end. Hanks' 'hello' sounded strangely weak to Steve.

"Mr. Greenspun. I trust you have the item we have requested?" Hank nodded before he cleared his throat and answered.

"Yes, yes I do."

"Glad to hear it. Now you are going to read it to me over the phone. If you're making it up as you go along, I will know." Steve turned and gestured for Murray to bring the paper into the office. Steve handed it across to Hank, who held it up and began to read. Five minutes later, Hank finished and laid the paper on the desk. There was a long pause.

"Okay, here is what you do. You get into your car, and only your car and you drive to Death Valley. Do you know how to get to Scotty's Castle?" Hank swallowed hard before he answered.

"I have only been there once, I will need extra time to get there."

Steve took out his notebook and was hurriedly drawing a map. There was a gap before the voice spoke again. From where he stood, Steve recognized it as Amis, though he was using something in an attempt to disguise it.

"No more time. You be there in two hours. When you get here, park in the main lot out front and blink your lights twice. Someone will come out to you. You got that?"

"Yes, I do." The line went dead. Steve looked into Hank's face that was drained of almost all of its' color. Steve held up the paper.

"This going to pass muster?" Hank leaned forward to steady himself on the desk before he sat down heavily into his chair. He rubbed his temples.

"Yes, it will." He looked up at Murray. "Get back downstairs and get the real edition out. Tell Clarence to get the word out to everybody that needs to know that it will be two hours late hitting the street." The man turned to go, when Hank continued. "And Murray? Thanks for all your help." Murray nodded and walked slowly back toward the stairs. Hank looked up at Steve who had ripped out two pages from his notebook. He moved behind the editors' chair and pointed to the map.

"When you get to this point, they will be able to see you. So start driving very slowly as if you are feeling your way along. That should give me the time I need to get into position. I am leaving now. You wait exactly fifteen minutes and then you start. Don't speed. You will get there in enough time if you drive sixty-five. Move slowly and talk slowly when you get there, but follow their instructions, no matter what they tell you to do. Our only chance is to make them feel comfortable and in control. You got that?" Hank nodded. Steve held out his hand.

"If we do this right, we'll have her back here safe and sound in four hours, OK?" Hank nodded again and forced a small smile. Steve patted his shoulder as he turned to go. The last glimpse he saw of the editor, Hank was holding the bogus paper in his hands, a wistful look in his eyes.

As soon as the Strip lights receded in his rearview mirror, the blackness of the desert night closed in on Steve as he sped along the highway toward the junction that would lead him to Amis and to Rita Malone.

*

An hour and forty-five minutes later, the red Jeep entered Grapevine Canyon and after a few winding miles came to a stop. The sharp coolness of the desert air hit Steve as he carefully closed the door of the Jeep, making sure that the final click was as soft as he could make it. He had been lucky to find the narrow road he remembered that ran behind the Castle and was used by the rangers to service the monument. By his reckoning, he was two hundred yards west and slightly above the castle. There would be a small junkyard in his path that held several old rusted-out cars and primitive mining equipment. He kept his pace slow as he waited for his eyes to grow accustomed to the dim starlight. In some places the desert was smooth and natural, but most of the going was over earth churned up by heavy equipment. The square grids that Steve passed over suggested that the Park service was building a series of new parking lots. The construction gave way to a strip of saltbush that immediately began to slope downward. Steve slowed his pace even more and then stopped to listen. For a brief moment the light breeze had brought the sound of two voices to him. He stood still for several minutes, but heard no more. He moved another ten yards before he saw the end of the saltbush just a few feet in front of him. He crouched low and took his time moving to the last one. He stopped behind the large bush and looked around. Just in front of where he stood, the slope dropped off sharply into a dry river bed. Across the twenty yard wide channel he could see the solid shapes of the old cars in the junkyard, and fifty yards beyond them the washed-out yellow stucco walls of Scotty's Castle glowed palely in the starlight. He breathed in deeply and then began to make a systematic survey of the entire area.

Twenty minutes later, he had located the positions of the two guards that seemed to be the only two posted, at least in the area that was visible to Steve. He had only spotted them because they kept moving out of boredom and they threw long shadows in the low light. Steve had just located the best place to cross the river bed unseen when he heard the sound of a car. He watched as both of the guards hurried to each other ten yards in front of the junkyard, and after conferring for a few seconds, one ran toward the castle and disappeared around the far side. The other stepped back behind cover and waited for Hank's car too make the last two turns before it reached the parking lot. Just as Steve had instructed, Hank was driving slowly and even stopping now and then as if he wasn't sure of the route. With the guard occupied, Steve began his journey across the dry riverbed. He slid noiselessly down the soft sand of the slope, the smooth rocks at the edge of the stream bed stopping his progress. He crouched down and swiftly moved along a line of low bushes that grew in the dry stream bed. He stopped when he got to the other side and looking through the windshield of a junked car just above him, he saw the two flashes of Hank's headlights. He immediately turned to his right and crept diagonally up the slope toward the spot where he had last seen the sentry. He peered carefully over the back of an old bucket loader to the spot, and ducked down slowly when the guard was not where he had expected him to be. Steve dropped near the ground and on all fours crawled past the next three wrecks before he saw the bottom half of the man's legs in front of a large trash bin. He carefully moved to a position where he could see better and raised his head just over the other side of the bin. From his vantage point he could see that the guard was intently scanning the area south of the castle, the same direction that Hank had just come. Steve could also see Hank standing beside his car, the paper clutched in his hands. Steve eased around the back of the bin taking care to stay out of the man's peripheral vision. When he was five feet away and directly behind the guard, the man's head turned suddenly as if he had heard something in the blackness. Steve recognized one of the two men who had broken into his motel room in Goodsprings. Steve smiled ironically to himself as he brought the barrel of the .45 down on the back of the man's head for the second time in two weeks. He dragged the unconscious body behind the bin and relieved the thug of his gun. He took the man's place and carefully positioned half of his body in the shadows so that anyone coming from the castle would take him for the absent guard. He wanted to signal Hank, but thought better of it, and just as he made his decision, he saw three figures come around the corner from the rear of the castle. They turned and walked in a straight line in front of the building and as they passed a large lattice gate, a security light illuminated the trio. Steve's hand tightened on the .45. Amis Kinsley was pushing Rita Malone forward. Her hands were bound behind her and she was wearing the same red dress she wore on stage. The other hood was several yards in front and Kinsley paused while the other man walked up to Hank Greenspun, gun in hand. He said something to Hank that Steve could not hear. Hank raised his arms as the man frisked him quickly. When he was done, he took the paper from the editor's hand and backed toward Kinsley, keeping his weapon pointed toward Hank. When the guard rejoined him, Amis held a flashlight on the newspaper for several seconds. From where he stood, Steve could see the mask of fear on Rita's face.

Steve held his breath as the trio returned to where Hank was standing near his car. On the way, the guard had waved toward Steve, who waved back hoping the man was far enough away and not looking too closely. Amis stopped five feet away from Hank. He had a gun to the back of Rita's head and he used her body to shield himself. Steve's position was slightly behind them, and out of their immediate sight. He swiftly ducked down behind a pile of rusty wire and crawled on all fours on a diagonal course arriving at a low concrete wall that curved out a small way into the lot. When he had crawled to the end of it, he was forty yards away from the group and he could hear Kinsley's voice, but could not make out the words. He held the gun up in front of his face, took two deep breaths and started walking as quickly and quietly as he could forward. His pistol sights were trained on the second man who was standing a few feet to the right of Amis and Rita. When he was twenty yards away, Steve adjusted his direction so that he had a clear shot at the guard without the risk of hitting Hank.

Steve looked down the barrel gleaming silver in the starlight and heard his own breathing as his last few steps brought him to within fifteen feet of Amis. He heard the second man exclaim before he was aware that he had been heard. The man wheeled around and Steve saw the short black barrel as the man's arm rose toward him. The .45 kicked violently in Steve's hand, the bright flash illuminating the faces of the four people in front of him, the sound crashing back around them from the walls of the castle.

A half second later, Steve stood ten feet from Amis who had his arm wrapped around Rita's throat. Steve looked into her eyes that still were decorated with small specks of glitter. He focused on her face and hoped that she understood that he wanted her to stay as still as possible. Amis's face was twisted in a sneer. With his left foot he kicked the dead man's gun under the car. He laughed as he spoke.

"You don't win this time, Cannon. Throw down your gun or I kill her right now." Steve responded by moving to his right until he was five feet away from Hank who was standing frozen by his car. Steve whispered toward him out of the side of his mouth.

"Stay where you are Hank and don't move unless I tell you to." He raised his voice toward Amis.

"I'm not dropping this gun, Amis. If you're looking for help from behind me, forget it. You should have brought more guys."

Amis quickly pulled Rita back three steps behind the front of the car. He tightened his hold around her neck, the pistol at the base of her skull. From the angle he was standing, Steve could only see part of Amis's face. He began to shift his weight and turn his shoes in the gravel, moving in small increments to his left. Amis' voice came from behind the red rose that Rita still wore.

"Your fault she is going to die, Cannon. We snatched her right after she came off the stage, and none of your lousy security was any the wiser." He moved the paper he held in his left hand that he had wrapped tightly around Rita's waist. "I got what I came for, and by the time they print the new retraction, nobody will care anymore." Steve hissed at Hank.

"Get down behind the car." Hank dropped to the ground and crawled backward until he found cover behind the rear tire. When Amis shifted his gaze momentarily in Hank's direction, Steve moved a few more inches to his left. He now had the best angle he was going to get, unless Amis moved again. Amis' black eyes stared straight into Steve's as he tightened his chokehold on Rita. Steve could see her face changing color and played his last gambit to distract Amis and get him into the right position.

"You know you can't get away, Kinsley, even if you kill all three of us. Do you think Hank and I would come here alone?" As he finished speaking, he held his breath, his eyes concentrating on the center white dot as it danced over Amis' face. His vision had narrowed to a small circle, outside of which light gray clouds swirled as if in a vortex. He heard his heart pounding in his ears, the sound getting louder as the trigger on the .45 began to travel backwards. In the black, cold desert night the two explosions sounded as one as they rolled back down the narrow canyon.

EPILOGUE

STEVE CANNON WALKED through the crowd of hotel guests and tourists and pushed through the revolving glass door in the lobby of the Casablanca, stepping out into the warm September night. He walked the fifty yards to where the red Jeep was parked. He had just unlocked the door, when he hesitated and leaned his arm for a minute on the frame of the open door. His eyes swept the parking lot and rested on the two-story tall marquee that sat at the corner of Flamingo Road and the Strip. He smiled to himself when he read the words just below the list of headliners: 'Rita Malone with Buck Monari and the Beale Street Blues Band'. The lights on the marquee blinked on and off as the Jeep turned underneath them and joined the traffic headed up the Strip.